FOREVERMORE

CLUB DESTINY

FOREVERMORE
CLUB DESTINY

NICOLE EDWARDS

NICOLE EDWARDS LIMITED
A dba of SL Independent Publishing, LLC
PO Box 1086
Pflugerville, Texas 78691

FOREVERMORE
Club Destiny, 12
Nicole Edwards

COVER DETAILS:

Image: © Wander Aguiar
Cover Model: David, Alana & Philippe
Design: © Nicole Edwards Limited

INTERIOR DETAILS:

Formatting: Nicole Edwards Limited
Editing: Blue Otter Editing | www.BlueOtterEditing.com

IDENTIFIERS:

ISBN: 978-1-64418-056-3 (ebook) | 978-1-64418-057-0 (paperback)

BISAC: FICTION / Romance / General

DEDICATION

Dedicated to the readers.

Back in November of last year, I released *Naughty Holidays 2021* and left it up to you to decide which of my characters you wanted to see more of. I was pleasantly surprised that the majority selected more of Sam, Logan, and Elijah. It reiterated that the path I've chosen is the correct one. That ten years after publishing my first book, those same characters still capture your hearts. The journey for Sam and Logan has been an interesting one. More importantly, it's been fun.

Dear Reader,

You might be wondering why there's another book for Logan, Sam, and Elijah when I said the series was complete after *Distraction*. Well, the answer's simple, really: the readers voted for it. If you already read *Cabin by Candlelight*, which was included in *Naughty Holidays 2021*, you're up to speed on the fact that something is changing with my first couple … er … throuple? I gave the readers an opportunity to vote on which of my past couples/throuples they wanted to see more of, and Logan, Sam, and Elijah won by a landslide.

But don't worry, if you didn't get a chance to read *Cabin by Candlelight* yet, I've included it at the beginning of this book. For those who have read it, it's here as a refresher; however, there is nothing new within the short story.

And I want to say thank you to everyone who voted for this threesome because it has brought my writing back full circle after ten incredible years of being a published author.

Enjoy!

~Nicole

Cabin by Candlelight

from Naughty Holidays 2021

Logan, Elijah, and Samantha from *Conviction* and *Entrusted*

After eight years of marriage, and seven years into their polyamorous relationship, Logan, Samantha, and Elijah are about to take things to the next level.

CHAPTER ONE

SAMANTHA MCCOY WOKE UP TO AN EMPTY bed. Not exactly unusual, regardless of whose bed she woke up in. Eight years of marriage and seven years into the polyamorous relationship they had with Elijah Penn, and she was still alternating bedrooms much of the time.

Not exactly a problem. Not most of the time, anyway. If she looked at it from a practical standpoint, she had two bedrooms and two bathrooms, both set up with her things as though it was as natural as breathing. So what if she had double the amount of things, at least her pillows were only getting half the use, right?

Oh, sure, they had the playroom where the three of them had fun, something she always looked forward to. But it wasn't the same. It wasn't the same because it wasn't *their* room. It was ... it was a sex room, not a bedroom, and by God, Sam wanted *one* room. Just one single room where the three of them could sleep together, dream together. Just *be* together. All the time.

As for what had prompted this crazy idea to combine their lives into one... Well, that was the bigger issue. The one where, on the mornings after a night she spent with Logan, she found herself waking up to an empty bed despite the early hour. The man was working too much, and she suspected she knew why. Only he was pretending that it was just business as usual, when in reality, she got the feeling he was working with his twin to come up with a new club design.

If the man only knew he wasn't nearly as subtle as he thought he was. Sam had long ago picked up on his tells, of which he had many. The way he glanced down briefly at the very beginning of an explanation told her he wasn't being entirely truthful. The way he tugged on his left earlobe and glanced to the side told her he was dodging her question entirely. And the way he smoothed his hair back, then rubbed his neck told her he was frustrated with her.

Yep. The man had many tells.

Add that to the fact he spent more time in his home office these days than he ever had before, and Sam was convinced he was up to something. As for why she suspected it was with Luke … well, that was because Sierra had told her Luke was doing the very same things. The twins were up to something.

"You're awake."

Sam peered over at the door and saw Logan leaning against the jamb. He was dressed in a black Henley and dark jeans, looking as remarkable as the first time she'd seen him. Logan could rock the casual look as easily as he could a suit and tie, but what impressed her more than his smoking-hot body and the washboard abs he hid beneath the designer labels was the sprinkling of gray at his temples. His once black hair was going salt-and-pepper as he aged, and she found it immensely hot.

"Sam?"

"Hmm?"

"Get your mind out of the gutter."

She frowned. "You've never minded that it went there before."

"And I wouldn't now except you've got to finish packing. Our flight leaves in a few hours, and we need you to be ready."

"I want a new bed," she blurted, propping herself up and allowing the sheet to slide down below her bare breasts.

Logan's gaze slid from her face to her breasts, just as she'd predicted it would.

"What do you think?" she prompted, discreetly straightening her spine to thrust her chest forward.

He smiled that sexy, mischievous smile that she loved so much.

"About the bed," Sam clarified.

It clearly took effort, but his gaze lifted to her face even as he adjusted himself as though she couldn't see him.

But rather than come at her like a starving man, Logan waltzed over and grabbed the garment bag he used when he was taking his suit on a trip.

"Wait!" she declared, sitting up straight and grabbing the sheet. "Why are you taking a suit with you? This is supposed to be a vacation."

"It is a vacation," he said. "Now get up and get ready."

He turned and slipped out of the room, leaving her fuming behind him.

He was most definitely up to something, but two could play that game.

Sam got out of bed, started toward the bathroom, but made a detour at the last second, heading out of the bedroom. She was naked, but that would only save her time in the long run.

"Good morn—" Elijah's words cut off as he looked up from the iPad in front of him. "Bloody good morning," he muttered, leaning back and watching her as she headed for the coffeepot.

No, Sam would never tire of that. Both of her men were blatant in their desire for her, and that was something she craved like air and water. They had the ability to make her feel like she was the only woman in the world. She had long ago expected the novelty to wear off, as she'd heard happened in many relationships, but it hadn't. And for that, Sam felt incredibly blessed.

Pretending she had no ulterior motive for being naked in the kitchen, Sam went to the coffeepot, found her favorite mug already sitting beside it, waiting for her. That was Logan's doing, she knew. Elijah's romantic gestures were more overt, and she honestly appreciated them both equally.

She could feel their eyes on her as she poured her coffee, doctored it with cream and sugar, and took a sip to test it.

"Perfect," she said, turning around to face them both as she held the mug with both hands.

She smiled at Eli, loving the way his eyes darkened as he blatantly stared at her nakedness. Something else she appreciated about him was that, even after seven years, he still found her sexy.

"Come here, love," he said with a grin, holding out his arm and gesturing her toward his knee.

Sam waltzed over, casting a sideways look at Logan, who was now standing with his arms crossed over his chest. Obviously he was in a hurry to get out of there, hence the reason she was going to take her time.

Oh, they wouldn't be late, she would make sure of that, too, but if she had to hurry through her shower simply so she could enjoy a little morning greeting from the men she loved, she would certainly rush to make it happen.

But first, the morning greeting.

Sam stepped into Eli's arm, let him guide her down to his denim-clad knee as she pretended to only care about the coffee in her hand.

"She thinks she holds all the cards," Eli said.

"She does," Logan agreed, still watching her intently.

"I think she might need a lesson in who's really in charge here." Eli chuckled. "What do you think?"

Sam's gaze swung to Logan as he approached slowly. When he reached down to take her coffee mug, she reluctantly handed it over.

"I think she won't be needing this right now."

LOGAN WAS FAIRLY CERTAIN HIS WIFE WAS going to be the death of him.

Not that he was complaining about the fact she was tormenting him with her naked form, wandering through the house without a stitch on as though it was an everyday occurrence. Sure, if he had his way, she would be naked a majority of the time. Her long, dark blond hair hanging down her back and over her shoulder, her light green eyes glittering with mischief and promise. Those sultry lips, her luscious tits, the gentle curve of her waist, the sexy swell of her hips, and the sweet juncture between her trim thighs. Every inch of her beckoned to every inch of him, even when he knew they didn't have time to waste.

After setting her coffee mug on the counter, Logan returned to where she was perched on Eli's thigh. Sam smiled up at him, clearly daring him to do his worst, and he suspected she thought he wouldn't.

But Logan wasn't the sort of man who backed down from a dare, and he damn sure wasn't about to start now.

"I haven't had breakfast yet," he said, holding her gaze. "And now I know what I'm hungry for."

He loved the way Sam's eyes glazed over at the promise in his tone.

Logan held out his hand to her, waited to see if she would take it. She glanced at Eli and smiled before laying her hand in his, allowing Logan to help her to her feet. It had been a while since they'd enjoyed an early-morning feast at this table, and today seemed like as good a day as any.

"What are you doing?" Sam asked with a giggle when Logan spun her around and backed her against it.

"Breakfast is the most important meal of the day, is it not?"

Her eyes remained locked on his face as he assisted her onto the table, urging her back until he could settle her heels on the edge. He wasn't rough, but he wasn't gentle, positioning her the way he wanted her, loving the way her nipples pebbled into hard little points.

"You do know if we miss our flight, I will paddle your ass," he grumbled, pressing her knees wide.

"Then you should let me take a shower," she countered.

"Too late for that."

Logan leaned in and breathed in the musky scent of her sex as he used his fingers to separate her slick folds, admiring her lovely pussy. He let his breath fan over her flesh, enjoying the way her stomach tightened and her legs trembled with anticipation. His wife did love having her pussy eaten, and since it was one of his favorite things, too, these encounters were a frequent occurrence in this house.

When Elijah reached over to cup her breast, thumbing her nipple until it drew up impossibly tight, Logan leaned in and swept his tongue over her. He lightly licked her entrance then her clit, but he wasn't about to give her what she wanted. He sucked on her labia, realizing she'd been waxed smooth very recently, something he found immensely erotic.

"Logan…"

He ignored her plea, taking his time, licking and laving her delicate flesh, alternating to ensure he didn't stimulate one spot too much. He was not about to make her come yet. That would take all the fun out of it.

Sam grunted, clearly catching on to his plan. She attempted to thrust her hips to get him where she wanted him, but he played her easily, moving with her and chuckling before finally stepping back.

"Damn you," she hissed, glaring up at him.

Logan smirked as he moved around to the other side of the table. "Eli, why don't you do the honors of finishing her off."

Sam wiggled as Eli got to his feet.

"My pleasure."

Logan curled his hand under Sam's chin, tilted her head back as he leaned down and pressed an upside-down kiss to her mouth.

"If you're really good, I might let you come."

"You wouldn't dare," she whispered on a moan when Eli's face pressed between her thighs.

Logan couldn't fight the desire to watch the man as he feasted on Sam's pussy. This was one of the highlights of his day, watching the two of them together. He couldn't explain why he was so fascinated with watching another man pleasure his wife, but it was there all the same. Had been since the beginning, but if he was being honest, it hadn't been until Eli came into the picture that his world had felt complete.

Sam's back bowed, her knees falling wide as Eli's tongue glided through her slit. He teased her clit momentarily, flicking the little bundle of nerves until Sam was writhing on the table.

"How does it feel, baby?" Logan prompted.

"Good. So good."

When she reached for Eli's head to hold him in place, Logan stopped her, taking both of her arms and positioning them over her head. He kept a firm hand on her so she was at Eli's mercy while the man drove her wild.

If they hadn't been pressed for time, Logan would've pulled his aching dick out and let his wife work him with her delectable mouth. But that would definitely stall them longer than was necessary. There would be time for that later when they were in their Colorado cabin. One week in the mountains was just what the doctor ordered. At least he hoped. Provided Sam and Eli didn't get angry when they realized he had business to tend to while he was there. It wouldn't take much time, but it would take him away from them for a short while. He figured they would have plenty to keep them occupied while he was away, though.

7

"Eli ... oh, God ... please ... I need..."

"Tell him, Sam," Logan ordered. "Tell him what you want."

"Make me come," she pleaded.

Logan's eyes never left Eli as he continued to suckle her clit while dipping one finger into her pussy. It was a sensual scene, one Logan would never tire of. Even these too-brief moments were worth it.

"I should make you wait," Eli mumbled against her smooth flesh. "I should make you wait for taunting us with this sweet pussy."

Sam's head tilted back when Eli thrust two fingers inside her. "No. Please. Don't make me wait."

"It would serve you right," Logan taunted.

"Eli ... oh, God ... please!"

Logan peered down at Sam's face, met her gaze when she opened her eyes. He held her stare and smirked. "Make her come, Eli."

Her eyes widened, and he could see the pleasure darken the light green of her irises. Her body shuddered, her fingers clutching his wrists as he held her arms in place.

"You ready, baby?"

Sam nodded, moaning louder now.

Logan didn't look away from her face as Eli sent her spiraling right over the crest and into ecstasy, Eli's name spilling from Sam's lips.

God, she was something else.

CHAPTER TWO

IF ELIJAH COULD'VE AVOIDED AIRPORTS, HE WOULD'VE done so. It wasn't so much the flying that frustrated him as much as the hassle and the time it took to get from one place to another. Two hours early, waiting, boarding, flying, getting luggage. He could think of a million things he would rather be doing. When it was work-related, he tended to pass the time easily, always connected to his email, his files. But this wasn't work, and he had long ago decided he would disconnect whenever he could. And since he enjoyed spending time with Logan and Sam far more than work, it wasn't a hardship.

The past few hours had stressed him more than he anticipated, and now that they'd made it to their destination, he was focused on breathing, relaxing, letting all that tension drain away. Now that they were finally at the cabin, he couldn't find much to complain about. Despite the concerning weather situation that they'd learned about upon their arrival, this was the perfect getaway. Quiet, secluded. Homey.

The cabin was a two-story log structure with vaulted ceilings in the living room, three bedrooms upstairs, a game room, media room, a fully stocked kitchen, and half a dozen fireplaces that could be used for warmth. It looked as though it would sleep a dozen comfortably, which meant the three of them would have it made for the next seven days.

And then there was the outdoors.

The snow was banked near the windows, but it was a sight to behold. Especially since he couldn't remember the last time he'd seen a snowfall, save for the ice storm they'd endured at the first part of this year. But he figured that didn't really count. It hadn't looked like this for more than five minutes.

Logan certainly knew how to plan a vacation, even if Elijah knew Logan wasn't here solely for vacation. The man had an ulterior motive, which was par for the course for the McCoy brothers. Elijah had long ago gotten used to the way that Logan and Luke managed to finagle time for work regardless of the event. If Elijah was right, this particular vacation was going to be expensed out. At least partially, anyway.

"What're you thinking about?"

Elijah glanced over his shoulder to see Sam approaching. She looked downright edible in her oversized black sweater, patterned leggings, and her favorite Ugg boots. She'd clearly come with the intention of getting cozy, and Elijah was grateful for that. He was looking forward to some downtime with her.

She stepped up behind him, pressed a kiss to his shoulder, and then stared out the window beside him.

"It's beautiful," she said, her voice reflecting the same awe he felt.

Elijah put his arm around her shoulder and pulled her to his side. He pressed a kiss to the top of her head. "It certainly is."

"We needed this, you know?"

He did know. There never seemed to be enough time in the day to really slow down. Between work and their busy social calendar, there wasn't a lot of relaxation. In the beginning, Elijah had kept himself somewhat separated from Sam and Logan's extended family, but over time his attempts became futile. The McCoy clan had welcomed him with open arms, making him feel as though he'd always been meant to be with them. And then there was Devotion, the club where they spent a good majority of their time, mingling with friends, indulging in one another.

The thought made him smile.

He had to admit, he'd never been happier in his life. And that was saying something, considering, at one point, he'd thought happiness was not something he would be blessed with again. Not the case. Sam had made sure of it.

"So what's on the agenda?" Sam asked, turning so that she was in front of him.

"I can think of a few things."

"I just heard the weather's supposed to be getting bad," Logan said as he strolled into the room, his phone in his hand, eyes glued to the screen. "Really bad."

"If we're lucky, we won't lose power," Sam told him, her gaze still fixed on the outdoors. "And I know we can think of a dozen ways to keep ourselves occupied indoors."

Elijah looked at Logan's reflection in the glass, knew he was thinking about whatever meeting he was supposed to attend while he was here. He hadn't said as much, but Elijah had learned to read Logan as easily as he could read Sam.

After pressing one more kiss to Sam's head, Elijah released her and turned from the window. "Who're you supposed to meet while we're here?"

Logan's eyes flew to his face and he frowned.

"There's no sense denying it," Sam added. "We're not dumb. We know you've got business while you're here. It's what you do."

Logan sighed. "It's not until Friday afternoon."

"Then I suggest we make the most of the days before then," Elijah told him, "and worry about Friday when it gets here."

"I like the way you think. How about lunch?"

Elijah peered down at Sam, smiled. "Are you offering to cook?"

She teasingly smacked his arm. "I'm a great cook."

"I wouldn't go so far as to say *great*," Logan joked, losing that frustrated look.

Sam stood taller, back straight. "That's not what you said when I made chicken piccata," she countered.

"If I recall, you gave me a blow job shortly after dinner," Logan noted, moving toward her.

Elijah chuckled. She had given him a blow job while Elijah had volunteered for dish duty. He certainly hadn't minded watching the show while he worked.

"What does that have to do with anything?" Sam's forehead creased as though she'd just understood. "Wait. Are you saying you praised my cooking so I would suck your dick?"

Logan laughed, a booming sound that was contagious, making Elijah laugh, too.

"Y'all suck," Sam pouted, stomping toward the kitchen.

11

Before she could get too far, Logan grabbed her around the waist and hoisted her up off the ground. "I'm kidding. Your cooking is … divine?"

Sam elbowed him, and Elijah laughed at them both. This was part of the appeal of their relationship. The fact that they enjoyed one another's company enough that they could joke about something as mundane as cooking made it so easy to be with them.

"Why don't I cook?" Elijah volunteered. "Then we'll take turns from here on out."

Logan put Sam back on her feet, and they both grinned wide.

It was Elijah's turn to frown. "Wait. You two did this on purpose."

Sam giggled and strolled his way, throwing her arms around his neck. "Your cooking is *so* much better than mine."

"You manipulated me?"

She planted a kiss on his cheek. "Never."

"You little minx," he mumbled, holding her against him. "You'll pay for that later."

Sam's voice was but a whisper in his ear when she said, "I'm looking forward to it."

THEIR LATE LUNCH/EARLY DINNER CONSISTED OF soup and sandwiches, something Sam could've easily prepared if they hadn't given her crap about her cooking skills. Not that she was denying she wasn't as brilliant in the kitchen as Elijah, but she could hold her own. Especially with tomato soup and grilled cheese.

However, she hadn't pitched a fit, enjoying the meal in the dining area while the three of them admired the view out the floor-to-ceiling windows that overlooked the mountain they were perched upon. This was the very reason she had agreed to come. The view was breathtaking and certainly not something she could see back home. Big, fluffy snowflakes floated down from the sky, layering the ground in white. It was serene, and she looked forward to cozying up with hot cocoa, a warm fire, and a good book at some point.

After lunch, Sam had left both men to take care of the dishes while she went to unpack her things.

Because there were enough rooms for everyone, Sam had commandeered one of her own, selecting one with a large vanity in the bathroom where she could put her stuff. She wouldn't sleep in a room by herself, but it would give her a space all her own where she could take naps, read, or just daydream. This was vacation, after all, and she fully intended to leave here relaxed and in good spirits.

No sooner did that thought flutter through her brain than the power blinked.

Frowning, Sam wandered out of the room to the second-floor landing that overlooked the main living area. From there she could see out the enormous windows that ran the length of the back of the cabin. Beyond, she could see thick, dark clouds looming overhead. Definitely a storm coming.

On the main floor, she heard Logan and Elijah talking, their voices hushed, something they did from time to time when they pulled that alpha male stunt of trying to protect the little lady.

"What's going on?" she insisted, her voice carrying as she started down the stairs. "Why are y'all whispering?"

"We're not whispering, love," Elijah answered, his tone placating.

Sam glared at him when she reached the first floor. "Don't do that, Eli. Tell me what's going on."

"It's just the storm," Logan assured her, his eyes on his phone. "This is the front side of it."

Sam glanced out the windows again, and for the first time since they'd arrived, she thought about what it would mean if they lost electricity while they were here.

"Is there a backup generator?" she wondered aloud.

"No," Elijah answered easily. "But we've got enough firewood to last us through the winter if we needed to."

She spun around to face him. "That's not funny."

Sam still remembered what it was like back in February when the ice storm hit Texas. They'd been without power for nearly a week and almost as long without water. It had been horrible, especially since they hadn't been prepared for that sort of storm. No one had because Texas wasn't prone to snow, only the occasional light dusting, but mostly they were iced over from rain when the temperatures would get low enough. Again, a rarity for them.

"Come here," Elijah urged, taking her hand and leading her over to the leather sectional sofa that faced the enormous rock-faced fireplace. "I'll start a fire just in case."

Sam plopped down on the sofa and watched as Elijah went to work. Admittedly, it was easy to forget her worries when she was watching him. The way he moved, the way he spoke … there was something enigmatic about Elijah Penn, something that called to her on a base level.

Like Logan, Elijah was a couple of years shy of fifty but didn't look a day over forty. His dark hair was thick and didn't have a single touch of silver. His brown eyes had softened over the years, losing some of the pain and storm clouds she'd noticed when they first met. And his body … she couldn't think about his very fine, very toned form without getting hit with a bolt of lust.

Warm hands settled on her shoulders, and Sam glanced back to see Logan.

"This should pass easily tonight," he said, as though that would assure her. "There's another storm predicted for tomorrow, but it should move through quickly."

"So you're our very own meteorologist?" She tried to keep her tone light, but it wasn't easy. Considering Logan had used this vacation as an excuse for work—or quite possibly he'd used work as an excuse for this vacation—Sam was irked.

However, the good news was, he would be all in for a couple of days since his meeting wasn't until Friday afternoon. Likely, that was the only reason Logan was paying attention to the weather at all. Otherwise, they would've been enjoying themselves, right?

Speaking of…

Sam shook off the worry and fear of the weather. It would do no good for them to sit here and fret over something they couldn't control. The last thing she wanted was to spend her vacation getting herself all worked up and in worse shape than when she'd left Dallas.

She took a deep breath and relaxed back against the cushion, allowing Logan to massage the tenseness from her shoulders.

Once the fire was burning, the warmth from the flames was immediate, relaxing her even more.

"What shall we do to pass the time?" Elijah asked when he came to sit on the sofa, patting the cushion, his request for Sam to put her feet in his lap.

14

Giddy over the idea of a foot massage, Sam twisted so he could have her feet. He easily slipped her boots from her feet, dropping them to the floor before peeling off her socks. Sam flexed her toes and smiled at him.

Logan joined them, taking his position so she could rest her head in his lap.

Ah, now this was what she'd been looking forward to.

"We could play a game," Logan suggested.

"Truth or dare," Sam blurted, glancing down at Elijah.

She watched him roll his eyes.

Sam chuckled. "What? You know you like that game."

"We *always* play that game," Logan said, likely speaking what Elijah was thinking.

She canted her head back to look up at him. "You said you liked it."

"That was until the last time," Elijah answered.

"When you chose *truth* every time," Logan finished.

Sam frowned. "I did not."

"Oh, yes, you did."

"I won't pick truth."

"Then that's not really truth or dare, now is it?" Logan commented.

Sam blew out a frustrated breath. "Fine. What would you prefer we did?"

It didn't surprise her when Logan reached for the remote.

Well, at least she was getting a foot rub out of this deal.

CHAPTER THREE

Friday, December 17, 2021

LOGAN WOKE UP EARLY ON FRIDAY MORNING, feeling relaxed from a full day of doing nothing. They'd spent the rest of Wednesday and all day Thursday lounging around, watching movies, eating popcorn, and chilling. The weather hadn't gotten as bad as they'd thought it would, and aside from a couple of blinks, they hadn't lost power, which had kept Sam in a good mood.

It had been nice just to relax and enjoy some time off.

Enough so, Logan had stopped fretting over the business meeting that was scheduled for later today. That was, until last night when he'd gone to bed alone since it was Elijah's night with Sam. Without her there to keep him company, he'd had no choice but to let his mind wander, and whenever that happened, it tended to gravitate toward work.

After an hour of tossing and turning, unable to go back to sleep, Logan decided it was time to get up. He could have some coffee and spend a couple of hours going over the proposal Luke expected him to give to a new set of investors.

He pulled on a pair of pajama pants and a long-sleeve T-shirt, then headed downstairs.

"I didn't think you'd be up this early."

Lost in his own thoughts, Logan jolted, his gaze slamming into Elijah, who was sitting at the small dining room table with a cup of coffee in his hand.

"I didn't think *you'd* be up this early," Logan countered.

Elijah smiled. "I'm still on Dallas time."

Logan understood that. If they went by the clock, they should've still been asleep, thanks to the one-hour time difference.

"Coffee's fresh," Elijah said, nodding toward the kitchen.

"Thanks." Logan caught a glimpse of Elijah's iPad screen. "What're you looking at?"

Elijah sighed, setting the tablet down and picking up his mug. "I think Sam's angling to have us in one room."

Logan poured his coffee, his eyes sliding over to Elijah. "She mentioned it to you, too?"

"In her roundabout way, yes." Elijah laughed.

That was Sam for you. When she wanted something, she rarely came out and asked. Instead, she manipulated and seduced until she got what she wanted. It was one of the things Logan adored about her. There was nothing simple about his wife.

Logan carried his coffee mug to the table, eased into a chair. "What're your thoughts on that?"

Elijah's dark eyes met his, holding steady. "I'll give her anything she wants, Logan. You know that."

"Even if it means sharing a bed with me every night?"

They'd never actually talked about what would happen if and when their relationship ever progressed to this point. They had separate bedrooms, and they shared Sam equally for the most part, although Logan was fairly certain Elijah gave up time with her because he didn't want to take from Logan. In the beginning, they'd given Elijah a wide berth because he had preferred more time alone. However, the past few years had changed him, and Logan had noticed that Elijah and Sam had grown rather close.

Elijah smirked. "I love her enough to deal with your snoring, too."

Logan laughed.

17

It was true, their relationship was unconventional. They both loved Sam, and they both lusted for her. Logan had a penchant for watching Sam be pleasured by Elijah, and he wouldn't apologize for it. There was nothing between him and Elijah, though. Well, nothing beyond the natural progression of a relationship such as theirs. They were close. They talked about work and personal things, did things together. All in all, Logan enjoyed Elijah's company immensely.

As far as an attraction to Elijah went, Logan wasn't sure he could explain what it was he felt. Not because he didn't want to, but more so because he didn't understand it himself. Over the years, he'd found he was attracted to Elijah, but he didn't think it was a sexual attraction. Simply put, Logan was comfortable around Elijah, more so than he'd ever imagined he would be. But regardless of what he did or didn't feel, he would never take that for granted.

Logan nodded toward the iPad. "So you were looking for a bed?"

"I figured if it would work, we'd need something bigger than a king."

They would. Logan's twin brother had a bed that'd been made for three, which offered more room than a standard king-size did. Considering Logan was six-five, the more space, the better.

"Are you thinking a Christmas present?" Logan asked.

Elijah met his gaze again. "If you think it's a good idea, it's definitely worth considering."

Logan peered up at the second floor. "Perhaps we should try sleeping in the same bed while we're here."

"Trial run?" Elijah nodded. "I think that can be arranged."

Logan glanced at the clock on the microwave. "Since it's still early, maybe we head back that way now. Grab a couple more hours, then wake her up appropriately."

Elijah's grin widened. "I like the way you think, McCoy."

SAM WOKE FEELING AS THOUGH SHE'D BEEN sleeping on the surface of the sun.

The heat was everywhere. At her front, her back.

It took a moment to orient herself, remembering they were in Colorado at the cabin Logan had rented for their winter vacation. She peeked open her eyes, saw her husband's handsome face. His eyes were closed, and he was breathing heavily, signifying he was still asleep.

Figuring she would get up and grab coffee, Sam rolled to her back, but she didn't get far. In fact, she didn't get anywhere thanks to the warm body pressed up against her on the other side.

She stilled instantly and realized that something was seriously off.

For starters, she'd gone to bed with Elijah, which made having Logan in bed with her the first strange thing.

Secondly, she'd gone to bed with Elijah, which meant having them both in the same bed with her—while sleeping—was another strange thing.

Despite the fact they did a lot of interesting activities together in a bed, they never fell asleep in the same room. Even when they were enjoying playtime at home and Sam would drift off, she knew one of them would always move her to their bed before they let themselves succumb to sleep. It was just how it worked.

So this ... *this* was weird.

"What's going on?" she mumbled, staring up at the ceiling as she shifted so she could lie on her back between them.

"Morning, love," Elijah whispered, his warm lips brushing her shoulder.

"Why are the three of us in bed together?"

"We thought that was what you wanted."

Sam frowned, looked over at Elijah, but she couldn't say anything.

Yes, it was what she wanted. More than anything, in fact. However, she hadn't mentioned it to either of them. Not outright anyway. Not yet.

"We've got your number, love," Elijah said, his words spoken softly near her ear. "We know what you're angling for."

"No, you don't."

"One bed. The three of us."

Sam narrowed her gaze, staring at him. Before she could give her own reasons, Elijah shifted closer. Close enough he put his heavy thigh over her leg, pinning her in place while he kissed his way up her neck while at the same time sliding the sheet down to bare her breasts.

"Mmm. This is a great way to wake up in the morning," Logan mumbled.

Sam's head snapped over, her eyes landing on his face. Logan hadn't moved, but his eyes were open, and he was watching as Elijah's oral ministrations worked their way to her breasts.

Her entire body flashed with heat as it always did when Logan watched. There was something innately erotic about her husband watching her with Elijah. She knew he loved it, and partly because of that, she did, too.

Elijah's finger tapped her chin before urging her to turn her head as he moved over her. She accepted the weight of him, spreading her legs to welcome him closer.

"You're so soft," Elijah muttered, his lips trailing over her chin. "So warm and wet."

Sam moaned.

"You ready for me?"

"God, yes."

It was the truth, although she sometimes didn't understand how easily her body prepared for her men. They could make her wet with just a look, and while she enjoyed foreplay, it wasn't always necessary.

Sam wrapped her legs around Elijah's waist and shifted her pelvis to welcome him into her body.

His thick cock stretched her perfectly, filling her slowly as he eased his way in. He grazed every sensitive nerve ending, lighting her up from the inside out.

The sheet slid lower, cool air wafting over her leg.

"Let me watch," Logan whispered, his face moving closer to hers.

Sam knew what he wanted, so she lowered her legs to the bed while Elijah pushed himself up with his arms, his hips rocking as he pushed in deep, retreated slowly. With the angle of his body, Sam could easily watch as he sank into her, which was what Logan was obviously fascinated by.

"Feels good," she moaned, relaxing as he did all the work to pleasure her.

"I love watching his cock slide into your cunt, your juices coating him," Logan said, his voice a rough, gravelly rasp.

Her skin tingled, her nipples pebbling tighter as his words caressed her in much the same way Elijah was.

This was what she longed for. The three of them together. Logan finding pleasure in watching them together, Sam seeking the comfort both men could give her, and Elijah letting her love him.

Elijah's dark hair fell over his forehead, and Sam brushed it back, staring up at him, accepting that he was going to torment her slowly this morning. She clenched her inner muscles when he pushed in deep, eliciting a ragged groan as his eyes met hers.

"Do that again," he ordered roughly.

Sam did it again and again, clasping him tightly each time he bottomed out inside her.

Before long, Elijah's slow and gentle ride turned frantic. He began pumping his hips, rocking into her harder, deeper, faster.

Logan's hand slid down over her belly, his fingers joining the party, ruthlessly rubbing her clit as she raced toward that inevitable peak.

"Eli ... Logan..." Sam let herself go, falling into the heavenly abyss as her orgasm crested.

Elijah growled low in his throat as he pushed up to his knees, gripping her legs. He didn't stop fucking her, his eyes locked on her face. Sam watched him, loving how sexy he was when he was chasing his release.

"Come for us," Logan commanded.

Elijah's gaze shot to Logan's face, and for the first time in their history together, he came while looking at Logan rather than at her.

And something about that moment triggered an eruption in her that had her crying out once more.

"My turn," Logan rumbled, wasting no time as he took Elijah's place between her legs.

Sam cried out when he filled her, slamming in hard and deep. Elijah moved to her side, his face close to hers, right there in the moment with them.

"Touch her," Logan bit out.

Elijah's hand cupped her breast, his forefinger and thumb pinching her nipple, sending heat bolting straight to her clit.

Logan leaned forward, his body hovering over hers but ensuring he didn't get in Elijah's way.

"Fuck, yes," he growled low in his throat, hammering away at her.

Sam's entire body was tightening again, another cataclysmic eruption looming. She loved this. Loved when they ganged up on her. It was such a rarity that she'd long ago stopped wishing for these moments.

Elijah's hand followed the same route Logan's had earlier, slipping between their bodies until he was strumming her clit, making her body vibrate with the impending release.

Sam gripped Logan's bicep with one hand, the other sliding into Elijah's hair as she held on, her body rocking beneath the onslaught of Logan's powerful thrusts.

Logan groaned, his head tipping back, and Sam peered down her body to where Elijah's hand was. Not only was he thumbing her clit, his knuckles were rubbing against Logan, gliding over his cock every time he retreated. Seeing Elijah touching Logan was more than she could bear. She screamed out their names as her orgasm obliterated her.

Logan followed her right over the edge, slamming into her one final time, pinning Elijah's hand between their bodies as he came with a roar.

WHILE SAM AND LOGAN FOUGHT TO CATCH their breath, Elijah remained where he was. He kept his hand on Sam's stomach as Logan slid to her other side. He was hesitant to look at the man, not sure what he was going to find. Touching Logan had been a serious risk, something he had never intended. He'd been so caught up in that moment, so turned on by watching Logan fucking Sam, he hadn't given it much thought.

Never before had he been inclined to touch a man, but he would admit—at least to himself—that it had been building for a while now. Years, maybe. But only where Logan was concerned.

He blamed his curiosity on the easy relationship they shared. They were bonded by their love for Sam, brought closer by their desire to take care of her, to love her, to pleasure her. And though Elijah had never been attracted to a man before, he found a curiosity about Logan that he couldn't seem to shake. It had grown more intense these past couple of years, and until today, he'd been able to ignore it.

"That was…" Sam exhaled. "That was so hot."

Elijah refused to look at her or Logan, instead staring down at his hand where it rested on her belly.

"I'd have to agree," Logan said, his voice rougher than usual.

Elijah's gaze darted over. Logan was lying on his back, his arm draped over his eyes.

"Which part?" Elijah asked, keeping his tone light.

"For one, waking up to both of you in my bed," she said.

Yeah, Elijah would agree. He did enjoy the idea of waking up every day to Sam, not just on his dedicated days.

"Then the taking turns thing..." Sam giggled. "A girl can get used to that."

Elijah choked on a laugh. "You sound spoiled."

"Oh, I am. Most definitely."

Figuring that was where the conversation would end, Elijah leaned in to kiss her shoulder, preparing to get out of bed and head for the shower, but Sam stopped him with a hand on his arm.

"The hottest part, though?"

He pretended to adjust the sheet to avoid eye contact.

"Was when you fucking touched me," Logan growled. "Holy fuck."

Elijah stilled.

"God, yes," Sam agreed. "I don't think I've ever come so hard before."

"Me, either," Logan chimed in.

Because he had no desire to get into an in-depth conversation about what prompted him to do it, Elijah forced a laugh and rolled out of bed. He padded toward the bathroom since this was the room he'd chosen for himself. He relieved himself then got into the shower.

He was grateful no one intruded on his moment because he needed a minute to get his bearings.

Chapter Four

When Elijah disappeared into the bathroom, Sam turned to Logan. She watched him as he lowered his arm and opened one eye to peer over at her, evidently sensing she was staring at him.

"Yes?" he drawled.

"That was insanely hot, right?" she whispered, unable to contain her excitement.

"It was."

She watched him, wondering if he would elaborate. Of course, he didn't.

"Wow," she said, falling back again. "Not sure what'll top that."

"Sam." His tone was etched with warning.

"What?"

"Don't push this."

She turned her head his way. "Push what?"

"Let it be. If it plays out, it plays out."

"Are you saying…?" Sam wasn't even sure what question she wanted to ask. Was her husband actually saying he was interested in something more from Elijah? Perhaps a little man-on-man action?

"I'm saying let it be."

"But—"

"I'm not discussing this with you right now," he grumbled. "Let it go for now."

She found herself left with no choice when Logan got up from the bed and padded out of the room. Her gaze bounced between the bedroom door and the bathroom door while her brain continued to process what had transpired.

Never in the seven years that the three of them had been together had Elijah or Logan touched one another so ... so intimately. Sure, there was touching involved, but it was the natural kind. One man moved against another when changing positions and whatnot. But that wasn't what had happened. Elijah had deliberately stroked Logan's cock with his knuckles while Logan had been fucking her.

Just the thought had a shiver racing through her and a torrent of dirty, filthy fantasies racing through her brain.

Of course, Logan's words were now echoing in her head, too. *Let it be. If it plays out, it plays out.* Let it be? Was he serious? Did he not know her at all?

By the time midafternoon rolled around, Sam was beginning to feel a bit antsy. Part of that was due to the fact they hadn't been able to get out of the cabin due to the weather. Instead, they'd passed the time relaxing. She had curled up with a book, taken a nap, vegged on chips, then taken another nap. All in all, she had managed to while away three whole hours. When Logan had woken her to see if she wanted a late lunch, she had opted for a shower while they cooked.

And now that the meal had been consumed, the dishes washed and put away, Sam was hoping they didn't intend to watch television for the rest of the afternoon. Especially not when they could be doing something together. For instance, playing a game.

"What time's your meeting?" Elijah asked.

Sam's gaze darted to Logan. How had she forgotten he was going to work? It had slipped her mind completely.

"They've rescheduled for Monday," he said, his frustration evident.

If they had rescheduled, that meant Logan was the one seeking something from them. Otherwise, Logan would've been in control of the time and location, and he was a stickler for punctuality. No doubt her husband would've tackled a blizzard head-on just to be on time.

"Did they say why?" she asked, wondering if he might share some details.

"The weather. They said it's predicted to get worse before it gets better."

"Enough that they're willing to postpone a meeting?" Sam didn't understand. "Aren't they used to snow here?"

"They are, but they know I'm not. It's my understanding I might get stranded one way or another if I attempt to head to Denver."

Well, that would suck. Sam didn't like the idea of Logan stranded anywhere. Certainly not away from her and Elijah.

"It'll wait until Monday," he said, his tone soothing. "I do need to call Luke, though. Give him a heads-up."

Sam watched Logan head up the stairs. The cell reception in the cabin was spotty at best, but they'd found it was best on the second floor.

"You okay?" Elijah asked as he walked past her on his way to the living room.

Sam nodded, then turned toward the windows. Only then did she realize it was rather dark outside. Since it was still relatively early—a little after three—she had expected there to be more light. A quick glance at the sky and she saw the reason. Thick, dark clouds loomed overhead, seemingly closer to earth than usual. She figured that had something to do with the altitude. Or maybe it was just a figment of her imagination.

"What do you want to do?" Elijah's voice echoed in the open space. "Movie?"

Sam put the weather out of her mind. There was nothing she could do about it, and since it had gotten Logan to stay here, she figured it might be a blessing.

"I think I'm TV'd out," she admitted, heading for the kitchen just as Logan made it to the bottom of the stairs.

What she wanted to do was play a game, but she wasn't sure how to broach the subject. She'd been shot down quickly the first night they were here, but now she had more motivation to get them to participate. *And* she had a new game she wanted to play, one that she'd found online and purchased for exactly a scenario such as this one.

"She's plotting."

Elijah's voice yanked Sam out of her thoughts, had her gaze darting over to where he was sitting on the sofa.

"She's always plotting," Logan agreed, grabbing two beers from the fridge then delivering one to Elijah on his way to sit down.

"I am not."

"Remember when we used to paddle her ass for lying?" Logan asked, grinning around the lip of his beer bottle. "I think we need to start doing that again."

Sam poured a glass of wine and joined them, but rather than sitting on the couch, she took a seat on the thick, plush rug laid out on the floor, her back to the fireplace.

Logan immediately reached for the remote, and Sam gritted her teeth.

"There's a hockey game on," he said, as though reading her shift in mood.

There was always a hockey game on. And when it wasn't hockey, it was baseball or basketball or football. She didn't know when it had happened, but at some point, her husband had developed a penchant for sports.

Almost as though a higher power was siding with her, the power chose that exact moment to flash off. Only this time, it didn't blink back on immediately.

Sam sat motionless as the darkness settled over them. The firelight and the dim light from outside were enough to see by, but the shadows grew heavier throughout the space.

She hated the dark. Like this, anyway. Especially in a place she wasn't completely familiar with. Add in the cold and the snow and—

"Looks like that storm's here," Logan said, sounding relaxed and not at all fazed about the lack of electricity.

"Good thing they postponed," Elijah chimed in.

Sam stared at them, feeling a mixture of anxiety and panic churning inside her. She did not want to spend days without electricity again. That had been brutal the last time. Sure, they had the firewood so they wouldn't get too cold, but that would only go so far.

"Sam, it's all right."

Her gaze shot to Logan's.

"The power'll be back soon, I'm sure."

He had no way of knowing that, but she didn't care to argue with him. It wasn't going to help the situation.

"What if we played a game," Elijah suggested.

She looked at him. "Seriously?"

"Anything but truth or dare," Logan added.

"I've got one," she admitted, letting her focus shift from the darkness to the small silk bag in her pocket. "And no, it's not truth or dare."

Logan's gaze was pinned on her hand. "What do you have?"

"It's called Naughty but Dice," she said with a grin. "I bought it online."

"Dice?" Elijah shifted, his eyes on her.

"Yes." She opened the bag and poured the dice onto the floor in front of her.

With her body blocking the firelight, there was too much of a shadow to see, so she moved to the side.

"This is a sex game."

It wasn't a question, but she responded to Logan anyway. "It's … yes, it's a sex game. You roll the dice and do what it instructs you to do."

"What exactly is on these dice?" Logan asked.

"One has the action, such as kiss or lick or suck," she said, turning the die to read the various sides. "The other has the location, such as neck, ears, lips…"

"So it's tame?"

"Well…" Sam smiled shyly. "There is a triple x side of the die, so you could have to, you know, suck something."

"Who does what?" Elijah asked.

"The person who rolls the dice gets it done to them," she explained.

Sam noticed that Logan looked at Elijah, but Elijah seemed to be avoiding looking at Logan.

"When you roll the dice, who does it to you?" Logan asked.

"That's where I want to improvise."

"Bloody hell," Elijah mumbled.

Sam smiled. "I want to spin the bottle to see who has to … perform."

"Samantha," Logan rumbled in warning.

Ignoring him, she continued to clarify. "The person whose turn it is will spin the bottle. Whoever the bottle lands on or is closest to is the performer. Then the person with the dice will roll them. The performer will then do whatever the dice instructs them to do for one minute, no longer than two."

Her gaze shifted to Elijah, and she saw that he was watching her closely. She couldn't read his expression, but she could tell he was uncomfortable, and she instantly felt like an ass.

"I'm sorry," she blurted, setting her wineglass on the nearby end table. "We don't have to play."

Elijah's eyebrows lowered, but he didn't speak.

And now she felt like complete crap for putting him on the spot like that.

Without thinking, she got to her feet and moved over to him. He was stone still, so she straddled his legs and tilted his chin up with her fingertips. "I'm sorry."

"For what?"

"For trying to get you to do something you don't want to do."

His eyes met hers. "I didn't say I don't want to do it."

Sam studied him, tried to process.

"Let's start slow," Logan suggested.

Sam looked over at her husband, saw that he was watching them intently. No way could she not see the interest in his eyes, even in the shadows.

"Without the bottle," he added. "If you roll, we take turns doing it to you. If we roll, you perform for us."

Sam nodded and looked back at Elijah. "I'm good with that."

Elijah met her gaze and nodded. "Me, too."

ONE THING LOGAN KNEW ABOUT SAM WAS that she was relentless in her pursuit of what she wanted.

And it was abundantly clear that she was on a mission for a repeat of what had happened this morning.

Logan wouldn't say he was completely on board with the idea, but he wasn't entirely opposed to it, either. He had been shocked by Elijah's touch and definitely not in a bad way. He would go so far as to say he had enjoyed it. It had added an element that had intrigued him, made him come harder than he had in a long damn time. However, if they had planned it, he couldn't say it would've played out the same way. He wasn't sure Sam understood that.

"All right. Who wants to go first?" Sam prompted.

"I think Elijah should," Logan told her. "Then me, then you."

Her pretty lips formed a pout as she got to her feet. Sam retrieved the dice, passed them to Elijah, then grabbed her wineglass and returned to her spot on the floor.

Elijah took a moment to study the dice, turning them in his hands as he read whatever was on them. Logan noticed the smile as it formed, and he relaxed a bit.

For most of the day, Elijah had been somewhat standoffish. Since Logan hadn't known what, if anything, he could say to make the situation any less awkward, he'd avoided it altogether, which probably hadn't helped in putting Elijah's mind at ease. And he had to assume that was the reason for the awkward tension. The touching this morning … no, it hadn't been enough to write home about, but it had been a significant shift for them. Something that Logan was curious to explore, but he wasn't willing to dive right in.

Elijah closed his hand around the dice, shook them, then let them fly down to the floor in front of Sam.

She leaned over and read them. "Lick. Neck." She looked up at Logan. "You call time."

Logan nodded, then watched as she got to her feet and moved back to Elijah, positioning herself on his lap once more.

He smiled to himself when she dramatically tilted Elijah's head to the side so she had better access to the spot she coveted. Logan watched as her little pink tongue dragged over Elijah's skin, and just like anytime the two were intimate, Logan's cock began to swell.

Elijah seemed to relax beneath the onslaught, and it didn't take but a few seconds before Sam was getting into the action, adding some sucking action.

"Stick to the rules," Logan commanded. "Lick, not suck."

She grunted, and Elijah chuckled.

"Time."

Sam immediately halted her ministrations, pulling away from Elijah. She grabbed the dice, handed them to Logan with a smirk.

For the next half hour, they each had a handful of turns, Sam having to perform twice as often. If the makers of the game meant this as foreplay, they'd certainly knocked it out of the park. Between stroking nipples, sucking lips, and putting ice below the navel, things escalated quickly. Enough so, Sam had shed a good portion of her clothing while he and Elijah were wearing only jeans.

"Another beer?" Logan offered Elijah when he finished his last round of kissing Sam's belly.

"Sure."

"I'll take the empty," he offered.

Elijah surprised him, glancing at the empty bottle, then back to Logan. "I think we'll need it for the next round."

Logan stilled, his gaze locked with Elijah's.

This was a major turning point in their relationship. One that, should they pursue it, they would never come back from. And that was what worried Logan the most. He was comfortable with their life together. The three of them. They meshed in a way most people wouldn't understand. Anything more ... well, anything more had the potential to knock over their delicate house of cards.

"If you're good with it," Elijah said softly, still holding his gaze.

"I'm good with it," he admitted, partially surprised that it was the truth.

"Me, too."

Sam's sharp inhale had them both looking her way. "I ... uh ... I think I'll get more wine."

Logan smiled as he realized how badly his wife wanted this to happen.

"I'll add some wood to the fire," Elijah stated, his attention shifting away quickly.

While he did that, Logan went to the kitchen, opened the fridge, and grabbed two more beers. The power was out, but the temperature was holding steady; however, he knew that wouldn't be the case for too long. If they didn't get electricity back soon, there was a good possibility their food would spoil.

But it wasn't something he could worry himself with now. Worst case, they could put it outside to keep it fresh, but he didn't want to point it out and risk Sam getting anxious again.

After opening the bottles, Logan went back to the living room and passed one to Elijah, then returned to his spot on the couch.

Sam was back quickly, downing half her glass before setting it on the table and easing down to her knees.

"Are you cold?" Logan asked, noticing her nipples were hard.

"I'm good." She sounded a bit breathless, which made him smile.

"Whose turn is it?"

"Elijah's," she said, tossing him the dice.

"I'll let you spin the bottle," he said, passing the bottle to Sam.

And this was the point of no return. Introducing that bottle meant they ran the risk of Logan having to perform on Elijah and vice versa. Since the dice held a variety of actions and body parts, there was no telling what it would lead to.

Logan watched as Sam leaned over and placed the bottle on the hardwood floor before spinning it. The anticipation of the moment was obliterated when it landed on Elijah. That helped to settle them as the three of them laughed before Sam did it again. This time it landed on Sam, and the rest of the tension dissipated. At least for the moment.

Elijah rolled the dice.

Sam read them. "Warm breath. Below navel."

She smiled as she crawled over to Elijah to complete her task while Logan observed. It was hot, but not as hot as it would've been if Sam had taken Elijah's cock in her mouth. Somehow they'd managed to avoid that particular action, although it was a possibility based on the dice. Or at least he assumed that was what the "xxx" referred to.

"Time," he called after allowing it to go on longer than a minute.

Sam huffed, grabbed the dice, and passed them to Logan.

This time, when the bottle stopped spinning, so did Logan's breathing.

Because it landed on Elijah.

CHAPTER FIVE

ELIJAH'S HEART THUMPED EXTRA HARD WHEN THE mouth of the bottle landed on him.

He had no idea what those dice would tell him to do, but whatever it was would be something he'd never done before because he would have to perform the action on Logan.

Was he nervous?

Damn straight.

Was he excited?

Surprisingly, yes.

Although he wasn't sure he wanted Logan to know just how much.

Things had been decidedly awkward between them since that morning, and he wasn't sure if it was all him or if Logan was just as freaked out by what had happened. He had tried his best not to make it weird, but no matter how hard he tried, it seemed inevitable. Probably had a lot to do with the fact they hadn't discussed what had happened. Not that he wanted to. Elijah wasn't sure he was ready for that just yet.

Then again, it was all moot because Sam had pulled one of her infamous stunts and managed to manipulate the situation to force it to happen again. And she'd managed to introduce a new game at the same time.

In the beginning, Elijah had been surprised by Sam's games, but over the years, he'd gotten used to them, so he hadn't been entirely caught off guard by the idea of this one. Nor with her modified rules. Didn't change the fact that he wasn't sure how this was going to play out or whether or not it even should. What happened between him and Logan would alter the course of their relationship regardless. Either they would enjoy it and continue down this road, or they would enjoy it and not continue. Or, what he prayed *didn't* happen, they would be turned off entirely, and things would only go downhill from there.

"Kiss. Lips," Sam announced when Logan tossed the dice to the floor.

Elijah's heart slammed against his ribs once more as he met Logan's gaze.

He had never been one to back down from a challenge, but he'd also never found himself in a position like this.

"I can roll again if you'd like," Logan said, and the way he said it made Elijah realize he was all right with the idea of Elijah kissing him.

"One rule," Elijah stated as he got to his feet and moved toward Logan. "If this gets weird, we talk about it."

"We won't let this destroy us," Logan said firmly.

Elijah nodded, then took a seat beside Logan, their thighs touching.

"Don't move," Elijah said firmly, deciding he was going to be in charge of this moment. Someone needed to be.

Logan remained perfectly still, but the problem came when Elijah found he couldn't move either.

He had never kissed a man before, and while he doubted it would feel much different than kissing a woman, he would *know* it was different. Especially because this was Logan. His stomach pitched, and he felt a moment of fear. Elijah did not want to do something that would ultimately ruin what they had. Not even something as innocent as a kiss.

"I can help."

Sam's soft voice drew their attention.

Elijah cocked an eyebrow. "How?"

Her expression was serious when she asked, "Do you trust me?"

"With everything that I am," he said honestly.

She nodded, then got to her feet and came over, positioning herself so she was sitting between them, forcing them both to sit at an angle.

They both turned their attention to her as she got situated. Elijah's breath expelled from his lungs when she leaned in and kissed his mouth. Soft, gentle.

He let her take the reins, giving himself over to her as she licked and sucked at his lower lip, her hand gliding over his bare back. When she pulled back, Elijah realized Logan was watching intently, as he always did.

Sam then performed the same maneuver on Logan while Elijah watched.

It went on for a couple of minutes while they took turns kissing Sam until she'd somehow gotten them closer together.

"I want to watch you kiss him," she whispered in Elijah's ear.

A jolt of heat speared him. Her words were a sensual seduction, and although he was far more dominant in the bedroom than Sam, he found he wanted to please her by doing as she requested.

Without thinking, Elijah leaned over and pressed his lips to Logan's. They both hesitated briefly, a brush of lips and nothing more.

Sam shifted, and Elijah felt her hand on the back of his head as though she was holding him in place. It wasn't necessary because he wasn't moving away. No, he was rooted to the sofa, to the moment, trying to remember how to breathe.

"Don't stop," Logan grumbled, his hand sliding onto Elijah's thigh.

That single command was enough to have Elijah going in for the kill. He crushed his mouth to Logan's and gave himself over to the kiss. He let the sensations overwhelm him, the feel of Logan's firm lips, his tongue, the whiskers on his cheeks. Elijah didn't hesitate to see whether Logan welcomed him because he didn't have to. Logan growled low in his throat and pulled Elijah into him.

The kiss was earth-scorching hot, unlike anything Elijah had ever experienced. There was a definite difference between kissing Sam and kissing Logan. Not only because of their gender but also because of their personalities. Sam was generously submissive while Logan was fully dominating. They were at war for supremacy as their tongues dueled, hands groping.

Elijah had no idea how long it went on. It lasted until Sam moaned, her soft, cool hands caressing his back, pulling him out of the moment.

"Christ Almighty," Logan whispered.

Sam's eyes were wide as she stared between them, as though she was waiting for one of them to do something.

Elijah wiped his lower lip with his thumb as he met Logan's gaze again.

Now for the moment of truth.

Sam was transfixed by the sight of Logan and Elijah looking at one another.

It was like watching two hungry wolves who'd gone head-to-head for their meal, and somehow they'd both come out the victor.

"Fuck," Elijah mumbled, his chest heaving.

That had been...

Unbelievable.

Freaking hot.

Sinful.

Sam wanted to watch them again, wanted to see her men give in to whatever this urge was to devour one another, but she knew better than to make the request. She wasn't in charge of this, no matter how much she wished that were the case. They had to find common ground for this to move forward. If, in fact, it was going to move forward.

"Enough games," Logan said, his gaze swinging to Sam.

She wasn't about to argue, but even if she had been, he gave her no time to do so.

Before she knew what was happening, Logan and Elijah were on their feet. A second later, Logan had her tossed over his shoulder and was marching toward the stairs. She squealed but remained still, not wanting him to drop her on his path to what she hoped was a bedroom.

Seemingly picking one at random, Logan strolled in and tossed Sam to the bed, making her laugh. It died off quickly when Logan stripped off the remainder of his clothes, then reached for her panties and jerked them down her legs. Elijah wasn't far behind, strolling into the room looking just as dangerous, his eyes flashing with heat.

"Don't move," Logan ordered her before looking at Elijah. "Start a fire? I'll get the lube."

Sam shivered, but it had nothing to do with the chill in the room and everything to do with what she knew Logan had in store for her.

She held her breath, watched as Logan disappeared into the bathroom and Elijah went over to start a fire in the fireplace in the bedroom. She wasn't sure they were going to need the added heat just yet, but she wouldn't complain, especially since the room was almost completely dark now that night was falling.

"This is your doing," Logan said firmly when he strolled out of the bathroom. "You got what you wanted, and now we're gonna get what we want."

Oh, boy. She loved that edge in his voice. He was in true alpha mode.

"Which is?" she taunted, her gaze drifting to Elijah as he stood tall before stripping off his jeans and joining her on the bed.

Logan didn't answer, but she wasn't waiting for it because Elijah's mouth crushed to hers as he rolled them so that she was on top of him.

"Put my cock inside you," he rasped, gripping her hair.

Sam reached between them and found his cock hard and thick. She stroked him once, twice before guiding him right where she needed him. He didn't allow her to ease down on him, though. Elijah gripped her hips and pulled her down, making her cry out as the ecstasy of pleasure/pain washed over her. She loved when he was rough, when he took what he wanted, when he was so overcome by his own desires that he took his pleasure from her.

She was vaguely aware of Logan moving around behind her, but she let Elijah distract her. With her hands planted on his chest, she rode him, rolling her hips and fucking him as though her life depended on it.

"Fucking tight," Elijah groaned, his eyes locked on her face.

"She's about to be tighter," Logan said from behind her.

Sam leaned forward when Logan's big hand landed in the center of her back. She didn't fight him, giving in because she loved when they did this. When they overwhelmed her, when they lost control. And they had lost control, there was no doubt about it.

When Logan shifted closer, Elijah stilled her with a firm grip on her hips. He lifted his head to get to her mouth, and she succumbed to the kiss, lying out over him. Strong hands gripped her butt cheeks, separating them. Cool lube dripped over her rear entrance, followed by a finger being inserted.

Sam tried to rock against the intrusion, welcoming it because she was on fire, and she needed them to quench this inexplicable need. Watching them kiss had done something to her, unraveled her in a way she hadn't expected.

Logan groaned, and then she felt the blunt head of his cock as he pressed against her hole. Elijah's tongue slowed, sliding against hers as he breathed her in.

"Tell him you like it," Elijah urged. "That you like having him fuck your ass."

"I *love* it," she whimpered, shifting so she could take him deeper. "I love the two of you inside me at the same time."

Sam could still remember the first time she'd taken Elijah and Logan at the same time. They had both fucked her pussy, and it had been an experience she had never forgotten. Since then, they'd experimented in so many ways. But having them like this ... there was something carnal about it. It made her feel alive in a way she couldn't explain. Sam loved when they double-teamed her because she felt so close to them both.

Logan's hands gripped her hips, and she realized Elijah's were still there, too. Together they held her in place while Logan penetrated her asshole, Elijah fucking her pussy. In and out, they alternated, slowly at first. It wasn't long before they had their rhythm, and they began plowing into her, sensation after sensation consuming her entire body. Her skin felt too tight as heat engulfed her. A ball of electricity formed deep within her, and the next thing she knew, it detonated, and she was soaring, her insides humming as her muscles tensed, letting the energy of her orgasm consume her.

"Fuck," Elijah shouted, his hips bucking upward as he stilled, buried deep inside her.

Logan growled, obviously following their lead as he rammed her backside, the two of them coming together.

Sam wasn't sure what this meant for the three of them, where things would go from here, but she knew without a doubt that she was looking forward to letting it play out, just like Logan had advised.

FOREVERMORE

CLUB DESTINY, 12

CHAPTER ONE

Thursday, June 16, 2022

ELIJAH PENN SAT QUIETLY ON THE LIVING room sofa, his attention on the man and woman currently laughing in the kitchen.

Logan, with his brooding hazel eyes and midnight-black hair—which, at forty-eight, didn't have a lick of gray coming in—towered over his wife, smiling down at her, his grin rich with promise. And Samantha, their beautiful Samantha, was making his jeans uncomfortably tight in that white, breast-hugging tank top and those dark jeans that rode low beneath her belly button. With her long dark blond hair, straightened to a glossy shine in preparation for her trip, Sam was like an erotic fantasy come true. She was laughing as she poked the bear, her light green eyes dancing with mischief as she said something to Logan.

"Keep that up, baby, and you're gonna find yourself over my knee," Logan's deep baritone echoed in the kitchen, keeping Elijah's attention riveted on them.

From his position, Elijah had the perfect view of their interactions, and like many times before, he found himself captivated. Not only by their physical appeal but by the easy way they communicated. They were comfortable with one another, laughing, joking, teasing. Just being near them was enough to brighten the darkest day, and there had been some really dark ones back in the beginning, but that was because Sam had come into his life during a dark point. Back then, Elijah had mistakenly believed he would be able to keep some space between himself and the promise of a future with someone else. He'd convinced himself that he would be satisfied with the physical aspects of their relationship and would remain emotionally committed to Beth and only Beth for the remainder of his days.

Oh, how wrong he'd been. As was her nature, Sam had been right there, showing him the error of his ways.

"Don't you dare, Logan McCoy," Sam giggled. "My butt's off-limits."

Elijah chuckled as he watched Logan's expression. The man clearly took her declaration as a dare.

The three of them had been in a polyamorous relationship for going on eight years now, and with every passing minute, they seemed to be getting more comfortable with one another. Of course, he wasn't talking in the intimate sense, because that had never been an issue. From the beginning, back when Logan invited Elijah to share his wife, there'd been a cataclysmic connection between him and Sam. Didn't seem to matter how many years passed or how many new things were discovered about one another, their connection continued to grow stronger.

"If I'm not mistaken, that sexy ass belongs to me," Logan countered. "And that rock on your finger is a reminder."

"That *rock* is a reminder that you're a pain in my butt," Sam teased, giggling when Logan reached for her.

Through the years, Elijah and Logan had grown accustomed to sharing Sam between them. Until recently, she had alternated which bed she slept in at night. Sometimes in Logan's, others in Elijah's. When one of them was away on business, the other was there to take her to dinner, get some quality time, and selfishly ravish her without a witness. He wouldn't say it was divided equally, but that had never been the point. What they had was both complicated and simple, depending on the day, and for them, it worked seamlessly.

"You're impeding my time with Eli," Sam added with a huff that ended in a squeal when Logan wrapped his arms around her middle.

"Perhaps Eli'd like the pleasure of spanking your ass."

Elijah rubbed his hands together when Sam glanced over. "Getting warmed up now," he teased.

Her eyes narrowed, and she flashed a brilliant smile.

Sam had once told him that, eventually, his heart would have room for one more, and she was right. Elijah had lost his beloved wife fourteen years ago to brain cancer. While he still reminisced, still reflected on the fond memories of their life before the vicious disease had stolen her from him, he had since moved forward, and he suspected his sweet Beth would've wanted that for him. Perhaps it was his acceptance of that or merely because Samantha had a magnetic appeal that drew him in. Whatever the reason, Elijah had come to want more. He loved Sam. That much was a given. After all, it wasn't difficult to develop feelings for someone you spent so much time with. Especially with a woman who was as fascinating as she was confounding. And yes, Elijah was also *in love* with her.

But she wasn't the only one who stirred a longing in him these days.

Six months ago, in a cabin lit by candlelight, as part of a game Sam had convinced them to play, Elijah had kissed Logan. It hadn't been a peck on the lips or a hesitant exploration of tongues, either. It had been a dick-hardening, mind-numbing, soul-rocking kiss that Elijah still thought about. They hadn't made any progress since, but Elijah continued to wonder whether they might. He figured they were moving in the right direction, and it had started when they'd granted Sam her Christmas wish and made a change to their sleeping arrangements. It had required them to custom order a bed that would work for them. After some research, they'd designed one that was a little wider than two queen-sized mattresses if they were put side by side and a little longer than a standard king to accommodate Logan's six-foot-five-inch frame. To put it simply, it was big enough for them to sleep without crowding, although they did that anyway. Plus, it provided all the room they needed for when one of them was feeling frisky. Which, believe it or not, was all the time.

Logan met his gaze over Sam's head and winked. "Looks to me like he's eager to get his hands on your ass."

I'm eager for something, all right, Elijah thought as he met Logan's heated stare.

As the saying went, things were a-changin'.

Elijah wouldn't say things between him and Logan were weird, but the dynamic had undoubtedly shifted, and it continued to do so day after day as the anticipation built. It probably had a lot to do with the sneaky woman whose goal in life seemed to be to manipulate a situation to her liking. It helped that she thought she was being coy and discreet, but Elijah could see right through her.

"I have a plane to catch," Sam squealed, giggling as she pulled away from Logan.

"Sierra's not here yet," Logan countered. "You've still got time for me to turn that pretty ass a nice rosy red."

"No." She laughed as she slipped out of Logan's grasp and made a beeline for Elijah. "My behind is off-limits. I've got just enough time to spend with Eli before I leave."

Elijah shifted his body to welcome her when she came and sat beside him on the sofa before falling against him, her arms wreathing his neck.

"I don't wanna go," she said, her nose nuzzling his neck, her soft fingers grazing his cheek reverently.

Elijah laughed. "Liar."

She pulled back, smiled. "You're right. I'm excited."

He'd known that she was looking forward to her girls' weekend for quite some time. Sierra, Ashleigh, Sam, McKenna, and Mercedes were off to Vegas for the weekend, a trip that had become a yearly event for the women seeking a little bit of time to themselves.

"You'll miss me, though, right?" Sam said, kissing his chin.

"Always."

"Good." She sat up straight, but he pulled her back to him. "I better get a real kiss before you go. To tide me over."

Sam hummed her approval, leaning into him. Elijah cupped the back of her head, molded his mouth to hers, and slipped his tongue inside. He tasted the cherry gloss on her lips and the subtle hint of mint from her toothpaste. Her soft sigh made his cock thicken, but he ignored the damn thing. She would be gone for four days and three nights, which meant he'd have to refrain until she returned.

"Careful," he whispered, his hand gripping her thigh, "or you will be late because I'll have those jeans around your ankles and my cock buried inside you."

Another moan, this one louder as she pressed her breasts to his chest. "You're a tease."

"It's a promise, I assure you," he corrected, releasing her, feeling lighter simply for her presence.

"I'd take you up on it, but I've got trouble to stir up in Sin City."

"If you get into trouble, we're not coming to bail you out," Logan said as he strolled into the room, his gaze hot, a sign he'd been watching their intimate kiss.

"You will, too," Sam countered.

He shook his head. "Nope. We've got things to do."

"Like what?" She looked back at Elijah as though he might reveal whatever their secret plans were.

Truth was, they hadn't intended to do anything. In fact, they'd agreed to do absolutely nothing while she was gone. Sam might be eager to jet off and enjoy some nightlife in a different city, but Elijah was looking forward to being home. He'd been traveling more than he cared to as of late, so being here would be a vacation in itself.

"Just promise me one thing," she said, glancing back and forth between them. "If you two decide to do something wicked and dirty … don't."

Elijah noticed the way Logan's eyebrows slowly rose as though challenging her authority.

"But if you do," she added, her grin widening, "then at least record all the dirty details and send the video to my phone. I promise not to share it."

Elijah chuckled, pulling her back so he could press a kiss to her temple. "We'll be perfect gentlemen."

She patted his stomach. "That's too bad because I really, *really* want—"

"Let it go, Sam," Logan said, his tone hard, all amusement gone.

Elijah had heard him tell her that numerous times since their return from the cabin. One of Sam's most prominent traits was her ability to push when she wanted something, and from what he'd gathered, she was eager for more of what happened that night between him and Logan. She'd been dropping subtle and sometimes not-so-subtle hints for the past six months. For whatever reason, Logan put the kibosh on it every time.

"Fine," Sam huffed.

She turned, planted another quick kiss on his mouth, then got to her feet. She sauntered across the room, came to stand directly in front of Logan, then waited until he leaned down so she could kiss him, too. He put his hands on her face, tilted her head back, and lowered his mouth to hers.

Elijah watched as she became putty in the man's hands, leaning into him as she hummed softly.

"Sierra will be here in a minute," she reminded him, patting Logan's cheek.

"Go on," he urged, smacking her butt when she turned. "Finish getting ready. I'll stall her if you're not out when she gets here."

Once she was out of the room, Elijah waited until Logan looked at him. "You know, we really do need to discuss what happened."

Logan seemed to consider that for a moment, his hazel eyes narrowed on him. "You're right. We do."

Rather than give him a time or place for when that discussion might occur, Logan did what he always did; he turned and walked out of the room.

Just another day in paradise.

LOGAN HELPED SAM LOAD TWO SUITCASES AND a carry-on bag into the trunk of the limousine the girls had hired to take them to the airport. For the life of him, he couldn't imagine what she could possibly need for three nights in Vegas that would require that much luggage, but he'd long ago stopped asking those types of questions. His wife was eccentric and free-spirited, and he loved her because of those traits, as well as a few hundred more, so he simply bit his tongue and learned to keep his mouth shut.

"Be good," he said, planting one last kiss on her lips. "We'll see you when you get back on Sunday."

"I won't make any promises," she said with a smirk. "On the being good part."

He rolled his eyes and kissed her nose, then helped her into the car.

Once the limo's taillights were out of sight, he ventured back into the house. He found Elijah still sitting on the couch, his nose buried in one of the many books he read. Tom Clancy, James Patterson, and Lee Child were his go-to authors, and more often than not, one of those books was in Elijah's hands. Logan knew the man could remain like that for hours, sometimes staying up late into the night before coming to bed.

Although he didn't share Elijah's love of reading, he got the feeling this hobby of his had only increased because of the situation they'd found themselves in—surrounded by a potent mixture of curiosity and desire. They'd gotten damn good at this game of pretend, the one where they both acted as though what happened had been just an ordinary day. Considering Logan had never kissed a man before that night, it was anything but ordinary, which he was reminded of every single time he looked at the man. By bringing it up, Sam thought she was keeping the dream alive, but her reminders weren't necessary. Not a day had gone by that Logan hadn't thought about that kiss.

The problem was, he wasn't sure which way to go from here. He'd developed a curiosity that drove him mad whenever he thought too long about that encounter. The more time that passed, the more he embraced the idea of exploring this bisexual inclination to see if the kiss was as good as he remembered. At the same time, he repeatedly told Sam to let things play out as they might, but they hadn't gotten around to tackling the subject, despite Elijah's repeated requests to talk about what had happened. Logan tended to shrug off the idea because he had no fucking idea what he was supposed to say.

Yeah, they'd kissed.

Yeah, Elijah had grazed his cock during one intimate moment.

Sure, he had liked it.

Fuck yes, he wanted to do it again. All of it.

However...

While he could fuck Sam nine ways to Sunday, didn't give a shit who watched—he was admittedly a voyeur and an exhibitionist—Logan didn't want to go that route with Elijah. He wasn't thrilled with the idea of making this—whatever *this* was—into a spectacle. And he certainly didn't want to get Sam's hopes up in the event they decided their imaginations had turned it into something it wasn't. But she was nothing if not persistent, another one of her quirky traits he loved.

Logan didn't want to interrupt Elijah's reading, so he went to the kitchen, grabbed a beer, then headed for the backyard. The pool lights were on, giving the water a deep purple hue. He never knew what color it would be because Sam remained in charge of that. He didn't really care because he rarely paid much attention. He usually had other things on his mind whenever he managed to get Sam out here. One of their very first sexual encounters had been poolside. Not this pool, not this house, but he remembered it clearly, how he'd introduced Sam to his twin brother, Luke. Back then, Logan had routinely shared women with his brother. It had been about the pleasure they could bring her, two-on-one, but with Sam, things had been different.

Different enough that his entire world had changed.

Logan had gone and fallen in love with Sam, and then Luke had settled down, married Sierra and Cole, and popped out some kids. There'd been a couple of other encounters after with other men Logan knew, but things had changed once again when Elijah came into the picture. Logan just hadn't realized how much they'd changed until that one lascivious encounter when Elijah had stroked his cock while Logan had been balls deep inside Sam. The brush of Elijah's knuckles along his shaft had set him off and left him questioning his sexuality.

He heard the back door open, glanced over to see Elijah sticking his head out.

"I know you don't want to talk about it," Elijah said, "but I figured we need to decide on our sleeping arrangements."

Sleeping arrangements?

Oh, shit. Logan honestly hadn't given any thought to what it meant for Sam to be gone. Since January, the three of them had shared a bed whenever they were all here. Which meant, without her between them…

"It's your bed, too," he grumbled, not sure what Elijah was angling for.

He heard a disgruntled huff, followed by, "I'll just sleep in my old bed."

"Eli, wait," he called before Elijah could close the door.

"It's clear I make you uncomfortable," Elijah said from the doorway. "Don't give it another thought."

"Just fucking wait," he demanded. "Come out here."

With his attention on the purple lights glimmering beneath the water, Logan listened for sounds Elijah was approaching. He didn't hear anything at first, but then a minute later, footsteps sounded on the pool coping. Elijah appeared, beer in hand.

It didn't matter that Logan wasn't ready to broach this subject; it appeared they'd found themselves in a situation that required it. Part of him wondered if Sam had played a part in that, too, with her earlier reference to wicked, dirty things.

He took a long pull on his beer, then let the bottle dangle from his fingers, his arm resting on the arm of the chair.

"I don't want you sleeping in another bed," he said, not looking at Elijah. "At the same time, I don't want…"

"A repeat?" Elijah filled in when Logan paused.

"Oh, I definitely want a repeat," he mumbled, then dared to look at Elijah, met his dark brown gaze. "I just don't want this scripted."

If he wasn't mistaken, that was relief on the Brit's face.

"We've got three nights. Let's just let it play out," he told Elijah, repeating the exact words he'd told Sam when she had pushed that night in Colorado.

"So should I expect you to rub up on me in the middle of the night?"

He heard the teasing in Elijah's tone, and he relaxed a little. "If anyone's gonna do any rubbing, it'll be you."

Elijah laughed softly. "You think so?"

Logan smiled.

That night, no one did any rubbing, but they did sleep in the same bed. Due to how big it was, they could've been sleeping in separate rooms. When Logan woke the next morning, he wasn't sure whether he was relieved or disappointed that they'd wasted one of those three nights.

CHAPTER TWO

Friday, June 17, 2022

"IF ANYONE TRIES TO TELL ME THIS morning wasn't better than even the best sex, I'll know you're lying," McKenna declared as they sat down for lunch at Diablo's Cantina, one of their go-to places whenever they were in Vegas.

Sam laughed, reaching for the first of many margaritas to come. They'd been in Vegas for less than twenty-four hours, and already their conversations were turning to sex.

"Ladies, I think our men might have to have a conversation with Tag. He's clearly not doing *something* right."

"I mean, it was good, but…" Sierra arched one smooth dark brow at McKenna.

"I agree with McKenna," Ashleigh said. "That massage was *heaven.*"

"An intervention for Tag and Alex it is." Sam glanced at Mercedes. "Looks like you're the tiebreaker. Which will it be? Team Sex or Team Spa?"

Mercedes's gaze swung across their faces before she smiled. "I agree with Sam and Sierra. The spa was nice, but…"

A round of laughter erupted.

Sam loved these getaways. The time she got to spend with her very best friends was priceless. At home, there wasn't as much time to get together as there once had been. Although they frequented Devotion on a monthly basis, those visits rarely offered them the chance to catch up. There were the weekend get-togethers, of course, but those food-filled encounters usually involved a handful of rambunctious kids and men who liked to disappear when it was time to clean up.

"Perhaps it's because we've got kids," Ashleigh said, brushing them off with a flick of her wrist and a goofy grin.

"Hey, I've got kids," Sierra countered.

"Then maybe it's because we're not sandwiched between two hot men every night," McKenna noted as she sipped her drink.

"I'll give you that," Sam conceded. "It is nice to sleep between two hot men every night."

"Sleep?" McKenna snorted. "How much sleep *do* you get every night, anyway? Like eight, nine hours?"

Ashleigh snorted. "God, I remember those days."

Sam smiled. She was the only one at the table without kids, and her friends never failed to point out that she was also the only one who had a regular sleep regimen.

"Don't let her fib her way through this," Sierra said, eyes pinned on Sam. "We all know you're getting less than us these days. Now that the three of you are sleeping in the *same* bed."

Sam felt her cheeks warm as she took a big swallow of her drink. She thought about two nights ago when she'd woken her snoring men with her hands on their cocks. Neither had complained. In fact, they'd rewarded her for her generosity by sandwiching her between them and ensuring she slept soundly for the rest of the night *after* wringing two orgasms out of her.

"How's that going, anyway?" Ashleigh inquired, her eyes dancing with curiosity. "The three of you in the same room? Is it weird?"

"No, it's good. I like having them both there." Sam hadn't yet told her friends about the encounter in Colorado between Logan and Elijah, but she hadn't been able to refrain from telling them about her desire to sleep in the same bed with them every night. Ashleigh had been the one to suggest they look into a family-sized bed, as they were awkwardly called, in order to make it a reality.

"Just *good?*" McKenna asked. She glanced between the girls, then back to Sam. "That sounds like the understatement of the century."

"I don't know how you do it," Mercedes said. "It's all I can do to keep up with Xander sometimes." She took a sip, then hurried to swallow as she nodded. "That reminds me…"

Sierra shoved a salsa-loaded chip in her mouth, nodding excitedly.

"What?" Sam asked, glancing between her friends, noticing they all had a sparkle in their eyes.

"Is there … um…" Mercedes looked at McKenna, who looked at Ashleigh, who looked at Sierra.

Sam frowned.

"Y'all always do this," Sierra accused. "Always leave it to me to—"

"To what?" Sam insisted.

Sierra sighed. "We've been wondering if…?"

Everyone was silent, their expressions sheepish.

"Oh, for the love of—Just spit it out," Sam declared.

"Is there something going on between Elijah and Logan?" McKenna blurted.

Sam froze, glass midway to her mouth. "What do you mean?"

Mercedes said, "We … uh … might've noticed they're acting a little differently around each other."

Sam cocked one eyebrow, waited for them to clarify. She knew exactly what they were hinting at, but she had no intentions of spilling the beans because, as far as she was concerned, their interactions were no one else's business.

Of course, if her friends could narrow it down, perhaps she could use that as the opening necessary to talk about it.

God, she wanted to talk about it. It killed her not to blurt it out and get their opinions, but she respected Logan and Elijah too much to gossip about something so intimate. She had no qualms talking about her own sexual encounters with her men, but that was different. Talking about the wicked things they did to her was a far cry from revealing the fact that her men might be bisexual.

Not that anyone at this table would judge them for it. They all had their various sexual proclivities, and as a group, they embraced them. That was one of the things Sam loved most about her circle of friends. They encouraged one another to be open about who they were.

51

"Different how?" she asked, reaching for one of the quickly dwindling chips.

"Did they have a fight?" McKenna asked.

"No, why?"

"Because when they're around, it's like watching two prizefighters gearing up for a showdown," Ashleigh explained.

She gulped down her margarita, reached for another chip. She'd noticed it, too, though she wouldn't describe it quite like that. Perhaps there was a little more distance than before the night in the cabin, but there was no toe-to-toe snorting and posturing.

"Maybe they're just getting used to sleeping in the same bed," Sierra said. "I mean, two men who've slept alone for so long. It's probably weird for them."

Oh, Sam didn't think *that* was the problem.

"Did they sleep in the same bed last night?" McKenna sounded more like the award-winning journalist she was, gearing up to write an article, than a curious friend.

Sam shrugged, studied the near-empty bowl of chips, the variety of salsas that came with it. At anything except for the inquisitive eyes peering back at her. She honestly didn't know. She had texted them both last night and had intended to call them this morning when she woke up, but their appointment at the spa had been the reason she'd crawled out of bed when she had. She hadn't yet had a chance to call and ask them that exact question.

"Wouldn't that be weird for them?" Ashleigh asked, eyebrows lowering as though she was mentally picturing it. "Without you there?"

Sam reached for her margarita, finished it off, wished the waiter would swing by with another pronto.

"Samantha McCoy," Sierra hissed, leaning forward. "What *aren't* you telling us?"

Oh, boy.

Sam scrambled for something to say that would make sense and not give away Logan and Elijah's secret. It would be wrong on so many levels for her to out them, even with her friends.

"She's definitely keeping something from us," Mercedes decided.

"First, we need to pinpoint when this began," McKenna said, glancing between the others. "Then we might be able to narrow it down to an event."

Sam shook her head. "No."

"What do you mean, no?" Sierra looked affronted. "Is there something wrong? Something you don't *want* us to know?"

Sam opted for the truth. Well, a partial truth, anyway.

"There's nothing wrong, and yes, there's something I'm not telling you." She hated the crestfallen looks her friends gave her. "Not because I don't want to," she added. "It's just not my place."

"Is it about Elijah and Logan?" McKenna asked, always in reporter mode. "And the new arrangement?"

"Yes." She waved a hand, pushed her empty glass to the edge of the table, hoping the waiter would see it as the white flag she meant it to be. "But that's all I'm gonna say."

"What—"

"Please," Sam pleaded, meeting each of their probing stares. "I promise it's not bad, but I can't talk about it. Not yet."

"You know you can tell us anything, right?" Mercedes noted, leaning in. "We don't judge."

Sam smiled softly. "I do know that. And I will tell you. Once I'm allowed to."

"Allowed?" Sierra snorted, her eyes twinkling. "Since when does Samantha McCoy let anyone tell her she's not allowed to do something?"

Sam relaxed a little. "Trust me, this is *way* harder for me than you think."

That was enough to settle her friends, and they spent the rest of lunch dancing around the subject but never overstepping. And yes, she was proud of herself for not blurting it out because, boy, this was harder than she'd thought.

"I TOLD YOU, LUKE, I'M STICKING CLOSE to the house this weekend," Logan informed his brother during his drive home from work on Friday evening.

It was his third attempt at politely declining his brother's invitation to join him and a few of the husbands at Devotion. Although he understood the appeal of the fetish club his brother owned, Logan saw no reason to go unless Sam was with him, and he'd told Luke as much.

"Just you and Eli?"

"Yes," he said, ensuring his brother heard his frustration.

"Things cool with the two of you?"

"Of course." He wanted to know why Luke would ask something like that, but he refrained from questioning him. The last thing Logan wanted was to get into a conversation with Luke, especially one that involved the topic of his newfound interest in Elijah. His brother was adept at dragging the truth out the same way a dentist extracted teeth—with precision and determination—and he damn sure didn't want to go into the details. Not now. Maybe not ever.

"Fine. I hope your old ass goes to bed early," Luke grumbled good-naturedly.

"I'm sure I will," he lied, ending the call with a promise to catch up the following weekend when the women were back from their trip.

Logan pulled into the driveway, looking forward to some downtime for the next two days. He was also looking forward to spending some time with Elijah. They rarely had a chance to catch up, just the two of them. He happened to find Elijah's job fascinating, and he wouldn't mind hearing how things were going.

Even as he thought about the safe subject of work, Logan could practically hear Elijah's request to analyze what had happened in the cabin.

He sighed.

Perhaps he should use their alone time to discuss what had happened, hash it out once and for all, and figure out what that meant for them and their future. God knows it weighed heavily on all of them, and Logan would accept that he was the reason they'd stalled out. And he would gladly take the blame. While he was usually the one who wanted to talk, to get Sam's take on the sexual aspects of their relationship, this wasn't something he cared to delve into. As far as he was concerned, talking was overrated when it came to things you had no control over, but maybe it would help.

Or he could simply pursue the man and see what transpired. Seriously, what was there to talk about? They'd both copped to enjoying the encounter, so dissecting it to pieces seemed like a complete waste of time. Logan had been serious when he told Elijah he didn't want to follow a convoluted script based on too much talking and planning. He had enough of that at work, and his biggest pet peeve was meetings to prep for more meetings.

"Let it be. If it plays out, it plays out," he muttered as he pulled into the garage and turned off the engine. That would be his motto for the weekend, he decided as he climbed out of the car. He opened the back door, walked into the house, and solidified that action plan in his mind. He vowed not to think too long or too hard on anything that pertained to Elijah and the strange—albeit ridiculously appealing—things that had happened between them that night in Colorado.

As he neared the kitchen, he was greeted by a sweet yet spicy aroma, his stomach rumbling in response. He set his laptop bag on the washing machine as he passed through the laundry room, then followed the delicious scent, wondering what Elijah was preparing tonight. It was rare for him to cook, considering he spent so much time at work—a good majority of it traveling—so Logan was looking forward to whatever was on the menu.

Logan stopped in the kitchen, his gaze settling on the man standing at the stove. He couldn't see what he was preparing, but it didn't matter when his gaze snagged on the rigid muscles that cut a path down the man's bare back, accentuating his broad shoulders and trim waist. Wearing only a pair of shorts, Elijah's sleek, golden skin was stretched taut over lean muscle, and every move he made had his back muscles shifting and bunching in a way that captured Logan's attention.

Definitely curious, that little voice in his head reiterated.

"Just in time," Elijah said, not bothering to look back.

Let it be, Logan repeated in his head, forcing his feet to carry him over to where Elijah stood.

He paused behind him, then leaned forward, the front of his shirt grazing Elijah's bare back as he peeked over his shoulder. "What're we having?"

He felt as much as heard Elijah's soft inhale as his body quivered slightly.

Was that because of Logan's proximity? And was it a shiver of anticipation, or was he put off by the touch?

Stop overthinking.

"Baked salmon with mango chutney and asparagus," Elijah said, his tone steady, making Logan wonder whether he'd imagined that initial reaction.

He kept his tone light when he said, "No burgers and fries for us tonight, huh?"

"Figured I'd make something light."

"Yeah? Big night of reading? Don't want to overdo it?" he teased, forcing himself back a step, keeping his hands at his sides and not sliding over Elijah's back so he could feel the heat of his skin or the play of those delectable muscles. "Do I have a minute to change?"

Elijah nodded, shoulders tense, hands paused over his preparations.

Logan took that minute and a couple more to get himself under control before pulling on a pair of shorts and a T-shirt, returning to find Elijah sitting at the small kitchen table where they had most of their meals, two plates, and two glasses of wine waiting with him.

The setting alone might've made most men feel awkward, but Logan thought it was nice. Then again, they shared meals often, usually the three of them just like this, so it felt routine. Comfortable, even.

Keep telling yourself that.

"Did you hear from Sam today?" Elijah prompted when Logan took his seat.

"Three times." He dragged his napkin to his lap and picked up his wineglass.

Elijah laughed. "She's been looking forward to this for so long, but I think she spent most of her day on the phone."

"She called you, too?"

Elijah quirked an eyebrow. "Three times."

That sounded like Sam. If he had to guess, she was looking for details from one or both of them, and when the other didn't offer it up, she would keep pushing.

"She did sound like she's having fun. They're going to a club tonight," Elijah mentioned.

"Is it wrong that I'm constantly imagining *The Hangover* scenario whenever I think about those women in Vegas?"

"Oh, boy." Elijah looked up, his eyes dancing with amusement. "Thanks for that. Now I'm going to imagine her waking up to a tiger in her hotel room."

The rest of the meal remained lighthearted. The food was good, the company equally so, and thanks to a couple of glasses of wine, Logan began to relax. Mostly.

After dinner, he cleaned up while Elijah grabbed another bottle of wine and disappeared into the backyard. Logan had plenty of time to think, but he managed to keep his thoughts from roving too far. Every now and then, he would see that image of Elijah's back muscles moving sensually as he worked at the stove, and he would hear that soft gasp he still wasn't sure had been real.

Not for the first time, he contemplated his response to Elijah that night in Colorado. He knew that if Sam hadn't instigated that kiss, hadn't urged them with her wandering hands and softly spoken words, it never would've happened. Up until then, Logan had never had any bisexual urges. Not the way he did now. Sure, he found Elijah appealing, but his assessment was usually during the times he was watching Elijah and Sam. Had he always been turned on by Elijah? He'd honestly never really given it much thought.

Thinking too hard, that voice in his head said, forcing Logan to shove it all down.

Once he was finished with the dishes, he decided to join Elijah. It was that or go to his home office, but he knew if he did, he'd turn to work to pass the time, and work was the last thing he wanted to engage in right now.

Opting for a beer instead of wine, he grabbed one from the refrigerator before heading for the back door. He found Elijah sitting on one of the benches in the pool, his arms stretched out, his head tipped back. The underwater lights danced across his chest, drawing Logan's attention.

Elijah Penn really was a good-looking man. Dark hair, dark eyes, and lean muscle packed on an almost-six-foot frame. Maybe Logan *had* been attracted to him all this time, because his current assessment didn't feel superficial. It felt … curious.

After pulling his T-shirt off and tossing it aside, Logan was quiet as he stepped down into the water, but apparently not quiet enough, because Elijah's head lifted, his eyes opening.

"Figured you'd be in the hot tub," Logan said, moving to the opposite side of the shallow end and taking a seat on the bench.

"A little too warm for me tonight."

Logan knew the feeling. There was a familiar hum just under his skin, and it was amping up his body temperature. It was usually a sensation he associated with Sam's presence, but it seemed it was there in her absence, too. At least tonight, anyway.

He settled back against the wall, stretched his feet out in front of him, the water hitting him mid-torso. He exhaled a long, slow breath, allowing himself to fully relax for the first time all day. To keep himself from ogling Elijah, he listened to the sound of the trees blowing in the gentle breeze and the soft cascade of the waterfall as it recirculated the water.

The entire time, Logan repeated the same words over in his head: *Let it be. If it plays out, it plays out.*

Only, every so often, he heard: *Just see where it's headed already.*

That voice was coming from his dick.

CHAPTER THREE

IT *WAS* WEIRD, ELIJAH DECIDED.

No matter how hard he tried to keep his thoughts reined in, to not look at Logan and imagine kissing the man again, Elijah couldn't help himself. Six months was a long time to dwell on that kiss, and he knew he wouldn't last much longer. He needed to figure out if this was something they should pursue or if he needed to put it in the past and bury it forever.

However, to do that, Elijah needed a replay. He needed to experience that soul-searing kiss once more before he could come to a final decision.

The question was, did he make the first move or wait for Logan?

As he sat there, feeling the weight of Logan's eyes on him, Elijah remembered what happened earlier when Logan had come up behind him in the kitchen. He'd thought for a second Logan was going to touch him, to be the one to make the first move. He could've sworn he felt the ghostly caress moving over his bare skin. He could still feel the warmth of Logan's body behind him, smell the rich scent of his cologne. His reaction to his nearness had been instinctive. He had welcomed the feel of him looming over him, had held his breath in hopes of something more.

Although time had stood still for those precious few seconds, it never came.

Resigning himself to an unsatisfactory end to a relatively pleasant day, Elijah tipped his head back and closed his eyes again.

"Do you regret that night?" Elijah asked as he relaxed.

"No."

There was no hesitance, no uncertainty. *Good to know.*

"Do you want me to regret it, Eli?"

Elijah didn't lift his head, didn't look up. "No. I'd like to know where I stand, that's all. Do you think about it? That night? *That* kiss?"

Silence settled heavily over them for a moment, but just when he thought Logan wasn't going to answer, he heard, "All the damn time."

That eased some of Elijah's anxiety over the situation. "Do you think about the kiss? Or about me rubbing your cock while you were fucking Sam?"

He honestly hadn't meant to speak that aloud, so he wasn't surprised when Logan didn't respond. The man had already said he didn't want to talk about it. Elijah should respect that.

Minutes ticked by while they sat silently, the leaves rustling, the waterfall cascading down from the elevated hot tub. On any given night, the silence would've lulled him into a semi-conscious state. Unfortunately, tonight, he was on edge, his body rigid, his cock pulsing as he mentally willed Logan to make the first move.

"Elijah."

The dark rumble of Logan's voice had Elijah's eyes snapping open. He hadn't heard the man move and wasn't aware of his nearness until he realized he was staring up into Logan's dark, brooding face as he loomed over him.

"Enough's enough," Logan said, his voice rich with seduction and promise.

When Logan leaned forward and planted one hand on the pool's edge behind him, Elijah didn't move. He remained perfectly still, his arms stretched out, his breaths stuck somewhere in his chest. It was like being underwater and kicking to the surface, the anticipation of air taxing his lungs as he waited to see what Logan would do next.

"No games tonight." Logan's voice was low, his expression stormy.

Heat swirled in his veins when Logan's thumb pressed on his chin, his fingers curling under his jaw. Logan held his head still as he leaned in closer, the gap between their mouths disappearing. For a brief moment, Elijah wondered if he was dreaming, if he'd conjured this up in his mind because he'd spent so damn much time fantasizing about it.

"Am I dreaming?" he heard himself say.

Logan smirked. "Do you want to be?"

Going with the truth, Elijah shook his head.

"Have you dreamed about this, Eli?"

Damn near every night. Instead of admitting that, he nodded.

"Me, too," Logan whispered. "Whatever happens is because we want it to happen. Understand?"

Elijah tried to nod, but Logan's grip on his chin kept his head still.

Admittedly, he wasn't a dominating man the way Logan was. He didn't feel the need to command a situation, but he also wasn't submissive in the sense that he wanted to be manhandled. However, there was something enthralling about the way Logan stripped his control and held it just out of reach.

He swallowed as air filled his lungs, his mouth opening as Logan's head moved nearer, their lips hovering mere centimeters apart.

They remained like that for the longest time before Logan exhaled heavily.

"Ah, fuck me," Logan rasped, followed by a strangled groan that sounded a lot like giving in.

And then Logan was kissing him.

Instantly, Elijah's arms came around, his hands reaching for Logan's neck. He'd refrained from touching him the first time they kissed but promised himself he would succumb to the full experience if and when it happened again. His fingers tangled in the long hair at Logan's nape, his thumbs sliding over that rigid jaw, the stubble abrading his fingertips, sending a bolt of heat coursing through him.

He wasn't sure if his touch resulted in Logan's flinch or if the man was simply trying to maintain control, because the next thing he knew, he was standing tall, Logan's hand palming the back of his head as they hungrily ate at one another. Their bodies weren't touching, although their tongues were involved in a sensual duel that spiked his blood pressure.

The kiss was precisely as he remembered. Sinful, passionate. Like he'd been submerged in molten lava, his skin too hot, his chest too tight, his cock hardening as though Logan's tongue was gliding along his shaft and not sweeping through his mouth. He was more than aware of the significant difference between Logan's kiss and Sam's. Where she was gentle and worshipful, Logan was hard and demanding. It was a give and take in equal parts, with Logan pushing for more and Elijah acquiescing as his body hardened.

Once they were in deeper water, Elijah pressed his chest to Logan's, his hands roaming over the broad expanse of Logan's back. He felt Logan shudder when he gripped him roughly, pulled him closer until their hips were pressed intimately together. Air was scarce, but his lungs didn't care. Every cell in his body was alive and alert, anticipation boiling in his veins as every drop of blood in his body gathered in his cock.

"This is not how I envisioned our relationship progressing," Logan muttered against his mouth.

"Then stop," Elijah bit out, not moving away.

"Is this where _you_ thought we'd be headed?"

"No," he admitted honestly, licking his lips, eager to get Logan's mouth back on his.

"But you want it?"

"Yes." He lifted his gaze to meet Logan's. "But I'll stop if you do."

"Fuck that," Logan growled, fusing his mouth to Elijah's once more.

The tension in their bodies coiled tighter as the kiss exploded. This was not a gentle mating of mouths. It was a roller coaster at warp speed, whipping them around curves, tossing them over the edge, and sending them into freefall as they feasted like savage beasts.

"There's no turning back from this," Logan warned.

Elijah didn't comment. He bit Logan's bottom lip instead, wanting more. He'd never touched a man before Logan, much less kissed one, but he found it erotic. Smooth, hot skin covering hard muscle shifted beneath his palms as he clutched at him, as though they weren't as close as they could possibly be.

Logan's mouth released his, leaving them both gasping.

"You think this is what she was referring to when she said wicked and dirty?"

"Knowing Sam…" Elijah drew air deep into his lungs and smiled. "Probably."

"I can tell you now, I'm not recording this, so you'll have to remember it so you can tell her."

Oh, Elijah would remember it, all right. Probably for the remainder of his days. He'd mistakenly believed that he had pursued every salacious impulse he'd ever had, but now that he'd felt the power and dominance of Logan's kiss, he could honestly say he'd been missing something.

The hand palming his head moved, Logan's fingers twining into his hair and tipping his head back. Elijah swallowed, waiting to see what came next. A shiver raced down his spine when Logan leaned in, his nose pressing against the pulse in Elijah's neck. He heard Logan's inhale seconds before he felt the warm press of his lips. For long, painful seconds, Logan hovered like that, his breath fanning Elijah's skin, making his cock throb and his muscles coil with anticipation.

"More?" Logan whispered.

Unable to find his voice, Elijah nodded.

"Good answer."

When Logan nipped his neck, Elijah groaned, his cock throbbing, his pulse pounding. Sliding his hands down to Logan's hips, he pulled him closer. Committed to this erotic experiment, he gripped Logan's ass firmly, drew his hips forward against his own, their cocks trapped between them. He rocked, seeking the friction that would alleviate the tension coiling inside him. It wasn't enough, but it was intoxicating.

They'd touched plenty over the years, their bodies coming in contact whenever they were with Samantha together. Elijah was familiar with the scrape of Logan's leg hair against his legs, the calloused brush of his knuckles as his hands grazed some part of his body. But those had been unintentional. This … there was nothing accidental about the way Logan was nipping and sucking on his neck or the way Elijah was groping him in the hopes of getting more.

Logan licked his way back up to his mouth, his unyielding lips settling over Elijah's once more.

"I can't stop this," Logan whispered, and it sounded like a warning.

"Neither can I," he admitted, ensuring Logan heard his need.

This time when their lips separated, their bodies drew apart. Elijah sucked air into his lungs while his cock remained a constant throb between his thighs.

"Even when she's not here, she's taunting us, Eli."

"How so?"

"She dangled you in front of me." Logan's hungry gaze raked over his face. "She made me *want*."

He couldn't deny he was surprised by the admission. He thought he'd known what made Logan tick, the kinks and fetishes that drove him. He was a libidinous man, and he never shied away from his hunger for Sam. Elijah knew the feeling because his desires were similar. It was the reason the three of them were so good together. They both had an overwhelming need to pleasure Sam and observe her in the throes, but he'd never considered there might be more to it. He wasn't sure they would be here right now if it hadn't been for that deceptive game they'd played that night in the cabin. The one that had set them on this path with a kiss.

Deep down, Elijah knew there'd likely always been a curiosity somewhere, though he couldn't remember ever feeling this way. He knew that kissing any random man wouldn't have created a need like this. But this was Logan, and while the intimacies they'd shared revolved around Samantha, something had been triggered along the way. Otherwise, he wouldn't fantasize about taking Logan's cock in his mouth or feeling that blistering tongue as it delved into places no man had ever ventured.

Elijah was so lost in his erotic fantasies that he didn't realize Logan was pursuing him or that he was backing up until he was pressed against the pool's edge, Logan's big body looming over him.

"Don't move," Logan growled, the dominance in his tone sending another shiver racing through him.

Time stood still once again when Logan submerged his hand in the water, his fingers dipping into the waistband of Elijah's shorts. That gentle, unhurried brush of his fingers tickled the tight muscles of his abdomen then generated heat when they grazed the swollen head of his cock. He stared up at him, their eyes locked as Logan slowly dragged his shorts down to his thighs, freeing Elijah's cock. It bobbed beneath the surface, and even the sensual caress of the water against the sensitive crown was nearly too much to bear.

As though attempting to read his mind, Logan's eyes remained locked on his as he reached down and fisted Elijah's cock.

So they were really doing this.

Pleasure tightened his groin, had his back arching as an electric current zipped down his spine. A growl rumbled in Elijah's chest as Logan's hand slowly stroked down his length, pausing briefly before gliding back up. Logan wasn't hesitant, but it was obvious he was taking his time.

"I've never touched a man like this," Logan admitted, his voice a dark rumble.

Elijah's eyes narrowed, his cock pulsing in Logan's hand. "I'm glad to be your first."

That earned him a smile when Logan's eyes flashed hot, his hand beginning a consistent stroke up and down Elijah's length. He focused on breathing as the pleasure consumed him, his cock throbbing against those deft fingers.

He wasn't sure how long he could survive this, but by God, he wasn't ready for it to be over.

LOGAN HADN'T INTENDED TO LET THIS GO any further than those blazing kisses. Hell, who was he kidding? He hadn't even expected to get his ass up off the bench, yet here they were.

He certainly hadn't anticipated getting to a point when his fingers were curled around Elijah's hot, pulsing shaft, his brain conjuring images of turning him around, bending him over…

Oh, Jesus.

Regardless of how they'd gotten to this point, Logan couldn't help himself, couldn't contain the need to explore this man. He was intimately aware of the velvet-smooth length of Elijah's cock against his palm, the shutter of Elijah's gaze as he stroked him firmly. He enjoyed the man's reaction as much as this exploration into the unknown.

Reaching down, Logan shoved his own shorts down with one hand, releasing his cock. Without hesitation, he reached for Elijah's hand, dragged it into the water, and settled it over his raging erection.

"Stroke me," he commanded with a startled gasp as his cock swelled from the brush of Elijah's fingers.

Elijah's hand curled around his dick, tightened as it glided up and down, mirroring the pace Logan had set. His brain registered every sensation, the firm grasp of his fingers as they slid over him. They remained like that for several minutes, their eyes locked as they jerked each other off. It wasn't a race to completion, and he wondered if Elijah was mentally logging how it felt to have a man's hand on him the way Logan was. Where Sam's touch was soft, Elijah's held an assertiveness that was foreign. Where Sam's eagerness generally sent him into the stratosphere, Elijah's confidence and curiosity kept him settled.

Logan watched the passion blaze in Elijah's dark eyes, the way his eyelids drooped when Logan grazed the head of his cock with his thumb. He wondered whether Sam had imagined they'd share a moment like this one. Had she fantasized about them touching one another the same way Logan fantasized about Elijah touching her? He'd never been able to explain his fascination with seeing another man pleasure his wife, but it was there all the same, and he'd long ago stopped trying to figure it out. He knew what he wanted, and he'd never been scared to go after it. And he'd found the perfect woman to indulge his every whim, because Sam craved it, too.

Elijah just happened to be the perfect complement, though Logan had never figured out why that was. From the beginning, he'd felt a connection to Elijah, but he'd always suspected it was a friendship born of similar desires.

This felt like more.

Hell, this *was* more.

"Show me how you like it," Logan instructed, nodding in the direction of their stroking hands.

Elijah's free hand covered his, tightening his grip.

Logan did the same, reaching between his legs as he guided Elijah's hand up and down the hard length of his cock. He was dangerously close to coming, but he'd long ago mastered the art of holding back. He'd never been one who was eager for the finish line, preferring a strong, steady pace instead. He was getting that now because he controlled the pump of Elijah's fist on his cock.

"I've watched you come a million times, filling Sam's pussy … her mouth … her ass," he said, keeping his voice low. "Now, I want to watch you come in my hand."

Elijah's eyes closed briefly, a deep, resonating growl sounding in his chest.

Logan added pressure on Elijah's cock, jerked him faster, rougher.

"Fuck yes," Elijah hissed, his back arching as he thrust into Logan's hand.

He kept at it, increasing the pace until Elijah was panting, the man's hand lax on Logan's cock because he was too distracted by the pleasure. Logan liked that he could do that, that he could control Elijah's pleasure the same way he controlled Sam's.

Elijah grunted. "Fuck ... uhh ... oh, fuck..."

Logan tightened his grip again, jerking hard, fast, watching Elijah's face contort, his mouth falling open on a strangled moan as his dick kicked and bucked in his hand as he came on a ragged groan that tightened the muscles across his neck and chest.

As soon as Elijah was steady on his feet, Logan took both of Elijah's hands, wrapped them around his dick.

"Make me come," he demanded, putting his hands on Elijah's head, forcing him to dip lower in the water to two-fist him.

He couldn't help it, he imagined Elijah's mouth wrapping around the head, and he came with a groan that scalded his throat and made him light-headed.

It took a moment for him to get his bearings after. His instinct was to walk away because he wasn't sure what to do now that they'd taken that giant step forward. Something kept him from doing so, because he stepped toward Elijah, leaned down, and sealed his mouth over his. The kiss didn't blaze the way it had earlier, but there was still an undercurrent that told him this was far from over.

In fact, he was pretty sure they were just getting started.

CHAPTER FOUR

"I DON'T THINK I'VE EVER DANCED SO much in my entire life," Sam exclaimed as they stumbled back to their hotel room.

She'd just spent the past several hours drinking and dancing at one of the hottest nightclubs in Vegas with the women she cared most for in the world. They had laughed, joked, and let loose by downing more liquor than she'd consumed in a year. She wouldn't deny she was grateful they'd made it back in one piece. She couldn't remember the last time she'd been that carefree, that relaxed. These escapes were few and far between because their daily routines took precedence. For her friends, it was husbands and babies keeping them busy day in and day out, while for Sam, her devotion was to her career and the two men she loved more than life.

"Thank God for separate bedrooms," Ashleigh slurred. "I plan to sleep all day tomorrow, so don't wake me up."

They'd gotten a fancy suite so they could all room together, and it was big enough they could've brought the husbands along and been fine. Not that they would have, because then it wouldn't have been a girls' weekend.

"I know *I* won't survive another night like that," McKenna said with a drunken giggle as she moved along the wall to keep herself upright.

"Me, either," Sierra announced. "That's more exercise than I get in a month."

Sam was right there with them. She'd had a great time tonight, considering it was the first full night they'd been here. Last night had been for them to get settled in. They'd ordered room service, catching up on everything going on in their lives. With only one more night to go, she figured they would find a way to enjoy themselves, even if it didn't involve teetering on breakneck heels on a crowded dance floor.

"Whose idea was it to do the spa *before* the dancing?" Ashleigh groaned. "I'm sure I'll be in need of a massage in the morning."

"I'm just hoping to make it to my bed," Sierra groused, clutching every piece of furniture she passed.

"I'm gonna call Logan and Eli. See how they're doing," Sam told them as she headed for her bedroom.

"You know it's almost four there, right?" Mercedes noted.

Sam frowned, then giggled. "Okay. So I'll wait till morning."

"Don't wake me up," Ashleigh said. "Seriously. I'm sleeping all day. It's the only way I'll make it another night here."

"Ditto, that," shouted Mercedes.

Laughing at her friends for being lightweights, although she was one, too, Sam went into her bedroom, shutting the door behind her. She managed to strip out of her dress but couldn't muster the effort to scrub her face. Instead, she fell into the bed face-first and passed out as soon as her feet joined her.

Sam came awake to the sound of laughter in the other room. Looked as though her friends weren't the lightweights; she was. If she had to guess, she was the only one still in bed, and she wasn't sure she was ready to get up yet.

She didn't move quickly, assessing the damage the night out had done to her body. A smile formed when she realized she was not hungover, and she reminded herself to thank Mercedes for whatever hangover remedy she'd given them on the return trip to the hotel. It had worked wonders. Although her muscles ached like she'd run a marathon in heels, at least she didn't have a headache.

Peering over at the clock, she noticed it was noon, which meant it was two in the afternoon in Dallas. She reached for her cell phone and dialed Logan's number first.

"Good afternoon, baby," he greeted with that warm, seductive tone she loved so much. "Or is it still morning for you?"

"I haven't gotten out of bed yet, if that matters," she said softly. "How are things?"

"We're good. You?"

"Tired." She yawned for emphasis. "We went out last night. Showed off our dancing skills."

"Yeah? Anyone make a move on you that I should worry about?"

She knew he was teasing, but she also knew that her husband was the protective sort. "Even if there was, I can assure you, I didn't notice. I don't have any room left in my heart for any more men."

His laugh thundered in her ear, and it made her nipples pebble. They were approaching their ninth wedding anniversary in September, and he still had the ability to turn her on with just the sound of his voice.

She propped herself up on pillows. "Where's Eli?"

"Around."

"Did you two sleep well without me between you?"

"We did."

Her body went stone still; her smile faltered as a new sensation warmed her. Was that some sort of revelation in his tone? Or was her wicked imagination getting the best of her? She figured it was the latter because that was generally the case.

"So you *did* sleep in the same bed?"

"We did," he repeated in that same tone.

Sam knew she should probably leave well enough alone since Logan constantly told her to do that very thing. Problem was, Sam was too curious not to pelt him with questions. She wanted to know everything that had happened since she'd been gone. Most of all, she wanted to know if anything had happened between her men.

"I can hear your brain working, Sam."

She laughed. "I'm just imagining the two of you in that giant bed … alone … together."

"Yeah, well. It's a big bed. We had plenty of room. Plus, I think *alone* and *together* contradict one another."

"No cuddling, then?"

"Are you trying to get me to kiss and tell?"

Her breath lodged in her chest. For the past six months, ever since that one incredible night in the cabin, Logan had repeatedly shut her down anytime Sam brought up what had happened. Not once had he joked about it.

Her anticipation weighed heavily on each word when she asked, "Logan, did something happen?"

"I'm sorry, I'm not at liberty to say."

"Oh, my God!" she huffed with exasperation. "You waited until I was *gone?*"

He chuckled, and the sound reverberated right through her.

"What's on the agenda for tonight?" he asked, effectively changing the subject.

Sam wasn't ready to give up, but she knew she had to. Logan wasn't going to reveal anything. However, she still stood a chance with Elijah, who would be her next call.

"I figure we'll go to dinner, maybe do a little gambling. No partying, though. We've got an early flight tomorrow."

"Enjoy it while you can, and don't worry about us. We'll manage to keep each other busy."

She gasped. "What?"

"I mean, we'll keep ourselves busy."

Oh, no, he didn't. Her husband was taunting her now. Something had definitely happened, and she hadn't been there to witness it.

"Sam?"

She growled although it sounded more like a purr. "Whatever. I don't want to talk to you anymore."

Another laugh. "Well, then, I guess I'll see you when you get back tomorrow. I love you, baby."

"I love you, too," she muttered, pouting as she hung up the phone.

No sooner did the call disconnect than she was dialing Elijah's number.

"Hey," he greeted softly, a soft chuckle signifying he was likely in the same room as Logan.

"Hey," she said back, smiling because his voice did that. It settled her, made her happy.

"You up and moving yet?"

"Nope." She stretched out on the bed. "I would be if you were here."

"Only one more night."

"Yep, then you and Logan won't have that big bed all to yourself anymore." She cleared her throat. "How was it, by the way?"

"Enlightening."

Sam bolted upright. "What?"

Elijah answered with a booming laugh. "Logan told me to say that."

"No, he didn't. Did he?"

"I guess you'll never know."

A knock sounded on her door, followed by Mercedes's commanding voice. "Get your ass up, woman. We're gonna have lunch without you."

"Sounds like you're being summoned," Elijah said in her ear. "You better enjoy what little time you have left."

"You're really not gonna tell me?" she asked, flopping back on the bed.

"I didn't say that."

Her eyes widened, and she felt heat curl between her legs.

"Just not over the phone."

"Spoilsport." She exhaled an exaggerated sigh. "Fine."

Another chuckle sounded. "I love you, Sam."

"Love you, too," she grumbled. "I'll call you later."

REGARDLESS OF WHAT HE DID, ELIJAH COULDN'T stop thinking about last night in the pool.

Currently, he was attempting to read while Logan cleaned up the kitchen after dinner, but his brain was not connecting with the words on the page. He'd read the same paragraph at least ten times, and still, he couldn't say whether anything had happened or not. Every single moment of last night was on constant repeat in his head and had been all day long. The kissing, the touching, but mostly, the sound of Logan's deep, gruff voice as he barked his sensual commands while they jerked each other off.

We jerked each other off.

Just thinking about it made his dick hard.

"What's on your agenda for the evening?" Logan prompted, coming out of the kitchen and stepping down into the living room.

Elijah held up his book, slowly lifting his gaze. "You have something else in mind?"

He hadn't meant it to be innuendo, but he'd be damned if that wasn't what it sounded like.

"Figured I'd grab a shower, maybe watch a movie."

Was that an invitation to join him? Or was he merely stating a fact? Elijah knew he was overthinking every fucking thing, but he couldn't help it.

"Sam's flight gets in at noon tomorrow," Logan mentioned. "I confirmed she's checked in and good to go. You talk to her any more today?"

"Not since earlier, no. She texted a few times." He figured Sam was done with calling them since she hadn't gotten the answers she was seeking. He figured that was for the best since he preferred they leave the details until she returned.

Would there be more details to share? Like a potential hot scene in the shower?

Yes, he was overthinking. He was doing exactly the same thing Sam did, nagging things to death when sometimes they were better left alone.

"Elijah?"

"Hmm?"

"I'm going to take a shower now," Logan stated firmly.

He nodded, glanced back down at his book.

Logan disappeared into the master bedroom. A second later, he heard, "You're welcome to join me if you'd like."

The book went to the coffee table before he realized he'd moved. Elijah was on his feet, but that was as far as he made it. He stared at the bedroom door. Should he join him? He wanted to, of course. He wanted to more than he thought was appropriate. But if he did, where would that lead them? Was he ready for something more than a hand job? Going in there would be accepting an invitation and ultimately admitting he was seeking more. Was Logan testing him?

Again, he was overthinking, which meant he needed to take a breather and think it through before he reacted. As tempting as it might seem, Elijah wasn't sure it was the right thing for them.

A minute later, he was sitting down, elbows on his knees, head in his hands. He wasn't sure how this was supposed to go. If he let his libido lead the way, his dick would always be in front. He would be in that shower, probably on his knees with Logan's cock in his mouth. God knows he'd fantasized about it enough. Was he ready for that? If Sam had been there, he would've gladly let her coerce him into exploring more. Without her, he was making that choice on his own.

Why the fuck was he complicating this? It was just sex. And he'd never been one to hesitate when it came to the pleasures of the flesh. That was how he'd ended up with Logan and Sam in the first place. He'd succumbed to his wicked desires the same way he had a million times before, although he'd intended to keep some space between them. Then things had changed, and he'd been caught up in the whirlwind that was Samantha McCoy. She fascinated and intrigued him, and he rarely considered the repercussions because he followed her lead. If he went to Logan now, it would be like telling Sam he wanted something that didn't include her.

Was he willing to do that? Willing to *admit* to that?

Elijah's ass remained planted on the sofa, and fifteen minutes later, Logan came out of the bathroom, his black hair wet, slicked back from his face. He had on a pair of shorts and a T-shirt, his feet bare. He didn't look at all disappointed that Elijah hadn't joined him. In fact, he looked indifferent.

Had it been a test?

There was no pressure from Logan for the rest of the evening, and from the outside looking in, everything seemed normal. They watched a movie—an action film of Logan's choosing. Elijah remained on his end of the sofa while Logan was reclined in his chair. Once the credits began to roll and the music faded, neither of them moved from their spots.

"Eli?"

"Yeah?"

"You don't have to feel bad about last night."

He looked up, saw that Logan was staring at him. "I don't feel bad."

Logan didn't look as though he believed him.

"I don't," he repeated.

"Good. Me either."

Elijah knew now was the perfect opportunity for them to discuss this, to agree on how things would proceed from here. Maybe Logan didn't want it scripted for him, but Elijah would feel better if they could at least have an honest discussion about their limits. If there were any.

Before he could broach the subject, Logan's cell phone rang.

With a smirk, Logan answered. "Yes, baby, we miss you," he said in greeting.

"You better," Sam replied, her voice coming from the phone's speaker. "We're about to go to dinner. I figure it might be late there before we're done. Thought I would call first, tell you I love you."

"I love you, too," Logan said, his eyes pinned on Elijah's face.

Elijah felt trapped in his gaze, like a wounded animal about to be charged by a predator. He wasn't sure how he felt about the anticipation that swept over him or what it meant.

"Is Eli with you?"

"He's here. We just finished watching a movie."

"Let me guess. There were a lot of things being blown up?"

Logan smiled. "It's the best kind."

Elijah listened with half an ear as Sam and Logan discussed her plans to go to the airport in the morning and when she would be home. His ears didn't perk up again until Sam asked whether or not they'd be sleeping in the same bed again tonight.

"We will, yes," Logan told her, his penetrating gaze once again locked on Elijah.

Sam's voice lowered to a husky whisper. "I wish I could see that. The two of you ... together."

Some of the amusement faded from Logan's tone when he said, "Is that what you want, Sam? To watch the two of us?"

"Will you be mad if I say yes?"

"Of course not. We want to know what pleases you. You know that."

"I won't push," she added. "I promised I wouldn't."

"Good. That's all we ask."

"We?" Her curiosity had been piqued. "Does that mean you've ... talked about it?"

"We've had a brief discussion," Logan said, still staring at Elijah. "Not a whole lot of talking, though."

Sam's sharp inhale made Elijah's cock twitch. "If there wasn't much talking, what *did* happen?"

"We'll be glad to walk you through it, in Technicolor detail if you prefer, but not until you get home."

Sam sighed, sounding disappointed that Logan didn't elaborate. It made Elijah smile. He loved how expressive Sam was, how she didn't keep her feelings locked down.

A mumbled voice sounded in the background before Sam said, "Coming!" She sighed into the phone. "Well, we're about to head down to the restaurant. I'll see you both tomorrow. I love you. Both of you."

"We love you, too," Logan replied before disconnecting the call and setting his phone on the end table.

Elijah's skin prickled as Logan's gaze heated. He'd picked up on every nuance of the man's expressions over the years, and that look usually preceded a hot encounter with Sam crushed between them. Only Sam wasn't here.

"She'll be home tomorrow," Logan mentioned, as though reading his mind.

"She will." Elijah wasn't sure where he was going with this.

"She's going to pick up on this tension."

Elijah nodded. "I know."

"We both know we're not through with"—he waved a hand—"whatever this is."

"Definitely not."

"What do you say we call a truce until she gets home?"

That sounded like a damn fine idea, although his cock wasn't as on board with waiting as he was pretending. "I think she'd appreciate that."

Logan's smirk was wicked. "But once she's home, all bets are off."

There was so much desire packed into that one single sentence, Elijah's cock swelled at the thought.

"Once she's home, we'll see where things go from there. That good for you?"

Elijah didn't speak, but he did manage a nod.

Chapter Five

Sunday, June 19, 2022

The following morning, Logan woke with a hard-on to rival all. He attributed it to sleeping in the same bed with Elijah and wanting to feel how hot his mouth would be on his cock, and also to the fact that Sam was coming home today.

He rolled to his back, slid his arm beneath the blankets, and curled his hand around his straining cock. He didn't even think about what he was doing, didn't consider the fact that Elijah was still in the bed, just a few feet away. At least, not until he heard a soft hum from Elijah.

"You're awake," Logan said, turning his head to look at him.

"For a while now," he said, his gaze lingering lower where Logan's cock was tenting the blankets.

He stroked himself while he stared at Elijah, then surprised himself when he said, "You want to watch?"

Elijah's gaze shifted to his face. "Yeah."

His lack of hesitation eased something inside him. Ever since he'd made the offer for Elijah to join him in the shower and the man had refused, he'd wondered what it meant. Overthinking was now his specialty.

Swallowing hard, Logan shoved the blankets down to his knees. He slept naked, as did Elijah, so there was nothing hindering the man's view. Neither of them moved from their spots, but Elijah's interest shifted back to Logan's hand as it moved up and down his steel-hard erection.

Watching Elijah watching him lent a salacious air to an otherwise normal activity. Logan's sex drive had always been high, and despite his very active sex life, he still succumbed to the pleasure of his own hand on a daily basis. He wasn't sure if that was normal, nor did he give a shit.

He continued to watch Elijah while he rubbed his dick, reaching down with his other hand to fondle his balls. His breaths grew labored as he imagined Elijah's sinful mouth filled to overflowing with Logan's throbbing cock, sucking him deep into his throat.

"What are you thinking about?" Elijah asked, his voice gravel laced.

"You sucking me," he said honestly.

Elijah groaned, then rolled to his back, shoving the blankets down to reveal his erection. Logan watched as Elijah wrapped his hand around it, stroked slowly, casually, as though he wasn't in a hurry. It allowed Logan to slow his pace, to let the pleasure build. It was hotter than he'd imagined it would be. Hot enough to make him moan as he pumped his hips, fucking his fist when the need to come overwhelmed him.

The only sound in the room was their rough groans and the silky glide of pre-cum being massaged into their cocks as they worked themselves up, watching the other. He imagined Elijah leaning over, wrapping that wicked mouth around the swollen head, and sucking him hard. He growled, his hips driving up, ramming his cock through his fist.

"Oh, fuck, yes," he hissed.

"Come for me, Logan," Elijah whispered. "Ah, fuck."

Logan growled, his gaze riveted to the way Elijah jerked his cock hard and fast, his hand moving rapidly over his swollen flesh. When Elijah's back arched, Logan bit back a curse, his release barreling down on him in a rush. He came with a groan at the same time Elijah did.

Two hours later, Logan was on sensory overload, his body still hard, even after the erotic tease this morning. Sure, he'd come, but it hadn't been as fulfilling as it could've been, considering. He needed an outlet, which was why he ordered a limo to take him to the airport so he could be there when Sam arrived. He figured he could get brownie points for the romantic gesture while at the same time getting Sam all to himself for the thirty-minute drive back.

Logan had the limo drop him at the pickup doors, then he went inside to the baggage carousels to wait patiently for her arrival.

He shouldn't have been surprised to find his brother, Luke, there, too, leaning against one of the columns as he waited for Sierra to return.

"Great minds," Luke said when Logan approached.

"Something like that." He clapped his hand on his brother's shoulder. "Where's Cole and the kids?"

"Home."

"Stealing all the glory for yourself?"

Luke's black eyebrows rose. "What? He volunteered."

"Yeah?" Logan chuckled. "What's he getting out of the deal?"

"He got his last night." Luke's eyes glittered. "Unlike you, I don't have to go without when my wife's out of town."

"No, I guess you don't," he said, averting his gaze when he recalled what had happened with Elijah in the swimming pool and again this morning in their bed. "Best of both worlds for you."

"Damn straight it is."

A few times over the past six months, Logan had considered talking to Luke about what had happened in the cabin. Not only did they share the twin bond, but Luke was also his best friend. Always had been. Sure, they fought like siblings did and got pissed off at each other often, but they still shared a bond. While neither of them was keen on sharing their innermost feelings, they did talk openly about many things, and Luke was the only person Logan would even consider talking to about something as private as these convoluted feelings he was developing for Elijah.

Granted, like every other time he'd considered it, he decided to hold off. Things were complicated, and he suspected they would get more so before this was all settled. He could honestly say he wasn't shying away from the idea of something more intimate with Elijah, but he didn't see them ever having what Luke and Cole had. What Logan and Elijah shared revolved around Sam, while Luke had a more intimate relationship with Sierra and Cole. It often felt a bit more separate than they'd likely intended initially. At least to Logan. Not that he was dissing it by any means, because it worked for them. He'd never seen his brother happier.

Luke chuckled, pointing toward the doors. "I don't think we're the only ones with great ideas."

Logan looked over, saw Tag and Alex strolling toward them, shit-eating grins on their faces. The only one missing was Xander, but Logan figured he likely had something more intense in store for Mercedes when she got home. The Dom rarely did things the easy way.

"Where's Elijah?" Alex asked when he neared.

"He said he had something to take care of," Logan told him.

He wasn't a complete dick; he had invited Elijah to come along. But after a moment's consideration, Elijah had told him he would see her when she got home and to enjoy himself during the drive back.

Logan wasn't the sort who had to be told twice.

"Their plane just landed," Tag informed them, his attention on the arrival and departure screen.

For the next few minutes, Logan listened while Luke, Tag, and Alex chatted incessantly about their children's most recent accomplishments. Luke had proudly announced that nine-year-old Hannah would be starting the fourth grade in the fall, and she was already a little too big for her britches, trying to sweet-talk her mother into letting her get her belly button pierced. His exact words: *over my cold, dead body*. He also mentioned that six-year-old Liam would be starting first grade. Something about the kid wanting to be a soccer player when he grew up so he could be rich and famous and date supermodels. At six, the boy was already planning to date supermodels. At least the kid had goals. Alex noted that his daughter, Riley, was also giving them a run for their money, acting like she was thirteen instead of eight. She, too, had tried to angle for a body piercing—her tongue.

Logan laughed along with them, silently enjoying that he did not have to endure the hardships of parenthood. While he had nothing against kids in general, he had never wanted any of his own. When Sam had admitted the same, he'd felt a sense of relief, although he knew he would've given her a dozen if that was what she'd wanted.

"There they are," Tag announced.

Logan followed Tag's pointing finger and laid eyes on his wife for the first time in three days. She looked tired but just as beautiful as always, with her long hair falling over her shoulders. As with every time he looked at her, he felt the warmth develop deep in his soul. From the day he'd met her, Logan had been ensnared.

"Isn't this a nice surprise," McKenna said, strolling right up to her husband and planting a kiss on Tag's mouth.

Sam approached, grinning mischievously as she passed over her carry-on bag for Logan to take.

He gladly took it, then grunted. "This is heavier than when you left. How's that even possible?"

"Souvenirs," she said, as though that explained everything.

He pulled her to him, kissed her lips. "You went to Vegas last year. Why'd you need more souvenirs?"

"Because that's what you do when you go on vacation without your husband. You shop." Her green eyes glittered as she stared up at him. "And to what do I owe the pleasure of your company?"

"Can't a husband just want to see his wife?" He wiggled his eyebrows. "Naked."

She chuckled, nodding in the direction of their friends. "All in due time. A little too much exhibitionism for my taste."

Logan loved how her eyes glazed when he said, "We've got our own ride home, which means you'll be riding me in the near future."

SAM COULDN'T SAY SHE WAS SURPRISED TO see Logan waiting for her at the airport. Her husband was always doing romantic things like that. She would've been more surprised *not* to see him. But regardless of whether it was a surprise, she was glad he was there.

"Where's Eli?" she asked as Logan helped the limo driver put her luggage into the trunk of the car.

"He said he had stuff to do around the house, said he'd see you when we got back."

She hoped so. Sam had missed him, too. She hadn't talked to him as much as she'd spoken to Logan, and she got the feeling that was by design. The only problem was, she wouldn't know for sure until she saw his face. Unlike Logan, Elijah wasn't good at keeping things from her. He had a shitty poker face, and she'd learned, if she wanted the truth, she just had to go to him to get it.

The limo driver opened the rear door, waited until she climbed inside. She heard Logan tell him something before he joined her in the car. While the driver was walking around to the driver's door, Logan pushed the button to raise the privacy window between the front and the back.

"I'm glad you're home," he said sweetly, patting his thighs. "But you're still too far away."

Sam smiled, recognizing the demand in his tone. It was subtle, but it was there.

Without hesitation, she shifted so that she was straddling his legs, her skirt riding high on her thighs. She'd long ago stopped playing coy, stopped pretending they weren't going to grope the hell out of one another when they'd been apart for any period of time. That was one aspect of their relationship she didn't take for granted. She knew it wasn't the case for all married people, so she was grateful their lust for one another still burned hot.

"Did you have a good time?"

"The best." She slid her hands over his shoulders, loving the contours of his big body. "What about you? You have a good time while I was gone?"

His eyes met hers, twinkled with mischief. "I did."

"Do you plan to tell me about it?"

Logan's hands settled on her thighs, grazing her skin as they moved higher, beneath the skirt she'd worn just in case her husband was too eager to get her out of her shorts when she got home. Little did she know when she'd selected the outfit that it would come in handy on the drive there.

"If you don't have panties on, I'm going to spank your pretty little ass," he growled softly, his hands venturing higher.

"I wasn't about to get on an airplane without them."

"That's too bad. Now give me that mouth."

"Only if you tell me what happened."

"Kiss me first," he said with a smirk. "Then I'll consider it."

When she leaned in, his lips brushed hers as his fingers slipped beneath the elastic edge of her panties. There was never any wasted time with this man. When he had his sights set on something, he wasn't hesitant to take it.

"You're wet," he whispered, dragging his thumb along her cleft. "And hot."

She tried to remain stoic, but his wandering fingers made it impossible. She wanted to hear what had happened, but resisting Logan wasn't an option. Sam sighed as he teased her lightly, his thumb grazing her clit as he stared up at her, obviously watching her reactions.

He slipped one finger inside her. "Ride my finger."

"Tell me what happened while I was gone," she retorted. Tit for tat and all that.

He added another finger.

She gently rocked her hips to appease him.

"I missed you," he rumbled, still staring up at her.

"Tell me," she repeated, desperate for him to reveal what had transpired between them. She'd thought about it endlessly, which was likely part of the reason she was so hot and bothered now.

His fingers retreated, and his thumbs began to gently knead her labia. "We ate, showered, and did all the normal things we do when you're not home."

Sam's eyes narrowed. "Did you do any of those things together?"

"We had dinner."

She canted her head to the side. "You know what I mean."

Logan's expression remained cool and reserved even though he was sliding his fingers along the slick seam of her pussy lips, tapping her clit because he knew it drove her crazy. "I don't, actually. I'm gonna need you to be more specific."

"Did you shower with Eli?"

"I did not," he said as his thumb pressed to her clit.

She inhaled sharply, enjoying the circular motion as he excited the tiny bundle of nerves.

"Did you touch him while you were in bed?"

"I did not."

"Did he touch you?" she asked, knowing he meant it when he said to be specific.

"He did not." He leaned in, nipped her bottom lip. "You're so fucking wet, and I'm so fucking hard, Sam. I want to feel your pussy on my cock."

She shivered, lifting when his hands fell away so he could unbutton his jeans. She settled her hands on his shoulders and stared down between their bodies as he deftly pushed his jeans down and freed his beautiful cock.

"Sit on my cock," he instructed. "Ride me while you interrogate me."

The dark rumble of his voice made her nipples pebble and her sex clench. She'd known he was going to make up for lost time when she got home, but she hadn't expected this. Not that she minded. She was sure there was a hefty tip in it for the driver, provided he gave them the privacy Logan sought.

Logan tugged her panties aside so she could sink down on him. She moved slowly, enjoying the glide of his cockhead along her slit, then the delicious stretch as he angled at her entrance. When his cock was pushing inside her, Sam eased down on him, moaning as she did.

"Oh, fuck, that feels good," she said softly, loving how his long, thick cock filled her, bringing all those sensitive nerve endings to life.

He grunted, pushing her shirt and bra up so that her breasts were bared to his hungry gaze.

Thank God for tinted windows.

Sam remained in control as she lifted and lowered, rocked forward and back, fucking herself on his cock. She'd worked herself up over the weekend with erotic thoughts of him and Elijah together. Because of those fantasies, she knew it wouldn't take much to get her off.

"Did you…" She moaned as he pressed on her clit again. "Did you kiss Eli while I was gone?"

"I did."

She sucked in a harsh gasp; her eyes widened at his admission. A mental image of their first kiss in the cabin flashed as heat swamped her.

"Was it as good as you remembered?" she asked, her hips moving faster, her pussy milking him.

"Better."

Oh, hell. Those mental images alone were going to make her come.

"Did you touch him?" she whispered, trying to focus on her questions even as the pleasure consumed her.

"I did."

"Where?" She moved faster. "Tell me, Logan. Tell me what happened."

His hazel eyes flashed with desire. "I fucked his mouth with my tongue, baby."

"Oh, God," she whimpered, her fingernails digging into his shoulders.

"And I stroked his cock until he came."

Her pussy clenched, pulling a moan from his chest.

"You like knowing that, Sam?"

She nodded. "I want to watch." She rocked forward and back, quickening her pace as her core began to tingle. "Did he touch you?"

"He jacked me off," he growled, his eyes hot as he stared at her breasts. "He made me come with his hands."

"Logan … I'm so close. What else?"

"What else do you need, baby? Doesn't the thought of us locked in a passionate kiss, our hands stroking … isn't that enough for you?"

It was more than she'd expected, yeah. But it wasn't nearly enough. She wanted to watch them. She wanted to see her powerful, dominant husband give and receive pleasure from her sinfully sexy lover.

"More," she moaned.

"Fuck me, Sam," he demanded, his control slipping. "Make me come the way Elijah did with his hands."

That was the more she needed. Sam cried out as those tingles ignited into a firestorm that ripped through her body. Her back arched as she came, her hands gripping Logan's shoulders as he drove up into her, taking control, bringing her right back to the brink before the first orgasm faded.

"We were waiting for you," he grunted as he fucked her, his hips bucking upward, driving his cock deep. "Waiting so you could watch us, so we can bring you pleasure while we explore."

Another orgasm lit her up from the inside out, and she slammed down on him. Logan erupted inside her, his growl muffled when he pressed his face to her chest.

"Jesus, Sam," he said, panting. "You're gonna be the death of me."

She smiled just like she did every time he said that.

CHAPTER SIX

ELIJAH WAS STEPPING OUT OF THE BEDROOM when the front door opened. He heard Sam's voice first. She sounded excited, which could've been due to any number of things—her favorite artist releasing a new song, the neighbor finally weeding their garden, an upcoming sale on shoes. She got excited by a lot of things.

However, he had a strong feeling today's excitement wasn't over any of those. Based on the rasp in her tone, he had a fairly good idea of what had happened during the drive from the airport. Logan had told him before he left that he would be filling her in on what transpired between them over the weekend. Knowing Logan, the man had turned Sam's inquisition into a give-and-take.

He wasn't sure which of them he was more turned on by as he joined them in the living room. Sam's glittering eyes and seductive smile or Logan's mischievous wink and that cocky, smug smile. So much for the cold shower he'd just taken. He knew he should've jacked off while he was in there. It would've eased some of the strain that racked his body. He honestly couldn't remember having been turned on this much for this long with nothing physically triggering the desire.

"Hey," Sam chirped as she hurried toward him, her eyes glittering as she planted a kiss on his lips.

"Did you have fun?"

"I did. It was exhausting, but we enjoyed it. I can't say I'm looking forward to going back for at least another year. It'll probably take me that long to catch up on my sleep."

She said that every year.

He kissed her once more, then released her before heading toward Logan to assist with the suitcases, taking them from the foyer to the bedroom while Sam disappeared into the bathroom.

"Is this more than she took with her?" Elijah asked, hefting one of the bags onto the bed so she could unpack when she was ready.

"I don't know how she does it, but yeah," Logan answered.

"Doesn't she realize she has enough souvenirs?"

"I'll let you be the one to make that suggestion."

He wouldn't be doing that. If Sam wanted to buy out all the tourist shops in Las Vegas, he would gladly walk her to each and every one.

"Did you tell her?" Elijah prompted.

Logan's expression said, *What do you think?*

"And?"

His voice lowered to a thundering growl. "Based on the way she came on my dick, I'd say she liked the story."

Elijah groaned. The cold shower had been a complete waste of time. He should've expected that vulgar explanation because that was Logan. He didn't mince words, and he definitely didn't hold back. Not to mention, if he could say something to spark a fire, Logan never missed an opportunity.

"I know this might make me sound old, but I could seriously use a nap after I unpack," Sam said as she joined them in the bedroom, clearly oblivious to Elijah's arousal. "Then I figured I could make us an early dinner."

"Sounds perfect," Elijah said, turning to face her. "It'll give me some time to run a few errands."

Sam's eyebrows lowered. "Is everything all right?"

Elijah could feel Logan's eyes on him, but he kept his gaze on Sam. "Perfect."

She did not look convinced as she glanced between them.

"I've got to run by the grocery store," he told her. "Is there something you need me to pick up?"

"Steaks and baked potatoes," Logan stated, stepping up behind Sam. "I'll cook tonight." He leaned over her shoulder, pressed a kiss to her neck. "And you can do the dishes. Naked."

87

She rolled her eyes, but there was a beaming smile on her face. "We'll see about that."

Unwilling to resist the opportunity, Elijah stepped up to Sam, effectively sandwiching her between them. "I'm glad you're home."

"Me, too," she whispered as he leaned in to press his lips to hers. He kept the kiss chaste before pressing another to her forehead.

"Get some rest."

"Sounds like I might need it," she teased.

Oh, if she only knew.

Three hours later, Elijah returned to the house to find Sam was still in bed, and Logan was laid out in his recliner, remote in hand.

"Need help with the groceries?" Logan asked.

"I got it," he told him, setting two of the bags on the counter before heading back to his car for the rest.

When he returned, Logan was in the kitchen, unloading the bags and putting things away.

"I figured you might want to wake her up. Maybe we could hang out in the pool for an hour or so before dinner."

"I'll see what she wants to do," he said, trying his damnedest not to think about what had happened the last time they were in the pool.

Elijah left Logan to put away the groceries and headed to their bedroom. He opened the door quietly, stepped inside, and shut it behind him. The blackout curtains blocked out most of the late-afternoon sun, but there was enough for him to see Sam in the middle of the bed, curled up on her side, clutching a pillow. He eased onto his side of the bed, spooning behind her. He roused her slowly, playing with her hair because he knew how much she loved that.

"Mmm," she mumbled, rolling to her back and smiling at him. "I missed you."

He pressed a kiss to her shoulder, slid his hand beneath her T-shirt, and rested it on the smooth, warm skin of her stomach. "Likewise."

They remained like that for a few minutes as she came awake fully.

"Logan told me what happened between you."

"I know."

"Is that why you were avoiding my calls?"

Elijah stared down at her. "I answered every one of your calls. I just avoided your questions."

She canted her head back, one of her adorable frowns pinching her features. "Are you upset with me?"

He searched her gaze, wondering what would've sparked that question. "Of course not."

Sam rolled toward him, her hands moving beneath his T-shirt. He groaned softly, not sure he'd be able to resist her if she kept that up. He was hard as stone, his body seeking a release that had been building for days now despite the fact he'd jacked off this morning right beside Logan. But he knew Logan's suggestion that they get in the pool had been more of a directive than a request. The man wasn't subtle when he wanted something, and Elijah knew him well. He wanted to watch Elijah and Sam together, and truthfully, Elijah needed that right now.

"Was it as good as the first time?" Sam whispered against his neck. "When Logan kissed you?"

"It was." He saw no reason to lie to her.

"Logan said it was better."

That made him smile. She was good for his ego, always had been. Sam seemed to know exactly what they both needed to hear from her.

Her voice took on that sexy rasp when she said, "What about when he stroked your cock?"

His cock jerked, hardening even more although he'd thought it impossible.

"I wish I could've watched. I want to see you touching each other."

Elijah cupped her ass, jerked her to him so she could feel the hard ridge of his cock against her thigh.

"Did you think about me?" she whispered.

"Always, love."

"Did you want me to watch?"

He groaned again, kneading her ass as he rocked her thigh against his cock. "Sam ... keep it up, and I'm going to fuck you right here."

"You make it sound like that's a bad thing."

Elijah leaned down, pressed his mouth to her ear. "Logan wants to watch you ride my cock."

Her throaty moan went right to his dick. "Did he say that?"

"He suggested we spend some time in the pool."

"Mmm. I like pool sex."

He chuckled, some of the tension in his body easing. Sam liked *all* sex. Didn't matter what time of day or where they were. She was a sexual creature, something he found intensely erotic. He never knew what to expect from her, and that turned him on, kept him in a constant state of arousal whenever she was near.

"I promise not to push you and Logan together," she said, her tone sobering. "But just so you know, I'm as eager to watch y'all as you are to watch me."

Elijah understood that hunger. He'd been plagued by that visceral desire for most of his adult life, but it had become a living, breathing thing when he'd met Sam and Logan. Sometimes watching was as pleasurable as being on the receiving end.

"What do you say we move this to the pool," he suggested.

"I like that idea."

It took tremendous willpower to pull away from Sam, but Elijah managed, leaving her to get ready.

WHEN ELIJAH EMERGED FROM THE BEDROOM, LOGAN had just finished preparing snacks and drinks to take poolside. He figured he could start dinner in a couple of hours but would give Sam something to tide her over until then.

"You okay?" he asked, noticing Elijah's wild eyes and the tight line of his lips.

"Peachy."

Logan chuckled. It was obvious Elijah was hanging by a thread, and he couldn't say he blamed the guy. Logan had already had Sam once on the way home from the airport, and he was hard and aching for another round. He never seemed to get enough of her, and there were times he'd certainly tried to sate that urge. It always returned, often more intense than before.

Until Sam, he'd never felt the emotions she stirred in him. Love and lust just barely scratched the surface. There was also a protectiveness that fueled his desire, a dark need to make her happy, to please her however he could. And every day with Sam brought something new for them. Sure, there was still the monotony that came with a solid, long-term relationship, but he wouldn't trade those comforts for anything, either.

"What can I help with?" Elijah offered.

Logan motioned toward the platter of vegetables and dip he'd prepared. "You carry that; I'll get the drinks."

He followed Elijah out to the backyard and set everything in the lounge area shaded by the trees. The backyard was designed to be an oasis, one that provided them with a place to relax and not to worry about the intrusive eyes of their neighbors. Thankfully, there weren't any too close, so he didn't worry about heads peeking over the fence or well-meaning people showing up on his doorstep.

He glanced over in time to see Elijah stripping out of his shorts and his T-shirt, wasting absolutely no time. The man wasn't the least bit modest. Logan doubted Elijah would care if they did have neighbors peeking over the hedges to see what they were doing. He was the same way at the club, game for whatever Logan had in mind, whether it be playtime with an audience or the more semi-private spaces for them to indulge. Regardless of where they were, Elijah's attention always remained raptly focused on Sam.

The back door opened, and Logan picked up a glass of tea, turning in time to see Sam coming out of the house. She had a floral-patterned silk robe covering her to mid-thigh, her long legs bare. Her golden hair was pinned high on her head, though he didn't know why she bothered. No matter what, Elijah always requested her hair be down. Maybe she preferred he do it himself.

The thought made Logan smile.

"Sleep well?" he asked, offering her a glass of tea as she approached.

"I needed that nap."

He pressed a kiss to her lips as she took the glass. She smiled at him before turning her attention to Elijah as he took the stairs down into the pool. Logan watched her reactions to Elijah. It brought back memories of when Logan had learned that Sam had deeper feelings for the man. He remembered the first date they'd gone on together when he'd been forced to stay home, to spend all his time thinking about what Sam and Elijah were doing together. He hadn't been sure he would make it through that night, but he'd forged ahead because introducing them had been his idea. He'd been the one to draw Sam into this lifestyle, and while it had taken a turn he hadn't expected, Logan couldn't say he was disappointed. It had taken time to come to terms with the fact that Sam loved another man as much as she loved him. And now it was their normal. Logan's initial jealousy and fear had been assuaged by Sam's actions. She loved them both, and Logan felt secure in the fact that she wasn't willing to lose either of them.

"I think I'll go for a swim," she said with a smile, passing back her glass.

Logan set her glass on the table, then eased into one of the chairs in the shade, watching as his wife strolled around to the shallow end.

She held his attention as she moved, the gentle sway of her hips, the shift of her body beneath the silk. But it was when she stepped down onto that first step in the water that he felt his heart kick hard. Her attention was on Elijah as she untied the belt around her waist, then slowly let the silk slide down her narrow shoulders, revealing every glorious inch of her sun-kissed skin. Her nipples hardened into tight little points as she took each step down, but he didn't think it was from the cool water or the gentle breeze. No, her gaze was still locked on Elijah, which meant her body's reaction was solely his doing.

Logan fucking loved this part though he couldn't pinpoint why that was. He craved seeing the two of them as they came together. For a brief moment, they were the only two in the world, at least where they were concerned, even though he knew they were aware of him.

Sam let the robe flutter to the patio behind her before taking another step down, her lithe form moving sensually.

"Come here," Elijah urged, reaching for her hand and pulling her toward him.

He whispered something to her that Logan couldn't hear, and then Sam turned to face him, her eyes skimming over Logan as she perched on Elijah's lap. She flashed him a knowing smile, and his cock twitched in response.

As he'd predicted, Elijah released the clip on her hair, set it outside the pool, then shifted the long, silky strands over her shoulder, out of his way. Sam leaned back, settling against Elijah's chest, her head on his shoulder, her beautiful breasts visible above the waterline.

Again, Elijah whispered something in her ear, and Logan's cock thickened. He wanted to hear what the man was saying, but he didn't dare move.

Sam's eyes closed as she moaned, clearly turned on by whatever Elijah whispered in her ear. Logan had heard the man talk dirty, knew he was skilled in that department. He had ways of drawing out Sam's pleasure that Logan hadn't even mastered yet. That, too, excited him.

Logan took a sip of his tea, kept his gaze fixed on the two of them, and settled in for the show. He knew, as always, it was going to be a good one.

SAM RELAXED INTO ELIJAH'S STRONG EMBRACE. THE water should've cooled her overheated skin, but it had nothing on the heat of Elijah's touch or the delicious things he was whispering in her ear.

She moaned softly when his hand cupped her breast, kneading gently as his breath fanned her neck.

"Put your hands under my thighs," Elijah instructed.

He positioned them where he wanted them, and she realized it was a way for her to keep from floating away. She tucked her fingers beneath his muscular thighs, her knuckles pressed against the smooth gunite coating on the seat.

"I want you to stay just like that, no matter what I do. You can't come until my cock's inside you," he whispered. "But I'm going to make you want to."

He punctuated the remark by lightly pinching her nipple, drawing another moan out of her.

"The other night, I was in the pool, sitting just like this," Elijah said.

Sam's body coiled tighter as she realized the story he was about to tell. Unlike Logan, who'd glossed over the details, she knew Elijah was going to let her relive it through his words. They were different in that regard; where Logan spoke right to the point, Elijah had a penchant for drawing things out. She loved that they complemented one another that way.

"I came out here to relax."

She leaned into him. "Were you hoping he'd join you?"

"Yes."

"Did you tell him that?"

"No. I was surprised when he came out," Elijah said, speaking close to her ear. "I didn't know what to expect, but I knew what I wanted."

"What did you want?" she asked, forcing her eyes open to peer over at Logan, who was watching them intently.

"I wanted to explore more of what I felt that night in the cabin, to have his tongue in my mouth, his lips on mine. But I wanted more … I wanted to *do* more, to feel his hard body beneath my palms."

Her pussy clenched against the emptiness. She understood because she felt the same. From the day she'd met Logan, she'd been intimately aware of him on a baser level. As though he was the soul her own was seeking. She'd fallen in love with him almost instantly, intrigued by his desires and his willingness to ease her into this world she hadn't realized existed. His powerful presence had attracted her, made her come alive for the first time in her life. She learned new things about herself thanks to Logan, tapped into pleasures she had never understood.

"He made the first move."

Elijah's softly spoken words vibrated against her skin as his other hand cupped her other breast. Logan's eyes heated as he watched the way Elijah fondled her. She knew Elijah was ensuring Logan could see every pluck of her tightly puckered nipples.

Elijah kissed the delicate skin where her shoulder met her neck before his mouth latched on, and he sucked gently.

Another moan escaped as she tilted her head to the side, offering him better access.

"I didn't realize he'd moved until he said my name. His voice alone made my cock hard as steel, just like it is now."

His hips rocked forward, and she felt the hard ridge against her lower back.

"When he kissed me, Sam ... when he kissed me, I thought I would come."

Her inner muscles clenched again as she remembered their kiss in the cabin. She'd been so turned on it had surprised her. Despite the fact that Sierra had told her how hot it was to watch two men together, Sam hadn't really understood it. She'd witnessed men in the throes of lust at the club, but nothing had compared to watching her men kissing.

Elijah released her right breast, his hand moving to her chin as he turned her head. His mouth pressed to hers lightly, then more insistently as his tongue plunged inside.

"His kiss is different than yours," he mumbled. "Where you're soft and sweet, he's hard and demanding."

Oh, she knew exactly what he was referring to. Kissing Logan was like delving into hell and succumbing to every sin imaginable all at once. And she understood the difference because there was a difference between Logan's kiss and Elijah's. They both had the power to control her every thought with the sweep of their tongue, to take over her body with that very intimacy, but their techniques were unique to them.

"He fucked my mouth with his tongue," Elijah whispered, releasing her chin so he could fondle both her breasts again. "Made me ache to feel that mouth in other places."

She closed her eyes, imagining how hot they'd been lip-locked. "I wanted it, Sam. I wanted more."

She rocked her hips back, seeking friction between her legs as her arousal grew more insistent.

"I thought I was dreaming at first. No way was I feeling an overwhelming desire for a man."

"You've never felt that before?" she asked.

"Not like that, no. But there's something about Logan. You woke the beast, Sam. And Logan was right."

"About?"

"This is your doing," he said, nipping her shoulder, his hands firming on her breasts. "You made us want something we've never wanted before."

Heat bloomed in her bloodstream as she met Logan's gaze across the pool. There was no denying that she liked that she had power over them. More so that it wasn't a physical power. Although, she doubted she could've convinced them to do anything they didn't want to do.

"What happened next?"

"We devoured one another, ate at one another. I couldn't get enough. I wasn't close enough."

Sam was aware of the tension in Elijah's arms, the way they banded more tightly around her as though he couldn't get close enough to her, either.

His hands released her breasts, sliding down her stomach, over her thighs. Then he was gripping her legs, forcing them apart. She knew what was coming, and she welcomed his touch as his fingers brushed her mound, delicately sliding between her labia, grazing her clit every so often.

Sam's breaths became more labored as she pressed back against Elijah, willing him to finger her, to fill her so she didn't feel empty anymore. But he didn't. Not right away. He merely teased.

She met Logan's gaze again, and she could see the passion blazing in his eyes, knew he was imagining what Elijah's hands were doing beneath the water.

"Logan palmed my head, kept our mouths fused as he moved away. I followed because I wanted to, not because he forced me to. I wanted his hands on me. I wanted to feel the difference between his touch and yours."

The fact that Elijah had consistently compared Logan to her was a heady feeling. She liked knowing that she'd been at the forefront of his mind during the encounter.

He tapped her clit, then rubbed light circles before tapping it again. She hummed her approval, wishing he would apply more pressure.

"A door opened that night," Elijah growled against her neck. "You are the key, and you unlocked that door, Sam. We need something from one another."

Present tense, she realized. "Does that mean you want more?"

"Yes," he answered easily. "I want to taste his kiss, to feel his touch. And I want his mouth on me."

She loved listening to the guttural rasp of his voice as he relived that encounter, replaying it for her benefit.

"He touched me first, slipped his hands into my shorts, fisted my cock."

Sam whimpered when Elijah's finger slipped inside her pussy. She clamped down on it, a silent plea for more.

"The way he stroked me … it was unlike anything I'd felt before. He's demanding, and I'd succumbed to the pleasure at his insistence."

Oh, she was well aware of how demanding her husband was. It was one of the most intriguing things about him. Regardless of where they were, Logan was the most powerful man in the room, and he didn't have to speak. He had an air of authority and dominance that you could feel.

"Oh, God," she moaned when Elijah pressed two fingers inside her, fucking her slow and deep.

She tried to ride his hand, but his arms kept her in place. He controlled her as he always did.

"When he shoved his shorts down, I wanted more. And when he placed my hand on his cock, I knew I was going to come. It was inevitable."

"How did it feel? Touching him?" she prompted as she panted, accepting his fingers, eager for more.

"Velvet smooth and so fucking hard." Elijah's breaths came faster. "He wanted my hand on him, wanted me to give him the same pleasure he was giving me."

"Eli … more, please."

As though he'd reached a breaking point, his fingers disappeared. His arms slipped beneath hers, forcing her to release his thighs as he gripped her hips and lifted her up.

"Put my cock inside you," he snarled harshly. "Let me feel the tight clasp of your sweet cunt, Sam. Now."

Sam reached between her legs, guided his cock where she needed him most, and moaned as he lowered her down.

"God, yes," she cried out, her voice echoing over the top of the water, her eyes closing as pleasure consumed her.

He shifted his hips forward, filling her so completely that she felt the pulse of his erection inside her.

"Watch him," Elijah demanded. "Let him see the pleasure we give you."

Sam forced her eyes open, locked her gaze with Logan's as she pleaded for Elijah to fuck her. She loved how her husband's eyes glazed, his hand pressing insistently over the erection concealed by his shorts. He was enjoying the show, which made it even hotter.

Elijah nipped her shoulder as he shifted her forward and back, moving her along his steely length, controlling the friction on his cock, using her to sate the unquenchable hunger.

"We jacked each other off right here in the water," Elijah continued, panting as he fucked her. "He wanted to know what I liked, so I showed him, guiding his hand while he guided mine."

She could only imagine how hot they'd been like that.

"Cup your tits, Sam," Elijah barked, his control slipping. "Pinch your nipples. Let him see you."

Her insides clenched and released as she did as he instructed. All the while, she watched Logan's expression, the hard lines on his handsome face as he watched what Elijah was doing to her.

"He worked me roughly." Elijah fucked her harder as he spoke. "Drove me fucking mad with his hand on my cock."

Sam was close. Her pussy clutched Elijah's cock, his vivid retelling driving her right to the edge.

His voice dropped an octave, rough and ragged. "He made me come in his hand, Sam. Made me come so fucking hard."

"Eli..." She whimpered, pinching her nipples to keep from coming because she needed to hear the whole story.

"Then he made me return the favor, using both of my hands. He palmed the back of my head..."

"Oh, God." Her pussy locked down on him as she imagined her dominating husband fucking Elijah's hands, taking his pleasure from him.

Suddenly, Elijah stood, his arm banded around her waist, their bodies remaining intimately joined. He turned, and Sam had just enough time to press her hands to the pool wall before he began fucking her from behind, his hands bracing her thighs to hold her where he wanted her. Hard, fast, deep. She locked her elbows to keep herself in place, feeling the heat of Logan's gaze as he watched them.

"I made ... him ... come," Elijah rasped, his words punctuated by the persistent thrust of his hips. "Come for me, Sam. Come ... all over ... my cock!"

Sam screamed, her head falling back as her orgasm ripped through her. It was cataclysmic, a violent eruption that consumed her from head to toe.

"Oh, fuck…" Elijah's hips slammed forward, his cock swelling seconds before she felt the delicious spasms deep inside her as he came. "Sam!"

It took a moment to catch her breath as Elijah pulled her back against him, holding her tightly. She dragged air into her lungs as she relaxed against him, aware of the fact that Logan had joined them.

"It was just the beginning, Sam," Elijah whispered in her ear. "You did that, love."

She covered his arms with hers, gripping tightly to show him how much she loved that he'd shared that with her. Logan stood before her, his eyes hot.

"Just as it should be," Elijah said, his voice louder. "No matter what, it's always about you."

"Always," Logan echoed, and she could see the dark hunger their encounter had ignited.

CHAPTER SEVEN

Friday, June 24, 2022

ON FRIDAY AFTERNOON, ELIJAH RECEIVED A TEXT from Logan, requesting that he meet them at Devotion in a couple of hours. He responded without hesitation, agreeing that he would be there as soon as he could.

Back when the three of them had started out, they'd gone to Devotion on a regular basis, generally once every couple of weeks, if not once a week. Then as time went by, their visits had become less frequent. There were a few occasions when they went simply to have a drink and talk to people rather than engage in play. Elijah wasn't sure what Logan had planned for tonight, but either way, he was looking forward to going. Anything to get them out of the house, away from the tension that loomed over them like a shroud.

After leaving the office, Elijah didn't bother going home to change. He merely removed his suit jacket and tie, rolled up the sleeves of his charcoal-gray dress shirt, and ventured inside. Admittance was for members only, and since Elijah had been a member for as long as he'd known Sam and Logan, he was greeted by familiar faces.

The moment he stepped into the club proper, Elijah relaxed. There was something about this place that soothed him, gave him a sense of peace and comfort. He knew in here there was no one who would judge him for his kinks or his life choices when it came to relationships. Considering the human race, in general, was judgmental by nature, it was nice to have a place to go where he didn't feel as though he was being ogled when he was out with Logan and Sam. So many people didn't understand the desires of the heart or the fact that not everything was as black-and-white as some narrow-minded jackasses believed it should be. Those who thought a couple should be a man and a woman didn't make it past the interview process. In fact, those who believed gender was defined as only male or female weren't allowed in, either.

This was a safe space, one that Luke McCoy had built through years of hard work and dedication.

Elijah found Sam sitting at a table with Mercedes and Sierra, the three women drinking cocktails and watching one of the enclosed stages where Mistress Serena, the Dominatrix who'd been managing Devotion for years, was currently engaged in a rather enthralling scene with not one, not two, but *three* male submissives.

"Hey," Sam greeted, pushing to her feet when Elijah approached.

He kissed her on the lips, smiling as her mere presence soothed the rest of the day's stress out of his muscles.

"Good evening, ladies," he greeted the two women still sitting at the table.

Sierra responded by raising her glass, her gaze locked on Mistress Serena's carnal scene. Mercedes gave him a cool grin and a wink before turning her attention to the same.

"Where's Logan?" he asked Sam as she returned to her seat.

She nodded her head toward the bar on the far side of the room. "He's engaged in a heated debate over the benefits of masturbation."

Elijah laughed. That didn't surprise him. "I'll go check in with him."

"Remind him I want to play later," she said with a beaming smile.

He took that to mean Logan hadn't yet committed to doing anything tonight. Otherwise, Sam wouldn't feel the need to get him over to her side so early in the evening.

"I'll do my best," he promised before strolling past the tables filled with a variety of people.

As he approached, Logan's gaze shifted as though he'd felt Elijah's presence. If he wasn't mistaken, there was a spark of interest in the man's eyes as he skimmed him head to toe before meeting his gaze again.

Then again, that could be all in his head. For the past week, ever since Sam had returned home, they were back to normal, pretending as though nothing had happened while she was away. That seemed to be Logan's default setting, and Elijah got the feeling he was going to get whiplash from the back-and-forth before too long.

Elijah ordered a scotch on the rocks before he came to stand near Logan, Luke, and Xander. He didn't get so much as a polite hello out when Luke prompted him with, "How many times a day do you masturbate?"

Thankful Sam had prepared him for this conversation, he answered easily with, "At least once."

"Every day?" Xander's dark eyebrows lowered.

"Every day," he confirmed, not ashamed to admit it.

"I told you," Logan said. "It's a stress reliever."

"And you have sex, what? Once or twice a week?" Xander inquired.

Elijah cut his gaze to Logan and smirked. "On average four, usually five."

"Your hand doesn't count," Luke grumbled.

"No one said anything about my hand." He took a sip of his drink, daring them to call him a liar.

"Jesus," Luke sighed. "How the hell does Sam put up with you two?"

Logan laughed. "Are you kidding? Who do you think instigates it?"

Elijah chuckled. That was only partly true. She didn't always instigate, but she rarely ever turned either of them down.

Luke rolled his eyes, his gaze moving through the space as he kept an eye on everything that was going on.

"Speaking of Sam," Elijah said, turning to Logan, "she said to remind you she wants to play tonight."

His eyes glittered. "I know."

Elijah tried to read him, but he couldn't, which meant that playtime was certainly still on the table, and if he had to guess, Sam was going to be in for a treat.

"THEY LOOK ... *FRIENDLIER* THAN THEY DID BEFORE," Sierra said, pulling Sam's attention off of Mistress Serena and that wicked crop she was using on one of her submissives.

Sam followed Sierra's gaze, noticed she was watching Logan and Elijah, who were standing nearly shoulder to shoulder as they laughed.

"Things better between them?"

She cut her gaze to Sierra. "Things weren't bad between them."

Her friend nodded, and she could see that Sierra didn't believe her.

Sam wished she could just tell them what was going on, but she had sworn herself to secrecy. Plus, she wasn't really sure there was anything to tell yet. While both Logan and Elijah had regaled her with the details of their brief interlude, she wouldn't have been the wiser otherwise. The past week had been back to normal, with both of her men acting as though nothing had happened between them.

They had been, however, intensely focused on her since she got back from Vegas. Not that she was complaining. Logan and Elijah were both very creative when it came to seduction. She figured that was part of the reason they had such a healthy sex life. It also helped that she craved them like a drug. Logan had once accused her of being addicted to sex, and while she wasn't sure she'd go that far, she knew for a fact she was addicted to both of them.

"I haven't seen Cole tonight," Sam said, purposely redirecting the conversation.

Sierra smiled knowingly and answered with, "He stayed home. Urged us to get out of the house for a little while."

"Everything okay?" Mercedes asked.

"Between us? Of course. It's Hannah. She's been a bit of a pill this week."

Sam had heard the stories. The fact that Hannah had hit puberty was a point of contention, something all parents likely had to deal with. According to Sierra, the nine-year-old believed she was a teenager already.

"Well, I hope you make it up to him when you get home," Mercedes teased Sierra.

"Oh, I plan to." She laughed. "Luke already promised him, and I have every intention of watching."

Sam jerked her attention back to the scene. She knew Sierra was baiting her, something she'd been doing because she clearly suspected that the tension between Logan and Elijah had to do with their attraction to one another. How the woman had jumped to that conclusion, Sam didn't know. She'd been good, keeping her thoughts to herself ever since Colorado, so it wasn't her fault. Not this time, anyway.

Sam spent the next hour watching as Mistress Serena interacted with her submissives. It was intriguing to watch a powerful Domme control the pleasure of three hot men. She didn't hesitate to make them pleasure one another, using every tool in her toolbox to put on a show for the members. Sam figured that was one of the main reasons they had such a packed house on Fridays. Mistress Serena always put on a good show.

When they first arrived, Sam had been hoping they might have an opportunity to venture into one of the main scene rooms like the one the Domme was entertaining in, but she hadn't mentioned it to Logan. She knew better. Whenever she tried to steer their playtime, it never worked out the way she envisioned. It was always hot, sure, but Logan rarely let her direct a scene.

Not that she minded. She happened to love the way Logan's wicked mind worked. Not only was he creative in the privacy of their home, he also had an arsenal of ideas to make their visits to Devotion memorable. She figured if and when he decided to play tonight, she would enjoy whatever he had in store for her. And if not, she knew there would be something in store for her when they got home. He never left her wanting.

Another hour passed while Sam mingled with other members she knew, working her way toward Logan and Elijah, who had moved to one of the lounge areas to congregate with the other husbands.

By the time she made her way over to them, she noticed a glint in Logan's eyes. He'd been watching her for a while because she'd felt his eyes on her. She loved that he was always aware of what she was doing and who she was talking to. It made her feel cherished that he wanted to know where she was at all times.

When she moved up behind him, setting her hands on his shoulders, he immediately reached up to touch her, caressing her hand with his. He peered up, smiled.

"I heard you wanted to play," he said, his voice seductively low.

"I always want to play," she countered, returning his smile.

"Good." He looked over at Elijah. "You ready?"

Elijah's eyes sparkled with interest as he set his empty glass aside and pushed to his feet. Sam stepped into him as he moved closer, his hand sliding down her back, pulling her against him before leaning in and pressing his mouth to hers.

"I'm seconds away from stripping you naked and taking you right here," he rasped against her lips.

He was in rare form tonight, she realized. Usually, he wasn't much into public displays of affection. Not *this* public, anyway. That didn't mean she hadn't been screwed silly right here in the main area, because she had. More times than she could count. Most of the time, Logan and Elijah were discreet about it, tormenting her endlessly as they fucked her while she sat on their lap.

"We're in the massage room tonight," Logan said when he stepped up behind her.

Sam's body warmed instantly. She loved the massage room because it usually meant she would spend at least an hour getting teased and tormented by their skilled hands. Add the fact that it was an observing room—which meant anyone who ventured to the second floor would have a clear view inside—and she knew she was in for something hot.

"Come on, baby," Logan said, taking her hand. "Let's get you loose and relaxed."

She sighed, smiling as she let him lead the way. With every step they took to the second floor, her anticipation grew exponentially. Sam couldn't count how many times they'd played at Devotion, but it didn't seem to matter. Every time felt like the first because she didn't know what to expect, and she suspected Logan did that on purpose.

"After you," he said when he opened the door to their designated room.

She stepped inside and sighed again. There was a padded table in the center of the room, the lights were dimmed, soft music playing overhead, and rose petals were scattered throughout. Although she knew it was going to be carnal by design, she sensed Logan had romance on the brain tonight. He did that. He was always looking at it from every angle, not just the lascivious one.

"Is this for me?" she asked, moving closer to the table.

Logan moved over to the small metal cart and lifted the drape that had concealed the contents. "These are for you, too."

Her eyes shot to the variety of tools displayed, several still sealed in their original packaging. "Is that...?"

Oh, God.

"A violet wand?" He chuckled softly. "It is."

"I thought you said massage."

"I never specified," he corrected, nodding toward Elijah.

In all fairness, he hadn't, but Sam would've appreciated a little warning. While she enjoyed the electric stimulation from time to time, it wasn't her favorite.

Elijah moved toward her, motioning with a twirl of his hand for her to turn around.

She turned her back to him, exhaled when she felt the warmth of his body against her.

"I think it's time to get you out of these clothes."

Sam didn't move as Elijah began to methodically strip every piece of clothing from her body. It was a sensual dance, one that was meant as a seduction, a distraction, and possibly a show for anyone standing on the other side of that two-way mirror. Sam couldn't see through it, which amped up the sensation of being watched, regardless of whether anyone was out there or not.

She tried not to focus on Logan, who was prepping the tools he intended to use. She paid attention to the gentle brush of Elijah's fingers against her skin as he seduced her with his touch and his wicked mouth.

When she was naked, Logan finished up what he was doing and motioned for her to get on the table.

"Facedown, first," he instructed.

With Elijah's help, she positioned herself on the table, her body humming with anticipation and a hint of fear. She knew the violet wand wouldn't hurt, but it did take quite a bit of effort to endure. She didn't know whether that was the case for everyone, but it was for her.

"I'll give you two choices," Logan said, his voice low, his fingers skimming her from shoulder to calf as he moved around the table.

If one of those options didn't involve that violet wand, she knew which choice already.

"Choose the violet wand, and we'll start slow and end with a one-hour massage. We'll focus entirely on you the entire time."

"Or?" she asked, hating that he would hear the concern in her tone.

"Or we'll skip the wand and—"

"The second one," she blurted before he could finish.

Logan chuckled. "You don't want to hear what we have in store for you?"

"Nope." She shook her head to emphasize.

"Not even to know it involves a butt plug and nipple clamps?"

She gritted her teeth, and her ass clenched tightly at the thought of the plug, but she stuck firmly to her decision. Sam admittedly enjoyed anal sex, but she wasn't all that keen on butt plugs. For one, they were hard, and two, Logan had been known to make her keep them in for longer than she cared to.

"Second option," she repeated.

"Very well."

Before she could turn her head to get a peek at the plug they would be using, a firm hand landed on the back of her head, keeping her from looking. A moment later, a blindfold was covering her eyes.

"Y'all are mean," she groaned, relaxing on the table as warm hands began caressing her back.

All thought fled as four hands moved over her, massaging her skin with a coconut-scented oil. Sam allowed herself to drift on the euphoria that came with the steady, smooth movements that relaxed her muscles even as they made her pussy wet with anticipation.

She was aware of the bed rotating, but she thought nothing of it until Logan said, "No reason not to let others watch while I slip this into your pretty little hole."

A chill snaked down her spine and made her nipples pebble. The thought of someone on the other side of that glass watching as Logan began fingering her ass, massaging the oil in to prepare her for the plug, brought her nerve endings to life.

"Relax, baby," he said softly. "This is the big plug."

Sam didn't know if he was screwing with her or telling the truth, but she suspected it was the latter. Logan enjoyed pushing her limits, and this was an opportunity he wouldn't pass up. After all, she'd chosen the plug over the violet wand, so it was only fair. At least in his mind.

Her moans grew louder, more insistent as he fucked her ass with two fingers, stretching her. With the blindfold on, she couldn't see anything, and it made her imagination run wild. She briefly pictured a plug the size of a watermelon, which did nothing to help her relax.

"I don't think she's ready," Logan said casually, as though carrying on a conversation about the weather.

She gasped when another finger sank inside her, then another.

"Fuck, she's tight," Elijah said.

Sam realized they were both fingering her.

"Relax," Elijah crooned. "You've taken more than this before."

She focused on breathing while they teased her ruthlessly, fucking her ass, stretching her impossibly. It felt good, more so because she imagined how debauched it looked for anyone watching.

It wasn't until she began to moan, rocking her hips to encourage more, that Logan said, "I think she's ready."

The fingers slipped out slowly, replaced a second later by the cold tip of the plug pressing against her anus. Her breaths became more labored as Logan—she assumed it was Logan—stretched her again with the toy.

"Relax that greedy little ass," Logan growled roughly. "Take the plug like you take my cock, Sam."

She shuddered as pleasure coursed through her, the plug inching in, filling her, stretching her. She took deep, even breaths as Logan pushed it all the way in until she felt as though she was splitting in two. Finally, the plug was situated, easing the stretch but making her feel full.

After Logan tugged on it twice, using the excuse he was getting it positioned better, she heard the water, figured they were cleaning up. When they returned, they resumed massaging her, teasing her flesh with wandering fingers as they stroked her clit, making her whimper as the pleasure intensified. If she was lucky, they'd forgotten about the nipple clamps.

"Did I forget to tell you that you can't come, Sam?" Logan said with a chuckle, the fingers disappearing from her clit. "Option one was about you. Option two is for us to use you however we deem appropriate."

Sam moaned, knowing she was in for it now. When Logan said the word *use*, he meant exactly that. The massage was going to be a moot point by the time they were done.

LOGAN HAD KNOWN SAM WOULD CHOOSE WHATEVER option didn't involve the violet wand. He'd been prepared for it. And now that she had the plug in, he was anxious to work her up until she was begging them to use her the way he'd promised they would.

He was generous with the massage, kneading her muscles, starting with her feet, and working his way up while Elijah worked on her shoulders and back. While they worked, they both stripped down, ensuring she was aware so she would know what their intentions were.

Once they were naked, Logan had her turn over. "Time for the clamps."

Sam groaned her displeasure, making him smile.

Elijah retrieved the clamps from the tray, then stood on her side, opposite Logan. With a look, he directed Elijah to follow his lead. They teased her nipples with their mouths first, worked her until she was moaning. When it appeared she had relaxed, they adjusted the alligator clips over her distended nipples and settled them on her, releasing them simultaneously.

"Oh, shit," she hissed, her back arching as the teeth clamped down on the puckered tips.

"Hurt?" he asked.

"Yes."

"Breathe through it," he instructed, sliding his hand over her thigh as encouragement.

She breathed through her nose for long seconds before finally relaxing on the table once more while they massaged her chest, her hips, her thighs.

"Good girl," he praised. "You ready to be used?"

"Mmm-hmm," she mumbled, clearly replete from her massage.

"Are you sure about that?"

She sighed, and he knew she was drifting between pain and pleasure, allowing the warring sensations to consume her.

He watched as Elijah moved to the head of the table, reached under, and adjusted it so that it lowered to a forty-five-degree angle, bringing her head level with his cock.

"Open your mouth, love," Elijah urged, tapping her chin.

Sam arched her neck and opened her mouth, her tongue darting out to lick Elijah's cock as it hovered over her face.

Logan guided her hand along his shaft while he watched her lick and lave Elijah's dick. He let his free hand stray down between her legs so he could tease along the seam of her pussy. Sam's legs widened, the wanton woman silently asking for more. He teased, never applying enough pressure to her clit, nor slipping his fingers inside her. She moaned and whimpered as Elijah adjusted his angle, pushing his cock past her lips to fuck her face.

Logan was transfixed by the sight, but that wasn't unusual. He loved watching Elijah and Sam together. He loved seeing how she worked to please him as much as he enjoyed the ecstasy that tightened Elijah's features.

"Such a sweet mouth," Elijah mumbled, tugging the chain between the clamps attached to her nipples as he pumped his hips. "Take me all the way, Sam."

She stopped moving and allowed Elijah to push his cock deep into her throat. When he was buried to the hilt, Logan pushed two fingers inside her, held them there. He could feel her cunt clutching him as she hummed softly.

When Elijah pulled out, so did Logan. When Elijah pushed in deep again, Logan followed suit, pushing two fingers in again. They fucked her from both ends, never rushing. It went on for long minutes, Logan keeping pace and following Elijah's lead.

Then they traded places, but this time, Elijah went to the foot of the bed, positioning Sam's feet flat and forcing her knees wide. While Logan slid his cock into the warmth of her eager mouth, he watched Elijah's tongue drag over her sensitive flesh. He moved slowly at first, which tormented Sam, her suction faltering as she tried to get Elijah to give her more. The entire time, Logan was raptly focused on the man's tongue as it flicked her clit, his lips as they sucked on her. Sam's hips bucked, but Elijah's arm was there, banding across her pelvis to hold her still.

When she began to groan, they traded places. Logan had Sam turn over onto her stomach again, then adjusted the lower end of the table while Elijah fixed the other end, collapsing it so that Sam's torso was draped across the narrow center, her feet on the ground.

"I'm gonna use this tight little pussy now, baby," Logan warned as he stepped between her legs.

"Please," she whimpered.

He guided his cock into the tight sheath of her cunt, pushing in deep and slow. With the plug in her ass, she was so fucking tight.

They worked together, fucking her from both ends—slowly, leisurely—while she mewled and whimpered.

They traded again.

"Taste yourself, Sam," he commanded as he pushed his cock, slick with her juices, into her mouth.

She hummed, the vibrations making his balls tighten.

While Logan fucked her mouth and Elijah drilled her pussy, they used her for long minutes, taking their pleasure from her delectable body. Logan kept his full attention on his wife, refusing to think about what it would feel like to have his cock tunneling in and out of Elijah's mouth. He hated that his thoughts had taken that turn for the past week. It felt like a betrayal to his wife, who was eagerly pleasing them as she let them take control.

Trading places once more, Logan slid back into her cunt, toying with the plug in her ass, inching it out, pushing it in, fucking her with it while his hips pumped more insistently, her pussy tightening around him as she sought more friction. Her body clutched at him as she whimpered, unable to move although he could tell she wanted to.

"You need more, baby?"

"Mmm-hmm," she mumbled around Elijah's cock filling her mouth.

This time when her pussy clamped down on him, Logan groaned. She was going to make him come. His gaze shifted to Elijah's face, and he realized the man was watching him. Their eyes locked, and Logan faltered. There was so much heat in his eyes, so much need. It reminded him of the night they'd gotten each other off in the pool.

"Fuck me," he growled softly, feeling the defeat wash over him. He was in too deep, he realized, his desire for Elijah building despite his efforts to keep it at bay.

"Suck me, Sam," Elijah bellowed, fisting her hair, his face pinching as he neared that inevitable cliff. "Oh, fuck ... oh, fuck."

Logan held his stare, waited until he witnessed that moment of no return. The instant Elijah careened over the edge, a dark, thundering growl escaping as he came deep in Sam's throat, Logan gripped Sam's hips with both hands and pounded into her. Hard.

He rocked her body on the table, her tits dangling down, bouncing from the momentum of his thrusts.

"Pull on the chain," Logan commanded Elijah.

He did, holding Logan's stare.

"Oh, God, yes!" Sam shouted, her pussy locking tight along his shaft.

Logan's control snapped, and he came with a rough growl, refusing to believe that Elijah's molten hot stare had been the reason for that powerful release.

CHAPTER EIGHT

Thursday, June 30, 2022

THE FOLLOWING WEEK WAS UNEVENTFUL. ELIJAH WENT to work, grateful for the reprieve from traveling. The second half of the year was generally when he was gone the most, so he spent time with his assistant going over his schedule, trying to figure out the best way to consolidate to keep him home more.

At the beginning of his relationship with Sam, Elijah used his job as a means of keeping himself level, taking the days necessary to balance himself when he realized he was falling in love with her. Somewhere along the way, he'd grown to hate leaving her, not getting to see her every day, wake up with her in his arms. In fact, in the past seven years, he'd turned down three job promotions because of it. Promotions that would've ultimately tripled his pay and added his name to the list of presidents of the company. For him, Sam was more important than money or any ridiculous job title.

With the last promotion they'd offered him nine months ago, Elijah had kindly informed them he would not be interested unless a role came open that kept him at home one hundred percent of the time. And now, there was a rumor going around that the regional vice president was slated to move up, which would leave his role up for grabs. On Tuesday morning, his boss had called, requesting Elijah to consider taking it. Nine months ago, he would've jumped at the opportunity. Shit, even six months ago. But now ... now, Elijah wasn't sure what the right move would be, thanks to the tension that his relationship with Logan was causing.

Because his office was gearing up for the July Fourth holiday, there were a lot of people out, taking advantage of a long weekend and extending it by a couple of days. Elijah had opted to do the same, taking off Friday, although he knew Sam and Logan had to work. He didn't mind being at home alone, and right now, he actually looked forward to it. His stress had reached astronomical levels due to his interactions—or lack thereof—with Logan. The man had shifted once again, keeping Elijah at arm's length in a way that was getting more uncomfortable by the minute.

He started his day by sleeping in, rousing when Sam and Logan were getting ready for work, but drifting off again when they left him alone. He woke and had coffee and a bagel around seven, then caught the late morning news. When the talk shows started, he got distracted by his own thoughts, so he headed to their home gym. He spent half an hour on the treadmill, another twenty minutes with weights. Rather than take a shower after, he ventured out to the pool. He exhausted himself by doing laps, then relaxed on one of the lounge chairs in the shade while he checked his messages.

Sam had texted him to let him know she would pick up dinner on the way home because she would be working late. She warned him that Logan was coming home early but didn't mention a time. Figuring it could be anywhere between three and five before he arrived, Elijah didn't make much effort to do anything else. Just shy of four, when he was still home alone, he got in the shower, keeping the water cool to see if he could do something about his overheated skin. Oddly enough, it had nothing to do with spending the afternoon outside and everything to do with what was churning in his soul.

Yes. His soul.

He wasn't sure what the hell was going on with Logan, and he wasn't sure he even wanted to know anymore. This thing between them had become complicated. One minute he'd get worked up, eager to go toe-to-toe with the man in whatever way possible. The next, he was relegated to sitting silently because Logan's brooding had darkened his mood.

Elijah washed up, intending to move on to the next thing he wouldn't be doing that day, but he distracted himself once more with thoughts of Logan. So much so, he didn't even realize he was stroking his soapy cock until he groaned, and the sound echoed off the tiled wall.

Leaning back against the cool tile, he spread his legs and gave his cock the attention it clearly wanted. His thoughts drifted to the night in the pool.

"This is not how I envisioned our relationship progressing."

"Then stop."

"Is this where you thought we'd be headed?"

"No."

"But you want it?"

"Yes. But I'll stop if you do."

"Fuck that."

Jesus. Why the fuck couldn't Logan just give in already? They'd both admitted they wanted to, but something kept holding Logan back. Elijah couldn't fathom what it could possibly be.

"I can't stop this."

"Neither can I."

No matter where Elijah thought it was going, Logan continued to pull back on the reins, stopping them from moving forward. It was making him insane because he didn't understand the man's reasons. He couldn't figure out if it was denial or fear, but there was a wall that was fortifying with each passing day.

Elijah grunted. "Why do you have to make it so damn hard, Logan?" He wasn't talking about his cock, either.

"Even when she's not here, she's taunting us, Eli."

"How so?"

"She dangled you in front of me. She made me want."

"Fuck," Elijah groaned, dropping his head back as he let the memory of Logan's hand stroking his cock take over. He could still feel the confidence in his touch, the way Logan stroked him as though he knew exactly what Elijah needed. He'd blown his damn mind in a way he hadn't experienced before. The need he'd felt that night had been all-consuming, but it wasn't just sex for him. At least he didn't think so. Why couldn't Logan see what was right in front of him?

He imagined Logan asking him what he wanted, what he needed, the way he did with Sam when they were pleasuring her.

"I need *you*, Logan," he said aloud. "*That's* what I need."

Too bad he didn't have the nerve to say it directly to the man. Perhaps if he did, they wouldn't be in this predicament.

LOGAN CAME HOME EARLY WITH EVERY INTENTION of changing and spending a couple of hours in the gym while he waited for Sam to get off work. He made it as far as the bedroom when he heard the shower running. Since his closet was on the other side of the bathroom, he had two choices: ignore the fact that Elijah was in the shower or wait however long it took the man to finish up.

Realizing he was too tense to wait, needing an outlet sooner rather than later, he started toward the closet. He stopped short when he heard Elijah mumble something incoherent.

To watch or not to watch, that was the question.

Without too much thought, Logan continued forward. He didn't consider it peeping since he figured Elijah would see him the moment he stepped into view, or at least that was what he told himself. He cut a quick glance over at the shower but stopped again when he realized Elijah was jacking off, highlighted by the LED light above, water sluicing down his rock-hard body.

"I need *you*, Logan. *That's* what I need."

Jacking off *and* thinking about him.

Logan moved over to the vanity and leaned back against it so that he had an unobstructed view of Elijah. His cock swelled, tenting the front of his slacks as he watched the sexy man. Elijah was leaning against the wall, head tipped back, eyes closed, his hand moving slowly up and down his soapy shaft. The muscles in his legs bunched as he bent his knees, his abdomen contracting. Seeing him like that brought back every feeling he'd shoved down for the past week. He was turned on by the man, that much he couldn't deny. But it was knowing that Elijah was thinking about him that had his dick jerking hard behind his zipper.

"Need me to what?" he said, his voice loud enough to be heard over the water raining down on Elijah.

Elijah didn't flinch, almost as though he'd known Logan was there. He lifted his head, opened his eyes, and met his stare across the steamy bathroom. His hand continued that slippery glide up and down his shaft while he cupped his balls with his other hand.

"Enjoying the show?"

Logan didn't answer the question, but he didn't look away when he said, "What is it you need from me, Elijah?"

They were at a standoff, staring at one another while Elijah continued to stroke his cock. His movements quickened, his arm muscles tightening.

"I need *you*," Elijah growled softly.

"Who said you didn't have me?" he countered hotly. "I'm right here. Watching you. Make yourself come."

He saw Elijah's throat work on a swallow, his chest muscle tensing, his legs trembling as he stroked faster.

"Will that make you happy?" Elijah retorted, his words heavy with frustration. "For me to get myself off?" His eyes narrowed, his hand jerking roughly. "Does it make you feel better to know I fucking think about you like this?"

Did it? Logan wasn't sure. But even if he did, he wasn't going to admit it. After their encounter at Devotion, when Logan had come while fucking his wife and holding Elijah's penetrating stare, he'd felt off. Confused. He'd realized that night that he didn't like the direction this was headed. This was supposed to be about Sam, but somewhere along the way, Logan's attention had been divided between them.

Elijah hissed. "I'm tired of the fucking games, Logan."

Games?

Logan snorted. "You're the only one playing games," he snapped, standing tall, feeling defensive.

"Yeah?" Elijah's grip tightened as he jerked his cock hard, his abdomen flexing, his chest heaving. "Is that what you think I'm doing?"

Logan was transfixed for a moment, captivated by the way Elijah chased his release, pushing himself to the breaking point.

"I'm not the one confused," Elijah bit out. "Oh, fuck ... oh ... fuck."

He came, a rough, grinding sound escaping his chest as his cock spurted.

"The only person playing games here is you, Logan," Elijah said as he remained pressed to the wall, his harsh breaths echoing in the space.

Logan swallowed hard and bit back the scathing remark that sat on his lips. He did not want to get into it with Elijah. Not now and certainly not here. Pretending he hadn't been affected by what he'd just witnessed, Logan marched into the closet, changed, and disappeared before Elijah shut off the water.

An hour later, after failing to work up a sweat, Logan collapsed onto the weight bench and stared up at the ceiling.

His cock was rock fucking hard, making it impossible to do anything. He'd tried the treadmill, lasted three minutes, so he had moved on to weights but ended up staring at himself in the floor-to-ceiling mirrors that lined one wall. He couldn't remember the last time anyone or anything had weighed so heavily on him that he couldn't focus.

It was pissing him off, but he refused to cave to the demands of his dick, so he focused on breathing. He had no idea how long he remained like that, but he didn't move until he heard footsteps. He lifted his head to peer over at the door, expecting to see Sam's beautiful smiling face, but she wasn't the one standing in the doorway.

"We need to talk," Elijah said, his tone lacking the easygoing vibe Logan was used to.

He dropped his head back down, stared up at the ceiling. "I've got nothing to say."

It was a lie. There were so many things he *wanted* to say to Elijah, but nothing he was *willing* to say. As far as Logan was concerned, this thing between them had played itself out. With time, he would ensure they went back to the way things were before he'd been tempted by something that wasn't Sam. It was the only way he could see things for them.

There was only silence and the rapid churn of his blood in his ears as he ignored the man who seemed intent on pissing him off. When he calmed, he took a deep breath, braced himself to sit up, but sucked in a harsh breath when Elijah's hands pressed to his thighs.

Logan lifted his head to see Elijah kneeling between his legs, his dark eyes pinned on his face.

"What are you doing?" he asked.

"What I've wanted to do," Elijah replied, his hands reaching for the waistband of Logan's shorts.

He should've moved then. Should've bolted upright and skirted around Elijah. Should've left the room and not looked back.

Logan did neither of those things as Elijah tugged on his shorts, jerking them down, freeing his throbbing dick.

"Elijah..." He'd meant it as a warning, but he'd be damned if it didn't sound like a request.

He stared down the length of his body at the man as Elijah gripped his cock at the base. He narrowed his eyes, swallowed hard, and mentally willed Elijah to keep going since he was too much of a coward to say the words aloud.

He felt the warmth of Elijah's breath as it fanned over his cockhead seconds before that wicked fucking mouth descended.

Logan dropped his head to the bench and groaned low in his throat, hips thrusting upward when the heated suction enveloped him.

"Jesus ... fuck," he ground out, gripping the bars near his head as he held on. "Fuuuuuck."

There wasn't an ounce of hesitation in Elijah's movements as he sucked his cock deep into his mouth, his tongue swirling around his shaft, caressing the sensitive underside as he drew him deep into his throat.

Logan's groin tightened, his balls drawing up close to his body. He'd never had the urge to come so fucking quickly, but he was dangerously close.

Elijah didn't make a sound, stroking the base of Logan's cock with one firm hand while he laved and sucked his cock. Logan refused to watch, hating himself for hiding from the pleasure, but more so for how much he wanted this. His heart pounded against his ribs; his blood boiled in his veins as his body was racked with undeniable pleasure. Despite his mental demands, his hips rocked as he fucked himself into the heat of Elijah's mouth.

"Oh, fuck..." His chest tightened; his abs contracted. "Eli ... goddamn you..."

With every grumble, Elijah seemed more intent, his head bobbing as he drove Logan straight to the precipice. He held on by sheer force of will and the denial he'd been harboring until it became clear he was helpless to deny what he so desperately craved.

"Make me come," he bellowed, his fingers turning white due to the death grip he had on the bars. "Fuck ... make me come down your throat."

Elijah's hand stroked faster, sucking hard as he bobbed faster.

"Ah, fuck me," Logan bellowed a second before the last of his control evaporated, and he came with a violence that rocked him to his core.

A minute passed, maybe two, while he pulled himself together, mentally preparing himself to hash it out with Elijah once and for all.

By the time he felt more in control, he forced himself to sit up so he could—

Elijah stood, his eyes hot as he stared down at him. "The ball's in your court now, Logan. You know what I want, what I'm willing to give. The rest is up to you."

With that parting shot, Elijah turned and strolled out of the room without so much as a backward glance.

THE INSTANT SAM WALKED INTO THE HOUSE, she knew something was wrong. The tension emanating from her two men was palpable, thick enough to cut with a knife.

She glanced at Elijah, who was sitting at the kitchen table with his iPad in front of him, then over to Logan, who was laid out on the couch, his attention on the television. Neither of them looked at her, although they both murmured greetings as though they'd been preprogrammed to do so upon her arrival.

Just for shits and giggles, she stood there for a moment, waiting to see if either of them would get with the program.

They didn't.

Looked like it was going to be a night for wine.

Or maybe vodka.

She wasn't sure yet.

CHAPTER NINE

Monday, July 4, 2022

LOGAN SAT BACK IN HIS CHAIR AND stared out at the swimming pool.

His brother was throwing his annual Fourth of July party, complete with barbecue, beer, and swimming. At the moment, kids and adults alike were splashing around, laughing, and having a good time.

Sierra and Sam were in the pool, floating on rafts, while the kids took turns doing cannonballs to see who could splash them more. Logan loved hearing his wife's laugh as she played along with them. His gaze shifted to Elijah, who was perched on the deck rail, deep in conversation with Xander and Alex about the pros and cons of electric-powered vehicles. Logan found his gaze straying that way every so often to see the animated expression on Elijah's face as the man fought to win them over to his side. He figured by the end of the day, someone would be ordering a Tesla.

"The water's not toxic, you know," Luke said, joining him as he passed over another beer. "You can get in."

He accepted the handoff with a sincere "Thanks," then glanced over at his brother. "It's more enjoyable this way. I don't see *your* ass in the pool."

Luke lifted a spatula. "Cookin'."

Logan laughed. "I thought Cole was cooking?"

"He who wields the spatula does the cooking," Luke said mockingly.

"Uh-huh. And how hard did you have to fight to get that away from him?"

"Cole doesn't fight me." Luke's grin was wicked. "He knows better."

Logan rolled his eyes. He wasn't going to touch that.

"So, how's work?" Luke inquired.

"It's work. You?"

"Same."

"Do you two ever have conversations that involve lengthy sentences? Or is it mostly the one- or two-word non-starters?"

Logan looked back when he heard the familiar voice to see Dylan Thomas and his wife, Sara, joining them.

"Well, I'll be damned," Logan said, getting to his feet and pulling Dylan in for a back-slapping hug. "How the hell are you, man?"

"We're good." Dylan offered a beaming smile as he drew Sara closer to his side, his free hand coming down to rest on the baby bump protruding from her stomach. "Damn good."

"It's about time someone else popped out a kid around here," Luke grumbled, offering Dylan and Sara both a hug. "We need some little critters around. These"—he motioned toward the kids in the pool—"are all grown up. Gettin' ready to head off to college."

Laughter erupted, but Logan knew his brother was only partially teasing. Luke's kids were getting older, but they were far from college age. Not that anyone could tell Luke that. He wanted his kids to stay little forever.

"How's the club?" Logan inquired.

"Goin' strong," Dylan confirmed. "I hear Trent's thinkin' about opening another one. Miami, maybe?"

Trent Ramsey, the world-famous Oscar-winning actor, was also a fetish club owner. Not only was he a silent partner in Devotion, Luke's infamous fetish club, he'd also created Dichotomy, one of the most profitable and well-known BDSM clubs in the country. Knowing Trent, before it was all said and done, he would have a location in every major city in the US. Now that he thought about it, that was likely Trent's goal. The man did not like to be outdone.

"We're glad you made it." Luke looked down at Sara. "I know my wife's eager to shower you with love and hand-me-downs."

"I won't say no to either," she said sweetly, glancing past them.
"Go on, then," Dylan urged his wife. "Go dip your feet in the pool. I'll bring you a drink in just a minute."

"Lemonade?"

"I made some fresh this morning," Luke said, deadpan.

"Really?" Sara asked hopefully.

Luke cast her that *what do you think?* look before smiling. "Of course not. But Sierra did. Just for you."

Her smile beamed up at him before she waddled toward McKenna and Mercedes, who were sitting near the shallow end of the pool.

"Grab a beer, have a seat," Luke encouraged, twirling his spatula. "I've got cookin' to tend to, and I'll grab that lemonade."

When Luke strolled off, Dylan stepped closer. "He does know Cole's cooking, right?"

Logan laughed.

Several hours later, after the food had been eaten and the fireworks had been witnessed, the party finally wound down. The majority of the people had dispersed, heading home to tuck little ones in bed, but a few brave souls remained. Luke had hired a babysitter to tend to the kids for the rest of the night, so they were the only ones with kids still hanging around. Xander and Mercedes had stuck around to chat it up with Leah Ingram and Shane Gibson, who'd both stopped by—separately, though they now appeared to be *together* if the fact that they were getting handsy was any indication. Logan had moved to join them, now occupying one of the lounge chairs near the pool, while Sam and Elijah had slipped back into the water with Sierra and Cole.

Logan figured he should head that way, too, since that seemed to be where the adults were congregating now that the kids had cleared out, but he wasn't moving quickly. For whatever reason, he was content to watch, though that was getting more difficult by the second. The party, which had been a family affair earlier in the evening, was taking a turn toward the taboo, something that frequently happened when they all got together.

"If I didn't know better, I'd think you were playin' it safe over here."

Logan looked up at his brother, then back over to where Elijah and Sam were talking to Cole. "Definitely not safe," he mumbled.

"All right, spit it out." Luke dropped into the seat beside him. "I've had about enough of your whinin'."

Logan couldn't help but smile. He'd been on his best behavior today, so he knew his brother was just giving him shit because he could.

"What's going on with you?" Luke asked. "Y'all having problems?"

Logan didn't look at his twin. "No problems."

"Then why the fuck are you keeping your distance from them? You've had your ass planted in that seat all afternoon."

Logan frowned, then pointed across the way. "Not true. I spent a couple of hours in *that* seat over there."

Luke huffed a sigh. "You can bullshit me all night long, brother, but I know when something's bothering you. And you've been acting fucked up for a while now. Spill it."

Logan watched Elijah as he leaned in and kissed Sam's shoulder. It brought back memories of the last pool encounter he'd witnessed between them. Two weeks ago, when Sam had returned from Vegas. He'd later learned that Elijah had told her in explicit detail what had transpired between them while she'd been gone. It hadn't surprised him that his wife had gotten off on the idea of the two of them touching one another. She'd already admitted to wanting to watch.

Not for the first time, he wondered what she would've thought if she'd witnessed Elijah sucking him until he came down his throat. Logan hadn't shared that little detail with Sam yet—wasn't even sure he wanted to—and since Sam hadn't brought it up, he knew Elijah had kept it to himself as well.

"Something's different between you and Elijah," Luke noted, his voice low enough that only Logan could hear.

"Something's different," Logan agreed.

He still wasn't sure he wanted to discuss this subject with his brother, but he also knew he had no one else to talk to.

"It's complicated."

"Yeah?" Luke snorted. "Meaning there's something between you and Elijah?"

He didn't cop to it, figuring it wasn't necessary. Luke was good at sensing these things.

"I didn't know until Cole," Luke said softly, drawing Logan's full attention. "He was my first and only."

125

Logan swallowed, realizing what his brother was saying. More so what he *wasn't* saying.

Daring a quick look over at Luke, he said, "Did you know right away?"

"Fuck no," he said dramatically, as Luke tended to do. "I'd known that man for years."

"And there was no one before him?"

"Maybe an inclination from time to time, but never something I considered acting on, no. Why? Is that what this is?"

"I don't know *what* it is," he admitted, keeping his voice low.

And that was the God's honest truth. Logan couldn't shake his newfound attraction to the man, sometimes to the point that it bothered him. He did not like the fact that Elijah was getting so much of his attention. In his thoughts, anyway. It pained him to think that anyone could come close to distracting him the way Sam did. The worst part was he didn't know what to do about it.

"If you live in a perpetual state of denial, you'll hate yourself," Luke relayed. "Just own up to it. It's the only way you'll figure it out."

"There's nothing to own up to," he lied.

"No?" Luke's laugh was mocking. "Then quit eye-fucking the guy. Everyone can see it but you."

Logan was about to launch into a tirade, to tell his brother to mind his own fucking business, but Luke leaned closer, met his gaze.

"I'm going to give you some sound advice," Luke said sternly. "It was given to me by a major pain in my ass many years ago."

"What's that?"

"Fucking figure it out," Luke said roughly.

Logan laughed as he remembered that conversation. It had taken place right after Luke had gone MIA for two months. His need to get away had been triggered by his first encounter with Cole and Sam together. Logan had been fed up with his brother's diversion tactics and told him to figure his shit out and address the issue. That issue being Luke's realization that he was bisexual and that what had transpired between him and Cole had only been the beginning.

"And if what I want fucks everything up?" Logan heard himself ask.

"Unfortunately, you won't know until you try."

Yeah. That was what he was afraid of.

For the past two weeks, Elijah had been wondering whether Logan was purposely putting distance between them. Even more so since the night Elijah had put his reservations aside and made the first move, sucking Logan's cock in their home gym. It had been both a shock and a disappointment that Logan hadn't so much as mentioned it in passing. In fact, he'd go so far as to say the man was pretending it hadn't happened at all.

And after today, he no longer wondered whether Logan was keeping him at arm's length. He knew it was true, but he wasn't sure what to do about it. Ever since the night he'd given Sam a vivid account of what had happened between him and Logan in the swimming pool, Logan had been taking small steps back, but until now, he hadn't realized how awkward things were becoming.

"Where's my lady?" Luke's voice boomed across the water as he left Logan to join them. "And why aren't we in the hot tub?"

"Hot tub!" Sierra shouted as she stood and headed toward the stairs. "Clothing prohibited," she declared as Luke approached.

He stopped instantly, set his beer on the edge of the pool, then shoved down his shorts. A second later, they joined the pile of clothing that had been discarded a short time ago when Xander decided skinny-dipping was the next order of business.

For the first time since he'd met the man, Elijah found his gaze lingering briefly, checking him out from head to toe. He was the spitting image of his brother, despite a few differences that came with age and lifestyle choices. So why didn't Elijah feel the same attraction to him that he did Logan? If it was merely about sex, wouldn't he at least feel something? Even if it was because Luke reminded him of Logan?

"You coming?" Sam asked, pulling his attention away from Luke.

"After you," he said with a smile.

As he got up to join everyone moving into the hot tub, Elijah's gaze swung over to Logan, who was still sitting at the side of the pool, now all alone. He was tempted to drag the man into the water and force him to join in the festivities. The festivities that had taken a very carnal turn in the past half hour. Although they thought they were hiding it, Elijah was more than aware of the fact that Mercedes was currently sitting astride Xander's dick while she did her best to pretend otherwise. Probably one of Xander's many directives he gave his submissive on a daily basis.

127

"Who wants to play Truth or Dare?" Luke asked when he took a seat beside Cole at the same time Sierra perched herself on Cole's lap.

Elijah was aware of the easy way Luke put his arm behind Cole's back as he shifted closer, and he wondered whether that was something he would ever have with Logan. Granted, if they couldn't get over their current hurdle, it wasn't something that even mattered.

"I do!" Leah shouted, followed by a giggle.

Needless to say, the wine had been flowing, and the women had been on the receiving end.

"I'm in," Sierra announced.

"Me, too!" Sam chimed in.

"Logan?" Luke asked his brother directly.

"Yeah," he grumbled. "I'll play."

Elijah was surprised by his acquiescence, and he openly observed while Logan stood, stripping out of his clothes before venturing down into the water to join them.

And just like that, the sight of all that smooth, golden skin on display made his cock swell. Definitely attracted on a physical level.

"No limits, no rules," Luke stated. "If you decline to do a dare, your partner has to fill in for you, and they have no option of declining."

"I take it y'all have done this before?" Mercedes asked, her voice trembling slightly as Xander's mouth glided up the back of her neck.

Sam laughed. "The first time was at Ashleigh's house." She looked at Sierra. "Remember that night?"

"Oh, I remember, all right." She giggled. "Good thing we got the naked part out of the way."

Luke cocked an eyebrow and smirked. "Who goes first?"

"Me!" Sierra insisted.

"All right, baby. Get us started."

Sierra looked at each of the faces in their circle. She started with Mercedes, moved to Xander, then Shane, Leah, Logan, Sam, Elijah, Cole, and finally Luke before shifting her gaze back to Sam. At the last second, she glanced over to Shane.

"Truth or dare, Shane?"

The man looked a bit surprised, but he masked it quickly. "Truth."

"Okay." Sierra smiled. "Have you ever faked an orgasm?"

"More than once," he admitted without hesitation.

"With anyone here?" Mercedes tacked on.

Shane's gaze darted to Leah before he looked away quickly. "No."

"That was boring," Luke declared.

"Your turn," Sierra told Shane.

Shane selected Cole. "Truth or dare?"

"Truth," he said quickly.

"If y'all are gonna play it safe, at least make the questions dirty," Luke grumbled.

Shane considered that for a moment, then asked, "Do you prefer the lights on or off during sex?"

"Jesus, Gibson," Luke groaned. "How fucking old are you? Twelve?"

The group laughed.

"On," Cole answered, his gaze shifting to Sierra. "Most definitely on." Cole glanced at Elijah. "Truth or dare?"

"Dare," he said, not sure he was ready to reveal any truths at the moment.

"'Bout time," Luke grumbled.

Sierra leaned in and whispered in her husband's ear. A moment later, Cole said, "Do a reenactment of the first time you had sex."

"That's more like it," Luke said with a wide grin.

Elijah had known he was taking a risk by selecting dare, but he'd been around these people long enough not to be surprised by what they came up with.

"Would you like me to get out to demonstrate?" he asked.

"Yes. God yes," Luke answered for Cole.

The group laughed behind him as he climbed out of the hot tub and moved to the nearest lounge chair. For dramatic effect, he turned it sideways so they'd have a good view. It took only a second for him to crawl on his knees into the missionary position, pretending there was a woman beneath him. He pumped his hips a couple of times, then threw his head back and pretended to orgasm.

Clapping ensued.

"And the Oscar goes to…" Xander bellowed.

When he got to his feet, Elijah bowed, smiling. "Thank you. Thank you very much."

His gaze slid to Logan, noticing the man wasn't even looking at him. The same could not be said for Sam. Her eyes blazed as she admired his nakedness.

"I think you just reenacted most of our first times," Xander noted, still laughing.

Elijah returned to the water to select the next person. He picked Leah; she opted for truth.

"How many times a day do you masturbate?"

All eyes shifted to her.

Her face turned a pretty shade of pink, highlighted by the white lights dancing through the water. "On average?"

"Quit stalling," Luke insisted with a chuckle.

"Fine." She smiled. "On average, once a day."

"Not so unusual now, is it?" Elijah remarked, smirking at Luke.

"Really?" Shane asked, his arm sliding behind her back along the edge of the hot tub. "Have you met your quota for the day?"

"It's not your turn to ask," she teased him with a grin.

"Answer," Luke demanded.

That went on for a good ten minutes. The truths and dares remained superficial. That was until Luke was called on.

He chose Xander. "Have you ever had a bisexual encounter?"

Elijah felt Logan stiffen beside him, and he had to wonder if Luke was baiting his brother. He'd seen the two of them talking earlier, and he had suspected the conversation had been about him. He'd connected with Logan's gaze once and had seen something in his eyes.

"Yes," Xander admitted.

"Explain," Luke insisted.

"In detail," Mercedes added.

Xander took a long pull on his beer. "I was nineteen, I guess. Somewhere around there, anyway. Spring break. A group of us had gone to Miami, ended up bunking in the same room to save money. There weren't enough beds, so we doubled up. I woke up to one of my best friends jacking me off."

"Did you enjoy it?" Mercedes inquired.

"If you mean did I let him finish me off, then yes." His smirk was roguish. "But it wasn't something I did again, nor did I care to."

"Were you the best friend jacking him off?" Mercedes asked Shane, her eyes glittering with amusement.

"Fuck no," Shane blurted.

"Let him tell you about *his* first bisexual experience," Xander belted.

"First?" Leah asked, eyes wide as she looked up at Shane. "Meaning there've been more than one?"

"Y'all don't wanna hear about it," Shane countered, not answering her question.

"The hell we don't," Luke said with a laugh. "Go on. Share."

"Fuck," Shane grumbled, tossing back the rest of his beer. "Fine. I was probably twenty-four, twenty-five. We were in San Diego at the time. One of my friends was telling me about this bathhouse he frequented. I'd never heard of the concept before, but apparently, it's pretty popular in the gay community. Or it was at one point. He insisted I go with him so he could prove it was real. When we got there, he told me the only way to gain admission was to spend half an hour at 'The Wall.' I had no idea what that meant, but I conceded when he called me a pussy."

Luke was chuckling already.

"Turns out," Shane continued, "'The Wall' was exactly that. A wall with holes in it." He cut his hand through the water about waist high. "You know, dick level."

Luke laughed again.

Shane continued. "Whenever a dick appeared through one of the holes, I was required to suck it. I took three that night. Thank fuck for condoms."

Elijah could feel Logan's tension rising at his side, and it was then he realized Luke was purposely shifting this in an uncomfortable direction. Never had they gone off on this subject, yet it seemed the goal was to force the straight guys to admit to a bisexual encounter. He only hoped Shane veered off in a different direction.

Otherwise, Elijah feared the night was going to end badly.

LOGAN WANTED TO STRANGLE HIS BROTHER. HELL, he already imagined wrapping his hands around his twin's throat—

"Sam, your turn," Shane said. "Truth or dare?"

"Dare," she said quickly. "Always dare."

"We like that about you," Luke quipped.

"I know you do," she teased.

"Since our host prefers raunchy," Shane noted, "I dare you to make one of your men come, but you've only got one minute to do it."

"One minute?" She choked on a laugh. "I'm not sure that's possible. You see, I'm not involved with minutemen."

The group laughed, and Logan relaxed a little.

"Fine. Five minutes. That's fair, right?" Shane joked.

"Five might be doable," Sam said, as though considering.

"Might I suggest you and one of your *men* gang up on the other one," Luke said, his eyes pinned on Logan. "It works for us."

Not for the first time in his life, Logan wondered why he hadn't taken Luke out in the womb. If he could've incinerated his brother with his eyes, he would've done so right then.

"I … uh…" Sam cleared her throat, her hand coming to rest reassuringly on Logan's thigh. "I think we've had enough for one night."

"No," Logan barked, still glaring at Luke.

Her eyes widened as she stared over at him. "Are you sure?"

He wasn't sure about anything, but he damn sure wasn't going to pussy out of this. He knew what Luke was angling for, and he would ensure his brother paid for it later. But right now, he wasn't going to let his friends down by taking the easy way out. That wasn't how they did things.

"Elijah," Logan said firmly, glancing over at him before he patted the ledge of the hot tub behind Sam.

Logan ignored the concerned look Elijah shot him as he slowly stood up, repositioning so that he was sitting on the ledge, his feet planted on the bench.

"Come on, baby," Logan whispered to Sam, blocking everyone else out. "Put that pretty mouth on him."

She sighed, and he noticed how her nipples pebbled tightly with her renewed arousal.

Turning his back to the group, Logan stood behind Sam when she kneeled between Elijah's legs.

"I've got the timer," Sierra announced, holding up her cell phone. She punched the screen a couple of times, then said, "Ready … set … start!"

Logan pressed up against Sam's back when she leaned in and took Elijah's cock in her mouth. The moment her lips wrapped around the flared head, Logan's body hardened, his gaze lifting to Elijah's face. The man was intently focused on the way Sam engulfed him, his hands planted behind him so he could lean back and observe.

Nothing quite compared to Sam's wicked mouth, Logan knew. Well, nothing except for Elijah's skilled mouth, anyway. Not that he was thinking about that now. Not with all these eyes on them. Last fucking thing he wanted was for anyone to see through him, to know that he was fighting this fierce attraction. He focused on the fact everyone *was* watching and let it stir the heat in his blood. Since they were exhibitionists by nature, it only intensified the scene, made it hotter.

Ignoring the soft murmurs coming from behind him, Logan let his gaze drift between Sam's oral ministrations and Elijah, watching the way Elijah's stomach muscles tightened almost instantly, his chest muscles flexing as he took the pleasure-soaked assault. Had this been any other time, they could've watched her for hours while she took her pleasure from giving it. Unfortunately, they didn't have hours, which meant Logan had to do something to spur things along.

He told himself that was the *only* reason he was doing this.

He started by putting his arms around Sam and planting his hands on the coping on the outside of Elijah's legs, letting his thumbs brush against him. The instant they touched, Elijah's gaze snapped up, met his. Logan watched Elijah's face as he moved his hands, settling them on Elijah's thighs.

Ah, hell. Touching the man wasn't smart. Not if he wanted to keep from doing something he'd promised himself he wouldn't do.

"Fuck," Elijah hissed, his thigh muscles bunching beneath his palms.

He couldn't deny that he enjoyed Elijah's reaction to his touch. It was a new sensation, and despite Logan's refusal to acknowledge how much he wanted this man, their recent explorations had created a new spark in the kindling that was their sex life.

A minute passed, then two—kindly tracked by Sierra. Sam continued to work Elijah's cock with her tongue and lips, their moans getting louder the more she sucked him.

"Spread your legs wider," Logan instructed Elijah.

When he did, Logan dipped his hand between his splayed thighs and cupped Elijah's balls, lightly at first, then more insistently when Sierra ticked off another minute.

"Logan…" Elijah whispered.

"Come right down her throat," he insisted, kneading Elijah's balls firmly while he stroked his thigh with his other hand.

Their eyes remained locked for several long heartbeats as Elijah's mouth opened wider each time Logan teased his balls, his sac tightening the more he touched.

"Ninety seconds," Sierra warned.

When Sam began fisting Elijah's cock as she sucked him, Logan took over, moving her hand and replacing it with his. With one hand on Elijah's balls, the other on the base of his cock, he stroked and caressed while Sam licked and laved.

"One minute left," Sierra whispered, as though not wanting to interrupt the show.

"Oh, fuck me," Elijah growled, his head tilting back. "Fuck ... Sam ... suck hard."

Logan tightened his fist as he stroked while Sam moaned low in her throat.

Elijah grunted a moment later, every muscle in his body clenching as he came on a strangled growl.

"Damn, that was hot," Leah said softly.

"Yeah, it was," Sierra hummed in agreement.

"Did you like that, baby?" Luke asked Sierra. "Because you know Cole and I are game to tag team you right now."

Logan remained where he was, his hands shifting down to Sam, cupping her breasts as she sat up. He teased her nipples while Elijah watched, not willing to stop. Not yet.

"Game over," Luke declared, followed by the sound of water sloshing before Sierra giggled.

"Xander..." Mercedes mumbled from behind them. "Fuck me. Now."

"Baby, you seem to forget who's in charge here."

"If you don't, I'm gonna take a page from Leah's playbook and get myself off."

"I don't think Leah's got to worry about getting herself off tonight," Xander told her. "Looks like Shane's gonna take care of it for her."

Logan leaned down, his mouth close to Sam's ear. "I think it's time we go home."

"I agree," she said softly.

While the others were preoccupied, Logan helped her up, then followed her out of the water as Elijah got to his feet. Their gazes met briefly, and he could see the banked fire still in Elijah's dark eyes.

This wasn't over yet.

Not by a long shot.

CHAPTER TEN

DURING THE SHORT DRIVE HOME FROM LUKE'S, Sam could feel the tension in the car. It was thick as molasses, neither of her men saying a word. She considered bringing up what had happened, how hot it had been to watch Logan touching Elijah, his big fist curled around Elijah's thick shaft, but she refrained. Something in their body language told her to leave well enough alone.

So she sat quietly until they got to the house, praying for the relief that would come once they were home. Before that incident, Elijah had been driving her mad by fingering her in the pool, teasing her relentlessly but never getting her to the finish line. She was eager for him to finish what he had started.

"I'm gonna take a quick shower," she told them. "Wash the chlorine off."

Logan responded with a curt nod before heading to the kitchen. Sam glanced at Elijah, thought about asking him to join her, but again refrained. Without another word, she disappeared into the bathroom, wondering if either of them would join her.

She took her time soaping up, washing her hair, conditioning it, still holding out hope. When the water lost some of its heat, and neither of them came in, she gave up the ghost, rinsing off one final time before shutting off the water and toweling dry. She took a few minutes to comb her wet hair, wondering whether Logan and Elijah had gone their separate ways and fearing she was going to have to run interference. She knew without a doubt that the only reason Logan had engaged tonight had been because Luke had pushed him.

Did he regret it? Was he angry?

Rather than get dressed, she wrapped the towel around her middle, tucking it in to hold it closed at her breasts, and made her way to the bedroom. She half expected to see them facing off, maybe having a knock-down, drag-out after the way Luke had manipulated that situation. She stopped short before stepping into the room when she saw them on the bed, Logan straddling Elijah's thighs, looming over him.

Definitely *not* what she expected to see.

Her breath caught in her throat as she watched the most intriguing scene she'd ever witnessed.

LOGAN KNEW HE WAS PUSHING THIS, BUT the adrenaline rush from their earlier encounter hadn't faded since they left Luke's. In fact, his dick was harder than it had ever been, and the longer he ignored the damn thing, the worse it got. For the better part of the last hour, he'd been intently focused on Elijah's mouth, remembering how good he'd tasted, how hot he'd been that night in the pool.

He probably should've gone to bed, left Elijah and Sam to figure out things on their own. Problem was, he couldn't brush this off, couldn't pretend things weren't progressing for them. Which was how he'd ended up here, with Elijah laid out beneath him while Logan straddled his hips, pinning his arms to the bed.

It was Elijah's fault. The man had come into the room as though going to sleep was a foregone conclusion. Logan begged to differ. The night damn sure wasn't over, and he seriously doubted sleep would come easily even if they went that route. When Elijah had come into the room, Logan had followed, not realizing his intentions until it was too late. One moment he'd been circumventing the bed to confront Elijah, the next, he'd had the man pinned beneath him. They were both panting, despite the fact that neither had made a move. And the moment the shower turned off, they'd simply stared at one another, waiting.

"Sam, join us, baby," Logan commanded when he heard her sharp inhale. His voice was rough because he was hanging by a thread, teetering on the edge of backtracking, forgetting this ever happened. He needed Sam there to bolster his confidence.

Or at least that was what he told himself.

Elijah stared up at him. "You wanna do it like this ... fine. But I can't promise I won't want more."

That was the last damn thing he'd expected the man to say. Logan had prepared himself for rejection, expecting Elijah to be pissed that Logan had brushed off their previous encounter. He would've deserved Elijah's anger because his response *had* been callous and petty. He damn sure didn't expect to see that look of longing in his eyes.

Logan planted his hands on each side of Elijah's head and leaned down. "Nor can I," he told him honestly. "One breath at a time, all right?"

"Is everything okay?" Sam asked, her tone wary.

"Lose the towel," Logan instructed, even as he kept his eyes on Elijah.

He could hear her breaths becoming choppy as the towel dropped to the floor. She eased onto the bed beside them, propping up on her elbow and resting her head on her hand as she watched them.

"You sure this is what you want, Eli?"

"Yes."

Knowing Sam was hanging on every word, Logan said, "I've never had a man touch me until you did." He knew Sam would think he was talking about their session in the pool, but Logan was referring to more than just that. He lowered his voice, leaned closer. "And I fucking liked it, Eli. That night … I've never felt anything like it…" He shivered, recalling how hard he'd come from Elijah's mouth on his dick.

"That was hot," Sam whispered. "In the cabin?"

Logan didn't respond, figuring it was safer for her to believe that was what he was referring to.

"She liked it, too," Logan told Elijah. "Wanted more right then." He leaned closer to Elijah until their lips were almost touching. "You made me curious, and now I want to explore you."

"I won't be dominated like Sam," Elijah whispered, his breath fanning Logan's lips.

Logan smiled because he knew that was a lie. Perhaps Elijah didn't want Logan to bark commands, but he certainly responded to the dominance in his tone. He'd seen it a million times in the years they'd been together. But that didn't matter because he had no desire to dominate Elijah. Whatever this was, it wasn't about that.

"Right now, I just want you to fucking kiss me," Logan growled.

As though accepting a dare, Elijah lifted his head up off the bed, their chests bumping as their lips brushed. They lingered for a moment, but then Elijah's mouth was on his, hot and hungry.

Sam moaned softly beside them.

Logan didn't waste time. He wasn't here to romance the man, he wanted to explore him, to see if this deep-seated need could be quenched. He pinned Elijah to the bed, grabbing his wrists, holding them flat while he plundered his mouth, swallowing every groan and rumble that escaped him. Unlike the times before this, the need was more powerful. As though their earlier game had unlocked a new desire.

He felt Sam's small, cool hand glide over his back, and he inhaled sharply, loving that she was touching him. He used it as a lifeline as he continued to feast on Elijah's mouth, holding him down, their cocks rubbing through their clothing. He wanted Elijah naked, wanted to watch the play of muscles as he writhed beneath him. He wanted to hold him down and feed his cock into his mouth, wanted to see Elijah's lips wrap around him again.

A bolt of lust spiked in his veins, had his body shuddering at the thought.

Moving his hands from Elijah's wrists, Logan remained on top of him but gave him the use of his hands when he said, "Take off my shirt."

Elijah dragged it up and over his head, passing it to Sam before she tossed it to the floor. She was watching them intently, even as she tossed it away.

"Now yours."

Elijah squirmed under him as he pulled his T-shirt up before jerking it over his head. Sam took it, too, tossing it to the floor before moving closer.

"You sure you wanna see this, baby?" Logan asked, looking her way for the first time.

"More than my next breath," she answered, her voice husky, her eyes glittering in the glow from the bedside lamps.

Logan looked back down at Elijah. "Push my shorts down."

Once Elijah had his shorts pushed to his thighs, Logan twisted his lower body until he could get them down before kicking them away. He helped Elijah out of his in a similar manner before moving back over him and pinning him to the bed. He sucked in a strangled breath when Elijah's hot skin pressed to his.

He was rough when he inched up Elijah's body, straddling his chest, pressing one knee on Elijah's biceps, effectively keeping him in place. Elijah stared up at him, panting as his chest rose and fell while Sam reached out, her hand teasing Elijah's hair. She was making herself a part of this, and that encouraged Logan to continue.

"I won't force you," Logan told him. "But I want your mouth on my cock." *Again.*

Elijah didn't fight him, didn't move beneath him, and the glint in his eyes seemed to grow hotter.

Logan shifted his hips forward, bringing his cock closer to Elijah's mouth. "Put your fucking mouth on me, Eli," he growled softly, fueled by passion and fear as he ventured into the unknown.

They remained like that for what felt like an eternity, his cock hovering dangerously close to Elijah's lips. The longer Logan waited, the harder he got, his cock pulsing in time to his heartbeat.

When Elijah lifted his head a fraction, Logan sucked in a deep breath.

When Elijah's tongue darted out and swiped over the sensitive head, Logan growled low in his throat. And when Elijah wrapped his lips around the head, he bowed his back and hissed. The pleasure was intense.

"Fuck ... Jesus, Eli ... oh, fuck. Suck me."

Not once did he look away from the man beneath him. He couldn't. He didn't want this to be another random encounter. He wanted Elijah to know he wasn't taking this for granted, and this wasn't a show just for Sam. It wasn't about shoving his cock into a willing orifice. He wanted that connection that he'd felt with this man. He wanted—

All sense fled when Elijah took him to the root.

"Goddamn, that feels so fucking good."

He held Elijah's gaze, pumping his hips, rocking into the blistering heat of Elijah's mouth while that tongue swirled and laved along the sensitive underside. Every now and then, he would bump the back of Elijah's throat, and a shiver would rack his body.

"Don't make me come," he warned. That was not how he saw this going. Not tonight.

The suction of Elijah's mouth didn't falter as he bathed him in delicious heat, the friction making Logan's balls tighten, drawing up as he hovered right there on the brink. Before he lost control, he pulled out of Elijah's mouth, then dropped down on top of him, flattening his body so that they were touching chest to knee. He kissed him hard, fucking him with his tongue, pleasure humming through his veins. He rocked his hips, their cocks trapped between them, and he loved the way Elijah moaned, flexing his hips to get closer.

For half a second, Logan forgot Sam was there.

"Put your mouth on me, Logan," Elijah insisted, panting heavily. "I want to know what it feels like."

Logan's muscles remained tense as he shifted lower, dragging his mouth over Elijah's jaw, feeling the gentle abrasion of the stubble there. He moved lower, noticing all the differences between kissing him and kissing Sam. Where Sam was soft, Elijah was hard. Where Sam was pliant, there was a constant tension drawing Elijah's muscles taut. Logan found he liked those differences far more than he'd ever thought he could.

He shifted lower, licking down his chest, following the lines of Elijah's abs. When Elijah's thick cock bumped his chin, Logan dipped his head and licked the wide crest.

Elijah growled, his hips lifting off the bed.

Spurred by the response, Logan drew him into his mouth, sucking hard, taking him deep. He'd never had a cock in his mouth before, but he didn't need a lesson. Elijah told him exactly what he wanted by his garbled groans and muttered expletives. Sam encouraged with her smooth hand sliding over his back, her soft moans echoing beside him.

Elijah's hands fisted the blankets beneath him, his body tightening, his cock pulsing in Logan's mouth. He knew he was close, considered pulling back but changed his mind and pushed Elijah closer to the fine edge of release by sucking him in deep.

"Logan ... oh, fuck ... oh, hell."

"Not yet," Logan growled before taking him deep again, tormenting him. Logan didn't relent, he pushed him higher. He wanted this man's complete surrender, and he didn't give a shit how he got it.

"I'm gonna come," Elijah warned, his hips thrusting upward. "You better stop. Oh ... fuck ... me."

Logan took him to the root, swallowed around the head, and held him there before pulling back completely.

"Suck him, Sam," Logan commanded, making room for her between Elijah's legs. "Don't make him come yet."

She moved like a goddess, her head lowering as she took Elijah in her mouth while Logan reached for the lube in the top drawer of the nightstand. While she licked and teased, Elijah moaned softly, his gaze following Logan's every move.

He made a show of lubing his cock, and he knew what Elijah was thinking even though he was wrong. His intention wasn't to fuck the man. No, they weren't ready for that yet. Hell, they might never be.

SAM WAS ALMOST CONVINCED SHE'D JUST ORGASMED by watching her men suck each other. She wasn't sure she'd ever seen anything hotter than that. The way they both moaned and groaned as they succumbed to the pleasure. She'd witnessed something pass between them, and there was a weird sensation that had swirled in her belly. She couldn't put her finger on what it was, but it hadn't been pleasant. Fear? Jealousy? Relief? She didn't know.

"Sam," Logan growled, banding his arm around her middle.

She released Elijah's cock, then sat up on her knees, not caring what he had in store for her as long as he didn't stop. She needed them now. She needed to know that she was part of this, and their attention was the only thing that soothed her.

Logan turned her chin so that she was looking back at him before he crushed his mouth to hers. He licked into her mouth, moaning as he kissed her. When he pulled back, there was a hint of warning in his tone.

"We're going to take you at the same time."

She whimpered when he gently pushed her forward. She went willingly, straddling Elijah's hips as she laid out over him.

"Oh, Jesus, fuck," Elijah hissed, and that was when she realized Logan's hand had fisted his cock and was angling it between her thighs.

"Take him inside you," Logan demanded.

Sam eased back, sinking down on Elijah's cock, letting him fill her.

"So tight," Elijah murmured, pulling her head down, so her mouth met his. "You feel so good."

She moaned, loving how hard he was, how on edge he seemed. Had Logan done that to him? Was his response reserved for him and not her?

Shrugging off the weird train of thought, Sam rocked on top of him while Logan drizzled lube over her anus, massaging with his thumb. He pushed inside her once, making her moan.

The next thing she knew, Logan's cock was sliding into her ass, Elijah's arms banding around her to hold her still between them. From that point forward, Logan was in complete control.

"Goddamn," Logan growled, inching back before driving in hard and deep. Her body rocked on top of Elijah, effectively shifting his cock inside her.

Logan's fingertips dug into her hips as he held her still and impaled her repeatedly. She couldn't remember the last time he'd been this rough, and she loved every second of it. There was nothing hotter than when Logan came undone. The man's control was something he clung to, so in the rare instances when it slipped from his grasp, she was usually on the receiving end.

"Did you like that, baby?" he rasped as he drilled into her, his hips slamming forward, retreating, rocking her on top of Elijah. "Did you like watching us suck each other?"

"Yes," she admitted.

"Jesus," he growled, his hand landing in the center of her back, pushing her down to change the angle of her hips.

His breaths were harsh, his grunts wild as he chased his release, using her body to accomplish his goal. It was so hot to be like this, crushed between them. Used by them. *Loved* by them. And she knew deep in her heart that they loved her even though she felt oddly like the third wheel at the moment.

"Tell him," Elijah insisted, his mouth close to her ear. "Tell him how much you liked it. Watching us."

"I loved it," she bit out, accepting every punishing thrust of his hips as he fucked her hard and deep. "I loved watching you fuck his face," she told Logan, then directed her next comment at Elijah. "Loved watching him suck your cock."

Elijah's hand slipped between her body and his, his thumb finding her clit and thrumming it roughly.

Sam screamed, her orgasm obliterating her while Logan drove into her ass deeper, harder. "Logan!"

Elijah grunted, his hips driving up once as he shuddered beneath her.

"Ah, fuck," Logan shouted as he slammed into her one final time and roared as he came.

A short time later, Sam fell asleep, still crushed between them, one on each side of her. As she drifted off, she couldn't help wondering what she'd set in motion and whether or not the three of them could survive it.

CHAPTER ELEVEN

Friday, July 8, 2022

OVER THE COURSE OF THE NEXT WEEK, Sam found herself at the center of both men's attention. And while she enjoyed every single second, she knew there was a reason they were directing all their energies at her. It was their way of avoiding what had happened between them. As much as she wanted to force them to hash it out, she knew better. Well, *that* and the fact they ensured she never had an opportunity.

On Monday, Logan came home while she'd been cooking dinner. She'd known the moment she saw him that he was on edge. It explained the reason he had fucked her right there at the kitchen counter, bending her over without preamble and taking her from behind.

On Tuesday, Elijah had insisted on taking her to dinner, just the two of them. Their conversation had primarily remained about work and an upcoming trip that he had to go on. It ended with him fucking her on the washing machine before they made it all the way into the house.

On Wednesday, Logan stayed at the office with her when she had to work late. She'd felt the tension in him, offered to release the pressure during the drive home. They never made it that far because he ended up making her come with his mouth while she was laid out on her desk.

On Thursday, Elijah met her for lunch before she drove him to the airport. Rather than let her drop him at the door like she usually did, he'd made her park in the short-term lot, then made her come on his fingers before he kissed her thoroughly and left her reeling.

On Friday, before Logan could get his hands on her, she informed him she was meeting Sierra for dinner, just the two of them. He'd told her to have fun and promised to be awake when she got home. She had no doubt that he would be.

"All right, girl, tell me what's going on," Sierra said once they'd been seated, their drink orders taken.

"Where do I start?" she said on an exhale, relaxing against the booth, eager for that drink. "I feel like I've been run through a deep-clean wash cycle. Ten times."

Sierra laughed, her crystal-blue eyes dancing with amusement. "I know that feeling. I've been on the receiving end myself. Does it have something to do with what happened at our party last weekend?" She leaned in, her left eyebrow slowly arching as she said, "I didn't know they ... uh..."

"They didn't. Until recently." Sam thanked the waiter when he delivered their drinks. "Can you give us a few minutes?"

"Sure thing. I'll swing back by," he said kindly before bolting to the next table.

Sam took a gulp of her drink, gauging how generous they'd been with the vodka. Unless it had been the whole bottle, she doubted it was enough. She took another sip, this one as a backup test. Eh. It would do. If she had about five of them.

"When did it start?" Sierra asked. "Between them?"

"Remember that trip we took to Colorado last year?"

"Your pre-holiday vacation. Sure." Her eyes widened. "It's been *that* long? And you didn't tell me?"

"There was nothing to tell." That was mostly true. "Nothing really happened."

"Why do I get the feeling you're glossing over the details?"

"They kissed," she admitted, keeping her voice low as she leaned closer. "We played a dice game, kinda like Spin the Bottle, I guess. They had to kiss. They did."

Sierra sat back as though that was the most shocking thing she'd ever heard. "How was it?"

"For me, it was great," she admitted, laughing. "I wasn't the one doing something outside my comfort zone."

Sierra laughed. "But it was hot, right?"

"So freaking hot," she whispered. "God, I thought I would spontaneously combust."

"They've never done that before?"

"Never."

Sierra smiled. "I figure it's safe to assume you instigated it?"

Sam cocked an eyebrow in that way that said, *What do you think?* A move she'd learned from Logan.

"Did you suspect they wanted something ... from each other?"

"No," she said, still feeling the remnants of guilt that had plagued her despite her curiosity. "I kinda forced their hand."

And she figured that was the reason she was feeling so guilty about the whole thing. But that was what she did. Right or wrong, Sam had impulse-control issues, and Logan and Elijah knew it, yet they still loved her. Sometimes she wasn't sure why.

"Well, they wouldn't've done it if they didn't want to," Sierra noted.

That was what Sam had thought, too. Granted, that didn't assuage the guilt she felt for manipulating them into it. Sometimes her ideas weren't the best ones, but that rarely stopped her from pushing. It had been selfish on her part; she knew that.

"Has anything *more* happened?" Sierra held up a hand. "Hold that thought."

The waiter reappeared so they could place their order. Sam asked for another drink while she was at it. After he'd jotted it all down and promised to bring them some bread, he disappeared again.

"When we were in Vegas, and they were alone"—Sam lowered her voice—"I think that was the first time since."

Sierra's eyebrows bounced, her silent request for more details.

"They jacked each other off."

Sierra fanned herself, grinning. "I can't believe you haven't told me already."

"It wasn't my place to tell."

Her friend laughed. "But it is now?"

"No." Sam took a gulp of her drink. "But I need some advice."

Sierra sat up straighter. "Well, you've come to the right place. I happen to be rather experienced when it comes to men fighting their attraction for one another."

Sam would definitely consider Sierra the resident expert. She'd heard the stories of how things had progressed between Sierra, Luke, and Cole back in the beginning. She knew Luke had fought his attraction to Cole, his desires for the man, and it had caused all kinds of problems between the three of them. Thankfully, they were able to figure it out without too much carnage left in their wake.

"I'm not sure it's the same between Logan and Eli," Sam admitted. "I mean, the way Luke and Cole look at each other ... I'm not sure Logan or Eli have those types of feelings."

"Maybe not, but you've got to let them figure it out for themselves."

That was sound advice, and Sam knew she had to back off. Didn't mean she could, because, again, impulse control wasn't her strong suit.

"They'll figure it out," Sierra reassured her. "Give it time."

"In the meantime, they're going to kill me," she said on a huff. "They're taking it out on me."

Sierra's eyes glittered. "That doesn't sound like a bad thing."

It wasn't. Necessarily.

While they'd always had an active sex life—on average, they had sex four times a week—it hadn't been nearly as intense as this past week had been. And while she loved sex, it was the volatility that came with it that was exhausting her. She was used to the laid-back, take-your-sweet-time-getting-to-the-finish-line kind of encounters. This week had been chock full of blisteringly hot, mind-blowing sprints that left her breathless and worn out.

"I think they need to talk it out," Sam said, finishing off the first of many drinks to come.

"Talk?" Sierra snorted. "Men don't talk, Sam. They bottle it up until they can't contain it, and then it erupts. The ensuing storm usually levels everything in its path. But thankfully, in the aftermath, they usually figure it out."

Sam wasn't sure she could handle the storm that was brewing.

"You said Elijah's out of town, right?"

Sam nodded.

"While you've got Logan alone, maybe the two of you can do some role-playing."

"What?" Sam's laugh burst free. "You want me to pretend to be Elijah?"

Sierra shrugged one shoulder. "Could it hurt? Maybe Logan can figure out what he wants that way."

Sam considered that option. She knew how much her husband loved role-play.

"Considering your only other option is to let them take it out on you until they get their shit together..." Sierra laughed. "I mean, you could survive that, right?"

No. She very seriously doubted she could.

Which meant role-playing might just be her best, if not only, option.

AS PROMISED, LOGAN WAS AWAKE WHEN SAM returned from her dinner with Sierra. She'd called a Lyft to take her to and from, so he knew that meant she would be nice and inebriated when she arrived. He found her amusing when she was drunk, mostly because she was usually feistier than usual.

Tonight, she didn't disappoint.

"How was dinner?"

"Good. Why? What did you hear?"

He laughed, patting the couch cushion beside him, urging her to join him.

She stumbled in his direction, though it was obvious she was attempting to walk a straight line.

"Did you and Sierra have a good chat?"

Her eyes widened, a sure sign that she had revealed some deep, dark secrets to her best friend. He had known she would. In fact, he was surprised she hadn't talked to Sierra before now. Sam was not one who could keep a secret, and since Sierra was the one Sam spoke to about their sex life, he figured she would've broken long before now.

"Give me your feet," he instructed, patting his thighs.

She shifted, reclining onto a pillow at the opposite end and propping her feet in his lap. He eased her shoes off, setting them on the floor. When he gripped one of her feet, she groaned as she always did. Funny how that sound was so similar to when she orgasmed.

"Tell me what you talked about," he urged.

Her eyes were on him, glassy and hooded. "What we always talk about."

"Sex."

"That's not true," she declared defensively, although her body was relaxing quickly. She was definitely feeling no pain, and if he had to guess, she would be snoring in less than five minutes.

He cocked an eyebrow, smiled.

"Fine. It *is* true. And yes, we talked about sex."

Logan focused on rubbing her feet, kneading her arches to earn him another sexy moan.

"She said it was hot to see you touching Elijah that night in the hot tub."

"I don't care what Sierra thinks about it," he said, keeping his tone level. He didn't want her to think he was being defensive, although there was an undercurrent of it. He wasn't interested in making a spectacle out of what was happening between him and Elijah.

"Well, *I* think it's hot," she said, her nose scrunching. "Do you at least care what I think?"

"Always." He glanced her way.

She huffed, then moaned again when he focused his attention on her toes. "I do think it's hot. What little I've been privy to."

Logan figured that was her way of hinting that she wanted more action between them. He decided to avoid going down that rabbit hole, knowing it would lead nowhere that he wanted to go.

"What else did Sierra have to say?"

Sam yawned, sinking deeper into the couch cushion. "She suggested we role-play."

"Did she?"

"Yup."

He smirked. "And what? You're gonna play the role of Elijah? See if you can seduce me?" He cut his gaze to her again. "I think it's a little late for that, baby."

"I haven't thought that far ahead."

"Why don't you tell me what's bothering you about the whole thing," he suggested.

"Nothing. I just think … I don't want it to be weird."

"*Is* it weird?"

"Seems to be, yeah."

"How's that?"

Her forehead creased. "Well, for one, y'all are screwing me silly."

He laughed. "And here I thought you enjoyed being screwed silly."

"I do," she declared. "Of course I do."

"Then what's the problem?"

"I just … it's like y'all are holding back … from each other."

Logan considered that for a moment, moving his hands to her other foot. He lingered on it for a couple of minutes, allowing her more time to relax. He finally said, "I think we're taking it slow."

"Understatement of the century," she mumbled.

He disagreed. Considering his age and this new thing he was just learning about himself, Logan didn't feel the need to rush things with Elijah. They were both venturing into new territory. As far as he was concerned, it would take as long as it needed to.

"So it's not all bottled up?" Sam asked.

He chuckled at her turn of phrase, answering the same way he took it. "I think I've effectively released what needs to be released this week."

"I'll say."

Logan kneaded the arches of both feet at the same time. "Are you complaining, Sam?"

"No." She yawned again. "No complaints."

"I didn't think so."

She was silent for a moment while he continued to give her feet the attention she enjoyed.

"You don't want to role-play?"

"Baby, I'm always open to playing. You know that." He glanced her way, met her gaze. "But if you're asking if I want you to pretend to be Elijah, the answer is no. I'm not willing to forsake my time with you to pretend to be with him."

That seemed to please her based on the way her face relaxed.

"Now, if you want to dress up in that little maid's outfit you've got, I'm definitely on board."

151

She snorted. "Last time I did that, you made me clean the oven. *For real.*"

Yes, yes, he had. He laughed, remembering how pissed she'd been that he had pushed the boundaries of their play. It had worked. The oven had gotten cleaned.

Their conversation died off as he continued to massage her feet and ankles. He didn't stop until her body had gone completely lax.

When he heard her softly snoring, he inched out from under her feet. He shut off the lights in the house, then returned, picked her up, and took her to bed. He wasn't exactly tired, but he crawled into bed beside her, phone in hand. He shot a quick text to Elijah to see if he was awake.

ELIJAH: *Still up. Everything okay?*

LOGAN: *Everything's fine. Sam went out with Sierra. They chatted about us.*

ELIJAH: *I bet that went over well.*

LOGAN: *She offered to role-play. She was going to star as you.*

ELIJAH: *Could've been interesting.*

Logan was about to text him back when he noticed the three dots continued to dance because Elijah was still typing.

ELIJAH: *I know it's cowardly to tell you this over text, but you've got the real thing. Whenever you want it.*

Logan's body hardened at the offer. He was surprised by his reaction, more so by the direction his thoughts went. He had liked the feel of Elijah beneath him the other night. More than he'd thought he would. Now the idea of having him beneath him in a more fulfilling way was consuming his thoughts.

LOGAN: *I want, Eli. I definitely want.*

ELIJAH: *Good to know… So what are you wearing?*

Logan laughed, then sent one last message before setting his phone aside and going to sleep: *Get your ass back home and see for yourself.*

CHAPTER TWELVE

Tuesday, July 12, 2022

ELIJAH MANAGED TO GRAB AN EARLY FLIGHT back to Dallas, coming in several hours before Logan and Sam would've been expecting him. Rather than call one of them to pick him up, he requested a Lyft because he was hoping to surprise them.

When he got home, he found it silent and empty, both Sam and Logan still at the office. He quickly changed, then headed to the kitchen to start dinner. Once he got the baby-back ribs prepared, he put them in the oven. They would need a couple of hours, which would be just enough time.

While those cooked on low heat, he headed for the bedroom he had slept in for the first seven years of his relationship with Sam and Logan. Until Sam had requested they sleep in the same bed, which meant ultimately the same room, Elijah had kept his life separate from theirs in this regard.

He opened the door and flipped on the overhead light.

Everything he'd left behind sat exactly as he'd left it. A few books were still on the small bookshelf, though many had joined those on the larger bookshelf in the living room. The lamp on the bedside table sat alone, his alarm clock having been moved to Sam and Logan's bedroom. The fancy watch case Sam had gotten him for Christmas one year sat on the dresser, filled with his many watches. The dresser drawers still held his clothes.

He skimmed every surface and felt a weird sensation bubbling in his gut. So many nights he'd spent in here, just him and Sam; others he'd spent alone wishing she was here.

Did he miss it? No. Not even a little bit. When it all began, he'd been the literal third wheel in their marriage. By design. But for the past six months, he'd been doing the trial run he'd promised Sam he would do, sleeping in their room, growing closer to them for the lack of space between them.

Technically, it wasn't *their* room anymore. It belonged to all three of them. Or it felt that way, anyway. At least to him.

While it would've been easy to keep that separation, to pretend he wasn't harboring this foreign desire for something he'd never even known he wanted, Elijah had decided this past weekend that his trial was over. He was ready to make that definitive step forward and take the plunge.

Figuring there was no better time than the present, he headed for the dresser and opened the top drawer.

Nearly two hours later, Elijah had transferred all of his things from that separate bedroom into the master. Sam had allocated space for him when she'd selected furniture, and he used it wisely, filling the drawers designated for him, utilizing the closet space. While there were still a few things stored in the extra bedroom, he could safely say it was no longer his. When he paused to take it all in, he felt a shocking sense of euphoria, similar to the feeling he got when he started a new book, not sure what would happen next but eager to find out.

As he headed for the kitchen to check on dinner, he heard the garage door opening. He glanced at the clock.

"Right on time," he said with a smile.

He headed to the refrigerator and pulled out the asparagus to arrange it on the pan. He started the second oven and had the asparagus roasting before the back door opened.

"Elijah!" Sam said with a wide grin. "Why didn't you tell me you were home? I would've picked you up."

"I wanted it to be a surprise," he told her, meeting Logan's gaze over her shoulder.

"And a nice one it is." Sam stepped up to him, pressed a quick kiss to his mouth. "I'm going to change. It smells delicious, by the way."

With that, she sauntered off toward the bedroom.

Logan was standing there, hands in his pockets, a mischievous gleam in his eyes. Then again, there was always mischief in the man's gaze; however, he'd never noticed it quite like he did now. There was definitely something different between them, and he felt the familiar hum just under his skin.

A squeal sounded from the bedroom a moment later.

Logan's grin turned into a grimace. "What did you do?"

"I moved my things into the bedroom."

And there it was, the moment of truth.

Elijah kept his focus on Logan's face, waiting for him to reveal his true feelings about what was happening between them. This had been a big step for Elijah; they both knew that.

"She's been waiting for that."

"I know."

The slow smile that formed on the man's handsome face sent a wave of relief through him. "As have I."

Elijah honestly hadn't been sure what to expect from Logan. Since their brief text conversation on Friday, they hadn't spoken much. And though Logan had been receptive to what Elijah had offered, he wasn't sure the man would still feel the same when they were face-to-face again. After all, this was not a situation he'd ever thought he would find himself in. He'd grown accustomed to the familiar, enjoying the routine and monotony that came with a relationship. It wasn't until the relationship had begun to change that he realized how comfortable he'd been.

"It's about time," Logan said softly, stepping forward, his hands slipping out of his pockets.

Elijah stood his ground, keeping his eyes pinned on Logan's face. He wasn't sure what would happen next. He hadn't made it that far in his thought process, always getting hung up on how Logan might react.

"I figured it was time to take the leap," Elijah told him, hoping the man understood the double entendre.

Since Logan continued his approach, he had to believe he got the meaning. And when he stopped directly in front of him, their chests nearly touching, he felt his resolve strengthen.

"Did you mean what you said the other night?" Logan asked, his voice low, a hint of gravel in the tone.

Elijah knew he was referring to his admission in the text message. "Every word."

Logan's eyes danced over his face as though reading his expression for a hidden meaning.

Behind them, Sam cleared her throat. "Am I interrupting?" There was a hopeful wisp to her tone, definite approval in her soft sigh.

"Not at all," Logan said, never taking his eyes off Elijah's face.

"Well, I'll just set the table then."

Logan's soft growl could've been an approval of her suggestion, or maybe it was his acceptance of whatever he'd intended to do, because the next thing Elijah knew, their lips were fused, and he was stumbling backward. He reached for the counter to keep himself upright as Logan kissed him fiercely. He groaned in response, sliding his hand behind Logan's neck and holding him there while the kiss ignited.

This was dangerous territory, this unknown path they were forging down, but Elijah had been hoping for this. They'd spent the past month dancing around what was happening between them. The night at Luke's had felt like a turning point, but Elijah knew better than to assume anything when it came to Logan. Hell, he hadn't been exactly sure which direction he'd wanted to go himself.

But here they were.

Elijah sank into the kiss, inhaling Logan's dominance with every breath he took. He'd never been kissed like this before, and it wasn't because Logan was a man. There was something deeper, far more complex than anything he'd ever felt. A tension he could sense, one that threatened to snap at any moment.

A throat cleared, then Sam said, "Would you boys like some privacy? Because I can … uh…"

They were both panting and breathless when they released each other. Logan's laugh was the tool that untightened that last knot of concern in Elijah's gut.

"We never need privacy from you, baby," Logan told her.

Elijah stared at him, wondering why Logan had yet to fill Sam in on their encounters if that was the case. He knew she wasn't privy to what had transpired in the gym the other day, but he wasn't sure why Logan was keeping it to himself. They both knew Sam would enjoy the hell out of hearing the raunchy details.

"Good to know," Sam said sweetly.

Logan's gaze swung back to Elijah. "Let me change; then I'll help with dinner."

When he slipped out of the room, Elijah turned to Sam, cleared his throat. He had a feeling his face was red, but he pretended it wasn't. "That's how I like to be welcomed home, by the way."

Her smile widened as she moved closer. "Is that so?"

"Absolutely." He reached for her, dragging her against him before sealing his mouth to hers.

She giggled softly, grinning up at him. He loved how pliant she was as she leaned into him, her tongue dancing with his. Elijah kissed her hard, letting her feel the pent-up tension coiling him tightly.

"Is it wrong to admit that I like that this"—she reached down and brushed her knuckles over his erection—"is also for Logan?"

Elijah growled roughly and kissed her once more, slow and deep, before releasing her.

She was breathless as she backed away, her eyes never leaving him.

It took tremendous effort, but Elijah managed to finish cooking and even made it through dinner without spontaneously combusting.

THROUGHOUT DINNER, SAM HAD FELT THE PULSE of arousal as it beat in time to her heart. She knew she wasn't the only one on high alert, waiting for something while pretending that all was normal. And by the time the meal was finished, she was a hairsbreadth away from losing her mind. They were driving her absolutely crazy with their subtle glances—at her, at each other.

"I'll do the dishes if you two want to … uh … you know … do whatever," Sam told them when Logan finally pushed his empty plate away.

His hazel eyes slid over to her, twinkled with amusement. "If we want to *do whatever?*"

Well, she couldn't very well tell them they were welcome to do whatever it was that was causing this insane heat to churn in the room. It was like a cloud that drifted overhead, clinging to everything as the tension rose.

It was killing her to keep her lips tightly sealed, but she was proud of herself. She'd made it through the entire meal without bringing up their kiss in the kitchen. While she'd mentally examined every detail, replaying it again and again, she'd refrained from asking them what it meant, where this was headed. She was nothing if not curious, and rarely could she bite her tongue, but somehow she managed.

Admittedly, she was quickly losing her grip on her tenuous control. She wanted them to make good on the promise she could see in their seductive glances, damn it.

"I'm not sure what *whatever* is, exactly," Logan told her, "but I won't argue with you doing the dishes."

Of course he wouldn't.

Without preamble, Elijah got up, began taking their plates to the counter. When he returned for more, Logan stopped him with a hand on his arm.

Sam's gaze shot to where they were touching as though expecting Logan to strip Elijah down simply because they were.

"She volunteered, Eli," Logan said firmly, still watching her. "Go on, baby."

Sam fully intended to stand, to pick up where Elijah left off, get the kitchen cleaned in record time, but her gaze remained locked on the spot where Logan was touching Elijah's arm. Was it her imagination, or were Logan's fingers moving over the crisp dark hair there? Caressing him?

She had no idea how to explain this insane desire that their intimacy spurred. Whenever she *thought* about them together, it was like someone had taken a flame to heat coils inside her veins. She'd thought about it so much that she'd begun to wonder if it was abnormal to have erotic thoughts about two men together. And yes, in her fantasies, she was always right there with them, observing every delicious touch, every kiss, every—

"Sam?"

She jerked herself out of her thoughts, her refocused eyes homing in on Logan's face. "Yeah?"

"Dishes."

With a dramatic huff, she got to her feet, began clearing the rest of the dishes from the table. While the two of them sat at the table, chatting about mundane crap like work, she completed her chore. Didn't they know she'd volunteered so they could get some alone time? After that kiss they'd shared, weren't they raring to go, eager to do ... well, whatever they were wanting to do?

God, she knew she was overthinking this, and if she had to guess, Logan was punishing her for it. He should've been impressed that she'd managed to keep her mouth shut all through dinner.

She quickly washed her hands, dried them with a towel, then turned back to see they were both staring at her.

Uh-oh. She knew that look, that heated gleam in Logan's eyes. It was a prelude to something raunchy he was intending to do to her. *Thank God.*

She considered faking a yawn, telling them she was going to bed early, but she knew better. Logan was a smart man, and he'd long ago figured out her game. On only the rarest of occasions could she slip something by him, but based on the hunger in his eyes, he wasn't going to take his chances, which meant she was resigned to whatever he wanted.

Yes, her core was tingling, and yes, she knew she was already wet, her body preparing for their delicious assault. She couldn't help it. There was something about being the center of their attention that just did it for her.

"It's my understanding you've been complaining about too much sex," Elijah prompted.

Sam's gaze darted to him. She frowned, feigned ignorance. "I've done no such thing."

His dark eyebrows popped. "No?" He glanced at Logan. "You lied?"

Logan chuckled gruffly. "I never lie."

No, he never did. Which meant she'd just put herself in the hot seat.

"I think we need to see just how much she can take," Elijah suggested.

A trickle of erotic fear coalesced with the anticipation fizzing in her veins. That was another thing she loved about them: she never knew what they'd cook up for her. She loved the spontaneity of their intimate encounters, the creativity of their actions. Even those moments when one of them made love to her were sinfully erotic because she never knew what to expect.

"You can start by going into the bedroom, stripping, and getting your blindfold. Put it on and lie down on the bed." Elijah lifted one eyebrow. "On top of the blankets. On your back."

Sam smiled as she turned away. The last time they'd told her to do that, she'd crawled beneath the blankets, pulled the covers over her head, and lay on her stomach. They hadn't found it nearly as amusing as she had. Her reddened ass that night had been proof.

"Yes, drill sergeant," she said mockingly as she sashayed away to prepare herself for whatever they had in store for her.

"SHE'S AWFULLY SASSY TONIGHT," LOGAN TOLD ELIJAH when Sam disappeared into the bedroom.

"She is. What do you think we should do about that?"

Logan had a few ideas, but he didn't want to take the reins from Elijah just yet.

"I suggest you make her wait." Logan knew she hated waiting, but it always enhanced their intimacy. "Perhaps put her senses on high alert."

"Sounds to me like you've got something specific in mind."

Logan had a lot on his mind, yes. The most prominent involved getting Elijah naked. Of course, he hadn't made it too much further in the fantasy yet, but he knew it would only require getting him stripped down to spur something. For the past few days, ever since that text from Elijah, Logan had been thinking about tonight, about Elijah returning home. Anticipation bubbled in his gut, made it churn like the sea during a hurricane. He was tired of pretending otherwise.

"Shower," he told Elijah as he got to his feet.

"Is that an invitation?"

Logan glanced back, smirked. "Get your ass in the shower."

Elijah's eyebrow cocked as though he was amused by the command. In all fairness, there hadn't been any conviction behind it. Logan had no desire to dominate Elijah. Sure, he'd considered it a time or two, but he happened to like the fact they were on even ground.

Without looking back, Logan continued to the bedroom.

He found Sam laid out on the bed exactly as Elijah had directed. She was naked, her beautiful body lit by the golden glow from the bedside lamps. Her blond hair fanned out over the pillow, her blindfold hiding her eyes.

"Beautiful," he said, ensuring she heard the approval in his tone. "Spread your legs for me, baby. Let me see the pussy we'll be feasting on tonight."

Sam put her feet on the bed, her knees up as she slowly inched her ankles apart. Her knees remained together until it was no longer possible. When they spread apart, his gaze zeroed in on the slick pink flesh between her thighs.

"Have you been touching yourself?" he asked as he pulled his shirt off over his head, not looking over when Elijah passed through the room on the way to the bathroom.

"No, but it wasn't easy," she said, smiling.

Logan stripped off his jeans, kicking them away before crawling onto the bed between her spread thighs. He kissed her ankle, her knee, slowly working his way up to the apex of her thighs. He blew warm air over her pussy but didn't linger. He moved higher, skimming her belly with the lightest brush of his lips. He dragged his tongue over her nipple when he moved higher. Once he was settled between her thighs, he let his heavy erection rest against her belly as he leaned down and pressed a featherlight kiss to her mouth.

"I'm going to take a shower," he informed her, keeping his words soft and low. "With Elijah."

Sam inhaled sharply.

"While we do that, I want you to stay right here. I want you to think about what we're doing to each other in there. Can you do that for me, baby?"

"Logan…"

"Can you do that for me?" he repeated.

"Yes."

"Good girl." He nibbled her earlobe. "Don't touch yourself. If you do, I'll spank that pretty ass."

She whimpered, making him smile.

Leaving her to think about them, Logan got to his feet, padded naked to the bathroom. He should've felt awkward about joining Elijah in the shower, but he didn't. Perhaps that was because this wasn't the first time. Sure, it was the first time without Sam with them, but certainly not the first time he'd seen Elijah naked, so why should he—

When he rounded the corner to the enormous shower, he stopped, his gaze lingering on the man beneath the spray. Something warm churned in his gut, and his cock hardened even more.

Elijah was standing beneath one of the overhead showerheads, his face tipped back, his thick cock bobbing proudly between his legs. Unlike the last time he'd observed him under that spray of water, Elijah wasn't touching himself, and Logan wondered if that was because he wanted Logan to do the honor.

Figuring it wouldn't hurt to make Elijah wait the way Sam was, Logan looked his fill, admiring every sleek inch of his well-toned body. Had he always admired him like this and not realized it? Had that stirring in his loins happened before and he not acknowledged it? Logan couldn't be certain, but this attraction didn't feel new.

Getting with the program, Logan stepped forward, his gaze lingering over Elijah's torso, the way his abs flexed when he moved, the water sluicing over his smooth, golden skin.

Yeah, it was safe to say Logan enjoyed looking at him.

He'd honestly suggested the shower as a way of inciting Sam. He knew she wouldn't be able to control herself, wouldn't be able to refrain from joining them. The question was, how long would it take her?

As he approached, Elijah's head tilted back down, his eyes opening. Logan saw the heat there, the desire that sparked as Elijah's gaze raked over him. When Elijah's Adam's apple bobbed slowly in his throat, he knew the man felt what he did. An unbridled lust had built between them, intensifying the more time that passed while they pretended not to want what the other was offering.

Logan went to the opposite wall, turned on the water so that both showerheads were raining down on them. The heat was instant, thank God, because he didn't waste a second moving beneath it, his gaze lingering on Elijah's face. He was curious as to which of them would make the first move. Did Elijah feel this powerful need that tightened Logan's muscles, made his cock swell impossibly? Was he holding back just as much?

He met Elijah's gaze. "I still want, Eli," he told him, reminding him of the offer Elijah had made in that text. "Now more than ever."

"Like I said, I'm here."

Yes, he most definitely was.

CHAPTER THIRTEEN

ELIJAH WAS AWARE OF THE WAY LOGAN'S heated gaze stroked him from head to toe. He'd felt it the moment the other man stepped into the space.

Admittedly, his nerves had rioted when he decided to take the plunge. The other day … when he'd instigated the blow job while Logan was working out … that had been a fluke. Elijah wasn't known for his bold moves when it came to relationships. Not friendships or romantic partnerships. He was rarely the aggressor. And for a brief moment, he had considered redirecting, ignoring Logan's request for the shower. Although the man claimed it was for Sam's benefit, he got the feeling it was more than that. A hell of a lot more than that. This hunger they'd been fighting was too intense for them to ignore any longer. The time for pretending had passed.

While Logan stood beneath the hot water, Elijah clenched his hands into fists, his fingers itching to touch. Had he ever met anyone who made him want something this badly? He couldn't recall. He'd fantasized about this moment, gotten himself off to it with his hand on his cock and his mind wandering in a direction it had never strayed before. In fact, he'd thought about it so many times, this felt like the millionth time they'd showered together, passing these heated glances.

He moved toward Logan slowly, his hands lifting so he could graze the man's abdomen. Logan groaned softly when Elijah dragged his fingertips over his ribs before flattening his palms and gliding over the rock-hard planes of his chest. He didn't rush, paying attention to the smoothness of Logan's slick skin, the subtle shift of muscle beneath his hands. He touched him everywhere, his fingers roaming over his torso up to his shoulders, back down. He wasn't teasing, merely enjoying this new sensation and the muted rumble coming from Logan's chest as he explored.

Elijah's eyes lifted to Logan's face briefly before he leaned forward. He was as interested in Logan's expressions as he was in the soft, encouraging rumbles coming from his chest. Feeling bold and empowered by the heat sparking in the man's gaze, Elijah leaned in and licked his nipple. He laved it, circling the small disc with his tongue, grazing it with his teeth.

"Fuck," Logan hissed, his hand instantly on Elijah's head when he nipped the tiny disc.

He didn't hold him in place, allowing him to tease his other nipple in the same manner. Elijah liked how they hardened beneath his ministrations, thoroughly enjoyed the way Logan's muscles coiled tightly as Elijah licked his skin as he inched higher. When he lifted his head, Logan looked down, held his stare for one heartbeat, two, before bringing their mouths together.

Elijah growled, the leash on his hunger snapping. He kissed the man with a ferocity that had been building to this heated crescendo. For months he'd thought about this, and the recent acceptance of what was transpiring between them only made it hotter.

It didn't surprise him when Logan became the aggressor, his tongue hot and hard as he plundered Elijah's mouth, his grip firm as he held Elijah's shoulders, backing him against the shower wall. The coolness of the tile was a direct contrast to the flames licking at his skin, making him groan low in his throat as he accepted Logan's weight pinning him in place.

But Elijah wasn't here to be dominated. He didn't want to relinquish control to this man. He wanted to show Logan exactly what he was in for by accepting this thing between them. He had no desire to be a male stand-in for Sam. She was irreplaceable in that regard, and Elijah wanted more from this experience.

He pushed his chest forward, gripping Logan's hips as he flipped their positions so that Logan was crushed between him and the wall. He took over the kiss, slanting his head to deepen the angle, thrusting his tongue against Logan's. He hissed when Logan's hands gripped his ass, jerking him forward, their cocks trapped between their hips. He could feel the aggression in Logan's touch, the desperation that hardened his body.

Elijah rocked his hips, stealing the friction of their bodies as his cock brushed Logan's.

"Oh, fuck. Keep doing that," Logan whispered, reaching between them to grip both of their cocks in one giant hand.

He pumped his hips, fucking Logan's fist in rhythm to the tongue thrusting into his mouth. He kept at it until Logan broke the kiss, his other hand sliding into Elijah's hair, yanking firmly.

"Put your mouth on me, Eli," he rasped, his voice low and then even lower when he said, "I've thought about nothing else since the first time."

To his shock, there was no command in his tone. It was more of a plea, an eager request to sate the physical ache that came with an attraction of this magnitude.

Elijah met his gaze briefly, then leaned in, pressing his mouth to Logan's overheated skin as he lowered to his knees. He dragged his tongue over every rigid muscle along the way. Never in his life had he imagined himself in this position, kneeling before a man, a cock hovering at his lips. He gripped the base of Logan's long, thick shaft, sliding his hand up, down, again and again, before he tongued the swollen crest.

"Fuck, yes," Logan bellowed. "Oh, fuck ... that mouth."

Elijah focused on the velvet-smoothness that moved beneath his lips as he drew Logan in deep. He licked and teased the spots he personally preferred, enjoying the rumbling grunts and harsh sighs coming from Logan.

He heard movement behind him seconds before Sam's soft, cool fingers were on his shoulders. A second later, she was kneeling behind him, her arms slipping beneath his as her hands roamed over his chest. She kissed his back, sucking on his skin.

He pulled Logan's cock from his mouth briefly. "Stroke me, Sam."

When she reached down and fisted his cock, he wrapped his lips around Logan again and sucked him in deep, earning a dark, thunderous groan in response. Sam jacked his cock while he sucked Logan, both of them panting as the pleasure assaulted them.

The hand fisting his hair tightened seconds before Logan said, "Stop!"

When Elijah pulled back, he stared up and noticed Logan's chest rising and falling rapidly, his head tilted back. He was riding that fine edge between euphoria and ecstasy. The idea of getting him off with his mouth again was tempting, but Elijah refrained. Barely.

Giving Logan a moment to rein himself in, Elijah got to his feet, pulled Sam up with him. He kissed her as he maneuvered her beneath the spray. He ran his hands over her hair, slicking it back from her face as the water rained down on them.

He loved the way she stared up at him, eyes lit with heat and hunger. She undid him with her smile.

"You like that," he told her. "Watching us together."

"Yes," she said on a breathless whimper when he bit the sensitive skin where her shoulder met her neck.

"Does it make you wet?" he asked, sliding his hand between her thighs and gliding his finger through the evidence of her arousal.

"Yes." She whimpered again, spreading her legs so he could sink his fingers inside her. "Eli…"

He loved how hot she was, how uninhibited she was. Sam had always been that way, accepting whatever they gave her, asking for what she needed when they didn't meet her expectations. She was the sweetest sin he'd ever imagined, and he knew he would never get enough of her.

As she trembled and moaned, Elijah went to his knees before her so he could feast on the sweet syrup coating her pussy lips. Like Logan's had, her fingers laced in his hair as she held him there. He suckled and licked along her cleft, enjoying her cries as she begged for more.

He was aware of Logan moving behind her, keeping her upright. When Logan lifted her leg, opening her to Elijah's hungry mouth, he tongued her entrance, fucking into her as deep as he could.

"Please!" Sam begged. "Lick my clit. Make me come, Eli."

"Not yet," Logan growled roughly.

Elijah pulled back, licking lightly rather than granting her request to keep her from coming. Considering she wasn't on the bed where they'd asked her to be, he figured it was only fair.

SAM WAS PANTING AND FRUSTRATED. SHE'D STAYED in the bed as long as she could, but their muted groans had triggered her curiosity. She'd known coming in here that they'd done this to tempt her. At least partially, anyway. However, the moment she'd seen Elijah kneeling before Logan, worshipping his cock with his mouth, she'd wondered if they'd been thinking about her at all.

On some level, she'd been disappointed in herself for intruding on their moment. Seeing them together had made her realize there was something they were seeking that didn't involve her. To her surprise, that strange feeling she'd gotten the last time wasn't there. No jealousy or fear, just unabashed wonder. This thing between them was real, more so than she'd even realized. Perhaps that was the reason they'd been fighting it for so long. And seeing them like that had given her an odd sense of peace. Knowing that they could find pleasure like that triggered a new emotion. Relief, hope? She couldn't really name it, but she also didn't care to.

Whatever this was, it felt right. The two of them seeking something from one another … it felt as though the scales had been balanced in some way.

She leaned into Logan as Elijah stood. For the next few minutes, she endured their teasing, wandering hands as they washed her from head to toe, Logan shampooing her hair, Elijah soaping her body. Every inch of her was tended to until she was a panting, writhing mess.

At Logan's command, she took care of them, soaping them both from neck to toe, doing her own teasing along the way. Once they were clean, Elijah shut off the water while Logan retrieved towels. Sam dried herself quickly, then raced back to the bed, giggling as she did.

"You think that makes up for it, huh?" Logan chuckled when he came into the bedroom.

She smiled.

He nodded his chin in her direction. "You forgot the blindfold."

"Well, crap," she muttered. She knew something was missing.

Elijah joined her first, crawling over her, his mouth trailing upward, starting at her knee and working all the way to her neck. She expected a kiss, but before he reached her mouth, he grabbed her, rolling them so that he was beneath her.

"Sit on my face," he instructed, his voice ragged with lust.

He didn't have to tell her twice.

She shifted up his body, prepared to straddle his face, but stopped when Logan's hands gripped her hips. He had joined them on the bed and was currently kneeling between Elijah's thighs.

"Turn around first," Logan ordered.

Carefully, she repositioned so that she was straddling Elijah's head, facing Logan.

She wasn't sure what his plan was, but the air was stolen from her lungs when her husband leaned down and sucked Elijah's cock into his mouth. With his hair slicked back, she could see everything, the way his tongue circled the broad head, his lips molding around it before he eased down on him.

Between her legs, she felt as much as heard Elijah's rumbling groan seconds before he grabbed her hips and pulled her down so that he could lick her right where she needed him. To keep herself upright, she reached back and grabbed the headboard, holding it with one hand as she stared down at Logan's head bobbing over Elijah's cock. The skilled mouth between her legs made it impossible to focus, but she couldn't look away. It was made all the more intense because Elijah was humming softly as Logan sucked his cock, the vibrations moving through her entire body.

When Elijah focused on her clit, Sam's body tightened. Logan likely suspected she was close because he stopped what he was doing. He repositioned, lifting his upper body, straddling Elijah's hips as he moved closer, aligning their cocks. She watched as he gripped both in one giant hand and stroked them simultaneously.

"Oh, God," she whimpered, pressing her hips down, grinding her clit against Elijah's wicked tongue.

"Come all over his face, Sam," Logan commanded.

Sam's attention was between them, where Logan was swiping his thumb over the heads of their cocks as he stroked. Elijah's insistent tongue flicked her clit relentlessly until she cried out, her body shuddering from the violent orgasm that stole the air from her lungs.

She sagged, but Logan was there to hold her up. He kissed her, pulling her toward him. She should've realized he had an ulterior motive, but she was still recovering, so she didn't notice until she was sitting astride Elijah's hips, his cock nudging her entrance.

"Sit on his cock," Logan rumbled against her ear. "That's it, baby."

She whimpered as Elijah filled her, his cock tunneling deep.

"Now, lean back."

It took some maneuvering because of the reverse cowgirl going on, but Sam unfolded her legs from beneath her, never dislodging Elijah from inside her because he was gripping her hips, holding her where he wanted her. Once she was reclined on Elijah's chest, she watched Logan move between her legs, repositioning so that he was straddling Elijah's hips. A moment later, she felt the urgent press of Logan's cock as he pushed in alongside Elijah.

They both filled her pussy, stretching her wide.

She closed her eyes and rode the wave of pleasure as he eased into her. As was the case every time, Sam recalled the first time Logan and Elijah had fucked her pussy simultaneously. It had been at Devotion all those years ago. From the moment they'd penetrated her at the same time, she'd craved the sensation of being fucked by them both. She loved this part. Loved the way her body stretched to accommodate the sensual intrusion. She still wasn't sure how they managed it, how her body could acclimate to two cocks, but it did.

"Oh, fuck," Elijah groaned near her ear. "I'm going to come like this. His cock stroking mine, your pussy gripping me. It's too good."

It was a warning, she knew. One that Logan didn't heed as he began fucking her, the momentum of his cock pushing in and pulling out, driving all three of them to that razor-sharp edge. Sam held on for as long as she could, but Elijah's thundering voice shouting Logan's name drove her right over the edge.

"Fuck," Logan groaned. "Ah, fuck, yes. Come for me, Elijah."

He said his name, not mine.

"Holy fuck, that feels good," Elijah groaned.

Sam felt them both pulsing inside her as another mini explosion erupted, leaving her breathless and sated.

Not to mention, for the first time in … ever … feeling like the third wheel and wondering if she hadn't gotten exactly what she deserved.

HALF AN HOUR LATER, AFTER THEY'D CLEANED up and fixed the bedding, Logan stared up at the ceiling in the darkened room, Sam's head cradled on his shoulder, her arm draped over his chest as she slept soundly. On her other side, he heard Elijah's deep, even breaths as he spooned her from behind, his arm over her, his hand resting on Logan's thigh.

His heart and lungs had long since recovered from that incredible moment, but his brain was still processing.

That moment when Elijah had taken control in the shower, touching him, teasing him ... Logan had felt something. Something very much like what he'd felt back at the beginning with Sam. It had been new and intense, and he'd wanted that single moment to himself. Just the two of them. It was then he realized that this thing he had with Elijah was something he wanted to covet for a little while. He didn't want to put it on display, didn't want to dissect it for anyone else. He wanted to see where it led without prying eyes.

Without Sam witnessing every intimate moment.

And that bothered him more than anything else. He loved his wife with a passion that was unrivaled. He would lay down his life for her. Hell, he *lived* for her. So what was driving this strange need to seek privacy with Elijah? Did that mean he wanted to cheat on his wife with a man? After all, he had yet to reveal to her what had happened between them the other day when Elijah had sucked his cock for the first time. The worst part was, he wasn't sure he wanted to share that moment with her.

Sam had actually accused him of taking out his lust on her for the week after their first encounter. She hadn't been wrong. However, she'd been incorrect as to his reasoning. It hadn't been his lust for Elijah he'd been trying to assuage. It had been this foreign desire to have Elijah for himself that he'd been fighting. Taking Sam, claiming her whenever he could, was the only way to prove to himself and to her that she would always be the center of his universe.

He needed to get a grasp on this so he could figure out how it would work between them. Logan couldn't keep doing this if it meant he was cheating on Sam. He couldn't move forward in good conscience, knowing he wanted something that didn't involve Sam. It wasn't fair to her, and if he were being honest, he would rather die than ever betray her.

Regardless of what he was starting to feel for Elijah.

CHAPTER FOURTEEN

Friday, July 15, 2022

"HAVE YOU GIVEN ANY MORE CONSIDERATION TO the offer?"

Elijah looked up from his computer screen as his boss strolled into his office.

He'd been expecting Jefferson Fellows to make an appearance. After all, it was Friday afternoon, and he doubted the man could go the entire weekend without getting a final decision from Elijah.

"I have," he said, leaning back in his chair and waiting for him to take a seat. "I still don't have an answer for you."

His boss, a portly man with a rotund face and shrewd brown eyes, stared back at him. "Why did I know you were going to say that?"

"Because you know I don't make decisions lightly?"

A small smile formed, but his eyes remained discriminating, as though he could will Elijah to make a decision with his cold stare.

"Is it the money?" He gave a one-shoulder shrug that made his round body jiggle. "I can see if there's wiggle room with the salary, but—"

"It's not the money," he interrupted. "There are other factors at play right now."

It wasn't like he could tell the man that he wasn't ready to make such a big decision when there were other things—more important things—going on in his life. Elijah wasn't sure he was ready for too much more right now with his relationship with Sam and Logan delving into new, unexplored territory. And the job, while it would keep him at home the way he wanted, would come with more stresses on top of the ones he was already carrying.

"I just need a little time to think about it," he said.

"I'm not sure how long the board will wait to get your decision."

Elijah had considered that. Knew they wouldn't wait for him forever. "Understood."

The man's beady eyes narrowed slightly. "But I can stall for a little while. How does a week sound?"

He figured it would have to do, so he nodded in agreement, wondering when he should broach the subject with Sam and Logan.

An hour later, Elijah was pulling into the garage. During the drive, he'd turned up the radio and done his best to shove thoughts of work and promotions and future decisions out of his mind. He was looking forward to dinner with Logan and Sam, followed by a weekend of doing as little as possible. He was mentally and physically exhausted, and some downtime was just what the doctor ordered.

When he stepped into the house, he was greeted with silence. He knew Logan was home because his car was parked in its usual spot, but he heard nothing to signal what the man was doing.

He set his laptop on the kitchen table and turned, noticing Logan was in his recliner, leaned back, staring at the dark television.

Oh, boy. The only time the man did that was when he had a lot on his mind.

"Hey," Elijah greeted, wondering if he needed to tread lightly.

Logan didn't move, and a grunt was his only response.

"Where's Sam?" he asked, making his way to the cabinet where they kept the liquor. It had been one hell of a week, and he wanted to kick off the weekend with a drink.

"Out."

He grabbed the Hennessy from the shelf, then retrieved one of the highball glasses sitting beside it. While he waited for Logan to elaborate—which he didn't seem ready to do—he poured two fingers of cognac and tossed it back.

Maybe that would help with the stress that tightened his shoulders and had a tension headache forming in the base of his skull. When Logan offered nothing more, Elijah sighed softly.

"Well, I guess I'll change and figure out something for dinner," he said, leaving the bottle and the glass on the counter before strolling past Logan toward the bedroom. He glanced back once to see that Logan was staring after him, his eyes dark, his expression unreadable.

Problems with work, maybe?

Figuring they could catch up over dinner, Elijah didn't bother making small talk. He went into the closet, which he shared with Logan, stripped off his suit before walking back toward the bedroom to grab a pair of shorts from the dresser. He stopped short when he saw Logan standing in the doorway, blocking his exit from the bathroom.

The look in Logan's eyes had adrenaline flooding his bloodstream. It was his fight-or-flight instinct kicking in, he realized. When was the last time someone had looked at him like that? With so much aggression and ... was it hunger that darkened the man's hazel eyes?

Keep it casual. "What's up?"

He took a step forward, intending to squeeze by Logan to avoid the impending storm he could feel churning. He didn't make it that far when Logan grabbed his arm. His grip was light at first but firmed as he turned Elijah so that they were face-to-face. With the doorjamb at his back, Elijah stared into his eyes, feeling the tension coming off him in waves.

"I told myself I wouldn't do this." Logan's voice was deep and dark. "But I lied."

"Wouldn't do—?"

He didn't get the words out because Logan slammed his mouth over his, pinning Elijah between his hard body and the wood at his back. Instinct kicked in, driven by a violent hunger that had been building for too long. He didn't submit to the tongue thrusting into his mouth, but he didn't break the kiss. He latched on to Logan's hair, gripping hard as he pushed him back, refusing to let the man dominate him.

He'd never felt anything even remotely as intense as this. The way Logan kissed him ... it was as though the choke chain on his control had snapped, and the vicious beast had been set free.

Despite his efforts to shove him back, Logan didn't budge, their tongues thrashing as they consumed one another. He wasn't sure what had brought this on, but he wanted more of it. More of this man unleashed, unbridled. The passion was savage, battering him from all angles. And it did what the liquor hadn't, relieving the stresses of work and resetting his focus.

"If this isn't what you want, you better tell me now," Logan said, a guttural growl emerging from his throat.

He didn't have to ask what Logan was referring to because he could feel it. The man radiated with need, his desire intoxicating, making Elijah's body tighten with anticipation.

"Tell me," Logan groaned, still holding his arm as he backed him toward the bed.

Even if he'd had traction, he was no match for Logan in this state. "Tell you what?"

"That you want me"—Logan nipped his lower lip—"to fuck you."

A rough groan rumbled in his chest, and while it was a definite answer, he didn't think it was what Logan wanted. For whatever reason, the man seemed to want his verbal surrender.

Elijah's words came out gravel rough when he said, "I already told you, I'm yours when you want me."

"Say. It."

Elijah frowned, confused by Logan's intensity. "Say what? That I want you to fuck me?"

Logan's eyes narrowed.

"Yeah," he said, holding Logan's stare and surrendering. "I want you to fuck me, Logan."

Before he could take his next breath, Elijah was flat on his back on the bed. Logan didn't waste a second jerking his T-shirt over his head and tossing it to the floor.

Elijah watched, his body hard, his cock throbbing. To prove he was on board with this plan, he stripped his underwear off, kicked it away before moving back on the bed, his gaze never leaving Logan. He watched as the rest of Logan's clothes disappeared before the man reached into the nightstand and retrieved a bottle of lubricant.

Yep. They were doing this.

Logan tossed the bottle beside Elijah, then crawled over him on the bed. Their mouths crashed together once more, teeth clattering as the hunger intensified. Elijah banded his arms around Logan, jerking him so he could feel hot flesh against hot flesh. His lungs worked overtime to keep up with the adrenaline surge that had him groaning.

The kiss seemed to go on forever until that single second when time stood still, and Logan pulled back, kneeling between his legs. Elijah watched, reaching down and stroking his erection as Logan flipped open the cap on the lubricant and squeezed a generous amount in his hand. Their eyes met as Logan slicked his cock. Elijah was shocked by what he saw in his gaze. Sure, there was lust and hunger, but there was something else. Desperation, maybe? Whatever it was, it lit Logan's eyes like a flame, his expression reflecting everything he was feeling.

Logan reached between them, his fingers sliding over Elijah's balls as he went lower, grazing his taint.

He was stunned silent, frozen by the pleasure that simple touch elicited. He knew what was coming, even had the common sense to fear the pain that would likely accompany having a cock shoved in his ass, but that didn't diminish his need. He wanted Logan to fuck him. He wanted to feel him inside him, to be as close to this man as two human beings could possibly be.

Elijah moaned when he felt the tip of one slick finger rim his hole. In that moment, it was all too real. He had wondered how he would react if ever put in this position—vulnerable and open for Logan—but Elijah had never expected this violent, mind-blowing need that would overwhelm him.

Logan's gaze never strayed from his face as he pushed one finger inside. Elijah's head fell back to the bed, his legs widening as he accepted that thick finger deep inside him. When Logan pulled his finger out and pushed it back in, Elijah was numbed by a haze of lust so powerful that it ripped a ragged groan from his chest. It felt so fucking good he could hear himself begging for more.

Logan gave him more, sliding two fingers in, fucking him slow and deep, stretching him. Elijah pulled his knees to his chest, watched as Logan's gaze dropped to where his fingers were thrusting inside him. His cock throbbed in time to his heartbeat, blood roared in his ears as heat churned in his bloodstream. He was going to come from this alone. He reached for his cock, gripped it tightly at the base to ensure that didn't happen. When he did, he saw the muscles in Logan's chest and arms flex as though it was taking every ounce of control he possessed not to pounce on him.

He wanted more. And he wanted it now.

"Fuck, you're tight," Logan hissed, the words vibrating in the air as his chest heaved. "I want my cock inside you."

Elijah rocked his hips then growled, "What are you waiting for? Fuck me."

Logan knew he wasn't going to get more of a green light than that. He upended the bottle and drizzled lube over his fingers, which were still fingering Elijah's hole, so he could massage it in. He didn't want to hurt the man, but he also knew he wouldn't be able to control himself once he drove into the blistering hot depths of his body.

He'd spent the past couple of hours telling himself that what he felt for Elijah was merely lust, and if he could get this out of his system, they could find a way to move forward without the tension that strangled them both whenever they were in the same room. It was a lie he'd gotten really good at telling himself. The moment he heard Elijah's voice, he realized he couldn't hold back any longer. He had to sate this need, or it was going to shred him.

"Need more," Elijah whispered, his hips rocking, urging Logan's fingers to slide deeper.

His ass gripped him, the smooth, tight channel relaxing as he pushed his fingers in, withdrew slowly. The man looked so fucking good laid out like that, completely at Logan's mercy and begging for more.

When he pulled his fingers out, Elijah's head lifted, his eyes meeting his.

Logan gritted his teeth, gripping his cock tightly as he angled himself toward his eager hole. He pressed the head against Elijah's anus and hissed as every pleasure receptor in his body came online. He watched the man's face as he fought the resistance, sinking in one centimeter at a time, stretching the tight ring that was determined to keep him out. He pushed his hips forward, his cockhead slipping inside. He grunted and hissed, consumed by a pleasure that bordered on pain as he inched forward.

He didn't pause, looking for Elijah to tell him when it was too much, but he never did, his chest rising and falling, soft moans rumbling in his chest as Logan pushed in deeper. He was panting, his skin slick with sweat by the time he was buried to the hilt.

Seated fully, he planted his hands beside Elijah's head, stared down at him as he pulled his hips back. He had dreamed about this moment. In fact, he'd had that dream more often than not these past couple of weeks, waking up to find his cock rock hard and aching. But the dreams had nothing on this. He wasn't sure he'd felt anything quite as wickedly hot as this in his entire life.

Logan's cock throbbed inside the snug channel clutching at him.

"Oh, fuck." Elijah's eyes closed.

"Hurt?"

"Don't stop."

He didn't like the idea of hurting him, but he'd long ago snapped that last tenuous thread of his control. He pushed in, retreated, letting Elijah feel the entire length of his cock every single time.

Never in his life had he imagined he would be here, fucking a man, caring about that man, wanting more even though there was no more to give. Once wouldn't be enough.

After a minute, Elijah began to relax, his expression softening as his eyes rolled back and his hips rocked beneath him. Logan fucked him slow and deep, aware of the smooth walls of Elijah's ass clutching him tightly. Thank fuck he had jacked off when he got home. Otherwise, he would've already come, and he damn sure wasn't ready for this to be over.

When more tension eased out of Elijah's body and his hands slid up Logan's arms, he began pumping his hips faster, driving in harder until he was fucking him, the bed rocking from the momentum of their joining.

"God, yes," Elijah rasped. "Oh, fuck … Logan."

His throat tightened when he heard his name fall from Elijah's lips. This wasn't about the physical act, although he'd told himself he could keep it that way. It was so much more than that. There was a connection, a bond they shared that had started because of their love for one woman. Who knows when it shifted or why, but here they were, and Logan knew he was fucked because this wasn't a one-time thing.

He glanced down, watching as Elijah jerked his cock in time to Logan's punishing thrusts. He savored the sound of Elijah's grunts every time he bottomed out inside him, the sexy hiss when he pulled out. He was lost to the sensation, overwhelmed by the pleasure that flayed him on the inside. It was incredible. The more he took, the more he wanted Elijah to give.

Logan slowed his pace, leaning down and pressing his mouth to Elijah's. He held himself there as he slid all the way in, pulled out again.

"You feel so fucking good," he whispered against Elijah's lips. "Tight. Hot. You want me to come inside you?"

Elijah's hand jerked harder on his cock. "Yes. Fuck. Make me come."

"You want more? Or less?" He gave him a sample of both options, slamming his hips forward, then dragging his cock out slowly.

"Oh, fuck." Elijah panted roughly, lifting his head to meet Logan's mouth.

He kissed him, impaling him again and again. Slow then fast.

"I'm going to come," Elijah warned. "Logan ... oh, fuck ... that feels..."

Logan picked up the pace, slamming his hips down. He worked him with shallow, deep strokes until Elijah's head arched back, and he shouted Logan's name.

He drove home one final time and let himself go.

In the aftermath, as the sweat on his skin cooled and he lay silently beside Elijah, he realized one devastating thing:

Not once had he thought about Sam.

CHAPTER FIFTEEN

Sunday, July 17, 2022

AFTER SPENDING THE MAJORITY OF THE WEEKEND doing absolutely nothing but lounging around the house and taking advantage of the pool on a hot summer's weekend, Sam's brain was coming back online. She had things to do to prepare for the upcoming week—laundry that needed to be finished, dinners that needed to be planned.

Forcing herself up from the couch, she went to the kitchen, where Elijah was sitting at the table, his eyes skimming his iPad.

She went to the refrigerator, opened the door. "I was thinking we might have—"

"I'm taking you to dinner tonight," Logan interrupted before Sam could finish her sentence.

She glanced behind her, stared at her husband as he pushed himself up from the couch, where he'd been sitting for the past hour.

She shut the fridge door, turning to face him.

"You are?" she asked, forcing a smile, feeling as though something was off.

"Elijah's on his own tonight," Logan said gruffly.

Sam tried to hide her wince at his tone, but she knew she had failed. Her gaze instantly shot to Elijah, who hadn't bothered to look up from his iPad. He didn't appear fazed by Logan's rudely spoken words, though she figured he should be.

Something was going on here, but she couldn't put her finger on exactly what. For the past several days, ever since the night Elijah and Logan had showered together, Sam had felt as though something was wrong with Logan. What she thought had signified a turning point between them hadn't gone exactly as planned. At least not in the aftermath. Logan was acting strange, far more growly than was normal. When she'd attempted to confront him about it, he had shrugged it off, told her it was her imagination.

"Is everything all right?" she asked, taking a step toward him.

"Of course it is," he grumbled.

Oh, it most certainly wasn't, but he could go right on pretending if that was his choice.

"Well, dinner out sounds great," she said, glancing between the two men. "I think that's my cue to get ready."

"Wear something nice," he groused as she was moving through the living room.

Sam refused to look back. This way, he couldn't see her roll her eyes.

Two hours later, Sam was sitting across from Logan in one of her favorite restaurants. It was an intimate setting, complete with candlelight and wine. It was unexpected, to say the least. Usually, Logan reserved this particular place for special occasions, which fortified in her mind that something was bothering him.

"So what are we celebrating?" she prompted when he refused to look up from the menu. He already knew what he was going to order since he always got the same thing—a rib eye, a lobster tail, and a baked potato—which meant he was avoiding her.

"Why do we have to be celebrating?" His gaze slowly rose, his eyes narrowed.

In that moment, he reminded her a lot of his twin. Back when Luke was always pissy, snapping at anyone who got in his path. He certainly didn't seem like her charming, romantic husband.

His eyes darted back to the menu when he said, "Can't I just take my *wife* out for a nice meal? Show her how much she means to me?"

Sam reached over, touched his wrist. "Logan."

He didn't look up, but she could feel the tension in his arm.

"Look at me," she said softly.

Logan put the menu aside and met her gaze.

"Please talk to me about what's bothering you."

He leaned in, his words gruff. "Nothing's bothering me, Sam. Let it go."

She swallowed hard, released his wrist. It was impossible to hide the hurt his harshly spoken words incited. She wasn't used to Logan acting like this, which was why she was so in tune with it. He was such a laid-back guy, going with the flow for the most part. Yet with every passing minute, something was eating at him, turning him into a man she didn't even recognize.

The waiter strolled over to take their order.

Sam sat up straight and offered him a smile, not wanting to ruin his night simply because her husband had just ruined hers. She rattled off her order, then waited as Logan did the same. At least his tone was somewhat more pleasant when he spoke to the waiter. She was grateful, although it made her own hurt feel more prominent.

Once the waiter disappeared to turn in their order, Sam sat silently, sipping her wine, looking at anyone except for Logan. He was doing the same, so it didn't take long before the tension was unbearable.

How was she going to make it through this dinner? She felt as though she was about to crack under the pressure.

Taking a deep breath, she set her empty wineglass down.

"I ... uh..." She pushed her chair back, set her napkin on the table. "I'm going to the restroom. I'll be right back."

Without waiting for Logan to make his gentlemanly gesture of standing when she got to her feet, she hurried away from the table, through the restaurant, and down the long, narrow hallway toward the restrooms. Thankfully, the restaurant was small, and so was the women's bathroom. There were only two stalls, and thankfully they were both empty.

Once inside, Sam went to the sink, set her clutch on the counter, and stared at herself in the mirror. There were tears pooling on her lower lashes, and she felt like an idiot for getting so emotional. Despite her requests for Logan to tell her what was bothering him, she didn't really need him to explain. She already knew. It was as obvious as a backhand across the face.

She'd screwed everything up. She knew it deep in her soul. She had pushed Logan and Elijah together, and it had backfired in her face. Now Logan was pissed at her, which served her right.

"What were you thinking?" she hissed at her reflection.

Her chest swelled as emotion bubbled down deep. She took a deep breath, trying to hold back the sob even as a single tear crested her lashes and slid slowly down her cheek. She'd known one day her desires, her wayward impulses, and yes, her selfishness would come back to bite her in the ass. She just hadn't realized it was going to cause a rift between her and Logan.

"Pull yourself together," she snapped at the woman in the mirror.

The bathroom door swung open, and she stood tall, sniffed to pull back the tears before reaching for a paper towel from the wall-mounted holder. Before she could reach it, Logan appeared behind her.

She turned in time to see him flipping the lock on the door, closing them inside.

"Baby," he said gruffly as he moved over to her.

His face was pinched, and if she wasn't mistaken, that was sorrow in his gaze.

Fear coiled in her heart, making it difficult to breathe. It was so much worse than she thought.

Sam swallowed, prepared to launch an apology for screwing everything up, to beg him to forgive her. She didn't get a single word out before he crushed his mouth to hers, his big arms curling around her, pulling her in tight.

She could feel the tension in his body, a subtle vibration that churned the emotion she was still battling. He was breathing heavily but not from desire. It was as though he was holding something in, afraid to let it out. She'd only seen him like this a few times, and never was it good.

"I need you, Sam," he whispered, reaching down between them to free the buckle on his belt, his mouth sealing over hers as he did.

There was a desperation in his voice, his movements. Sam didn't know how to react, but she knew better than to push him away.

She was aware of him unbuttoning his slacks moments before he lifted her dress. The next thing she knew, her butt was perched on the edge of the countertop, and Logan was driving deep inside her. There was no seduction in his technique, but her body welcomed him all the same, softening instantly. She loved this man with her whole heart and had long ago learned that there was no such thing as resistance when it came to him.

He buried his face in her neck as he pumped his hips, fucking her as though he'd been deprived for years.

"Hold on to me, baby," he growled.

She wreathed his neck with her arms, their bodies bumping with every stroke of his cock inside her. She held on, biting her tongue to keep from moaning as the pleasure shoved the hurt and the pain down. At least for a little while.

"God, baby," he groaned. "Do you know how much I need you? So fucking much, Sam."

She cupped the back of his head, slid her palm over his silky hair as he pulled her hips toward him, changing the angle and giving him better traction to drive in deeper.

"You're everything to me, Sam," he continued. "The only thing I've ever needed."

Her chest constricted because she could feel his pain. This was Logan at his most vulnerable, something she rarely ever saw. The man went to extraordinary measures to show her how important she was to him. She never doubted his sincerity, which was why she was questioning his motives now.

He fucked her hard, his rhythm shifting, his thrusts shallow and rough as he kept her tight against him. Despite her worry, her body sought what he was offering. It didn't take long before she felt the first wave of her orgasm. It washed through her on the tide of love she always felt for him.

"Yes, baby," he growled. "Come for me, Sam. Oh, fuck, yes."

She bit her lip but couldn't hold back the moan that escaped as she succumbed to the tsunami that engulfed her. A moment later, Logan was right there, slamming in deep as he came with a groan that rumbled against her neck.

When he lifted his head, he cupped her face, met her stare. "I love you, Sam. Never, ever forget that."

The Sahara Desert took up residence in her throat, making it impossible to swallow. She saw a myriad of emotions burning in his hazel eyes, and it choked her. For some reason, that sounded far too dire for such a declaration.

Little did she know, but that one intimate moment was the prelude to the storm she'd been fearing.

AFTER LOGAN AND SAM LEFT FOR DINNER, Elijah decided he needed to get out of the house. He figured he'd done a damn good job hiding his reaction to Logan's strange behavior. He'd made it through the weekend without confronting the man, but when Logan had abruptly declared he was taking Sam out tonight, Elijah had known the worst wasn't over yet.

So he decided to come to the one place where he knew he didn't have to pretend or hide what was weighing on him.

"Hey, honey, it's me," Elijah said as he took a seat on the cool grass that surrounded his wife's headstone. "I know it's been a while."

He reached forward, brushed a stray leaf off of the marble before he laid out the flowers—a dozen white roses—he'd purchased on his way over here.

"I needed someone to talk to, figured you wouldn't mind listening." He leaned back, planting his palms on the ground and stretching his legs out before him. "It's about Sam and Logan."

For the longest time after he had gotten involved with Sam, Elijah had never mentioned her to Beth when he came to visit her grave. He always kept his conversations on safer topics like work and the club. Then time had moved forward, and he'd used Beth as his sounding board. Although she was no longer of this earth, he could still feel her when he was here. As though she visited when he did, just so they could have a little time together. The more he had revealed, the stronger he'd sensed her until he had convinced himself that she was glad to know he'd gotten a second chance at love.

It was probably all in his head, but Elijah had come to enjoy the time he was here. He still missed Beth, still thought about her, but the pain that had come from the loss had eased until he was left with only fond memories. He figured he had Sam to thank for that. From the very beginning, Sam had made a point of ensuring Beth was as welcome in their lives as he was. She'd even put her picture in the living room, among the photos of Logan and Sam. As time moved forward and their lives became intertwined, more pictures appeared alongside it, many of him and Sam, one of the three of them smiling. After a while, Elijah had stopped staring at the photos of Beth, his gaze straying toward Sam more and more.

"Things have gotten … complicated," he said aloud, letting his gaze stray to the trees that surrounded the area. "I'm not sure when things changed for me, but I've recently learned something about myself. Something I doubt even you could've predicted."

Elijah swallowed, smiled as he swore he could feel her presence.

"I recently had an encounter with Logan," he admitted for the first time aloud. "Well, technically, there've been a few now, but it started last year. When we went to the cabin for the holidays. I told you about it, remember? Sam was up to her usual games, convinced us to play." He chuckled softly. "Little does she know, but we put up a fight more for her benefit. I love her games because they seem to make her happy.

"Anyway, I ended up kissing Logan that night."

He let that admission hang in the air for a minute while he decided how to explain it.

"Something shifted inside me that night, Beth. Like a switch had been flipped on."

He took a deep breath, let it out. Saying the words aloud felt like acceptance, and he wondered if he should feel guilty for burdening Beth.

The breeze kicked up briefly, stirring the flowers lying on the headstone.

"To say it was strange is an understatement. I mean, kissing a man. Odd, right? I could've never imagined kissing James."

Elijah thought back to the polyamorous relationship he'd been in with Beth and his best friend, James. What the three of them had shared was significantly different than what he had with Logan and Sam, but it had been a high point in his life for a while. But never had he felt even an inkling of attraction to James.

"Kissing Logan ... I'd been hesitant but not scared." He laughed. "Okay, that's a lie. I was terrified, but not because I was going to kiss a man."

He stared ahead and continued, "I've done some interesting things in my life, Beth, and I doubt that ranked at the top of the list. But it was when I was kissing Logan that I realized I'd been wanting to ... I guess the right word is *explore*."

He took a deep breath, crossed his ankles. "It changed me. Made me see a side of myself I hadn't realized was there. After that, nothing happened for the longest time despite Sam's constant encouragement." He smiled as he thought about Sam. "I told you, that's her way, and I love her for it."

Usually, this was the point when he paused, filled with regret for admitting that he loved another woman when he'd always thought Beth would be it for him. But somewhere along the way, his love for Sam had become so important to him, he'd felt the need to share it with Beth. He felt blessed by the fact that he'd known the love of two incredible women in his life. Some people didn't get lucky enough to have the love of one, much less two.

He swallowed past the lump in his throat. "She thinks she's discreet, but I know what she's up to. I didn't mind her subtle interference, but I think Logan did. Then, about a month ago, Logan and I were alone. We explored a little more, and it ramped up my curiosity. I knew then that I wanted something from him. I don't know what yet, but I know it's more than I've gotten so far."

He took a deep breath, glanced over as a car passed along the narrow road that wound through the cemetery. He watched it until it was out of sight.

"You're probably wondering if it's a physical thing." He sighed. "Yes and no. That certainly spurred it, I'm sure. I just don't think that's all it is. It feels like more for me, Beth. More than a mere physical attraction."

He took a deep breath, let the warm breeze move over him, and admitted what had been bothering him for the last few weeks.

"I think I've fallen in love with Logan. I don't know when it happened, didn't even realize it was a thing until recently. You're probably wondering what Logan thinks about that." He chuckled. "If I had to wager a guess, I'd say he's terrified. It's one step forward and two steps back for him every time. I can feel him pull away after. His full attention shifts back to Sam as though he's done something wrong.

"He took her out tonight. Spur-of-the-moment. He doesn't usually do that. I think Sam noticed the shift in him, too, but he's closed himself off to both of us. I don't know what I'm supposed to do about it. The thought of this attraction coming between Sam and me… I can't bear the thought of losing her. I don't know if it'd be easier to pretend nothing happened and go back to the way things were. I've considered it plenty."

He sat silently, wishing he could hear Beth's voice. He knew without a doubt she would have the right answer. She always did.

The breeze kicked up, strong enough to blow the roses onto their side.

Follow your heart. It never steers you wrong.

Elijah sat up abruptly, staring around. He could've sworn he heard her voice. His gaze shot to the trees, to the street. No one else was around. No one living, anyway.

"Beth?" he whispered, feeling his chest constrict.

Another gust of wind bent the limbs of the trees, but that was the only response he received.

CHAPTER SIXTEEN

Monday, July 18, 2022

THANKS TO ENDLESS MEETINGS THAT DRAINED EVERY spare second of time she had, Mondays usually went by quickly for Sam. Today was no exception. From the moment Logan had walked through the doors of their building, she'd been otherwise engaged, which she figured was a good thing. Work was a way for her to focus her energies and keep her mind from worrying endlessly.

Unfortunately, those meetings only lasted so long, and by four thirty p.m., Sam was ready to leave it all behind and go home, where she could hopefully spend a few uninterrupted hours with the men she adored. Perhaps she could make lasagna. Sierra had sent her a recipe that she swore was foolproof, and since Sam was a disaster waiting to happen when it came to the kitchen, she'd wanted to give it a go.

Maybe she could make some garlic bread, too. How hard could that be?

As she was packing up her things, she dialed Logan's office, not surprised when his assistant, Deanna, answered.

"Hey, girl," Deanna greeted with a smile in her voice. "I was about to head your way."

Puzzled, Sam said, "For?"

"To drop off Logan's keys?" She sounded confused, too. "He said you'd swing by to get them this afternoon."

"He's not in?" Sam asked.

Deanna huffed. "I told him not to forget to call you. He had to go out of town for the week. Urgent meeting. Something about fires that needed to be put out. He seemed scattered when he mentioned it. That's why I told him to call you on the way to the airport."

Sam swallowed hard as she eased into her chair, unable to feel her legs, her chest painfully tight.

"He didn't call you," Deanna said, clearly oblivious to Sam's impending panic attack. "Well, don't worry. I'll bring the keys over on my way out. It'll take me only a minute."

"Mmm-hmm," she managed before hanging up and staring blankly at the phone.

He'd gone out of town? Worse, he'd gone out of town without bothering to tell her? When had he ever done *that*? She was usually his first call, and never—absolutely *never*—had he gone out of town without kissing her goodbye.

Sam rubbed the spot over her heart, tried to ease the unbearable ache. She hadn't felt the urge to curl up into a ball in a really long time, but right now, she was seriously considering it. Shit. She knew there was something wrong, but she hadn't realized it was quite this bad. Bad enough her husband would disappear without a word?

Her mind went wild with speculation. Was he gone forever? Would he start a new life somewhere else, fall in love with a different woman? Have kids? Live happily ever after?

A sob broke free, but she choked it down, refusing to fall apart yet. There had to be a really good reason for this. Logan wouldn't just bolt on her.

She swallowed the tight lump forming in her throat, drew in a shuddering breath, and squared her shoulders.

"There's a good reason," she whispered, bringing her phone up so she could dial Logan's number. She took another fortifying breath, prepared to interrogate him about where he was and why he didn't bother to tell her he was leaving. He owed her that much, right?

She got voicemail.

When she was prompted to leave her message, Sam kept her tone pleasant when she said, "Hey, it's me. Just thought I'd check in. Deanna said you had an emergency to deal with. Call me when you get this. Please."

She disconnected, getting to her feet, when she heard the sound of footsteps coming her way. No way would she let Deanna see her on the verge of a breakdown.

"Here you go, honey," Deanna said, dangling the keys before passing them over. "Oh, hey, what's wrong?"

Sam met her gaze, forced a smile. "Just have a lot on my mind. It's nothing."

Deanna didn't look convinced, but thankfully, she didn't press. "Okay, then. Have a good evening."

"Yeah. You, too," she said, setting the keys on top of her purse. "Thanks."

Deanna's gaze remained on her as she backed out of the room. The moment she was out of sight, Sam clutched her chest again, rubbed the ache. She needed to talk to Elijah. Maybe he knew what the hell was going on.

LOGAN DISEMBARKED FROM THE COMPANY JET AND strolled to the town car waiting for him. He probably should've felt guilty for using company resources for personal business, but he didn't. Hell, he had far too many other things to feel guilty about at the moment.

Taking this trip to Chicago had been a spur-of-the-moment decision, one he wasn't ready to regret just yet. He told himself he was on a fact-finding mission, so it made it all right. The fact that he didn't tell Sam or Elijah was a definite misstep on his part, but he decided he would worry about that later; otherwise, he would find himself back on the plane taking a return trip home.

You need to be here, that little voice in his head said.

"Would you like to go to your hotel first, sir? Or straight to the club?" the driver asked when he was settled into the backseat.

"The club."

"Very well. We should be there in about twenty minutes."

Logan nodded, pulling out his phone to check his messages. He noticed one from Sam, so he tapped the screen to play it.

Hey, it's me. Just thought I'd check in. Deanna said you had an emergency to deal with. Call me when you get this. Please.

He replayed it two more times, hating that he heard the concern and perhaps a hint of fear in her tone. That was his fault. Leaving abruptly wasn't something he'd ever done before, but the phone call from Trent Ramsey early this afternoon had given him the perfect excuse to make this impromptu trip.

Deciding it would be best to wait to call Sam back, Logan tucked his phone away and stared out the window as the Chicago skyline came into view. It didn't take long before the car was pulling up to the building that housed Trent's infamous BDSM club, although, from the outside, it looked more like an industrial hideout than a place someone went to explore their deepest, darkest desires.

"I'll have your things delivered to your hotel, sir," the driver informed him as he exited the car.

"Thanks."

As the car pulled away from the curb, Logan strolled up to the door, then took a deep breath before opening it. The moment he stepped inside, he was given a warm welcome from the young woman perched behind a desk. To an unknowing observer, the space would look like nothing more than a regular reception area. To someone who knew what lay beyond the secured door to the left, there were a few things that stood out. First was the armed security guard sitting casually in one of the chairs, a magazine open in front of him. Logan would bet millions the man hadn't bothered to skim a single article despite his attempt to pretend otherwise.

"Mr. McCoy," the receptionist greeted with an enormous grin. "Master Ramsey said you would be stopping by."

She pulled a drawer out of her desk and held it up.

Knowing the drill, Logan deposited his cell phone inside. She then returned it to its hiding spot and locked it with a key she kept around her wrist before getting to her feet. She moved out from behind the desk, holding something in her hand.

"This denotes you as a personal guest tonight," she informed him as she secured a bracelet around his wrist. "Just be sure it's visible if you decide to play."

Logan could've told her there wasn't a chance in hell of him playing tonight or any other for that matter, but he didn't bother. He wasn't here to enjoy the amenities.

"The bar is on the main floor. There's a two-drink maximum if you intend to play." She motioned toward the door. "You'll be screened on your way in, and I'll let Master Ramsey know you're here. Enjoy your evening."

He nodded in thanks, then turned toward the door, which was being opened by the magazine man.

Logan stepped through, allowing a submissive to wave a wand over him, ensuring he wasn't carrying a weapon or trying to sneak in a camera or cell phone.

He knew the drill, understood it even. Like Luke, Trent was big on security for his members. Providing a safe place to relax and engage in salacious activities was the main objective.

Once inside, Logan headed for the bar and ordered a vodka on the rocks. While the submissive manning the bar prepared his drink, he skimmed the interior of the space. The area was geared toward submissives. There was a lounge area where they could go if they weren't looking to play. Another section reserved for submissives whose Dominants wanted them to relax. And lastly, an area where submissives could go to kneel on pillows in the hopes of being selected by one of the shopping Doms.

"It's been a long time, my friend," came a deep voice from behind him.

Logan slowly turned to see Trent strolling his way with a smirk plastered on his movie-star-handsome face.

"It has," he agreed, greeting Trent with a back-slapping hug reserved for old friends.

"You didn't bring Sam and Elijah?" he asked, his gaze scanning the room.

"Just me this time."

Trent's light blue eyes sparkled with curiosity. "Tell me there's no trouble in paradise."

"I wish I could," he admitted with a sigh, turning back to retrieve the drink the submissive set on the bar behind him.

"Come on," Trent urged. "Let's get comfortable. You can tell me what the hell has you hightailing it outta Dodge."

Trent led the way to a lounge reserved strictly for Dominants and their submissives. It was currently empty, but he figured that wouldn't be the case for long. It wouldn't matter that it was Monday; the club's members didn't live by strict routines. They came to play when they felt the urge, regardless of the day of the week.

"Are Clarissa and Troy here?" Logan inquired as he got comfortable in one of the oversized leather armchairs.

"Not tonight. Clarissa is working late, and Troy's at home. They do have a life of their own without me."

Sure they did. He knew Trent's version of having a life had a different definition than most people. The first time Logan had visited Trent's Dallas club, he'd been shocked by what he'd learned. Having been a member of a fetish club for most of his adult life, he hadn't been prepared for the strict rules and regulations. It wasn't just the privacy of members that Trent was protecting. He was also offering a safe place for submissives to interact with Doms and satisfy whatever kink they were into. Most important was keeping the submissives on a tight leash. Pun intended.

Trent waved someone over, then requested another drink for Logan as well as a Glenlivet for himself. The submissive scurried off to do his bidding.

"How's Sam and Elijah?" Trent inquired when they were alone again.

The pleasantries ensued for a few minutes, just two old friends catching up. It wasn't until Trent leaned forward, his piercing blue eyes locking on Logan's face, that he knew he was not going to get away with any bullshit tonight.

"Tell me why you're here."

"I want to see how it works," he told him.

Trent's dark eyebrow rose slowly, forming a perfect arch on an otherwise perfect face. "Since I know you don't live by a strict lifestyle, I can only assume you're referring to something else."

No, he wasn't referring to Domination and submission. While he enjoyed varied aspects of play, his interests were not as defined as the lifestyle enjoyed by Trent and those he associated with. However, there was a trend that he'd noticed. Many of those within Trent's social circle were in polyamorous relationships. Successful ones, from what he'd heard and seen.

He met his friend's gaze and decided to go for broke. "I've recently learned something new about myself."

"Do tell." Trent leaned back in his chair, nodding his head as though he was a therapist encouraging his patient to continue.

"I think I'm bisexual."

"The operative word being *think*?" Trent's smile formed slowly, amusement glittering in his eyes. "I take it you've developed an interest in Elijah?"

Logan nodded, took a sip of his drink.

"Am I to assume he also *thinks* he's bisexual?"

"It's complicated."

"It always is." Trent chuckled. "But complicated can be interesting. So what's the problem? Sam not into it?"

"Oh, she's into it. She's the one who instigated it."

Trent laughed. "You give her far too much credit. There's nothing to instigate. She can't make you want something you don't want, Logan. You know that. Nor is there much *thinking* involved. You're either bisexual or you're not. If you're not, you can be bi-curious. Sounds to me like you've surpassed that part. Have you fucked him yet?"

Logan forced his gaze to remain steady on Trent's face when he nodded.

"Has he fucked you?"

He shook his head.

"Is that something you want?"

A small shrug was his only answer.

"So you're still in the exploration phase? And yet you're here, a thousand miles away from home." He laughed. "Tell me you haven't fucked it up already."

Logan thought about the fact he'd slipped out without actually telling Sam or Elijah. "Wish I could," he grumbled. "Really wish I could."

WHEN ELIJAH WALKED INTO THE HOUSE A little after seven, he knew something was wrong.

The house was too quiet, most of the lights off, and there were no scents coming from the kitchen, which meant he was on his own for dinner.

"Have you heard from Logan?"

Sam's voice drifted toward him from the darkened living room. He set his computer on the kitchen table and walked toward her. He saw her sitting on the couch, her elbows resting on her knees, her back bowed as though she was holding herself together from the position alone.

"No. He's not with you?"

She shook her head. "Deanna said he went out of town."

Elijah stepped down into the living room. "I didn't realize he was supposed to."

"He wasn't. She said it was a spur-of-the-moment thing."

"You haven't talked to him?"

Her head lifted, and he noticed her eyes were red-rimmed, as though she'd been crying. "I left him three messages. He hasn't called me back. I think he hates me."

Instantly, he was at her side, pulling her against him, holding her because it made him feel better to console her. "Logan could never hate you."

"You don't know that."

It was futile to argue with Sam. She was the type to insist on getting the last word.

"Did Deanna say *where* he went?"

Sam shook her head, relaxing against him.

It was strange behavior for Logan, that was for sure. Then again, this entire year had consisted of strange behavior between all three of them.

"I pushed too hard," Sam whispered against his neck. "I asked for something he didn't want."

There was an uncomfortable pull in Elijah's chest. He wasn't sure what to think about Logan's abrupt departure, but if he knew anything about the man, he knew Logan didn't make decisions like this lightly. Wherever he went, whatever he was doing, he had a good reason. Or at least he believed he did.

"Would you like me to make dinner?" he offered.

"No." Sam nuzzled closer. "Could you just sit here with me for a while?"

"Anything you need," he whispered, pressing a kiss to her temple.

Elijah put his arm around her, pulled her close to his side, and let her warmth and her proximity soothe him.

An hour later, after Sam had gotten up to go change into her pajamas, Elijah pulled out his phone, dialed Logan's number. The call went right to voicemail, which meant he'd turned his phone off. He didn't bother leaving a message.

Now he was damn curious about what that *good reason* might be.

CHAPTER SEVENTEEN

Thursday, July 21, 2022

"HAVE YOU HEARD FROM LOGAN THIS WEEK?"

Luke hadn't even managed to get through the front door of his house when Sierra pelted him with the question. He knew from the glint in her eye and the way her fists rested firmly on her hips that his answer was going to play a huge part in how the rest of the evening went.

He thought back on the last couple of days. "No. Why?"

"He's gone," she exclaimed, and it was then he realized her eyes were wild, and there were lines pulling at her mouth. The only time she ever looked like that was when she was stressed or anxious, and usually only when it pertained to the kids.

He managed to shut the door, then set his keys on the table beside it. "What do you mean *gone*?"

Sierra threw her arms in the air and spun on her heel, marching toward the kitchen. "I mean *gone*, Luke. What else could I possibly mean?"

All righty then.

Following behind and wondering when Cole would be home so perhaps he could take the brunt of Sierra's mood, Luke braced himself for more of her frustrations. He ensured his tone was smooth and even when he joined her in the kitchen. "Maybe you could start from the beginning."

He headed to the refrigerator, pulled out the pitcher of iced tea, and turned to the island.

Her tone simmered somewhat as she perched on one of the center island stools opposite him. "Sam called me today. She said Logan left on Monday. Didn't tell her he was leaving."

That didn't sound like Logan. The man wasn't prone to running scared. However, now that Luke thought about it, a lot of Logan's actions these days had seemed uncharacteristic for him. The constant brooding, the sour mood, keeping his distance from Elijah.

"Has she talked to him?"

Sierra shrugged. "She said he texted."

"And where did he say he is?"

"Chicago," she snapped, speaking the word as though it was blasphemy.

"Well, that's not completely out of character for him," he said, grabbing a glass out of the cabinet and returning to the refrigerator for ice. "XTX has a branch in Chicago."

"That's not the point, Luke," she insisted, her eyes flashing with fury. "He left without telling her!"

Well, at least now he understood what was really bothering his wife about the whole thing. And it made sense. Kinda. Luke couldn't imagine leaving town without giving Sierra and Cole a heads-up. He recalled a time when Cole had pulled a stunt like that, disappearing in the middle of the damn night. Luke had been furious. Enough that he'd gone after the man and all but dragged him back by his hair.

As he poured his iced tea, he felt Sierra's gaze on him. He looked up to see she was glaring daggers in his direction. Clearly, she wanted him to do something about this conundrum. On a good day, Luke wouldn't mind being Sierra's knight in shining armor. He rarely got to play that role. But when it came to Logan, he wasn't sure there was anything he could do. Or *should* do.

"Why don't I call him?" he suggested, dragging his phone out of his pocket.

He dialed Logan's number, waited as it rang. The entire time, Sierra stared at him as though boring her gaze into him would make Logan answer the phone.

It didn't work. Logan didn't answer.

Luke set the phone down, took a sip of his drink. "I'm sure he's busy, probably wor—"

"He went to Dichotomy," she spat.

"Then you know he's all right if he went to—" He frowned as her words processed. "Wait. What?"

"Dichotomy," Sierra repeated slowly, clearly for the imbecile in the room. "Sara texted me, said she talked to Trent, and he mentioned seeing Logan on Monday. At the club. In Chicago!"

Son of a bitch.

"You have to do something, Luke," she insisted.

"Me? What the hell do you want me to do? Logan's a big boy. He can take care of himself."

Clearly *not* the right thing to say. Sierra's eyes flashed blue fire as she stared at him.

"Let me rephrase that," he said carefully. "What would you *like* me to do?"

"Go after him."

Luke cocked an eyebrow. She was serious. She wanted him to hop on a plane and traipse across the country to get Logan and what? Drag him back by his hair? No, thank you very fucking much. Luke knew better than to stick his nose in his brother's business.

"It's the least you can do," she tacked on.

Jesus. How the fuck did he always end up in the middle of everyone else's shit?

The door from the garage opened, and Cole stepped into the kitchen. He must've sensed the tension vibrating from their wife, because his eyebrows rose slowly. The man was brave; Luke would give him that. Had their positions been reversed, Luke would've turned right around and gone back the way he'd come.

"What's goin' on?" Cole drawled, glancing between them as he slowly closed the door, sealing off his safe exit.

"Logan abandoned Sam," Sierra accused, her words laced with venom.

"We don't know that for sure, Sierra."

Cole's gaze darted to Luke for more details. He offered a slight shrug. Truth was, at this point, Sierra knew a hell of a lot more than he did.

"Luke's gonna go after him," Sierra said, evidently having decided for him.

Again, Cole looked at him.

Since Sierra was looking at Cole, she didn't see Luke adamantly shaking his head even as he said, "Yeah. I'm goin' after him."

Two hours later, Luke was pacing the back patio, his phone to his ear. It was the fourth time he'd called his brother since he got home. He figured at some point Logan would get pissed enough and turn off his phone, or the asshole would just answer. He was praying for the latter.

The ringing stopped, but the call didn't disconnect. There was no response on the other end.

"Logan?"

There was a grunt that *could* be deciphered as a greeting. You know, if the guy on the other end of the line was an asshole.

Eh. Fitting.

"It's about fucking time," Luke blasted, exhaling his relief. Maybe now he could get this resolved without getting on a plane. "What the fuck is wrong with you?"

"I knew I should've ignored your call," Logan grumbled.

"Where are you?"

"Chicago."

So at least that much of the story was true. Luke belted out his next question: "Does Sam know?"

"She does," he said in that irritating way of his that made Luke feel like an idiot.

Hmm. Maybe Sam was being a drama queen, getting Sierra riled up for no reason.

"So you didn't slink out of town without telling anyone?"

His brother's lack of response told him at least another part of the story was true.

"What the fuck, Logan?"

"Look, I don't have it in me to listen to your shit right now," Logan growled roughly.

"Well, I don't have it in me to be the voice of reason," Luke countered. "That's your job, brother, so we're even."

A heavy exhale sounded. "I've got enough shit on my mind, Luke. I don't need you harping on me. Say your fucking piece so I can get on with it."

Luke could hear the wariness of his brother's tone. Had he ever heard Logan so distraught?

It was enough to sober him somewhat. "Is everything all right?"

"No, goddammit, it's not. But that's not your business."

The storm stopped churning inside him as though he'd prepared his whole life for the one time when his brother might need him to be reasonable and considerate. Logan was the solid one, the guy everyone could lean on when they needed to bend an ear. Not that Luke had ever done much leaning, but he'd always known his brother would be there for him if and when it came down to it.

Which meant Sierra had been right in suggesting he go after him, and now Luke had to be the strong one. The one with the right words that would coax the problem out so he could fix it.

"Fair enough," Luke conceded. "But when you're ready to talk, you'll call me?"

Okay, so he wasn't going to take the plunge all at once. That was just stupid.

"Yeah." Logan sighed. "Sure. I gotta go, Luke."

He didn't bother trying to keep the man on the phone. Something had crawled up Logan's ass, and he obviously wasn't interested in sharing the details, which meant Luke had to suck it up and go after him. It was part of the role of being Logan's twin, not to mention his best friend.

Luke tucked his phone back in his pocket and turned to see Sierra standing by the house, her eyebrows low, face scrunched with worry.

"Did you talk to him?" Her tone was far calmer than when she'd barked at him earlier.

"I did." He moved toward her, put his hands on her shoulders, and pulled her closer. "He *is* in Chicago."

"So you're going to get him?"

Luke peered down at his wife. He loved her with everything he was, which was the only reason he was willing to make an impromptu trip to talk to his brother. He seriously doubted Logan was going to break down and share his gooey, mushy feelings, but the least he could do was try.

"If it'll make you feel better, then yes. I'll go up there to talk to him."

She sighed, leaning into him. "I'll tell Sam. She'll be relieved."

"No," he insisted, pulling back to stare down into her face. "We have no idea what's going on between them, and it's not my place to get in the middle of it." He lifted his chin, cutting her off before she could argue. "I said I'd go, and I will. But only to talk to him. Let them work this out between them. You don't need to get in the middle of it, either."

"She's my best friend."

"I understand that."

"And Logan's gone and lost his mind."

Luke wondered how many people had thought that about him back when he'd been confused about what he wanted from Cole. Regardless, he didn't want Sam blowing up his phone because she knew he would have Logan's attention once he arrived.

"Keep it to yourself for now," he told her.

The look she gave him was one he was familiar with. He knew the instant he was out the door, Sierra would be on the phone with Sam, filling her in on every detail right down to how much iced tea he'd poured into his glass during their conversation earlier.

Cole opened the back door, peered over at them. "Everything cool?"

He knew the man was asking about Logan, so he nodded in response. "I'm gonna go to Chicago. See if I can talk to him."

Cole stood up straight. "Want me to go with you?"

Luke had considered it. He wouldn't mind the company, and he enjoyed any time he spent with either of them alone. However, this wasn't one of those times when he thought it wise to have more eyes on the situation.

"I'm good," he said. "It'll only be a couple of days, tops."

Cole nodded. "I'll get you a flight for tomorrow morning."

"First class," he reminded him.

He received a smile before Cole disappeared back into the house.

"It'll be fine," Luke assured Sierra.

"It better be."

He laughed, couldn't help it. Leave it to Sierra to hold him accountable for her best friend's happiness and his brother's idiocy.

ELIJAH CAME HOME ON THURSDAY EVENING TO find Sam curled up in Logan's recliner. She wasn't asleep, nor was she watching TV. She was simply staring at the bookshelf where all the framed pictures sat, proudly reflecting on a much happier time.

He offered to make her dinner, but she turned him down the same way she had every other day that week. He hated seeing her so distraught, which was why he had decided tonight he would tell her his thoughts on what Logan was doing. Although he knew it wouldn't help her forgive Logan for running away, he hoped she might have a bit of sympathy for the situation.

Then again, it could also come back to bite him in the ass. Revealing the fact that he and Logan had been intimate on more than one occasion—and they'd both kept it from her—was a risk. One he was willing to take if he could ease her mind a little bit.

Elijah shored up his nerve by going to the liquor cabinet and retrieving a bottle of single malt scotch. He poured two rocks glasses, then delivered one to Sam before taking a seat on the sofa.

"There's something I need to tell you," he said, not realizing how horrible that sounded until he saw Sam's eyes widen with shock.

"It's not about Logan," he hurried to clarify. "Well, not anything about his trip."

She relaxed somewhat, taking a sip and not speaking.

That was another thing he'd gotten used to this week. Sam had been quiet, as though she was mourning the loss of something vital. He understood her reasons, which was why he hadn't pushed for her to open up to him.

He took a drink, set his glass aside, and shifted to the edge of the cushion. Planting his elbows on his knees and clasping his hands together, he met Sam's stare.

"Not too long before Logan left, something happened between him and me."

Sam shifted, sitting up in the chair and lowering the footrest, her full attention on him.

"Last Friday, before you got home"—Elijah cleared his throat—"Logan and I ... had sex."

She inhaled sharply as though he'd slapped her. "Sex?"

"Yes. You were out with McKenna and Ashleigh."

Her tone was hard when she ground out, "I remember."

He took a deep breath and kept his eyes pinned on her face. "Neither of us meant for it to happen, but it did. One thing led to another and ... well..."

"You had sex," she repeated.

Elijah nodded.

"In our bed."

He nodded again.

"And neither of you mentioned it."

That was what he felt bad about, and he suspected that was what was eating at Logan.

"Was that the first time?"

"Yes."

Her gaze shifted to the photos briefly before returning to him. "Was that the only time y'all were intimate that I don't know about?"

"No."

He could see the hurt in her eyes. "Let me guess. Whatever it was happened right before Luke's party."

"Yes." Elijah could tell she wanted more details, so he explained how he had given Logan a blow job when Logan had been working out. "I reacted," he tacked on. "I was fed up with how he was acting, so I pushed. He didn't reciprocate, so it's completely on me."

Her eyebrows dipped low. "You're not to blame for this, Eli. This is on me."

"Sam—"

She held up a hand. "It's true. I'm the one who instigated this at the cabin. I set it in motion."

"We shouldn't have kept it from you."

"No," she agreed. "You shouldn't have. What did you think I would do? Get angry?"

He didn't respond. The last thing he wanted to tell Sam was that he didn't tell her because those moments had felt private between him and Logan. And yes, partly because he didn't want her to get upset. They had yet to define how this was supposed to work.

"Y'all seem to forget that I understand how complicated this is." Her voice wavered slightly. "It wasn't too long ago that I fell in love with you. And what you and I have ... I don't always share it with Logan."

He honestly hadn't thought about it that way, but yeah, he could see her point. It was almost the same thing, but now in reverse.

"I get it, Eli. I do. What I don't understand is why Logan is shutting me out. I don't need the details, damn it."

He cocked an eyebrow because he wasn't sure he believed that.

"I don't," she repeated hotly. "What I need is honesty. I need some reassurances. Not for my husband to run away because he's confused about his feelings."

"Did he say that he was?"

"No, but I'm not stupid. You two might think I don't notice the heated glances, but I live here, too. I can feel the tension coming off both of you all the damn time." She sighed heavily. "What kind of idiot would I have to be not to see that y'all want some privacy? I mean, seriously. Logan waited until I was in Vegas before making a move on you."

He had no idea what to say to that, so he sat silently, watching the defeat on her beautiful face.

"I'm gonna go to bed," she finally said, setting her glass on the coffee table. "I appreciate you telling me, though it might just be too little too late."

His chest constricted, the pain those words incited was breathtaking. The thought of losing Sam because of this... It was more than he could bear.

Two hours later, after he made himself a sandwich and managed to choke down half of it, Elijah decided to go to bed. He considered sleeping in the other room but changed his mind. He was not about to put more distance between him and Sam than there already was. He needed to work on a way to salvage what the three of them had, not cause more problems.

He quietly entered their bedroom, stripped out of his clothes, then crawled into bed behind Sam. She was curled up, hugging Logan's pillow. It wasn't until he was pressed up against her, spooning her, that he felt her body shudder, heard her soft sobs.

"Sam," he whispered, gently gripping her shoulder and rolling her to her back. He propped himself up and peered down into her face. It was too dark to make out much, but he saw the tears streaming down her cheeks. He brushed them away with his thumb, turning her face to look at him.

"You're breaking my heart," he said softly.

"Since mine is shattered, it seems fair," she retorted, turning toward him and burying her face in his chest.

He slid his hand over her hair, consoling her the best he could, although there was a cold chill deep in his bones. It was fear, he realized. Fear of losing the most precious thing in his life.

For the past four days, Elijah had dissected every second of his time with Sam and Logan. He'd thought about the good times, stressed over the bad. As he was doing that, he'd realized this was possibly the worst position they'd ever been in. At least as far as their relationship went.

"Sam?"

"Hmm?"

"I love you."

She sniffled, her arm sliding under his, her hand clutching his back. "I love you, too. Nothing will change that."

He took a full breath for the first time in hours.

She inched closer, so he held her tighter. Elijah pressed a kiss to her temple as he leaned over her, holding her against him, wanting to feel her warmth, to let himself believe that they could work through this.

Her lips pressed to his throat, dragging a rough moan from his chest. "Sam."

"No talking," she whispered, her arm banding around his back as she attempted to pull him over her.

Elijah didn't hesitate, shifting so she was beneath him, her soft skin pressed to his. Their mouths found each other in the dark. The kiss that ensued was slow and sweet, a gentle, intimate mating that he felt in the depths of his soul.

When her hands gripped his ass, Elijah knew what she wanted. He didn't hesitate, sliding his hand between them, caressing between her thighs, ensuring she was ready for him. It took only a moment before she was slick, her moans growing louder as he inhaled them, their tongues still doing a sensual dance.

"Make love to me," she mumbled against his lips.

Shifting his lower body, he angled his cock at her entrance, pushed his hips forward, and sank into the blessed heat of her body. Sam sighed, and he groaned as the pleasure consumed him. They didn't rush. There was no chasing a release this time. It was a sweet descent into heaven as he rocked his body into hers, loving her as he had a thousand times before.

Her soft fingers teased over his back as her hands roamed, her hips rolling to accept his gentle thrusts. God, he loved this woman. Loved her in a way he'd never thought possible.

"Eli..." Sam whimpered. "God—Eli..."

Sam shuddered beneath him, her pussy clutching him as she succumbed to her orgasm. He continued to thrust inside her, allowing her body to milk his release from him.

When he was spent, he rolled to his back, bringing her with him until she was draped over him, a soft, warm weight that soothed every part of him.

"I love you," he whispered, pressing his lips to her shoulder.

"I love you, too."

For a brief moment, there was a lull in the storm. At least for him. Elijah knew it would take time and a hell of a lot of communication, but he felt more confident that they could weather this one just like all the others.

CHAPTER EIGHTEEN

Friday, July 22, 2022

LOGAN SPENT THE ENTIRE WEEK IN CHICAGO.

On Monday night, after he'd left Dichotomy, he'd texted Sam to let her know everything was fine and explained he had some things to take care of for XTX. On Tuesday morning, feeling somewhat less frazzled, he had called her to explain, only for his call to go to voicemail. The same on Wednesday and Thursday, too. She wasn't answering, nor was Elijah, and he honestly couldn't say he blamed them. That first night he was here, he had missed numerous calls from both of them, and he figured they were pissed because of it.

However, they were responding to text messages, which he took as a good sign. He hated himself for lying to them, claiming he had business up here that needed his attention. In all fairness, he did go to the XTX offices every day, putting in his time. And each night, he ventured to Dichotomy, never straying farther than the Dom lounge on the main floor despite Trent's suggestion that he wander through so he could feel the energy coming from the play. Since energy wasn't what he was after, he'd politely declined and settled for conversing with some of the Doms he'd met over the years.

And here he was again on Friday, still searching for something he wasn't even sure existed but too scared to leave before he found it.

NICOLE EDWARDS

He'd come straight from the office, checking in with security at the front door and being granted entry. After being told they would let Trent know he was there, Logan ventured over to the bar. The submissive working behind it offered a smile and then started making his drink without him having to ask for it.

Someone cleared their throat behind him, then Trent's voice followed. "I figured you would've gone back by now. Should I be worried?"

That was the question of the day. Logan knew he should've gone back long before now, and he wanted to, but he knew he wasn't mentally prepared to deal with the situation he found himself in. At this point, he was already in the doghouse, so he figured he might as well see if he could find some clarity before he went back to Dallas.

"Don't get me wrong, I'm happy to see you," Trent said, his grin widening as though he harbored a secret. "I'm just not sure what to do with *two* of you at the same time."

Logan's eyes darted behind Trent when the man stepped out of the way. "Son of a bitch."

"Nice to see you, too," Luke greeted with a shit-eating grin. "It's kinda weird that our roles are reversed, don't you think?"

Trent chuckled. "I was thinking the same thing."

Logan rolled his eyes, then turned back to the bar, thanking the submissive when she passed over his drink.

"I've been giving some thought to your situation," Trent said, motioning for Logan to follow. "But I need to make my rounds first. You boys can sit down and be good, or you can go with me."

Logan felt Luke's eyes on him. He knew if he opted to sit down, his twin was going to read him the riot act. On the other hand, he knew Trent was intent on him taking the tour, and when Trent wanted something, the man didn't stop until he got it. Perhaps it was the lesser of two evils.

He sighed, letting them see how put out he was by his options. "Come on," Trent urged.

"Why're you here?" Logan asked Luke when he forced his feet to move, falling in step with Trent with Luke moving up to his side.

"Figured you needed a shoulder to cry on." Luke patted his shoulder. "I've got two. Pick one, and once you let it all out, you can get your panties out of the knot they're in. I *won't* be helping with that part."

Logan groaned. This was not how he'd seen this night going.

211

"I haven't told him anything," Trent said, chuckling. "Although he's a persistent fucker, this one."

"One of my finer qualities," Luke quipped. "I already know what your problem is."

"Do you?" Logan grumbled.

Luke looked proud of himself when he said, "I do. I think you're hung up on the bisexual nature of your urges."

Ah, hell.

"I was thinking the same thing," Trent added.

Logan didn't respond. He could see how they would jump to that conclusion, although it couldn't be further from the truth. At this point, accepting that he was bisexual was the least of his worries.

"I can hear that hamster wheel turning," Luke said. "We might be off on our diagnosis, Trent."

Trent stopped, peered over at Logan, and frowned. "That was only one of my thoughts."

Of course it was.

"What else were you thinking, Dr. Freud?" Luke asked Trent, never looking away from Logan.

Trent held Logan's stare, and there was a hint of sympathy in his blue eyes. "If it's not that, then you're hung up on the fact you've got real feelings for someone who's not Sam."

Well, hell. Maybe the guy was a mind reader after all.

Luke nodded slowly. "I think that hamster just had an aneurysm, so you might be onto something there."

Thankfully, Trent continued to walk toward the stairs that would lead down to the dungeon, giving Logan a moment's reprieve from the scrutiny of their gazes.

"Is that it?" Luke asked.

"I've never loved anyone but Sam."

"But you do now."

It wasn't a question, so Logan didn't respond.

"I'm no expert on matters of the heart," Trent said from in front of them. "You of all people should know that. But I did find what I was looking for. Troy and Clarissa did, too. With each other and with me."

"But you were always looking for that," Logan countered.

"Was I?" Trent barked a gruff, disbelieving sound. "Shit. For the longest time, I had no fucking clue *what* I was looking for. Neither did you, if I recall correctly. You met Sam, fell in love, married her. Then Elijah came along and disrupted the whole process."

"He didn't disrupt it," Logan said defensively.

Trent chuckled as though he'd expected Logan's rebuttal.

"Sam fell in love with Eli," Logan corrected, swallowing hard as he recalled how difficult it had been at the time to acknowledge that. But he had. Not only acknowledged but accepted and welcomed Elijah into their lives. If he was being honest with himself, he couldn't imagine his life without Elijah in it. And not only because of this thing between them.

"So you fought her tooth and nail?" Trent snorted. "You weren't the one to introduce them? To bring Elijah into your relationship?"

Who knew the guy had a memory like a fucking elephant?

They reached the bottom of the stairs, and Logan avoided the questions by looking around, taking it all in. Although he wasn't into BDSM to the degree these people were, he found the interactions highly erotic. There were various scenes underway. On one side, there was a woman draped over a spanking bench while a man stood several feet behind her wielding a long, leather whip. Most of the onlookers were here, watching as the Dom skillfully and carefully snapped the leather against her bare ass. Two dungeon monitors were standing nearby, keeping an eye on things.

In the center of the space, he noticed Benjamin Snowden—one of the partners of Chatter PR—strapped to a St. Andrew's Cross while Justin Parker set up the scene with their submissive, Addison.

"If you want to get into a discussion about complex relationships," Trent said, gesturing toward the trio with his chin, "think on that one for a while. Addison's a submissive, and Justin's a Dom. Clear, delineated boundaries. However, Ben's a Switch, which means he needs to dominate and submit. They live the lifestyle full-time, which, as you can imagine, is a delicate balance to ensure everyone gets what they need."

Logan could see how that could get complicated.

"But I think your situation compares more to this one," Trent said, moving on to another scene.

Logan followed with Luke acting as his shadow as he surveyed the scenes.

"Jamie's a submissive," Logan said, referring to the woman sitting astride a Sybian machine while her two Doms looked on. "How's that compare?"

Trent stopped, angled toward Logan while still watching the submissive riding the sex machine. "She is definitely submissive," he said approvingly. "And while Edge and Cav are Doms, neither has a submissive bone in their body. Yet they manage to work things out between them because they love each other." Trent looked back at him. "All three of them."

"You mean Edge and Cav..." Luke prompted. "They what? Dominate each other?"

Trent grinned. "As I said, they make it work."

Logan wasn't sure what to say to that because, yes, he could relate in that regard. If he were to compare his relationship to one, it would be this one. Two dominant men loving one submissive woman. Not that Sam was submissive in any way other than the bedroom. The woman was a force to be reckoned with. She had a backbone of steel and a will of granite. When she wanted something, she didn't hesitate to go after it.

One of the many things he loved about her.

"Is that what this is?" Luke asked, all amusement gone. "Things are serious between you and Elijah?"

"Hell if I know," he mumbled under his breath, unable to look at his brother for fear the man would see right through him.

As though realizing he wasn't ready to talk, Trent led the way through the dungeon, past a few more scenes underway. Logan skimmed each space, not seeing much of anything. His mind was as chaotic as when he stepped foot on the plane in Dallas, hating himself for running away but unsure how to handle the significant shift his life had taken in recent months.

"Are you worried you won't give Elijah what he needs?" Trent asked, keeping his voice low as they continued back toward the stairs leading to the main floor.

Logan glanced at Luke, hating the fact his brother was here. While he appreciated that he'd come all this way, he wasn't sure he wanted to burden Luke with what was going on in his life.

"If it's what I think it is, I've already been through it," Luke said, his tone sympathetic.

He glanced between the two men, then decided fuck it. He still hadn't found the answers he was looking for, so maybe this was his chance.

"I'm not worried about Elijah or whatever this is we've got going," he said, admitting it aloud for the first time. "It's Sam I'm worried about."

Trent's eyebrows V'd over scrutinizing eyes. "It's more than sex for you. With Elijah, I mean."

Logan took a deep breath, exhaled slowly. "I have no idea what it is."

Luke chimed in. "But you wouldn't be worried about Sam if you didn't already know you have feelings for Elijah."

He didn't respond. He didn't need to. They had nailed it.

"So tell me this," Trent said as they reached the top of the stairs. "Is Sam on board with what's going on?"

"I told you, she instigated it."

"Sure. She instigated the intimacy, you said. Some women like the idea of two alpha men going at each other. Hell, some men like that, too. Everyone has a kink or two, regardless of whether they'll admit it. Is she okay with the two of you being intimate when she's not there?"

"She didn't mind hearing about it," he said, feeling a bit uncomfortable that he was having this conversation.

"So you've told her about…?" Trent waved his hand, letting the sentence hang.

"Told her about what?" Luke inquired. "You and Elijah hook up?"

Logan's eyes narrowed on Luke.

He didn't dignify that with a response, but he didn't need to. Recognition had already dawned in Luke's eyes.

WELL, HELL.

Admittedly, Luke had suspected there was something going on between Logan and Elijah. He'd first noticed something different between them back at the beginning of the year. Nothing overt. Just some stolen glances from time to time, the way Logan watched him the same way he watched Sam. It was obvious they'd gotten closer, but he hadn't figured it was intimate between them.

Luke had always admired the relationship the two men had. It was born of a fondness for the woman they loved. And Luke understood it because, while his relationship with Cole was intimate and forged in love, they shared the same sort of bond as well. They both loved Sierra, and they did what was necessary to make her happy. In turn, Sierra acknowledged that they shared something between them, too. Something that had modified the dynamic of their relationship.

And it looked as though the universe was playing the same game with Logan.

"I need another drink," Logan grumbled, avoiding looking directly at either of them.

"Come on then," Trent said.

Luke considered what he'd learned in the last few minutes while he followed Trent and Logan into the Doms' lounge. They found an empty spot in the back corner, away from a few others who were chatting quietly over drinks.

With a simple snap of his fingers, Trent summoned a submissive over. A guy wearing a leather chest harness and tight leather briefs hurried over. Luke watched him, smiling to himself as he noticed how eager the guy was to please the man he referred to as Master Ramsey.

When the guy scurried off to do Trent's bidding, Luke looked at Logan. "Get me up to speed here. Something happen between you and Elijah?"

Logan nodded.

"And Sam doesn't know?"

Logan shook his head.

"Because you don't want her to know?" Trent inquired.

"Because it just happened," Logan said defensively. "And only once."

Luke barked a laugh. "What? You tripped and fell, and on your way to face-planting on the floor, your dick landed inside Elijah?"

Logan glared at him.

"What? That's how you make it sound. Like it was a fucking accident."

The submissive returned, and Logan's hand shot out to grab one of the drinks from the tray. He brought the glass to his mouth and guzzled.

"Have Troy and Clarissa arrived?" Trent asked the submissive.

"Not yet, Master Ramsey."

Luke took his drink from the tray, then watched with amusement.

"Let them know where I am when they do."

The guy's eyes glittered with so much worship, it was like he'd received a request from a deity. "Of course, Master Ramsey."

Oh, what it must be like to have your ass kissed so hard it left an imprint.

Amused by the situation, Luke waited until they were alone again before addressing Logan. "Has it only been the one encounter Sam doesn't know about?"

Logan took another gulp of his drink, then swallowed. "No."

Luke didn't need the details, nor did he want them. The only reason he asked was to try to understand just how complicated Logan's feelings had gotten for Elijah. He knew from this little excursion of Logan's that the man was dealing with some serious matters of the heart.

"You obviously came here for a reason," Trent said, leaning back in his chair and regarding Logan. "Might as well get it all off your chest. Otherwise, you've wasted a trip."

Logan downed what was left of his drink and set it aside before focusing on them. "Fine."

Luke raised an eyebrow, silently urging his brother to talk.

"It started last year. I kissed Elijah."

"Was it a random thing?"

Logan shook his head. "We were playing one of Sam's games."

Luke grinned. That didn't surprise him.

"I kissed him, but that's as far as it went. I knew something changed between us that night, but I managed to shrug it off."

"Or you thought you did," Trent corrected.

"Yeah." Logan sighed, his eyes shifting to the floor. "I was curious. Elijah was, too. He wanted to talk about it, but I shut him down every time." He looked up. "Then Sam went to Vegas, and an opportunity presented itself. Things progressed from there."

If Luke knew anything about his brother, it was that Logan didn't wait for opportunities, he made them.

"I have yet to hear the concerning part," Luke chided.

"I thought I was doing it for Sam's benefit," Logan said gruffly.

"But it's not for her," Trent acknowledged.

Logan shook his head. "What I want from him…"

"You don't want it to always involve her," Luke said, understanding.

Logan's gaze slid over, and Luke saw the pain of that acknowledgment.

"What did you think you'd find by coming here?" Luke asked, curious how it had evolved into such a mess.

"I have no fucking clue. I thought ... I thought if I could understand the dynamic of others in a similar situation, it might help me figure it out."

Luke chuckled. "And I'm not enough of a role model for you?"

For the first time tonight, Logan smiled.

Trent leaned toward Logan, resting his elbow on the arm of the chair. "You want my honest opinion, or did you come here for me to placate you?"

"Honest opinion," Logan replied, keeping his gaze intently focused on Trent.

"I think you're complicating matters."

Luke would agree with that assessment.

"You don't even know what you want from Elijah yet."

"I know *exactly* what I want from him," Logan countered, his voice low. "And what I want doesn't involve Sam. Not all the time."

Trent's blue eyes widened infinitesimally. "You think you're betraying her because you want Elijah to yourself."

Luke watched Logan, saw the guilt plastered all over his face.

"I could never betray her," he argued.

Trent's expression reflected his agreement. "I'm sure the same could be said for her, could it not?"

"She wouldn't betray me, no."

Trent's voice lowered once more. "Yet she's in love with another man."

"She's... Yes. But that's different."

A smirk formed as Trent's eyebrows rose slowly. "Is it?"

Luke knew from experience that it wasn't easy to accept the simplicity of it. Trent was right in that regard. Logan's relationship was no longer that much different than Luke's.

"Master Ramsey?"

Trent looked up at the submissive who'd delivered their drinks.

"Troy and Clarissa have arrived."

He nodded, then turned back to them. "If you'll excuse me. I haven't seen them all day."

Luke smiled.

As Trent was getting to his feet, he looked down at Logan. "I suggest you do some serious soul searching. There's only so much you can learn from anyone else's situation." He nodded in Luke's direction. "But if you look in the mirror sitting beside you, you might already see exactly how it can play out. If you'd stop being so goddamn stubborn."

"Thanks for the advice," Logan muttered.

"Anytime. I'll check in with you both later. Stay, drink. Enjoy yourselves."

Luke waited until Trent strolled away before shifting in his chair, angling to face his brother more fully. It didn't surprise him that Logan didn't look him in the eye. He knew all about retreating from the complicated stuff. Back before he'd settled down, gotten married, and had babies, Luke had mastered the art of it.

Which meant he also had a fairly good idea of what not to do.

"You need to tell her how you feel about Elijah," Luke suggested. "Come clean about what's happened between the two of you."

"It feels like cheating."

"Maybe. But I don't think you give your wife enough credit. She knows there's something going on with you. Y'all've been together long enough she can read you like a fucking book. And she's scared right now."

Logan's gaze lifted. "Why do you say that?"

He huffed, unable to believe his brother was too blind to see that his actions were raising red flags all around.

"You left her without saying goodbye. Jesus Christ, Logan. What woman do you know who wouldn't think it was her fault?"

His eyes widened. "It's not."

"No," he agreed. "It's not. But until you tell her otherwise, she's gonna continue to think it is."

Logan didn't respond.

"Look around you," Luke said, motioning to the space. "You came here to see how others make it work. Has it helped?"

Still no response.

"I didn't think so. And you know why? These people—me included—haven't gone through exactly what you're going through. It might seem similar, but you can't model your reactions based on anyone else's relationships. Think about all the people who couldn't make their complicated situations work. It wasn't because they modeled themselves on someone else's outcome. It's because they didn't include the people who mattered most."

Logan's eyes narrowed. "Since when did you get so fucking smart?"

Luke laughed. "You don't give me enough credit, brother. I've always been the smart one."

CHAPTER NINETEEN

Saturday, July 23, 2022

WHEN ELIJAH SUGGESTED THEY GO TO DEVOTION, Sam hadn't been sure she could deal with seeing so many of her friends. Since the thought of sitting at home and waiting to see if Logan would show up had felt like an even worse option, she hadn't been able to refuse.

As she sat at one of the small tables with Sierra, she couldn't remember if she'd ever been here without Logan. It didn't matter. Right now, she didn't care that he wasn't here. Well, that was only a small lie. She did care because she wanted him to explain why he'd disappeared and what he'd accomplished while he was gone. Thanks to Sierra spilling that she'd convinced Luke to go after him, the fear and anxiety she'd had when she first learned that Logan went to Chicago had been replaced by anger, which grew increasingly stronger as each day passed and he didn't come home.

Since the moment she learned that Logan had been spotted at Dichotomy, she had purposely ignored every single one of his phone calls. It was a petty way of paying him back for hurting her, but she couldn't help it. Sam was a lot of things, but she was loyal and committed, and she never would've considered pulling the stunt Logan had. No matter how difficult things got between them. He'd left without so much as a word to do what? Hang out at a BDSM club? Who did that? Certainly not any married couples she knew. Add to it the fact that Logan hadn't bothered to tell either of them when he was coming home—then Friday had come and gone—she had finally reached her tipping point.

So she spent a few hours at Devotion, hanging with her friends and pretending nothing was wrong. She watched Elijah from across the room, not wanting to interrupt since he seemed to be in a deep conversation with Cole. She wondered what they talked about. Were they comparing notes, maybe? Like how Logan was pulling a stunt that Luke was famous for? Or rather, he had been before he'd settled down and accepted who he was.

Was that it? Was Logan confused about what he wanted? Or maybe he'd realized what he *didn't* want and was too scared to tell them? The most troubling question was: what if he didn't want *her* anymore?

Her chest constricted, making it hard to breathe. She reminded herself that there were others here. She damn sure didn't want them to see her fall apart.

"Ummm … Sam."

Pulling herself from her scattered thoughts, she glanced over at Sierra. Her best friend was staring behind her, so she turned to see Logan walking in, his hands tucked in his pockets and the full heat of his gaze on her.

Her heart kicked hard in her chest. At least he was alive and well. The relief was potent but not nearly strong enough to chase away her anger.

As she stared at him, she considered launching to her feet and storming out, but she remained still. Sierra was the only person who knew that Logan hadn't simply gone on a business trip this week, and she didn't want everyone to know her business.

She cast a dismissive glance his way, then turned her attention back to the Sierra. Unfortunately, her friend chose that moment to excuse herself. Rather than grab Sierra's arm and force her to remain in her seat, Sam sighed heavily and resigned herself to confronting Logan here and now.

"Hey, baby," he said when he approached.

Her chest tightened at the soft hum of his words even as the knife edge of her anger dug into her soul.

She tried to be flippant when she said, "Hey," back, but the quiver in her voice clearly gave her away.

"Can I join you?"

Her breath shuddered. When had they gotten to a place where he had to ask something like that?

She managed a nod as she stared up and drank in the sight of him. He looked good, although she could see storm clouds brewing in his hazel eyes. She prayed that was remorse and not guilt etched into the hard lines of his face.

Not trusting her voice, she gestured toward the chair Sierra had vacated.

Logan pulled it around closer to her, then sat down. He left her no room to move when he spread his knees wide and scooted even closer.

"Baby, I'm sorry," he said, his voice so low she could barely hear him.

"You should be," she bit back, intending to let him hear her fury, but a sob came out and ruined the effect. Not in all the time she'd known him had he hurt her quite this much. They'd been through so much together, but never once had he done something like this. Turned his back on her. Abandoned her.

"Sam."

She took a deep, shuddering breath.

"Baby, look at me."

She couldn't, but he stole her choice from her by lightly gripping her chin and turning her head toward him.

When their eyes met, she felt the tears forming, hated herself for being such a wuss when she wanted to blast him for doing this, for jeopardizing all they'd built over the years.

Sam pulled back, shook her head, and swallowed the hot ball of emotion clogging her throat. "I can't do this here, Logan. I can't."

She pushed to her feet and walked away, heading right for Elijah.

Either he could take her home or she would drive herself. It didn't matter, but she needed to get away from all the prying eyes.

ELIJAH LOOKED UP IN TIME TO SEE Sam hurrying toward him, her face pinched in a frown, her eyes glittering with what looked a hell of a lot like tears.

He was on his feet in a second, moving toward her. "What's wrong?"

She shook her head but didn't respond. Elijah looked past her to see where she'd come from, and that was when he noticed Logan standing at the table Sam had been sitting at, his focus on them.

Well, damn. That was the last person he expected to show up here tonight.

Their eyes met across the distance, and Elijah saw the man's pain. Whatever he'd done, or for whatever reason, he was beating himself up about it. Probably deserved to be, but Elijah couldn't fault the man entirely.

Yes, he was angry that Logan had left for a fucking week without warning, but more so because he'd hurt Sam in the process. Elijah didn't fully understand Logan's reason for doing something so drastic, but he knew it had everything to do with him. Unfortunately, Sam had been caught in the crossfire.

"Please take me home," Sam finally said, leaning in but not quite touching him.

"Of course."

After a quick goodbye to Cole and without a word to Logan, Elijah steered Sam out of the club and to the car. He had expected the man to follow them, but he wasn't behind them. Not even when they were pulling out of the parking lot.

Half an hour later, they were home, and Sam headed straight for the bedroom, claiming she was tired. He considered following her to calm her down but decided it was best to give her some space.

Elijah grabbed a beer from the refrigerator and headed out to the back porch. He sat in one of the chairs near the back door, staring out at the red lights in the pool. He wondered if Sam had been angry when she changed the color this time. She rarely used red, but it seemed somehow fitting to her mood. If he had selected the color, it would've been dark blue because it reminded him of her tears.

Where the fuck had things gone so horribly wrong? Not counting the beginning of their relationship, this was the biggest hurdle they'd ever come up against. Never had he considered that one kiss in the cabin all those months ago would've led them here, caused such a massive rift between them.

Where the hell were they supposed to go from here? Elijah saw only two options: move forward or move back. There was no standing still, because if they did, there was a good chance it would all implode. He loved Sam and in no way wanted to risk losing her, but as he'd admitted at the cemetery, he was sure he'd gone and fallen in love with Logan somewhere along the way. By taking a step back, rewinding to the point before they'd changed the very foundation of their relationship, Elijah would still have them both. Even if that meant loving Logan from afar and pretending his feelings didn't exist. He could do it, and he would if it came down to it. Above all else, Sam held his heart, and he would do nothing to forsake her.

The back door opened, drawing his attention. He looked over, expecting to see Sam, but found Logan standing in the doorway, his eyes downcast, his shoulders slumped.

"She's not out here," Elijah told him, settling his gaze back on the water.

"Can we talk?"

"If you're asking whether we're capable…" Elijah sighed. "It's long overdue."

However, if they were going to have a heart-to-heart, Elijah was going to need another beer. Rather than mention it, he got to his feet and headed into the house, moving past Logan without so much as brushing the front of his shirt.

He grabbed another beer from the refrigerator and popped the top, then turned and leaned against the counter.

Elijah decided not to pull his punches. "You hurt her. Badly."

The man who usually kept his emotions masked looked like he'd been sucker-punched with that one. Elijah didn't feel bad about it because that was his main point of contention with this entire fucked-up situation. Sam was their heart and soul, and he'd long ago understood that the main objective in keeping this thing between them working smoothly was to ensure she was happy. With his actions, Logan had taken that rule, snapped it in half over his knee, and tossed it into a fire.

Could they even come back from this? Would it take Elijah making the sacrifice in order to fix things?

Fuck, he hoped not.

Elijah refrained from telling Logan that he was willing to go back to the way things had been before. Although it was an option, it wasn't something he wanted to resort to unless absolutely necessary.

Minutes ticked by until it became apparent that Logan wasn't going to talk. The man was a fucking wreck, and Elijah couldn't help but feel some sympathy for him. He was about to tell him as much when Logan cleared his throat.

"I remember the first night you took Sam out. Just the two of you."

Elijah took a pull on his beer, keeping the bottle low so he could hold Logan's stare.

"An art gallery of all fucking places. You and your class and sophistication and that goddamn accent." Logan swallowed hard. "It was hard for me, although I put on a good front. I knew before that night that Sam had feelings for you. We talked about it. Talked about everything because that's how Sam does things."

She did. And it worked for them. Even if it was a touchy subject, Sam insisted they discuss it openly and honestly. Too bad they hadn't given her the same consideration. Elijah knew he was as much at fault for holding back when she deserved the same from them.

"I wasn't jealous, I was … scared," Logan admitted.

"It's not like I could give her anything you couldn't," Elijah told him, remembering all too well how Sam had changed his entire life.

"Exactly." Logan stood taller, squaring his shoulders. "But we can give each other something she can't give either of us."

Elijah tried to figure out what he was saying.

"And I want that, Elijah," Logan declared, his tone stronger than before. "I fucking want you in a way that feels like a betrayal to her."

"Physically, you mean? Because otherwise—"

"Yes, physically. What I want from you … I can't get from her."

"And you think that means we're betraying her?"

"Doesn't it?" Logan snapped.

"*That's* why you ran away?"

Elijah's gaze shot over to Sam, her words snapping like a whip.

"You *abandoned* me because you think you're *betraying* me?"

Logan's throat worked on a swallow as he slowly pivoted and faced off with Sam across the room.

"How can it be a betrayal, Logan, when we all went into this with our eyes wide open? I'm not an idiot." She thrust her hand through her hair. "Jesus. You honestly believe I've got blinders on? That I think the whole fucking world revolves around me?"

Elijah stood tall, set his beer down. He was prepared to intervene if need be. Tempers were high because this was a long time coming.

"That's not what I'm saying, Sam," Logan countered.

"Then what *are* you saying?"

Logan glanced back at Elijah, then turned to Sam once more. "I'm saying I want him."

Her eyes narrowed. "That tells me nothing."

Logan expelled a heavy breath, his voice deeper, harsher than usual when he said, "I fucking want him, Sam. I want him in a way that doesn't involve you."

Elijah expected Sam to jump back from the power of those words, but she remained stone-still when she said, "I know. Like I said. I'm not an idiot."

LOGAN WASN'T A MAN PRONE TO SHEDDING tears, but at that moment, he could feel the heat in his sinuses and the water pooling in his eyes. Every inch of his body was tight, the emotional turmoil lashing at him.

He'd fucked up.

Royally fucked up.

"Sam, I don't think you understand," he said, choking back the emotion clogging his throat.

"Are you telling me that you're gay? That you no longer want to be married to me?"

"Fuck no," he barked. "That's not it at all."

She rolled her eyes and planted her hands on her hips. "Then trust me, Logan. I get it." Her gaze darted to Elijah then back. "Because one of you had the decency to tell me what the hell is going on."

More heat swamped his sinuses. "I wanted to tell you," he said quickly.

Fire burned in her eyes. "The hell you did. Your ass wouldn't have hopped on a plane if that was the case."

Fine. She had a point.

"You can't do shit like that, Logan," she snapped, waving her hands in the air. "That's not how this works. How the *three* of us work. Without trust, we've got nothing. And you broke that trust by proving you don't trust us. If you did, you would've talked it out."

Her words felt like a slap, but he took it like a man because she was right. Sam had always been open about everything. From the moment Elijah came into their lives, and they decided they wanted something permanent with a third, she'd ensured they were always on the same page. Rather than take a page from her book, Logan had taken the coward's way out, using excuses to put space between them.

"I'm sorry, Sam."

"For what?" She put her hands on her hips again. "For leaving? Or for not telling me you were?" Her eyes narrowed. "Or for holding back when you know I deserve better than that. *We* deserve better than that." Her gaze shot to Elijah. "I'm not the only one you owe an apology to."

Logan exhaled heavily. He owed them both more than an apology. It wasn't until the flight home that he'd realized what he was running from was the same thing he stood to lose because of his actions. He hadn't known whether either of them would even talk to him when he returned, so the fact that he was here now was something of a miracle. He'd half expected to be bunking at his brother's house tonight.

He heard a door shut, and he turned back to see Sam had disappeared, the bedroom door now closed.

He was about to go after her when Elijah moved past him. "Give me a minute."

One minute turned into two, then a few more. Finally, Elijah returned, but Sam didn't appear.

"You want a beer?" Elijah offered.

Logan met the man's gaze, nodded.

A few minutes later, with a beer in hand, Logan followed Elijah out to the pool.

Without preamble, Elijah began stripping off his clothes. "I'm getting in the water. You can sit out here, or you can join me. Your choice."

Logan watched Elijah as he undressed completely. He let himself openly admire rather than look away, which he'd done many times over the past seven months. When he saw that Elijah's cock was semi-hard, something loosened inside him. He figured that wouldn't be the case if Elijah were appalled by his presence, so he took it as a good sign.

When Elijah descended into the water, Logan set his beer aside, stripped out of his clothes. He grabbed the bottle and joined him, sitting opposite him in the shallow end the same way he had the first night they'd explored. He couldn't believe it had been over a month ago when he'd touched this man for the first time. That night had been a turning point for him in so many ways. What he'd anticipated being a pleasurable encounter had been so much more than that. It triggered something inside him and made him want something he'd never expected.

"Did you find what you were looking for, at least?" Elijah prompted.

Logan took a long pull on his beer, forced himself to hold the man's stare. "No."

A slight nod was the response he received.

"What I was looking for was right here all along," he admitted.

"Did it at least give you clarity?"

Logan considered that. "Somewhat, I guess." Figuring Elijah deserved some explanation, he continued. "I didn't go to play."

"I didn't figure you did."

"I went to see the dynamic of the relationships." Logan relaxed, stretching his arm out behind him. "Thought maybe if I understood more, I'd be able to rationalize this ... feeling."

"What feeling might that be?"

Logan could see the interest on Elijah's face. It was more than curiosity. There wasn't an ounce of amusement on the man's face, and Logan realized then that Sam hadn't been the only one he'd hurt by leaving.

"It's not just sex for me, Eli."

"Yet you went to a sex club to find the answers."

"Only because I knew they all went there."

Another slow nod from Elijah.

Logan could tell he was trying to understand, so he opted for the truth. "When I... When *we...*" He swallowed. "Something changed in me that night."

"The night you fucked me," Elijah said. His words weren't harsh but very direct.

"Yes. The night I fucked you, something changed." Logan shook his head. "That's not true. Something changed before then. That night confirmed it."

Elijah didn't speak, just stared, waiting.

"I didn't fall in love with you because we kissed or touched ... or fucked," Logan clarified. "I think I fell in love with you before that, and what happened between us brought it to the surface."

If Elijah was shocked by his admission, he didn't show it. "And that's a bad thing?"

"No."

That much Logan knew to be true. He didn't question his feelings for Elijah. How or when they developed was moot at this point. Logan was beyond trying to figure it out or explain it away. If the trip had done anything for him, it helped him accept that what he felt for Elijah was real. As real as what he felt for Sam. He loved them both and wanted to spend the rest of his life with them.

"I wasn't trying to run from my feelings for you, Eli." He glanced at the back door, ensuring Sam wasn't standing there. He looked back at Elijah. "That night when I fucked you, not once did I think about Sam, and that scared me."

"I didn't think about her either. But why would I? She wasn't there. She didn't need to be there, Logan. That was between the two of us. She would understand that."

"Maybe, but I still felt like I was betraying her."

"You weren't." Elijah took a drink. "We betrayed her when we kept it from her."

Logan hadn't thought about it that way. It made sense, though.

"You mentioned my first date with Sam," Elijah said. "I remember it, too. I spent that night getting to know her and trying to understand how I would possibly fit into her life. Do you remember me calling you that night?"

Logan frowned, trying to recall. "It was so long ago."

Elijah smiled, his gaze drifting away from his face. "Sam invited me back to your house that night. I told her I had to call you first. She told me she had already talked to you, but I needed to hear it for myself. She's *your* wife, Logan. Since the beginning, Sam has been *your* wife. I share her with you, even if she doesn't see it that way. It's still true. I wanted her so badly, but I couldn't go any further until I knew you were okay with what was happening. That's why I called you that night. To get your blessing. Not because I wanted you to be there with us. I didn't. I wanted her to myself."

Logan listened intently, willing Elijah to keep going.

CHAPTER TWENTY

ELIJAH LOOKED BACK AT LOGAN AND DECIDED it was time for the hard truth.

"Trust me when I tell you, what I feel for Sam doesn't include you. And if you honestly believe that Sam thinks about you when she and I are together, you're wrong. Very, very wrong." He let some of his frustration bleed into his tone. "Your name isn't the one she cries out when I bring her to orgasm. Your name's not the one she says when she whispers that she loves me. And she does love me, Logan. I know that with everything I am. And I love her. I love her the same way you do. With my heart and soul. I would die for her, and I never thought I would feel that for anyone but Beth. I've accepted it over the years. She's the reason I'm here."

Logan flinched, which was exactly the response he'd expected.

"But she's not the only reason I stay," he clarified, letting his tone even out. "I don't know when things changed between us. I don't know if it was that night at the cabin when I kissed you or if it was before that. But that night, I realized something was different." He tapped his chest with two fingers. "Something in here. I can honestly say that if I'd been in that position with anyone else, I would've backed out. I didn't have a buried desire to kiss a man, but when the opportunity to kiss you presented itself, I wasn't appalled by the idea. I was intrigued. I wouldn't have done it otherwise."

When Logan didn't have anything to contribute, Elijah continued.

"I was pissed that you left, but not because I didn't understand why. I've got experience with this because I share something with Sam that she doesn't share with you. What angered me was the fact that you hurt Sam. While you were off seeking answers, I was the one who listened as she cried herself to sleep. I was the one who watched as she stumbled through this past week with her heart in her eyes. She loves me, and I know that, but she's not complete without you."

"I know," Logan said softly. "I screwed up."

"The good news is, you can make it up to her." Elijah tipped his beer to his lips, swallowed the rest, then set the bottle aside.

"But can I make it up to *you?*"

Surprised by the question, Elijah frowned. "Do you want to?"

Logan didn't respond.

Elijah sighed. He'd hoped by revealing this, Logan might understand that their situation truly was unique. What they had was complicated, more so now that the lines of the triangle were equilateral.

Elijah decided it was time to call it a night, feeling emotionally wrung out by what little conversation had taken place. He started to get to his feet but stopped when Logan said, "Please don't go."

It would be too easy to stay, Elijah realized. Too easy to get caught up in this riot of emotion that he could feel coming from Logan. The man was a mess; that much was obvious. However, now that he'd said his piece, it was up to Logan to figure out how they would proceed.

"When you figure out what you want, Logan, you know where to find us."

With that, he got out of the pool, grabbed a towel on the way into the house. He wanted to sleep next to Sam tonight, but he considered going to the guest bedroom he'd slept in for so long. Just one night, he told himself. He could endure for one night in hopes of giving Logan the chance to go to her. Maybe then he could figure out what he truly wanted and how Elijah fit in.

He didn't make it through the living room before he detoured back to their bedroom. Elijah didn't mind playing the martyr when necessary, but he had no desire to hurt Sam any more than she already was. If he put distance between them now, she might take it as a slight, and he couldn't allow that to happen.

As silently as he could, he slipped into the bedroom and decided to leave the rest up to Logan.

LOGAN REMAINED IN THE POOL AFTER ELIJAH went inside. He replayed everything Elijah said over and over again in his head. There was one thing he was hung up on, something he'd never really thought about before.

Trust me when I tell you, what I feel for Sam doesn't include you. And if you honestly believe that Sam thinks about you when she and I are together, you're wrong. Very, very wrong. Your name isn't the one she cries out when I bring her to orgasm. Your name's not the one she says when she whispers that she loves me.

He knew every single word Elijah said was true. Knew to the depths of his soul that Sam loved Elijah, and what they shared didn't include him. He'd never thought it did.

Or had he?

No way he could've been screwed up enough to believe that, when they made love, Sam always thought about him. Why would she? If she did, that meant that when they were together, she was also thinking about Elijah, which he knew for a fact wasn't the case.

Logan exhaled, dropped his head back, and stared up at the inky-black sky and the glitter of stars dusted across it.

"WHERE'S LOGAN?" SAM WHISPERED WHEN ELIJAH CRAWLED into bed behind her.

She settled against him, welcoming his warmth even as she worried that he'd left Logan alone. She'd heard the pain in her husband's voice when they'd talked earlier, and since then, she'd been replaying every word, again and again, trying to make sense of it all to no avail. It had pained her not to go back out there, not to insist Logan talk to her, but she knew that they wouldn't make any headway until Logan and Elijah figured out what they felt for one another.

"He'll be here," Elijah said, his tone soft and reassuring.

When he settled onto his back, Sam rolled toward him, resting her head on his shoulder and her palm on his chest. "Did y'all talk?"

"I gave him my thoughts on the situation."

"Which are?"

His head turned, his lips pressing to her forehead. "You and I both know it's complicated, Sam. We've been living with that for a while, but he's just now learning what it means to have feelings for someone who's not you."

She frowned, confused for a moment, but then she realized what he was saying. When they'd gotten together, Elijah had still been deeply in love with his dead wife, but he'd opened himself up to her, allowed her in. In a lot of ways, she figured that was the same as what she'd felt when she realized she was falling in love with Elijah. And now, here she was, in love with two men. And she loved them equally, couldn't imagine her life without either of them.

What she found most interesting was that she wasn't jealous that Logan and Elijah had developed feelings for one another. She hadn't considered it even a possibility back in the beginning, but it made perfect sense how they could. They were both extremely passionate men, and though they were often driven by their lust and desires, their hearts were as much a part of who they were as anything else.

Nor was she jealous that they'd had sex without her there. She couldn't count how many times she'd had sex with them without the other present. That was the way their relationship worked.

What bothered her the most was that Logan thought his feelings were a betrayal to her. It pained her to think that the reverse could be true. She had never considered falling in love with Elijah as a betrayal to Logan because they'd talked about it again and again. Sam remembered wanting to ensure that Logan understood where their relationship stood as things progressed.

She wondered why he hadn't done the same for her.

"Do you love him?" she whispered in the dark.

Elijah put his hand over hers. "I do."

"Do you think that's what drove you to want him?"

His head tilted toward her. "I never thought about it like that, but I guess it could've played some role in it."

For the past week, when she was attempting to rationalize Logan's behavior, Sam had tried to put herself in their position. She had imagined a scenario where the roles were reversed, and she was sharing Logan or Elijah with another woman. In all fairness, she wasn't sure she ever could've done it, but for the sake of understanding, she had pretended. Would she have fallen in love with a woman she'd grown close to like that? She honestly didn't know, but she could see how it could happen. People changed because of the situations they found themselves in. She certainly had. At one point, she'd never imagined she could love someone nearly as much as she loved Logan, but she did. Her heart was divided right down the middle, with each of them holding a half.

With that thought comforting her somewhat, Sam allowed herself to drift off, hoping Logan would find his way back to them, because deep down, she knew this was where the three of them belonged.

WHEN ELIJAH HAD GONE INSIDE, LOGAN HADN'T been tired, which was why he'd spent the past couple of hours doing mundane chores. After getting out of the pool, he had picked up the clothes he and Elijah had discarded, dumping them in the laundry room. He'd then emptied the dishwasher, surveyed the refrigerator, and added things to the grocery list Sam kept pinned on the door. After that, he had wandered through the empty house, taking it all in. It was the first time he'd noticed how much things had changed in their lives over the past seven years. The ways in which Elijah's presence had altered everything.

Funny how he hadn't noticed until now. He figured that was because it was normal to him. The pictures of Elijah and Sam on the bookshelf, cards that they'd given each other over the years. It was all on display the same as the photographs of Logan and Sam, the cards they'd exchanged.

Elijah was right to say that Sam loved him the same way she loved Logan. The proof was all around him, and Sam had never asked his permission to merge their lives in that way because his permission wasn't needed. She'd done it because it felt right to her and because she loved Elijah.

And because they'd been open with each other from the beginning. Elijah hadn't randomly appeared in their lives. Logan had set that in motion, and Sam had talked to him every step of the way as things progressed. In some way, Logan had always been a part of her relationship with Elijah. And vice versa.

Yet he'd never really noticed since Elijah's presence in their lives was as natural as breathing.

It was a little after two when he finally forced himself to go to bed. He wasn't tired, and he wasn't sure what he would find on the other side of that bedroom door, but he knew he couldn't let his fears keep him away any longer.

When he slipped into the room, he was greeted by the soft, even sounds of their breathing. They were asleep, Sam curled up to Elijah. He stood there for a second and watched them as he'd done so many times before. It was normal, he realized. There was no pain, no confusion because his wife wanted another man. He'd long ago accepted that she was in love with Elijah, that he could provide her with the same comfort and love she got from him.

Would she feel the same if she was in his shoes? If she walked into this room and found him and Elijah in a similar embrace?

Logan frowned, realizing that was the first time he'd wondered that. This thing with Elijah … it wasn't about exploring their sexual boundaries or finding pleasure in one another. It was more.

With a sigh, he stripped off his boxers and crawled into bed on his side. He moved toward Sam, spooning behind her. He exhaled his relief when she sighed, her hand sliding off of Elijah's chest so she could reach back and touch him. She rested her hand on his hip, still sleeping soundly.

Testing the waters, Logan draped his arm across her, resting his palm on Elijah's stomach.

It wasn't until Elijah's hand moved over his that he relaxed enough to fall asleep.

CHAPTER TWENTY-ONE

ELIJAH CAME AWAKE SLOWLY, HIS BODY STIFF from not moving during the night. He realized Sam was still curled up against his side, her head on his shoulder. But it wasn't her familiar weight that had brought him out of a deep sleep. No, he suspected that had something to do with the hand resting on his stomach, inching dangerously close to the hard-on raging between his thighs.

Checking to see if Logan was still asleep, he lifted his head and saw the man watching him from his casual pose, his head resting on his propped-up hand.

Before he could say anything, Logan pulled his hand away from Elijah's aching dick and held one finger over his mouth to signal for quiet.

Elijah watched as Logan leaned down and pressed a kiss to Sam's shoulder. "Baby?"

"Sleep," she mumbled, eyes closed.

Logan smiled, then jerked his chin toward the bathroom before he turned and gently climbed out of the bed so as not to wake Sam.

Elijah followed suit, easing out from under her and tucking a pillow nearby so she would have something to hold on to. He padded naked into the bathroom at the same time the shower came on. He debated going straight to the shower but detoured to the double sinks, pulled out his toothbrush and toothpaste. For some unknown reason, brushing his teeth felt like the thing to do. He just wasn't sure if it was because he was stalling or getting ready. After all, he had every intention of sealing his mouth to Logan's when he joined him.

It only took two minutes—dentists' recommendation—and then he rinsed his mouth and shut off the water.

Without hesitating or contemplating what he should or should not do, he joined Logan, watching him intently as he approached. He didn't give the man space, didn't linger on the opposite side of the shower. He moved right up to Logan, reached for his head, and pulled him in for a kiss. The soft moan that escaped him was involuntary as he leaned into the kiss.

He had wanted to do this ever since Logan walked in the door last night. He couldn't explain it; he wasn't even sure he wanted to. Whatever this was, whatever Logan did to him, Elijah had accepted it. He wanted this man with a passion he didn't understand but no longer wondered about.

"Eli," Logan whispered against his lips, his hands sliding up his back, hooking over his shoulders and pulling him in until they were chest to chest.

Their tongues stroked and licked, neither of them rushing. There was an intimacy here that Elijah hadn't felt with Logan yet, despite the fact the man had been inside him already.

Acceptance, maybe? Could that be what had them slowing the pace? Elijah was content to do this and only this.

Logan backed up until he was against the wall, allowing Elijah to put more of his weight on him, their hands lightly skimming.

"Elijah..." Logan pulled his mouth away, resting his forehead on his "I'm sorry."

Elijah swallowed and nodded. He knew that already.

"I'm sorry for leaving, sorry for hurting Sam and you." There was both pain and promise in his words. "I never expected this, but I'm not willing to give it up."

Elijah ran his hand over Logan's hair, brushing it back from his face and pressing his mouth to his once more. He tilted his head, changed the angle, and used his tongue to express his understanding. The kiss was languid and hot, likely the most intimate one he'd had in years. It remained that way, even as Elijah pressed his palm along Logan's steel-hard erection. He rubbed slowly, up and down, listening to the man moan softly, the sound muted as Elijah swallowed it.

This was what he wanted. This man and the woman who was still asleep in the bed. He knew if he had both of them, he would be content for the remainder of his days. He didn't expect everything to be roses and champagne all the time, nor was he anticipating a fairy tale. He wanted this man with all his complexities, his brooding, and his insecurities. And he wanted Sam, the woman who kept them both on their toes with her impulsiveness and her innate ability to love like no one else.

The kiss continued, carrying on the silent conversation because words weren't necessary. Elijah pressed against his slick skin, rubbing lightly along Logan's cock. This moment would forever be etched in his mind because it was the first time they were admitting this was so much more than either of them could've anticipated.

This was love.

He pulled back suddenly, met Logan's gaze. His eyes were hooded and glazed with passion. "This is more than sex."

Logan's eyes suddenly cleared, but he didn't pull away. "It is."

Elijah swallowed, preparing to announce his feelings, but didn't get the words out before Logan spoke.

"I want more, Eli. I want everything." Logan's hand paused on his chest over his heart. "I love you, and I want more with you and Sam. I know it won't be easy—"

"I love you, too," Elijah blurted, pulling Logan's mouth back to his.

He kissed him, willing him to feel everything he'd been holding back.

WHEN LOGAN AND ELIJAH SLIPPED OUT OF bed, Sam remained where she was.

She'd been awake for at least an hour, unwilling to move while she basked in the comfort of having both men with her.

The only reason she'd feigned sleep when Logan spoke was because she had wanted that sense of peace and calm to last for a bit longer. It hadn't surprised her when they'd gotten up. Neither was all that keen on staying in bed when there were other things to do. And the moment she'd heard the shower come on, she knew they were taking a minute to themselves. Alone. Together.

Still content with the calm that had finally chased away the anger and pain, she opened her eyes and rolled to her back, listening for the sounds again. Yes, there were definitely two different voices echoing off the tiled walls in the bathroom. She couldn't make out what they were saying, but she heard the hushed rumble of their voices and the answering moans.

Despite the fact she hadn't yet made up with Logan, she felt a sense of relief wash over her. She wasn't sure if she should, considering what she knew about the reasons Logan had left and now the fact that he was in the shower with Elijah. In his defense, he had tried to wake her, and she was the one who'd pretended to want to stay in bed. Maybe she wasn't ready to face the hard truths that were sure to come out when they hashed things out once and for all.

Shaking off the runaway train of questions that came with what she'd learned last night, she decided it didn't matter. Although she still wanted to have a conversation with Logan, her chat with Elijah before drifting off had brought a few things home for her. One of those things was that she was going to have to learn to share them with each other. And unless they invited her to join, now was a good time to test her ability to do just that.

"Logan…"

The sound of Elijah's voice sent a shiver down her spine, but she resisted the urge to see what they were doing. Instead, she got out of bed and grabbed one of Elijah's T-shirts from the dresser. She pulled it on, then slipped out of the bedroom, careful to close the door silently behind her.

There were plenty of things she could keep herself busy with until they were finished.

In her defense, she tried really, really hard to focus, but in the end, she found she had absolutely no willpower. Rather than do something constructive like clean the refrigerator or dust, she ended up making a pot of coffee, then took a seat at the table.

Her attention never strayed from the closed bedroom door as she wondered what was taking place on the other side.

It was a wonder her stare didn't burn a hole clear through the closed door.

LOGAN MANAGED TO MAKE IT THROUGH THE shower without groping Elijah too much. He didn't seek more than the kisses and light touches as they washed each other, letting the moment drag on for long minutes.

He'd needed this. A moment to settle his thoughts and accept that what he wanted was right here under this roof.

"I need to talk to Sam," he whispered against Elijah's mouth as they let the water wash away the lather they'd created with wandering hands.

"Yes, you do."

"Could you give us a minute?" he asked, pulling back to stare into the man's eyes.

Elijah nodded, then stepped back, releasing him.

Logan hated to pull himself away from Elijah, but he had to talk to his wife. Before they took this any further, Logan needed to ensure she understood how sorry he was for what he'd done.

He left Elijah in the shower, grabbed a towel, and dried off. He snagged a pair of shorts from the closet, pulled them on, and headed for the bed only to realize Sam wasn't there.

Logan frowned, then made his way out of the bedroom.

He found her sitting at the kitchen table, her eyes locked on him the moment he stepped out.

She didn't say anything, but he could see a million questions burning in her eyes. On a normal day, she would've pelted him with them, and he hated that he'd taken that from her.

Her eyes followed him as he neared, remained locked on his face as he stepped up to her and reached for her hand. She didn't speak, even as he helped her to her feet and urged her to follow him. He led the way to the sofa, took a seat, and pulled her down on his lap. She came willingly, and his heart swelled in his chest, a relief so potent he was surprised he could still breathe.

"God, baby," he whispered, wrapping his arms around her and pulling her against him.

His entire body shuddered with relief as the warmth of her breath fanned his neck. A sob escaped her, and his chest tightened, his arms banding more firmly around her.

"I'm so sorry, Sam."

Her arms wrapped around him, clutching him tightly. "I know."

"I love you." He pressed a kiss to her cheek, spoke softly near her ear. "I love you with all that I am. That will never change even when I do stupid shit."

She chuckled, but it was broken by a sob. "Why'd you go?"

He exhaled heavily and decided to admit the truth. "Because I couldn't breathe. I didn't anticipate feeling..." Logan paused, ordering his thoughts. "I didn't anticipate falling in love with Elijah. But I didn't leave for that reason."

Her fingers teased the ends of his hair, her nose still nuzzled against his neck.

Logan ran his hand over her back, comforted by her nearness. "I left because I felt like I was betraying you. I've only ever been on the other side, and I didn't want to feel something for anyone who wasn't you."

"I know how that feels. I understand, trust me. It's not easy falling in love with someone else when you're already in love. I've been there."

He palmed the back of her head, needing to have her as close to him as he could get her. "I hope you can forgive me."

"Of course I can," she whispered.

"And you'll let me make it up to you."

Sam pulled back, meeting his eyes, her expression serious. "But you have to know it's going to take some time for me to adjust."

Logan nodded. "I know. That's the part *I* understand."

Her gaze skimmed over his face. "I'll do my best to give you both the space you want."

He shook his head. "We don't want space, baby. That's not what this is about."

"But it is," she countered. "And I get that. I do. There are times when I want you all to myself. Others when I want Elijah. I expect no less for you and him. I want you and Elijah to find with each other what I've found with both of you. If that means you need to be alone, I'll find something else to do." She smiled. "But if you want me to sit quietly ... and, you know ... *watch* ... I can do that, too."

He pulled her back to him and laughed. That was his Samantha. Honest to a fault, with a heart big enough and strong enough to handle a man like him. Just one of the millions of reasons he loved her.

Logan held her against him for several minutes, content to do only that for the rest of the day. It was movement out of the corner of his eye that had him looking over. Elijah was standing in the bedroom doorway, his shoulder resting against the doorjamb. He had a towel wrapped around his hips and a look in his eyes that warmed Logan to the depths of his soul.

He couldn't believe he'd run from this, but he knew in his heart he'd found his way back because this was where he was meant to be.

For him, home wasn't a place but the two people who'd burrowed into his heart somewhere along the way.

Chapter Twenty-Two

Elijah wouldn't go so far as to say things were back to normal, but the tension between the three of them had certainly lessened since that morning. At least the emotional stress, anyway. As for the sexual tension, that was drawn tight as a bowstring, threatening to snap at any minute.

He figured it likely had something to do with the fact they'd opted to spend part of the afternoon in the swimming pool. Sam, wearing that skimpy white bikini that gave him a hard-on without fail, was floating on her favorite raft in the center of the pool, fingers teasing the top of the water. Logan was cleaning the grill, preparing it for the burgers he intended to make for dinner, while Elijah was content to sit in the shallow end, sipping a beer and watching the two of them.

When Logan peered over for the hundredth time, Elijah got the feeling he was hoping to catch a glimpse of him and Sam doing something wicked and dirty. Or maybe that was him projecting, because Elijah had been hoping for the same thing. He'd been anticipating Logan joining them in the water at some point, and if he had to guess, Sam was waiting for the same.

So basically, it meant someone had to make the first move.

"Sam?" Elijah called out to her when she used the side of the pool to push herself back to the center.

"Hmm?"

Before Elijah could make his request, Logan spoke up. "Take off your bathing suit."

The man had read his mind.

Her eyes opened, and she shielded them with her hand, peering up at Logan. She then turned and looked at him, so Elijah gave her a nod of encouragement.

She smiled wickedly, then did as her husband requested, removing the tiny scraps of fabric that had been covering so very little. Once she was naked, she settled back on the raft, this time dropping her feet into the water on either side, which gave them an unobstructed view of the slick pink flesh that beckoned.

Elijah groaned as he got to his feet, unable to resist the temptation she presented.

No sooner did he move than Logan was joining them, stepping down into the water, a glass of wine in one hand, the other adjusting his cock in his shorts.

"Here you go, baby," Logan said, passing her the glass as he approached. "Don't spill it."

"Have you ever known me to let wine go to waste?" she teased as she took a sip.

Logan chuckled softly, turning her in the water so that he was standing between her parted thighs at the end of the float.

Elijah came to stand at her side, smiling as she began to glance between them. Her expression relaxed, and he knew she realized what they were angling for.

"I think this pretty pussy needs some attention," Logan mused, his big hands gliding over her thighs, higher, until his thumbs were kneading her mound.

"Her breasts, too," Elijah noted, covering her left breast with his hand, trapping her nipple between two knuckles, and lightly pinching it.

Sam sighed, the wineglass teetering precariously.

"Don't spill the wine," Logan commanded, his thumb sliding between her pussy lips.

Sam righted the glass, then took another sip.

Elijah's gaze fixated on Logan's hand, watching as he pinched and plucked her clit, drawing it out from its hood.

"Logan…" Sam tried to buck her hips but couldn't.

"Yes, baby?" he crooned, grinning. "Did you need something?"

"More."

He chuckled. "More what?"

She groaned when Logan flicked her clit with his fingertip.

Elijah pinched her nipple at the same time, which made Sam jerk on the float. She quickly tightened her grip on the wineglass, ensuring it didn't fall in the water while they teased her. Each time the glass began to fall over, Logan would stop what he was doing and wait for Sam to pay attention. That lasted a few minutes before the woman figured out it was easier to down the wine and eliminate the risk.

She was a smart one; Elijah would give her that.

With a thrust of her hand, she passed the glass over to Logan, who took it and set it on the pool's edge before returning to his post between her thighs. Elijah moved to stand at her head, giving him better access to her breasts. He used both hands to torment her supple flesh, watching Logan as he fingered her pussy until Sam was writhing, her jerky movements threatening to topple the float at any moment.

Logan must've had some sympathy for her because he eliminated the float altogether, pulling Sam off of it and into his arms. She went willingly, wreathing his neck, their lips melding as she attempted to climb his big body.

Elijah wasn't interested in being a bystander in this encounter, so he moved closer, crushing Sam between them. When Sam and Logan broke for air, Elijah claimed Sam's mouth, turning her head for a better angle.

"You want to hear a story?" he prompted when she slid one arm around his neck, keeping him close.

"What's it about?"

Elijah met Logan's gaze, saw approval flash in his eyes.

"I think he'll need encouragement first," Logan interjected, moving toward one of the long benches and turning Sam in his arms.

She went willingly, her gaze locked on Elijah as Logan positioned her so that she was in his lap. There was another adjustment, and then Sam's eyes rolled back in her head. Elijah wasn't privy to what was taking place under the water, but he could tell by the way her mouth opened and she sighed that Logan had just buried his cock inside her pussy.

"That's better," Logan said gruffly.

Elijah felt heat flood his veins.

"I think I'll be the storyteller today," Logan added, motioning Elijah closer.

He took another step toward them, stopping when he was directly in front of Sam.

"I think he's wearing too many clothes," Logan whispered near Sam's ear, his eyes raking over Elijah's face.

"I agree."

Without preamble, Elijah shoved his shorts down, letting them float away while he waited patiently for what would happen next.

THE INSTANT ELIJAH WAS NAKED, SAM FELT Logan's cock pulse inside her. She sighed, leaning into him while watching Elijah. She wasn't sure what they had in store, but she was eager to find out, and she definitely liked the fact that neither of them could hide their physical reactions from her. Not like this, anyway.

"It was the night you went out with McKenna and Ashleigh," Logan said, his voice rough as he reached around her, his big hand sliding over Elijah's washboard abs.

Sam inhaled sharply, her gaze riveted to the spot.

"Elijah came home from work," Logan continued.

Sam noticed Elijah's eyes flash with acknowledgment and realized she was going to hear about their first time together.

"I was in a mood," Logan admitted. "Anxious and restless."

Sam felt his cock as it thickened inside her, and she knew he was reliving the moment in his mind.

"He was," Elijah chimed in, reaching for Sam's hand. "Grumpy."

He positioned her hand so that her fingers curled around his thick shaft, but he didn't instruct her to do anything, so she just let herself feel.

"I decided to give him space, so I took a shower. Figured I would start dinner after."

Beneath her fingertips, Elijah's cock flexed and pulsed.

It was then she realized she was reliving the moment with them. Their bodies couldn't deny how they'd felt even now.

Sam moaned when Logan's hips shifted, his cock pushing deep inside her. "Keep going."

Logan chuckled, covering her hand with his, guiding it up and down Elijah's cock.

"When I got out of the shower, Logan was in the bathroom, looking pissed off."

"More like determined," Logan corrected.

"I could practically taste your need."

Sam was watching Elijah's face, so she saw his eyes glitter as he looked at Logan before turning his focus on her again.

"The second he looked at me, I knew what was coming."

Logan's mouth pressed close to her ear. "I needed him. I needed to feel him, baby. I wanted to slide my cock in his ass and feel him all around me."

She moaned, tingles erupting over her skin as she imagined them together.

"There was no foreplay that night," Elijah added. "But it didn't matter. We were too far gone at that point."

Logan's arm banded around her middle, and he pulled her hips back, driving his cock deeper inside her.

She whimpered, her hand tightening around Elijah's cock as Logan's hand moved hers more rapidly. She could feel their need now, knew they were as affected by the memory as they'd been during the encounter.

"How did it feel?" Sam asked, turning her head, directing her question at Logan. "How did it feel to bury your cock in his ass?"

Logan grunted roughly, his cock pulsing inside her while Elijah's jerked in her hand.

"Fucking heaven," Logan growled roughly. "He was so fucking tight."

Sam moaned, shifting her hips, changing the angle of Logan's penetration. She needed more.

Although she hated to break the connection, she released Elijah's cock. Before Logan could drop his hand, she grabbed his wrist and guided it back to where it was, only this time, his fingers curled around Elijah's thick shaft.

"Ah, fuck," Elijah groaned.

"I want to watch," she told them, unable to look away as Logan began to stroke Elijah faster.

Logan nipped her earlobe. "And I want to fuck you while he's fucking me."

Sam nearly came from that admission, her pussy clenching tightly around Logan's cock.

"Oh, fuck," Logan groaned. "Baby ... do that again, and I'll come."

Elijah stepped even closer, his fingers tangling in her hair while Logan continued to stroke him faster. Sam couldn't help herself; she was rocking on Logan's lap, fucking him while he was jerking Elijah off.

"I want that, too," she admitted. "I want to hear you say his name while he's fucking your ass."

Logan growled roughly.

Sam knew she was being more vulgar than usual, but it seemed fitting for the situation. Usually, they were the descriptive ones, but she wanted them to know that she could be part of this with them. That this didn't have to be awkward between them. She understood the need because she felt it for both of them. There were times she wanted them at the same time, others when she selfishly wanted each of them all to herself. She wasn't ashamed to admit it and didn't want them to be, either.

Looking back at Logan, Sam smiled. "And one day, I want to suck his cock while you're fucking *his* ass."

"Oh, Jesus," Logan growled harshly, driving his hips up. "Fuck, baby."

Sam felt his cock swell and pulse, knew he was coming.

"Fuck her, Eli," Logan bellowed as his body shuddered violently.

The next thing Sam knew, Elijah was pulling her to her feet. He jerked her to him, and she went willingly, sliding her arms around his neck as he lifted her. A second later, he thrust inside her, his hands rough as they gripped her hips. She clutched his shoulders as he stumbled back, taking them to deeper water even as he bounced her up and down on his cock.

Sam was so close.

"Come for me, Sam," Elijah groaned, the muscles in his arms and chest flexing as he guided her along his steely erection. "I want to feel that sweet cunt milk my dick."

That did it. She dropped her head back and cried out both their names as she came.

LATER THAT NIGHT, AFTER THEY'D EATEN DINNER, cleaned up, and gotten everything in order for the week ahead, Logan felt his exhaustion hit him. Or maybe it was relief from all the chaos that had the adrenaline fading from his system.

For the first time in months, he felt like himself again. He figured that was weird since he was no longer the man he'd thought he was. Well, in a sense, he was still the same. At his core, sure. His morals and values hadn't changed, just his outlook, he figured.

Sam was coming out of the bathroom when he came into the bedroom. She smiled over at him the same way she did most nights.

Yes, it was relief, he decided.

"I've got an early meeting tomorrow," she informed him as she pulled the blankets back on the bed. "I'll need to go in early. You want me to drive myself?"

"I'd prefer to do the honor," he told her, adjusting his pillow as he prepared to get in bed with her. "Will Elijah be in town this week?"

"To my knowledge," she said as she crawled into the big bed, situating herself in the middle.

"I've been meaning to talk to you both about that."

Logan looked over to see Elijah standing in the doorway, his shoulder pressed to the doorjamb. "About what?"

"I've been offered a VP position."

"A promotion. It's about damn time. Congratulations," Logan said, getting into bed with Sam.

"I haven't accepted it yet." He crossed one ankle over the other. "In fact, I've turned down several other promotions in the last few years."

"You have? Why?"

"They didn't feel right."

"But this one does?" Logan prompted.

"It does."

"That's fantastic," Sam said, patting the other side to encourage Elijah to join them.

He didn't move from his spot. "If I take it, I'll be home more than I am now."

Logan got the feeling Elijah was gauging their reactions to the news.

"That's even better," Logan told him.

"Are you sure?"

Logan frowned. "Why wouldn't I be?"

His only response was a slow quirk of one eyebrow. Logan could feel Sam's eyes on him, too, and he wasn't sure what they expected him to say.

He glanced over at his wife and then to Elijah before deciding he would lay it all on the line for them. "Things are different. I've accepted that. But at our core, we're still the same together."

"Are we?" Sam asked, her skepticism evident.

"No," Elijah said firmly, moving away from the wall. "We're not the same together."

Logan watched him, expecting him to move to the other side of the bed. He didn't, instead coming to Logan's side.

"We'll never be the same as we were," Elijah continued, shoving the blankets down and putting one knee on the bed.

Logan had no choice but to lean back when Elijah crowded him.

"He's right," Sam agreed, shifting so that she was laid out at his side, her head on his shoulder.

"I don't want us to be the same," Elijah said softly, moving over him.

Logan relaxed on the bed, the heat of their bodies enveloping him. He pulled Sam in closer, resting his hand on her hip as he stared up at Elijah. "What do you want, then?"

"I'm not just your wife's lover anymore."

Sam's hand moved up Elijah's arm, the movement drawing Logan's attention. He loved watching her touch him.

"And I don't want to just be your lover, either."

Logan's gaze snapped over to Elijah. He wasn't sure what was happening here. Were they ganging up on him?

"I want more," Elijah continued, his gaze shifting to Sam. "More from both of you."

"Anything," she said sweetly.

Elijah's dark gaze moved between them for a moment, and Logan sensed that what was coming next would ultimately change the dynamic of their relationship.

He probably should've let Elijah continue, heard the man out because what he was about to say was important. However, Logan had never been the sort to take a backseat to anything, and he damn sure wasn't about to start now.

Before Elijah could speak, Logan moved. He heard Sam's squeal of surprise seconds before Elijah grunted as Logan flipped their positions so that Elijah was flat on his back and Logan loomed over him.

"You're right," Logan told him, his voice rougher than he intended.

He pulled Sam closer, shifted so that he was straddling one of Sam's legs and one of Elijah's. They remained where they were, flat on their backs, staring up at him as he sat on his haunches.

"If we're gonna do this, it needs to be more permanent."

Elijah turned his head, peered over at Sam. "He's stealing my moment."

She laughed. "I think you're right."

Logan smiled. "Do you want a wedding?"

Elijah's head snapped back, his eyes slamming into Logan's face. "What?"

Sam inhaled sharply, and Logan could practically feel her vibrating. She clearly understood what Logan was getting at.

"You heard me." Logan tapped Elijah's knee. "Do you want a wedding?"

"Wha— I don't—"

"The three of us," Logan clarified. "It's not legal, of course, but we can still stand on ceremony. Do it the right way."

Elijah's eyes widened. "You would marry me?"

"For the record, so would I," Sam declared with a huff.

Logan smiled down at his wife. "Would you marry me again?"

There was no hesitation when she said, "In a heartbeat."

He ensured she saw his relief before turning his attention to Elijah. "And you?"

"Are you asking me to marry you?"

Logan felt his chest warm. "I'm telling you that I love you." He looked at Sam. "Both of you." He glanced between them. "And I want to spend the rest of my life making you both happy."

"And you don't mind everyone knowing?"

He smirked. "I have a penchant for shock and awe, you know that." Logan took a deep breath, then met Elijah's stare and held it. "I love you, and I don't have any intention of pretending otherwise."

"I love you, too." Elijah then looked over at Sam. "You hold my heart in the palm of your hand, so I need to know that this is what you want before I answer him."

She grinned, so much love in her eyes. "I think it's a great idea."

"Me, too," Elijah noted, and Logan felt those words warm his soul.

Sam tapped Logan's thigh. "I'll agree to be married—at least in theory—to both of you, under one condition."

Logan suspected he knew what she would say, but he arched an eyebrow in question when she peered up at him.

"I get to watch sometimes."

Shaking his head, Logan laughed, leaning down and pressing a hand to the bed beside her head. "We'll consider it. Under one condition."

Sam's hands cupped his face, her eyes bright. "What's that?"

"You wear the maid's outfit at least once a month."

"Once a week," Elijah corrected.

With a giggle, Sam lifted her head, bringing her mouth to his. "But I'm *not* cleaning the oven."

Logan looked to Elijah for a final decision. He nodded, grinning wide.

"Deal."

"Good." Sam yawned dramatically. "Now, if y'all are done with the mushy stuff, I'd like to get some sleep."

Logan laughed, his relief overwhelming and potent.

EPILOGUE

Friday, July 29, 2022

ON FRIDAY AFTERNOON, SAM WAS SITTING IN her office, finishing up an email so she could call it a day. It had been a long week, and she was looking forward to the weekend, some time alone with Logan and Elijah, who'd both gone out of their way this week to return things to normal.

Well, mostly normal. She was still getting used to the fact that she'd caught them kissing on more than one occasion. Hot kisses. Mind-blowing kisses. Ones she found herself captivated by, watching when she didn't think they were aware she was there. But they always seemed to know, and it pleased her that they weren't trying to hide it.

Of course, it helped that she'd had to deal with good ol' mother nature. For the past week, her period had put a damper on her sex life. But that was finally over, and now she could focus on getting Logan and Elijah to make up for the teasing they'd made her suffer.

A knock on the door had her glancing up.

Logan was standing in her doorway, looking as ridiculously hot as he always did in his bespoke suit and that beguiling smile.

"You about ready?"

She nodded, glanced back at the email, and hit send. "I am now."

"Elijah's waiting for us."

"Are y'all taking me to dinner? Or to the club?"

Sam reached for her laptop but stopped when Logan said, "You won't be needing that."

She stood tall, stared at him as she slowly closed the laptop. "Why not?"

"It's a surprise." He gestured her toward him with a wave of his hand. "But if we want to make our flight, we need to leave now."

Sam tried to process what little information he'd just relayed, despite his tone giving the impression he'd just gone into detail. "Where are—"

"Baby, quit wasting time."

Spurred into action by his curt but amused tone, she opened her desk drawer, grabbed her purse, left her laptop locked in place, and asked again, "Where are we going?"

He chuckled. "I told you, it's a surprise."

"I don't like surprises."

Logan put his arm around her shoulder and guided her out of her office. "Yes, you do."

Fine. She did. But that wasn't the point.

"I need to pack. How will I know what to—"

"We packed for you," he explained as he led the way down the stairs to the main doors.

"Well, at least tell me what you packed for me?"

He laughed. "Then you'd know where we're going."

Yes, that had been the point.

Sam huffed, ensuring he heard her frustration even as her belly churned with excitement.

Half an hour later, they arrived at the airport. The first surprise came in the form of an enormous plane that put all other private jets to shame. And the second was the arrival of so many people on the private landing strip.

Sam looked at Logan. "Please, please, *please* tell me we're going to Sapphire Island."

He chuckled, shaking his head. "Never can keep it a secret for long with you. Happy birthday, baby."

The excitement made her chest swell and exhilaration surge into her bloodstream. She couldn't count how many times she'd asked Logan and Elijah to take her to Sapphire Island, the private island owned by Talon, the mysterious Dominant with only one name. Ever since she'd learned of its existence, she'd been dropping hints that it would be the perfect place for them to vacation. Who wouldn't want to visit a private resort, aptly named the Sapphire, that had once been restricted to Owners who were seeking their very own possessions? She wasn't talking about material valuables, either. These were living, breathing people looking for the one person who would own them, heart, body, and soul, for eternity.

Sam had been obsessed with the need to see Sapphire Island for herself, to experience the wonder that could only be had by people who were willing to give themselves over to another human being and be, in essence, their slave for life.

And Logan and Elijah were taking her for her birthday.

"Go on up," Logan urged when Elijah joined them at the back of the car. "I'll ensure the luggage gets loaded."

Sam took Elijah's hand and walked beside him toward the plane, then up the stairs to the open door.

The moment she stepped inside, she gasped. "Holy shit."

This was not your mother's regular 737. This was a luxury hotel with wings.

"This way," Elijah said, tugging on her hand.

She followed him, not sure where he was leading her and not caring, either. She couldn't believe what she was seeing. There was so much to take in, so many—

"Happy Birthday!"

Sam jumped, startled by the chorus that rang out as soon as she stepped into what appeared to be a dining/conference room.

Her eyes pooled as she took in the faces of all her friends. Sierra, Cole, and Luke, Ashleigh and Alex, Xander and Mercedes, Tag and McKenna, Trent, Clarissa, and Troy, even Dylan and a very pregnant Sara ... they were all here, holding up glasses of champagne as they watched her with wide grins.

As they greeted her with hugs and welcomes, Sam couldn't help but think she was the luckiest woman in the world.

LOGAN RECLINED IN ONE OF THE LEATHER chairs while the plane made its approach to Sapphire Island. He'd spent the five-hour trip in the same spot, watching movies on the big screen while friends relaxed and chatted around him.

Elijah tapped his arm, pulling his attention away from the TV.

"You know there's a good chance she's going to want to take a possession home with her."

Logan laughed. He'd had the same thought when he initially started planning this trip for Sam's fortieth birthday many months ago. With Elijah's help, they'd managed to pull off the surprise for as long as was physically possible.

"Well, we'll have to keep her too busy to do any browsing."

"I'm certainly up for the challenge."

A man wearing a collar and claiming he was the flight attendant began making his rounds, ensuring everyone was buckled for landing. If Logan had to guess, he was one of the many possessions owned by the resort, explicitly sent to ensure their safe arrival. Logan had never been to the taboo resort that Trent spoke so highly of, but he'd heard plenty of stories. At one point, it had been restricted to a certain caliber of guests, but in recent years it was converted into a fetish resort that put all others to shame. Even Alluring Indulgence Resort couldn't boast the kind of taboo, kinky things that the Sapphire could.

He heard Sam giggling from somewhere behind him, and he smiled to himself.

Definitely going to be an interesting trip.

Two hours later, after they'd arrived at the Sapphire, they were checked in and given an impromptu tour of the main facilities before being escorted to their private bungalow. Logan had known when he'd set everything up that the accommodations would be five-star, but he'd never anticipated this. The three-thousand-square-foot space was magnificent. It even had a bed that would work for the three of them, a request he'd made at the very last minute. Between that and the private pool, he wasn't sure they would need to leave for the entirety of the trip.

They would, of course, because Sam was already begging to go to the main pools. Evidently, she'd heard that they held scenes in the area throughout the day and sometimes into the night.

"I've got a scene for you," he said, pulling her in close and pressing a kiss to her lips.

"Oh, yeah?" She smiled up at him, her light green eyes glittering with anticipation. "Does it involve lunch? Because I'm starving."

He laughed, glancing over at Elijah. "You hungry, too?"

The spark in Elijah's eyes said he was, but not necessarily for food.

Logan knew the feeling. He'd spent the better part of the past week doing his best not to ravish either of them. It wasn't easy, but he'd known this day was coming, and he'd been hoping to grant Sam her request as one of her gifts. Her request being to watch the two of them together.

"I can make lunch if that's your first birthday request," Logan informed her.

"*My* request?" Sam glanced between them. "You mean I get to ask for stuff?"

"This trip's all about you."

She put her finger on her lip and tapped, her eyes darting back and forth between them. "If I have a say in the matter, I'd prefer something … a little more intriguing."

"Such as?"

Her eyes glittered. "I want to watch."

Logan looked at Elijah. "I guess we better strip."

Sam laughed. "Not yet."

Smiling, he peered back at his wife. "No?"

She shook her head.

Elijah was perched on the arm of one of the sofas, watching them closely. He slowly stood, grinning wide. "Why don't you go down to the pool while we get unpacked." He glanced at his watch. "If you were to return, in oh, say, one hour, perhaps you'll find a show you approve of."

Sam's gaze bounced between them, her eyebrows lowered in suspicion. "This is the honeymoon phase, isn't it?"

Logan smirked. "Baby, that phase never ended. We're just renewing our vows."

She giggled and danced away when he reached for her. "You're insatiable, you know that?"

He most definitely was. And he wasn't ashamed to admit it.

"Okay, fine," she said, moving toward her suitcase, which was standing near the door. "Let me change, and I'll head down to the pool. I told McKenna and Sierra that I'd meet up with them as soon as I could."

Logan leaned against the center island in the open kitchen, crossing his arms over his chest. This trip was about her. Her friends were all here, and he knew she needed to get in some face time with them. Despite the fact he'd prefer to get her naked and under him for the foreseeable future, he wasn't about to be selfish with her time, no matter how much he wanted to be.

AFTER SAM LEFT, ELIJAH DRAGGED THEIR LUGGAGE into the bedroom. With Logan's help, they put away their things, getting settled in for the week they'd be spending in paradise, celebrating Sam's fortieth birthday.

When they'd first started planning for this trip, there was no way he would've imagined things would've changed so drastically between them. Certainly not like this. For the past week, there'd been talks of a vow-exchanging ceremony and a few more *I love you*s being said between them.

And while they hadn't actually nailed a date for that ceremony, Sam had nailed it when she said this was the honeymoon phase because that was exactly what it felt like. The last time he'd felt this much anticipation churning in his bloodstream had been back when he'd first started dating Sam. And while there wasn't necessarily anything new about their situation, it felt as though they were starting over, the dance beginning once again, only this time, there was one more pair of feet doing the box step.

As he was filling one of the drawers with the rest of his things, he felt the heat of Logan's body when he stepped up behind him.

Elijah slowly closed the drawer, remaining as still as he could when Logan leaned down, his mouth close to his ear.

"I need to know the rules."

"Rules?" Elijah asked, not sure what he was referring to.

Logan stepped closer, eliminating the space between them. "Are we playing this cool for everyone else?"

Elijah had actually given some thought to how they were going to come out to their friends. Would they go to Devotion? Would it be one of the get-togethers? He agreed with Logan in that he had no intention of hiding this from anyone. He'd never been ashamed of his desires before. He didn't want to start now.

However, he'd wondered whether or not they would own up to the new dynamic during this trip or if they would maintain the status quo for outward appearances. It wasn't that he was looking to molest the man in public, but he wasn't sure he could pretend to be aloof when it came to Logan anymore. He'd never expected to have feelings for someone other than Sam, much less for a man who'd become his best friend over the years.

"Let me start by telling you what I want," Logan said softly, his hands sliding over Elijah's hips as his lips pressed lightly to the spot just beneath his ear.

Gas furnaces didn't burn as hot as what was currently roaring to life inside him.

"I don't care to hide this, Elijah. And even if I did, I'm not sure I can."

He swallowed, stepping back until he was pressed fully against the man behind him. "Then don't."

"You're okay with that?"

Elijah knew he wouldn't be able to safely answer that question until he was in a situation that required him to do something out of his comfort zone, but he nodded anyway. It wasn't like their friends hadn't figured out something was going on already. Hell, Luke had all but called them on it that one night and since Logan's brother had gone to Chicago to talk Logan off the ledge, there was a good chance he knew exactly what was going on.

The warmth at his back disappeared. A moment later, Logan turned him around with a gentle tug on his arm. Elijah backed against the dresser, now face to face with Logan.

He sucked in a ragged breath when Logan began unbuttoning his jeans, slowly inching the zipper down.

"You're saying you won't be embarrassed if I get the urge to suck your dick while we're sitting out by the pool?"

Elijah exhaled sharply when Logan's hand curled around the iron-hard length of his cock and squeezed. To prove he was onboard with the idea, Elijah shoved his jeans down his hips, freeing his cock.

Logan chuckled, his eyes glittering with both heat and mischief. "You definitely like that idea." He stroked Elijah's cock. Down. Up. "You don't think I'll do it?"

Two weeks ago, he would've said no, but now Elijah wouldn't put anything past Logan.

To his shock, Logan lowered to his knees before him, his hand still moving firmly over his raging erection. Every muscle in his body was tense with anticipation of that wicked mouth on him.

Gripping the edges of the dresser, Elijah fought to remain upright when Logan licked the swollen head of his cock. Seeing him like this … he'd never seen anything even remotely as enthralling. Such a big, powerful man on his knees, succumbing to his desires.

Logan sucked him into his mouth then released him, licking from root to tip, his eyes lifting to Elijah's face. "What if I want to bend you over and slide my cock into your ass?"

A violent tremor rattled his body.

"Would you bend over for me then, Eli?"

He nodded because, right here and now, he wanted that more than his next fucking breath.

"You like when I fuck you?"

Elijah couldn't deny that he did. This past week had proven he was a slut for this man, wanting something he'd never wanted before in his life. Although they'd only done it twice now, it was something he fantasized about immensely.

Logan's eyes narrowed. "What if I want you to fuck me, Elijah? Fuck my ass while I fuck Sam's tight, wet cunt?"

He swallowed, his cock jerking in Logan's fist. He'd fantasized about that, too, ever since Logan had brought it up.

"Fuck," Logan hissed, releasing his cock and jerking at the denim confining his thighs. "Take off your shirt."

Elijah didn't hesitate. He jerked the T-shirt over his head and tossed it to the floor while Logan stripped off the rest of his clothes.

When Logan was on his feet again, Elijah yanked at his shirt, wanting him as naked as he was. It took no time at all before they were skin to skin on the enormous bed, their mouths fused, hands roaming, hips pumping as they sought what the other was offering.

They ended up sixty-nining, Elijah feasting on Logan's throbbing cock while they lay on their sides. It was wickedly hot to surrender to something he'd wanted for so long without fearing the aftermath.

"Don't you dare make me come," Logan growled, the rumble sending vibrations through Elijah's balls. "You gave her an hour. I expect you to keep to the timeline."

Feeling more at ease than he'd been in forever, Elijah slowed his pace, savoring every second.

"ARE YOU WATCHING THE CLOCK?"

Sam's attention shifted from her phone to her friends. They were sitting poolside in one of the many cabanas that were set up. When she'd walked out of the bungalow, she'd been eager to hang out with her friends, to take in the sights of a fetish resort of this caliber. However, the more she replayed what Elijah had said, the more eager she became to go back to see what they were up to.

"Of all of us, I thought Sam would be the one to go crazy for the scenery," Mercedes noted.

Sam followed her gaze to see she was watching Talon's wife, Braelyn, as she strolled out of the hotel with three men clad only in jeans following close behind. The woman was absolutely stunning. She wore a gauzy white sundress that billowed around her bare feet as she moved, her long, golden-brown hair cascading down her back. From what Sam had understood, it was a real reverse harem going on with them. At least on some occasions. Evidently, the possessions they owned belonged to Talon—all except for one—but they'd established loyalty to the woman who held their hearts when she came along.

"Every woman should have herself one of those," Sierra mused.

"A bare-chested man who follows her everywhere?" McKenna asked, giggling.

"Absolutely."

Sam smiled. Although she found the entire thing intriguing, she couldn't imagine it for herself. She preferred her men less obedient, and she'd certainly hit the jackpot.

Glancing at her phone once more, she realized it had been almost an hour since she left.

"I ... uh..." She swallowed, setting her drink on the table and scooting to the edge of the seat. "I think I'll go check on Logan and Eli."

Sierra laughed. "Check on them? Or do you mean molest them?"

Sam smiled at her friend. "Most definitely the latter. I'll be back."

With her friends laughing behind her, Sam made the trek from the pool to their bungalow, admiring the beautiful scenery along the way. She couldn't imagine a more perfect place to spend her birthday.

Sam walked into the bungalow as quietly as she could, closing the door behind her. Neither Logan nor Elijah was in the living room or the kitchen, so she made a beeline for the bedroom. She approached slowly, smiling when she heard deep moans coming from inside. They'd invited her to watch, and she'd be damned if she would miss this opportunity.

She stopped at the door, her gaze settling on the two men currently on the bed. A jolt of electricity shocked her womb when she saw them sucking each other. If they knew she was there, neither of them acknowledged her, so she leaned her shoulder against the jamb and settled in to watch the show.

LOGAN COULD FEEL SAM'S EYES ON THEM. Knowing she was there watching ramped up his lust by a thousand degrees, sending molten lava coursing through his veins. It was enough to have him pulling back, dragging his cock from Elijah's wickedly skilled mouth for fear he would come before he was ready.

It took effort not to acknowledge her, but Logan managed to turn around on the bed without making eye contact and settle himself over Elijah, kissing him roughly as he took his hands and lifted them over his head. He could've spent the entire day like this, naked with Elijah at his mercy, his hot, hard body grinding against him.

"I'm all for foreplay," Elijah rasped against his mouth. "But I want to be inside you."

An electric current sparked at the base of his spine, making his cock jerk as every drop of blood in his body pooled between his legs. His cock was so fucking hard it hurt, and the thought of Elijah fucking him wasn't helping.

"You're gonna have to work for it," Logan teased, nipping his lower lip.

"I'm up for the challenge," Elijah growled roughly.

A second later, Logan felt the power in Elijah's body as he rocked Logan off of him, trading places so that he was on his back.

He huffed a laugh when Elijah glanced back at Sam. "You're welcome to join us if you'd like."

"I've got a pretty damn good view from here."

"Suit yourself," Elijah replied as he reached for the lube conveniently sitting on the nightstand. When he'd put it there, Logan didn't know, but apparently, he'd been thinking ahead while they unpacked.

Tucking his hands behind his head, Logan glanced over at Sam, smiled when he saw her raptly focused on Elijah as he got back on the bed. He could see her pebbled nipples beneath the thin fabric of her bikini. The sheer eroticism of that act … her watching them as they indulged fanned the flames of his arousal.

"Turn over," Elijah commanded, his tone steel hard with dominance.

There was a flash fire in his groin. No one had ever used that tone of voice with him, and oddly, coming from Elijah, he found it appealing.

Lowering his arms, Logan slowly rolled so that he was on his stomach. He tossed the pillow aside, pressing his cheek to the mattress and turning his head so he could see Sam's face. Behind him, Elijah kneed his legs wide so he could settle between them. Logan's cock throbbed, trapped against the cool silk of the comforter.

For several minutes, the only sounds he heard were the insistent pounding of his heart and Elijah's gruffly spoken instructions as he got Logan into the position he wanted him—on his knees, legs spread wide, chest pressed flat to the mattress. He felt vulnerable and alive, his breaths racing in and out of his lungs as he watched his wife watching them.

He groaned when Elijah's palms flattened on his ass, kneading him urgently as though holding back was painful. Logan understood. He was amped, his body on high alert as he waited with bated breath for Elijah to do something … anything.

Elijah leaned forward, the warmth of his chest along his back seconds before his lips pressed to his shoulder. His words were so soft when he said, "I don't want you to move from this position."

Logan grunted his agreement.

Those lips began a slow trek down his spine, his tongue gliding over his skin, making sparks dance under his skin. His body tightened when that devilish tongue reached the crack of his ass, and a second later, when it dipped lower, Logan's hands fisted the comforter as pleasure sang throughout his entire body.

Sam's gasp was erotically sharp, but it faded quickly as Logan moaned low in his throat as Elijah's tongue grazed his anus. His body reacted on impulse, his legs widening to give him better access. The sensation was invigorating, the warmth that invaded him so intimately as Elijah rimmed his hole, tormenting him with light licks at first, followed by gentle probing as he tongue-fucked him. As though that wasn't enough, Elijah massaged him with one deft finger, then two, stretching him, preparing him.

Logan grunted, weathering the assault that had precum dripping from his cock. He wasn't sure he'd ever felt anything quite like having his ass teased by Elijah's tongue and fingers.

He remained as still as he could, heeding Elijah's command to the best of his ability. It took effort not to rock against those intruding fingers. Thankfully, the man didn't make him wait long, fucking those fingers into his ass, stroking every nerve ending to life. When Elijah brushed his prostate, Logan groaned, the sound tearing from his throat.

"More," he demanded. "Eli ... fuck me."

The man's response was a rough growl that sent chills dancing down Logan's spine. The bed shifted, Elijah's fingers disappearing, replaced by the thick head of his cock. Logan pressed back against the intrusion, unable to remain still any longer. He breathed through the bite of pain, accepting everything Elijah was willing to give him. He welcomed him into his body, his hands white-knuckling the comforter as he rocked himself on Elijah's cock.

"Next time," he told Sam on a ragged breath, "I'll be fucking *you* while he's inside me."

Her mouth was open, her eyes glittering with heat as she watched Elijah fuck him.

"More," Logan insisted.

Elijah gave him more, sliding in balls deep in one mind-numbing thrust.

The pain sucked the air from his lungs. "Fuck."

Elijah held still.

"Don't stop," Logan snapped.

Elijah's fingers dug into the flesh of his hips as he held him there, retreating slowly. "So fucking tight."

"Fuck me. Now."

"I'm gonna come if I move," Elijah warned.

"Fuck. Me."

Elijah thrust forward and retreated slowly. Logan could hear his labored breaths, knew the pleasure he was feeling. He'd felt the same way the first time he fucked him. It was intense, not only the physical sensation on his cock but the acknowledgment of their intimacy.

Logan began fucking back against Elijah, stealing the pleasure, forcing the man to drive in deeper, harder. Every muscle in his body vibrated from the adrenaline that flooded his system. All the while, he stared at Sam, loving that she was here with them. He wasn't sure how he'd ever thought this wasn't about her. It was about all three of them. Always had been.

"Oh, hell," Elijah growled, his fingers digging into Logan's hips. "I'm coming."

Logan exhaled sharply when Elijah's cock swelled inside him before erupting. He dragged air into his overtaxed lungs as Elijah drained himself. The second Elijah's cock softened and retreated, Logan moved. He grabbed the bottle of lube sitting on the bed beside him, then manhandled Elijah down onto his stomach. He took position behind him, barely restraining himself long enough to pour lube along his throbbing dick. He stroked himself once, twice, then pressed the head to Elijah's hole and pushed in deep.

"Bloody hell," Elijah groaned, his accent thicker than usual.

"Take all of me," Logan demanded, willing him to relax.

Elijah reached back, his hand curling around Logan's thigh as he pulled him closer.

Logan let go, impaling him roughly, fucking in deep and hard. He was out of his mind, his body taking over, shutting off all common sense and reason as he used Elijah for his own selfish needs.

"Oh, God," he groaned. "It's too fucking good. I'm gonna come."

A second later, he did, a strangled roar piercing the air.

AFTER THAT INCREDIBLE BOUT OF MIND-BLOWING sex, Elijah managed to get to his feet. He padded toward the bathroom, but not before grabbing Sam and dragging her with him. She didn't resist, stumbling along, panting as though she'd run a mile and not simply watched two men fuck each other senseless.

Once they were in the shower, Sam took over, washing him up while he fought to catch his breath. Elijah found some semblance of balance—both mind and body—as her hands moved over him, her eyes bright with excitement.

When Logan joined them a few minutes later, more of the tension eased out of his body.

"Did you enjoy watching?" Logan asked, stepping up behind her and gripping her long hair in his fist.

"God yes." She peered back at him over her shoulder. "Did you enjoy me watching?"

"Fuck yes." Logan pressed a kiss to her lips then took a step back, his eyes meeting Elijah's.

There was something there he wasn't sure he'd seen before, and it soothed him in a way he hadn't realized he needed.

This thing between them was new, so many paths untraveled. Eventually, with time it would become second nature, but until then, he was looking forward to the journey, to exploring everything that came with being in love with two people, sharing their lives.

"My turn," Logan told Sam, pulling her soapy hands from Elijah's chest. "After you wash me up, we'll hang out at the pool and have some lunch delivered."

"Oh, thank God," she moaned. "I'm starving."

"And later," Logan said, his voice dropping an octave, "I want to watch you and Eli."

"Down by the pool?" she asked hopefully.

"Wherever you wanna be, baby. This is your birthday weekend. It's all about you."

Her grin widened, her eyes taking on a wicked gleam as she peered back at Elijah. "In that case, you might be doing some watching, too."

Elijah smiled, feeling the contentment consume him right down to his soul.

What they had was certainly untraditional. It was also complicated. He figured that was part of the reason it worked for them. They weren't ordinary people living ordinary lives. But who wanted ordinary when you could have a life full of adventure and excitement? If they were lucky, it would take them a lifetime to navigate the unexplored terrain on the path to their happily ever after.

Because he loved both of them, Elijah would gladly be along for the ride forevermore.

ACKNOWLEDGMENTS

My writing career started with Logan and Samantha and it's hard to believe that it's been ten years since then. Never in my life did I imagine I would be living my dream, but writing this book has brought it all back. I've never taken a single minute for granted. It's a blessing to do this day in and day out and I have *you* to thank for that.

Okay, now on to the acknowledgments. I know that I will likely leave out someone important, but here goes.

First of all, I have to say thank you to my amazing husband who puts up with me every single day. If it wasn't for him and his belief that I could do this, I wouldn't be writing this today. He has been my backbone.

Chancy Powley … it hasn't quite been ten years yet for us, but it's coming up quickly. Thank you for always being there for me. It's an honor to call you friend.

Jenna Underwood … You, my friend, make answering the phone almost enjoyable. If it wasn't for my anxiety and my busy schedule, I would answer every single time you call. But thank you for thinking of me and checking in to ensure I'm still kickin'.

I can't forget my copyeditor, Amy at Blue Otter Editing. Thank goodness I've got you to catch all my punctuation, grammar, and tense errors.

A huge shout out to Wander Aguiar for always providing me with the hottest selection of covers. When I saw this one, I knew it would be perfect for this book. Wander, you're a rock star behind the camera, and I hope you never stop doing what you're doing.

Nicole Nation 2.0 for the constant support and love. You've been there for me from almost the beginning. This group of ladies has kept me going for so long, I'm not sure I'd know what to do without them.

And, of course, YOU, the reader. Your emails, messages, posts, comments, tweets… they mean more to me than you can imagine. I thrive on hearing from you, knowing that my characters and my stories have touched you in some way keeps me going. I've been known to shed a tear or two when reading an email because you simply bring so much joy to my life with your support. I thank you for that.

ABOUT NICOLE EDWARDS

New York Times and *USA Today* bestselling author Nicole Edwards lives in the suburbs of Austin, Texas, with her husband, their three fur babies, and the youngest of their three children, who has threatened never to leave home. When Nicole is not writing about sexy alpha males and sassy, independent women, she can often be found with a book in hand or attempting to keep the dogs happy. You can find her hanging out on social media and interacting with her readers - even when she's supposed to be writing.

CONNECT WITH NICOLE

I hope you're as eager to get the information as I am to give it. Any one of these things is worth signing up for, or feel free to sign up for all. I promise to keep each one unique and interesting.

NIC NEWS: If you haven't signed up for my newsletter and you want to get notifications regarding preorders, new releases, giveaways, sales, etc, then you'll want to sign up. I promise not to spam your email, just get you the most important updates.

Ramblings of a Writer Blog: My blog is used for writer ramblings, which I am known to do from time to time.

NICOLE NATION: Visit my website to get exclusive content you won't find anywhere else, including sneak peeks, A Day in the Life character stories, exclusive giveaways, cards from Nicole, Join Nicole's review team.

Nicol Nation ON FACEBOOK: Join my reader group to interact with other readers, ask me questions, play fun weekly games, celebrate during release week, and enter exclusive giveaways!

INSTAGRAM: Basically, Instagram is where I post pictures of my dogs, so if you want to see epic cuteness, you should follow me.

TEXT: Want a simple, fast way to get updates on new releases? Sign up for text messaging. If you are in the U.S. simply text NICOLE to 64600. I promise not to spam your phone. This is just my way of letting you know what's happening because I know you're busy, but if you're anything like me, you always have your phone on you.

NAUGHTY & NICE SHOP: Not only does the shop have signed books, but there's fun merchandise, too. Plenty of naughty and nice options to go around. Find the shop on my website.

Website:	NicoleEdwards.me
Facebook:	/Author.Nicole.Edwards
Instagram:	NicoleEdwardsAuthor
BookBub:	/NicoleEdwardsAuthor

By Nicole Edwards

THE WALKERS

ALLURING INDULGENCE
Kaleb
Zane
Travis
Holidays with The Walker Brothers
Ethan
Braydon
Sawyer
Brendon

THE WALKERS OF COYOTE RIDGE
Curtis
Jared (a crossover novel)
Hard to Hold
Hard to Handle
Beau
Rex
A Coyote Ridge Christmas
Mack
Kaden & Keegan
Alibi (a crossover novel)

BRANTLEY WALKER: OFF THE BOOKS
All In
Without A Trace
Hide & Seek
Deadly Coincidence
Alibi (a crossover novel)
Secrets
Confessions

PIER 70
Reckless
Fearless
Speechless
Harmless
Clueless

SNIPER 1 SECURITY
Wait for Morning
Never Say Never
Tomorrow's Too Late

SOUTHERN BOY MAFIA/DEVIL'S PLAYGROUND
Beautifully Brutal
Without Regret
Beautifully Loyal
Without Restraint

STANDALONE NOVELS
Unhinged Trilogy
A Million Tiny Pieces
Inked on Paper
Bad Reputation
Bad Business
Filthy Hot Billionaire

NAUGHTY HOLIDAY EDITIONS
2015
2016
2021

Made in the USA
Monee, IL
28 July 2022

10439600R00157